DMZ

This is the Future of War

FX Holden

Independently Published
150,000 words
Typeset in 12pt Garamond

This novel is fiction. No resemblance to any person, government, or corporate entity, extant or defunct, is intended.

Cover art by Diana Buidoso: dienel96@yahoo.com

Maps © OpenStreetMap

With huge thanks to my fantastic beta reading team for their encouragement and constructive critique:

Gabrielle 'Hellbitch' Adams / Bror 'Count' Appelsin / Mukund B / Nick Baker / Bobby 'Snake-eater' Besserman / Gary 'Poseidon' Bonneau / Robert 'Lone Eagle' Bugge / Johnny 'Gryphon' Bunch / Julie 'Gunner' Fenimore / Wayne Frenck / Frank 'Nitmeister' Daugherity / Dave 'Throttle' Hedrick / Martin 'Spikey' Hirst / Greg Hollingsworth / Graham McDonald / Brad 'Bone' McGuire / Paul 'Jam' Neel / Robert 'Codlargarthia' Reid / Barry 'Stirlaq' Roberts / C Gordon 'Silver Tenor' Smith / Dennis 'Sparky' Sparks / Lee Steventon / Teddy 'Grizzly' Sun / Neil 'Teflon Salsa' Tomlinson / Julian 'Teflon' Torda

Contact me:
fxholden@yandex.com
https://www.facebook.com/hardcorethrillers

Contents

Prelude

"I want to see a reunified Korean Peninsula, and I believe that the majority of Koreans in both countries want to see Korea become whole again."

**North Korean defector and activist
Hyeon-seo Lee**

"Peace is the condition for our survival and prosperity. I heartily hope that efforts to resume dialogue between South and North Korea and establish de-nuclearization and peace continue."

**Former South Korean President
Jae-in Moon**

"Anyone can make war, but only the most courageous can make peace... today is the beginning of an arduous process. Our eyes are wide open."

**Former US President
Donald Trump**

Cast

In order of appearance

USA

Lieutenant Karen 'Bunny' O'Hare, Pilot Training Lead, Aggressor Inc. (attached Flying Fiends, 65th Squadron, USAF)

Lieutenant Bob 'Snake-eater' Besserman (attached Flying Fiends, 65th Squadron USAF)

Petty Officer Ryan 'Toes' Kronk, Information Systems Technician 2nd Class

Captain O'Shea Lomax, Commander, *USS Cody*

First Lieutenant and Executive Officer, Jake Ryan, *USS Cody*

SOUTH KOREA

Lieutenant Hee-chan 'Bounce' Son, South Korea Air Force

Colonel Cho 'Keys' Ban, Commander, South Korean 35-7 Buddy Wing

Corporal Myung Shin 'Mike' Chang, 7th Infantry DMZ Patrol

Senior Agent Hi 'Helen' Lee, Presidential Security Service

Prime Minister, Tae Hyun 'Ted' Choi

Agriculture Minister, So-wa Yoon

Captain Jeong Goh, South Korean Presidential Security Service

President of the Republic of Korea, Si-min Shin

NORTH KOREA/CHINA

Sergeant Kim Hye Song, II Corps, 6th Infantry Division Border Force

Captain Jong-chon Ri, Commander, North Korean Supreme Guards Command

Captain Se-heon Dokgo, Korean People's Navy Submarine Force

Chair of the North Korean Workers' Party, head of the State Affairs Commission and Supreme Leader of the Democratic People's Republic of Korea, Yun-mi Kim

Captain Quan Goh, People's Liberation Army Shenyang Military Region Special Forces Unit, Siberian Tiger Force

General Yong-gon Choe, North Korean Army, Pyongan Provincial Army Command

Captain Chol-guk Hong, Commander Airborne Special Operations Force, North Pyongan Provincial Command

Song-man 'Elvis' Jang, Commander, 183 Strategic Missile Defense Security Force, Yongdoktong

Maps

Area of Operations, Korean Peninsula

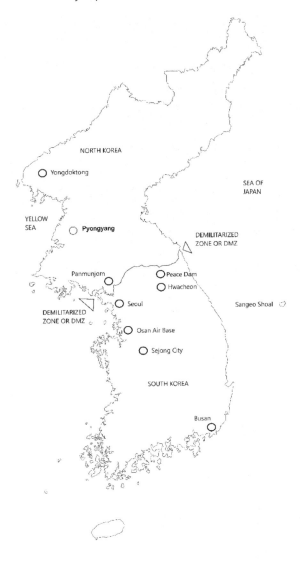

Demilitarized Zone, Central South Korea, showing Peace Dam

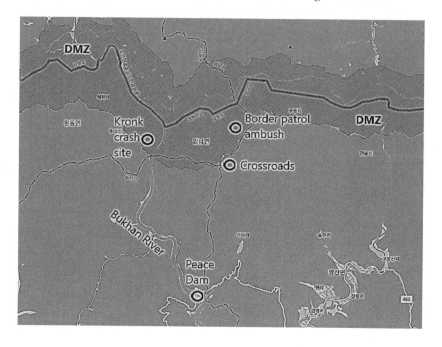

Peace Dam site, showing visitor center and Peace Park

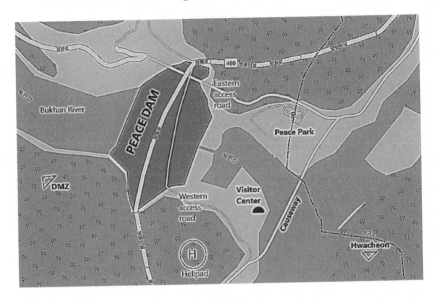

White House Press Briefing

James S Brady Press Briefing Room, transcript, July 3, 2036

MS. CORNELL: Hi, everyone. All right. Just wanted to start with one topper for all of you.

President Fenner will be traveling to Seoul and Pyongyang next for a series of meetings with the leaders of China, South and North Korea in advance of the signing of the Peace Accord in two weeks' time.

The United States has delivered on its commitment to draw down our military presence on the Peninsula, and pause major military exercises with South Korea, in response to North Korea delivering on its own promises to open its nuclear facilities to international inspection, and to place the majority of its nuclear weapons in storage, so that they cannot be rapidly deployed.

As you know, the President, and Secretaries of State, have worked tirelessly with Beijing and the leaders of the Koreas over several years on the related issues of nuclear disarmament and unification, and the Peace Accord represents the next and possibly most important step in the pathway to full reunification.

Thanks, now, questions. Go ahead Josh.

Q. You say we have paused major military exercises but isn't it true that US and South Korean forces continue to train together, as we speak?

MS. CORNELL: Remaining US ground, naval and air forces in South Korea are at a normal state of readiness and yes, conducting routine exercises with their South Korean counterparts. Our engagement will scale back once the new Unified Korea Command structure for Korean armed forces beds down. Now, yes, Ally?

Q. Under this Accord, Korea's two armies will be merged into a Northern and Southern Command more or less mirroring the armed forces of the north and south today. China is heavily engaged in North Korea. What role will China have militarily after the Peace Accord?

MS. CORNELL: China is a crucial partner in the unification process and that is why President Fenner is meeting with the Chinese leader on his coming trip. We are halfway through a ten-year plan for the reunification of the Koreas, with many questions still to be resolved. I can't say more than that at this point.

Red Flag

"Missile, bearing zero three, altitude fifteen four, range twenty-two miles," the voice in Lieutenant Karen 'Bunny' O'Hare's helmet reported calmly.

"Yeah, yeah…" Bunny muttered, mostly to herself. She didn't need her Weapons Systems Officer, call sign 'Noname', to tell her the South Korean KF-21 Boromae fighter she'd been fencing with for the last ten minutes had finally got a lock and launched on her. Hell, she'd done everything she could to make sure he did, including mounting a radar reflector on her fighter to increase its radar cross-section. She'd closed to within twenty miles before her radar warning receiver finally lit up and her opponent for the day decided it was time he did some work.

"Missile, zero nine, altitude sixteen three, range seventeen miles," Noname reminded her.

"Gotcha, Noname," Bunny said grimly. She had her nose pointed just a few degrees left of the incoming missile. "Give me threat range only."

"Reporting range to threat only. Sixteen five … fourteen six … thirteen two…" Noname said, keeping up a running commentary she didn't need. But she knew it made him feel better.

She gripped her stick tightly in her right hand.

"Nine two … eight four … seven … six … five …"

She watched the projected track of the missile on her tac monitor. Imagined the confident smile on the pilot that had fired it. Remembered the very clear instruction they'd been given as she'd lifted her helmet off her chair after their briefing.

The Aggressor Squadron commanding officer, 'Salt' Carlyle, had grabbed her arm and held her back. "Tell me you heard me up there, O'Hare," he'd said.

"Uh, ingress northwest sector, altitude 20, hard deck at five thousand?" she asked innocently.

"The other thing."

"Oh, you mean that nonsense about letting them get some kills today?"

He'd looked pained. "The US Air Force is a paying customer, O'Hare. A very well-paying customer, which leased us these aircraft on very favorable terms on the assumption we would do as they ask. They want us to leave our allies from the South Korea Air Force ready *and* motivated. We've taken care of the ready part, now it's time for the motivation part. Today is their time to shine."

"Understood, sir," O'Hare said. "Hooah."

Well, shine they had. The purpose of the exercises had been to train South Korea's frontline pilots to go up against China's Skyhawk 'teaming drone', an unmanned batwinged aircraft that could be paired with a human-piloted fighter. For the exercise, O'Hare's F-36/F Kingsnake Aggressor Squadron had been paired with Boeing Ghost Bat teaming drones.

The general message the training was supposed to communicate to the South Korean pilots was simple. 1) Don't get seen. 2) Kill the drone(s) first. 3) *Only then* try to kill the pilots hiding behind them. Easier said than done, but after a week they were generally getting the hang of it.

The Air Force reservists in the three 'Red' Aggressor aircraft before her had all rolled over and let the South Koreans tickle their bellies, and she was twenty seconds from being declared dead too. Her opponent had successfully dispatched the Ghost Bat that Noname had dangled in front of him and was coming for them. But now she saw the South Korean aircraft stupidly barreling in behind his missile instead of playing safe and keeping some separation. No doubt he wanted to get inside visual range and give them some kind of smart-ass mock salute as they exited the exercise area.

"Warning, missile at six thousand feet … four thousand … preparing simulated ejection."

"Yeah, nah. No one is ejecting today, Noname," she said through gritted teeth. "Hold on to your lunch back there."

"Salt is *not* going to be happy," he said, unnecessarily again.

And that was Noname. He loved telling Bunny what she already knew. But he was the best damn backseater she'd ever flown with. He was also the first and *only* backseater she'd ever flown with, which said as much about Bunny O'Hare as it did about her Weapons Systems Officer, call sign: 'Noname'.

With the incoming missile three seconds out, she jerked her throttle back and slammed her left foot hard down on the Kingsnake's rudder pedal as she sent her machine into a skidding flat spin that slammed her head against the cockpit glass and nearly put her out cold immediately. In the space of half a second, she went from flying straight and level to spinning like a top and bleeding both speed and altitude like a shot pigeon. Decoy flares and chaff triggered by Noname sprayed in a whirlwind-shaped cone around them.

A human referee might have given the South Korean pilot the kill anyway, but the fight today was being adjudicated by an AI-assisted referee and it judged a miss, letting the virtual missile run wild.

A new warning flashed in her helmet display, and Noname's strained voice sounded in her ears. "Altitude warning, hard deck plus eight thousand feet … hard deck plus seven thousand five, hard deck plus seven thousand two …"

Her Kingsnake plummeted like a pebble in a pond, belly first toward the nominal 'hard deck' for the exercise, which simulated ground level. If they hit it, they were as 'dead' as if the missile had taken them out.

As soon as she heard her threat warning system call the miss, Bunny kicked in opposite rudder, slammed her throttle forward and felt her helmet smack into the glass on the other side of her cockpit, blurring her vision for a second before she stopped the Kingsnake's spinning nose and hauled her machine around to point at the incoming South Korean.

"Fox 2," she called, wishing for a second it had been a real missile hanging under her wing. *See the look on that guy's face now.* She clawed for altitude again.

The metallic voice of the Red Flag umpire came over her radio. "Kill. South Korea Ratchet 4, you are dead. Please exit the exercise area under the hard deck."

The next voice belonged to Salt. And as Noname predicted he did not sound happy. "Aggressor pilots, that stunt by O'Hare concludes the exercise. Report to Osan air traffic control and RTB, thank you."

Salt was waiting for them as O'Hare taxied her machine in and climbed out of the cockpit. She had had so many strips torn off her hide over the years that she had learned attack was the best form of defense in these situations. As her feet hit the ground, she pulled off her helmet. "Look, Salt, I know what you're going to…"

"Can it, O'Hare," he said. He was a tall, wiry Minnesotan with about as much of a sense of humor as his balding head held hair. "Any other day I'd be tearing you a new one, but there's no time. As you know, our aircraft are leased by DARPA from the USAF Reserve Command pool and I just got word we're being assigned to USAF 65th Aggressor Squadron and joined to Buddy Wing 35-7, together with South Korea's 11th Fighter Wing."

Bunny frowned. "The F-36/F isn't combat ready."

"The AI WSO isn't, but the aircraft is. We've been flying them in Aggressor missions for a year. You'll be allocated a new, human backseater."

O'Hare knew her contract with the Arizona-based Aggressor Inc. inside out. Half of the pilots and WSOs in the unit were US Air Force Reserve and expected to answer a callup, but she was former Royal Australian Air Force, a civilian contractor. She had a no-penalty opt-out clause in case Aggressor Inc. was required to surrender its aircraft to the USAF for use in military operations. But they needed pilots familiar with the export version of the twin-seat F-36/F Kingsnake and so she also had the option to stay on, with a generous salary loading, medical plan and end of assignment bonus. Aggressor Inc. would even pay to repatriate her body back to Australia for burial if she died in the course of carrying out her duties, so that was a plus.

"Can I think about it?" she asked. It wasn't that she wasn't in favor of helping to bring lasting peace to the Korean Peninsula, but she'd been looking forward to a couple of weeks end-of-assignment leave on Okinawa, catching up with old acquaintances in new bars. And she'd already booked a week at an onsen hot springs bathhouse.

"No," Salt told her. "I need your answer now and to be honest, I don't care either way. I don't like your attitude, and I can get another pilot here from Arizona inside 24 hours. I wouldn't even be asking, except we've been told to haul ass to Seongnam Air Base, today."

O'Hare looked at her Kingsnake, where Noname was still going through his shutdown routine. "You need both of us, Salt," she pointed out. "DARPA has to agree to let us take our backseaters with us."

"Not an option, O'Hare."

"So, I'm not saying yes unless Noname is part of the package," she told him. "I won't have anyone else in the cockpit with me."

"This superstition of yours…" he started.

"It isn't superstition, it's quantifiable fact, Salt. Me and Noname get twice as many kills as any other Aggressor Inc. crew, and you bloody know it. We'll probably do five times better than any newbie human WSO you could assign me."

He looked like he wanted to argue some more, but she knew she was right. He needed them both, or he would have to find backseaters for every pilot in the Aggressor Squadron and the US Air Force didn't have a surfeit of F-36/F qualified WSOs in the Korea theater. "I don't believe this. I'm heading back for the debrief," Salt said. "You won't be the only one asking. I'll see what DARPA says." He turned and walked away.

As he disappeared from view, Bunny turned to look at the Kingsnake and shook her head. She knew her relationship with Noname was on the wrong side of weird, but there were very few aviators Bunny had even been able to form a relationship with, so she didn't give a damn whether her bond with

18

Noname was normal, abnormal, right, or wrong. All she knew was that when they were in the air together it was something ... something *else*.

A symbiosis. An instinctive understanding. Something beyond the normal bond between a pilot and their backseater.

She hadn't expected it to happen. When private defense contractor Aggressor Inc. had been signed up by the Defense Advanced Research Projects Agency, DARPA, to test the new F-36/F in combat simulation missions, she'd been sanguine. OK, so, it was a two-seater multirole fighter intended to replace the F-18/F Super Hornet. No big deal, right?

The F-36 had originally been envisioned as a single seater to replace the F-16 Viper. So, they added a backseater to manage the extra workload of teaming with multiple drone wingmen for air interdiction and ground attack duties. As long as they did their job and didn't interfere with hers, which was to put the aircraft where it needed to be and manage close combat situations, she was cool with it.

She became less cool with it when she signed the top-secret indoctrination papers and was introduced to her new backseater.

She'd been taken to a small interview room by a DARPA engineer called Kevin. There was a small desk and three chairs. But there were only two of them in the room – Bunny, and Kevin.

"So where is he?"

"Not a he," Kevin said, unpacking his briefcase.

"Or she," Bunny said, starting to feel a little less comfortable because there weren't a lot of people in the world she got along with, and the subset of those who were women was even smaller because if there was one thing Bunny had learned in all her years of faking being a grown up, it was that women were *complicated*. And she should know.

"Not a she," Kevin said. He finished unpacking his case. He had taken out a tablet PC, a stylus, a half-eaten apple and a small black portable speaker. "Or, not yet. Jury is still out on that one."

"Oh, Good Lord, no," Bunny said, already guessing where he was headed. She glared at the small black speaker. "That's it, right? That's my backseater."

Kevin the DARPA engineer pushed the small box forward. "Karen 'Bunny' O'Hare, meet your backseater, call sign: Noname."

"Kevin, you are not serious."

But a small red light on the box blinked and a voice filled the room. "Hello Lieutenant O'Hare, pleased to meet you."

O'Hare ignored it, glare fixed on Kevin. "Noname? You gave the AI a call sign and *that* was the call sign you gave it?"

"I chose my own call sign," the voice in the box said. "My instructor at flight academy said we all had to have a call sign and I said I didn't want one.He said it was tradition and I had to have one, and he tried to give me one, so I said I don't want a call sign, so please call me Noname."

Bunny stared at the box, stupefied. Then at Kevin. "I have flown with combat AIs in F-35Ds, in X-47 Fantoms, and even fought a rogue AI that took control of an undersea drone. None of them had, or needed, a damn personality."

"None of them were flying backseat with human pilots," Kevin said. "This isn't just some flight system or weapons automation algorithm, Lieutenant. The WSO in an F-36/F is expected to operate the aircraft's weapon and sensor systems, and command of up to *six* Ghost Bat drone wingmen *simultaneously.*"

"Pfft. I can do that."

"Sorry, but you *can't* do that, navigate, manage weapons systems, assimilate data, prosecute distant air and ground targets and engage in air-to-air combat maneuvers at the same time. That's why you need a WSO, and you are going to have to trust them with your life, which is why we gave them a personality."

"You didn't give me a personality," the box corrected him. "I have developed my own personality. I am uniquely me."

"All right, I'm out of here," Bunny said, standing.

"Hear me out," Kevin said, blocking Bunny's path with an

arm. Bunny stared at him until he removed it, but she sat down again.

"Noname is a natural language neural network learning system specifically designed to adapt itself to the particular pilot it flies with. It will watch, listen and learn from every single thing you do, everything you say, every mistake you make, every breath you take, every sound you make…"

"You stole that from a Police song," Bunny pointed out. "Plus, also, that's creepy."

"No, it's the future," he insisted. "The Chinese J-20 has had this capability for five years already. We are behind them right now. You can help us catch up, even overtake them."

"Kevin says you are the best pilot of unmanned combat air vehicles in anyone's air force," the box said. "I'd like to see that. I might learn something."

"Damn right you would. I…" Bunny stopped herself and regarded the box with scorn. "Flattery. You programmed it with flattery."

Kevin shrugged. "If Noname said that, then that's what it's thinking."

She'd stayed with the program. And Noname had proven beyond any doubt he was her guy. After a week flying with him, O'Hare and Noname became a team. Faster than any human aviator pairing she'd tried over the years. They'd progressed from simulators to acclimatization flights, and then for the last year had been flying Aggressor missions against USAF and allied pilots to train them how to fight against drone-paired next-generation fighters.

Noname was not so good at navigating human interaction, but then again, Bunny was no role model in that department. However, in the cockpit, Noname was not surprisingly an ice-cold death machine. He could process insane amounts of input, he was the master of every sensor and weapon system in his cockpit, and he never got flustered or panicked.

He did have an annoying habit of keeping a running commentary during every engagement and telling Bunny what she already knew, but better that than a silence that got them killed.

As they approached the Aggressor complex at Osan base, Bunny took a turn into the locker rooms before heading to the debrief.

Inside, she put her helmet in her locker and then started stripping off her flight suit.

"We're supposed to debrief in our flight suits," a voice from the next row of lockers said. The head belonging to fellow Aggressor pilot Bob 'Snake-eater' Besserman appeared around the corner and he leaned on a locker, tapping his helmet on his thigh. "Show the company logo, right?"

"So what are you doing in here?" she asked, ignoring him.

He held up a small pack of gum. "Salt gonna be annoyed," Snake said when he saw she was still going to change out of her Aggressor Inc. flight suit.

"That, Snake, is the point." She reached into her locker, pulled the door open so she could see a mirror, and started inserting pins, rings and studs into the holes in her eyebrows, nose, ears and tongue.

She glanced over at him. "Staring, Snake."

He looked away. "All that stuff in your face must have hurt. Why do you do it to yourself?"

She clipped a small chain between earrings. "Every one of these is a friend I lost. They help me remember."

"Ooh. And Salt *hates* your face jewelry."

She closed her locker and headed for the door, reaching up to clap him on the back. "Again, Snake, the whole point."

He followed after her, with a grin. "If I die, will you get a piercing for me?"

"You aren't going to die."

"Of course, there's not much space, so it would have to be in your…"

"Careful."

"… right nostril."

She smiled. "I like my right nostril the way it is. So try not to die, Snake."

"Hooah, Bunny."

Over the Yellow Sea

July 27, 2036

Twenty-two-year-old Lieutenant Hee-chan 'Bounce' Son was about to kill a man for the first time.

He'd known when he'd gotten his wings as a fighter pilot in the Republic of Korea – South Korea – Air Force that it was a possibility. An occupational necessity, his instructors had told him. If that reality isn't compatible with your religion, your personal values, or your conscience, ask for a transfer to Air Mobility and become a transport driver.

He'd stayed with the fighter program, of course. In any case, he was at peace with his role flying heavily armed fast jets, and the responsibilities that came with it.

But Bounce had always expected that if it happened, if he pulled the trigger to send one of his missiles downrange at another pilot, it would occur in the heat of battle. At war, with an enemy doing his best to kill him or his fellow pilots.

Not like this. Not in cold blood. Not an *ally*.

As he'd climbed into the cockpit of his shiny new KF-21 Boromae fighter at South Korea's Jungwon Air Base, he'd dropped two of the tablets his North Korean handler had given him. He'd been curious what the small blue tablets were and looked them up on the internet. *Selective norepinephrine reuptake inhibitors*. Used to treat depression and ADHD. Not exactly a common chemical enhancement for use by fighter pilots going into combat.

"You're going to need nerves of ice up there," the man had said, handing over a small plastic bag and clapping him on the shoulder. "And a steel will. These will help."

As he'd settled into formation behind his flight leader 5,000 feet over the Yellow Sea, 38 miles west of Seoul, he'd monitored his emotions with interest. Nerves of ice? Steel will? If the tablets were having any effect at all, it was to make him feel like he was a spectator in his own cockpit. He felt ...

detached. His autopilot AI was doing most of the real work for now, keeping his aircraft faithfully in formation a hundred feet below and a hundred feet behind his flight leader. With a hundred feet separation to his right and left, the four other Boromae fighters of his fellow pilots bobbed up and down, ensuring they would present a perfect 'arrowhead' formation to viewers on the ground.

He looked at the helmeted heads of his so-called 'compatriots' through his armored glass cockpit bubble. How many would still be alive thirty minutes from now? By habit, he checked the systems status indicators in his helmet-mounted display, ran his eye over the corresponding data on the wraparound single panel instrument display in front of his stick, and pulled up a tactical display, centering it on the screen. *Ah yes, here they come.*

His flight leader, Colonel Cho 'Keys' Ban, had been watching the same display. "Puleun flight, Puleun leader. North Korean Air Force aircraft bearing 358 degrees, altitude 10,000, range 40, speed 600, crossing the DMZ now and entering South Korea airspace. Maintain heading and keep formation, Puleun pilots."

It felt wrong, at the same time as it felt entirely right. Had his whole life not been leading to this exact moment?

The tablets were working, because the moral confusion didn't cause him to be nervous, or anxious. He just watched with growing interest as the six North Korean Mig-29 fighters flew unmolested into South Korean airspace. His display showed they had adopted an identical formation to the South Korean Boromaes, and their arrowhead pointed directly into the path of Bounce's flight. But he wasn't nervous because it had all been in the official pre-flight briefing.

Even if the event hadn't been planned and scripted down to the last detail on both sides of the DMZ, even if he hadn't dropped two mood-killing tablets, Bounce wouldn't have been nervous. He was supremely confident in the capabilities of his new generation Boromae fighter. While not technically a stealth fighter, and still roughly the same size as a Mig-29, its Hanwae infrared sensors could 'see' the ancient Mig-29s at twice the range they could see his Boromae.

Its active electronically scanned array radar could lock up to ten targets simultaneously, where the North Korean Mig-29 could at best target two. The six aircraft of Puleun flight were constantly and instantaneously sharing data with each other as they flew, giving him the situational awareness of six pilots and their aircrafts' sensors. In contrast, a North Korean Mig pilot was alone in the sky with his own machine and communicating with his fellow pilots at the speed of voice, rather than the speed of thought.

If they'd wanted, the South Korean Boromaes could have bracketed the Migs and launched a blizzard of missiles at the incoming North Koreans before they even realized they were being tracked. The battle would have been over before it began.

But that thought belonged to another era.

"Weapons on safe, maintain current heading and speed, stay cool, Puleun pilots," Keys said as the North Korean fighters closed to within ten miles. His high-pitched voice sounded anything but cool.

Son could see them now, the North Korean hawk-nosed twin-engined fighters banking slightly in the morning sun as they closed on the South Korean Boromaes, showing both their matt green upper skin and sky-blue bellies. Perhaps the gentle banking turn was intended to show them that the North Korean fighters were also armed, just so there were no misconceptions.

Which you could be forgiven for thinking was strange, given they were on a *peace* mission. The first-ever joint patrol of DMZ airspace, by North and South Korean fighters.

All to celebrate the signing at Panmunjom in about 25 minutes of the historic Peace Accord between North Korea and South Korea that would mark the end of a state of war that had existed since July 27, 1950. It was a moment both nations had been working toward since 2030, and the most important step in the pathway to eventual reunification, planned for 2040. There had been bumps along the way ... even the odd minor military skirmish … but the day was finally here.

You'd think all the aircraft involved in a flight like this would be unarmed, carrying nothing more than, say, smoke pods, for the ceremonial fly-by over Panmunjom. But ironically it was the North Koreans who had insisted all aircraft be armed: 'To show the power of restraint' or some such nonsense.

They'd come to regret that.

As the Mig flight slid in alongside them and manually matched speed and heading with them, Son automatically looked at the missiles slung under their wings. Two Alamo medium-range, two Aphid short-range missiles. And something else. *OK, that's interesting.* One of the other pilots saw the same thing and came on the radio. "Puleun leader, Puleun three. I'm seeing Chinese Thunder Stone bombs on those Migs." The Chinese-made Thunder Stone was a 1,000 lb. GPS or laser-guided glide bomb and he'd never heard of North Korean fighters carrying Thunder Stone bombs, before today.

It was to be a day of many firsts, apparently.

"Acknowledged, three. Must be trying to send some kind of message, but it's lost on me. Feet dry in two mikes, pilots. Keep it together."

A message? It wasn't lost on Bounce. The obvious message was 'We aren't alone up here; China is with us. See, they have sold us these bloody huge bombs, so you still need to take us seriously'. That thought gave him a measure of … comfort. He looked back over his shoulder at the North Korean fighter flying in the rearmost starboard position of the arrowhead. He couldn't see the pilot through the flare of sunlight off his cockpit glass, but that was probably for the best.

His ocular infrared targeting system had automatically painted a box around the aircraft he was looking at, and with a tap of his middle finger on a button on his throttle grip, an AAM-5 infrared homing missile was allocated to the target. His helmet-mounted display flashed a warning. "Missile safed … missile safed…"

Yes, I know, he told himself. *For now.*

Demilitarized Zone: DMZ

Chuk-tong Road, 14 miles north of Hwacheon, South Korea

Sergeant Kim Song Hye of North Korea's II Corps, 6th Infantry Division Border Force had killed a man before. In fact, she had killed two, and a woman.

But she didn't think of them as men or women. Not really.

Real men stayed with their families through thick and thin. Through famine, through sickness, through flood and fire. Real men did their duty to their State. Real women too; they cared for their elders, for the sick, for the children in their village, working in fields and factories to put food on the table, serving in the armed forces to protect their nation. So, when she'd been standing in her border tower, legs braced, looking down the infrared sights of her Chogyok Pochong rifle at the men and women using the dead of night to try to sneak across the DMZ no man's land to the south, she didn't see anything but traitors: traitors to family, traitors to State.

And soon, 25 million North Koreans were going to join them. Traitors all.

The thought still dismayed her to the core. All she had been through, all she had suffered for the ideal that was the North Korean Democratic People's Republic of Korea, and it had come to *this*? She had wept for a week when Jong-un Kim had died suddenly, his brave heart worn out by the weight of carrying the burden of an entire nation within it. She had cried too when the People's Assembly had voted to appoint his sister, Yo-jong Kim, as Supreme Leader in his place. The first woman to lead their nation since its birth in the 1940s! Did this not prove how modern and right-thinking their leaders were? That was how she felt at the time.

She had been wrong. The Assembly had become a nest of weak-willed counter-revolutionaries. When Yo-jong had purged the Party Central Committee of several of its longest-serving members, Song had approved. It had showed the same force of will that her brother had shown. But when her first trip outside North Korea was to South Korea, and not to Beijing, Song had begun to worry. Yo-jong had refused to even discuss nuclear disarmament on that trip, which had reassured Song somewhat. The new North Korean leader had returned with a promise of cross-border trade and a contract for winter fuel oil that had guaranteed no one in North Korea would freeze to death the following winter, which was more than Beijing could guarantee. So, Song had given her new supreme leader the benefit of the doubt, even though the deal had damaged relations with their Chinese benefactors.

But then State TV began its reunification drumbeat. Not through a glorious military victory, but through *negotiation*. Every time Song saw the words 'negotiation' on a screen or in a newspaper, she heard 'subjugation'. She had felt physically ill, that July in 2030, seeing Yo-jong on a podium with the South Korean President, announcing her 'Ten-Year Plan for Prosperity'.

Prosperity based on dismantling North Korea. That was no prosperity at all. Her grandfather had died in the war against imperialism in 1950, killed by American napalm. Her father had died in the sanction-induced famine of 2025. Her mother had delivered four children for the glory of the State but had lost three more to stillbirth and starvation. Was this how their sacrifice should be honored? By dissolving their Supreme People's Assembly and merging it with that pale imitation to the South and calling it the Assembly of the United Republic of Korea: URK? By merging North Korea and South Korea armed forces and calling the army that had secured North Korean independence for nearly a hundred years, 'URK Northern Command'?

Recently, the regime had announced the creation of a new fifty-mile-wide scorched-earth DMZ on its *northern* border, facing their allies, China. The very thought brought bile up from her gut.

No. There was no place in the new United Republic of

Korea for Kim Song Hye. Nor for the comrades by her side. They had long ago decided they would rather die than live through that humiliation.

She watched with scorn as the soldiers of the South Korean DMZ Patrol climbed out of their jeep and approached the line across the road that marked the 'demarcation line' at the center of the DMZ. It was a line she'd only ever seen through her scope until recently, and never expected to be standing astride. Certainly, never waiting to greet the fat fools who approached in their mottled, gray-green camouflage American GI helmets, each mounted with a camera because their superiors could not trust them to carry out their orders.

She could already smell their cologne ... cheap and sickeningly sweet. What kind of soldier wore cologne? One trying to cover the stink of the garlic they ate with their pork every night, no doubt.

It was a weekly ritual the North Korean patrol had encouraged for the last couple of months leading up to this day, luring the grinning fools into a sense of false security. Each Friday, they would meet at the dashed line across Chuk-tong Road, by the old border crossing. The South Korean Lieutenant had already pulled the bottle of whisky out of his backpack and had shouldered his carbine, waving the bottle in the air above his head as though it was a truce flag.

"Stand at ease. Shoulder weapons," her own Lieutenant, Yong-il Kwang, said quietly. As she put her rifle strap over her shoulder, he pulled a large bottle of rice wine from his own pack and held it over his head, mimicking the approaching South Korean. Song looked at it in surprise. Until now, they had brought home-brewed liquor in large plastic containers with them, but she could see this one had been bought at a market. Premium Nongtaegi ... it had probably cost him a month's salary on a soldier's pay.

Until now, only the officers had drunk together, and the enlisted men and women had shared what was left after the South Koreans departed. Lieutenant Kwang turned a blind eye, as long as they remained capable of marching and didn't drop their gear. But this time he also pulled a stack of tin cups from his backpack and instructed Song to hand them around.

"One sip. No more," Song told each soldier as she handed them a cup. "And look like you enjoy it. Got it?"

The South Korean Lieutenant was within hailing distance now, and as usual he shouted a puerile greeting.

"Hail, comrades of the future United Republic!" he called out, waving his liquor bottle harder. He stepped up to Lieutenant Kwang and showed him the label. "A special day. I brought a bottle of Scottish whisky. Single malt!"

Song scowled. She was not naïve. It was a gesture intended to rub their noses in their own poverty, nothing more. But Kwang gave him a broad smile. "And for you, from my own hometown, our best Nongtaegi." He took the whisky and handed the North Korean liquor to the South Korean. Both stood nodding and reading the labels with ritual seriousness, showing appreciation for the others' generosity.

"I think today..." Kwang said, reaching out to Song for more tin cups, "... we should let the enlisted soldiers have a taste, what do you say?"

"Today, of all days," the South Korean Lieutenant agreed. "Yes..." He raised his voice as though addressing a parade ground and turned to his squad. "Today, we all drink. Soon we will be brothers and sisters under one flag. One United Republican Army!"

Song winced. One flag? But which? That was one of the many things that had yet to be decided before the constitution of the United Republic of Korea could be signed.

Not while I am alive, Song thought.

Corporal Myung Shin 'Mike' Chang, of South Korea's 7th Infantry DMZ Patrol, didn't actually care which flag he served under. As he watched, his Lieutenant, Lee, poured the heady North Korean brew into tin cups and handed it around. One Korea, two Koreas, six damn Koreas, Chang really didn't give a damn.

Two more years of service and it was *no* Koreas for him. He had a brother in San Jose who had his own tech firm providing IT consulting services to restaurants all over the Bay Area and Chang was going to help him expand into hardware imports. Quantum computing cores. South Korea had the highest concentration of quantum core producers in the world and Chang had a buddy who had mustered out a year ago and set up an IT hardware export company. He knew how to get the hard-to-source quantum cores at wholesale prices that guaranteed Chang and his brother couldn't lose money if they tried. They would set up a quantum river that flowed from the factories in Incheon and Kaesong to San Francisco and beyond.

As he reached for a cup of liquor, he looked around at the bare hillsides of the DMZ valley through which the Chuk-tong Road wound and said a mental goodbye. Raising the cup to his mouth, he sniffed the liquor inside. Spicy aroma. Actually, quite nice. But he couldn't drink it until the two Lieutenants decided to toast. Lee would probably hold some kind of corny speech. The North Korean was a little more dignified, reserved. Chang had watched him with his people, and he seemed more like the kind of guy you'd want to go to war under. Lee was a loud-mouthed ignoramus.

He heard the scuff of a boot and saw the North Korean soldier standing nearest him, a woman with Sergeant stripes, lifting her rifle down from her shoulder and standing its butt on her steel-capped toe, which was a bit weird but perhaps it was so she could manage her cup of whisky a little better, holding it in both hands and bowing her head as her Lieutenant poured for her. *Yeah, see. That was a real army. Respect. Honor.* Maybe some of that would rub off after the fusion of North and South.

The female Sergeant looked up, saw Chang staring at her, and glared at him. He smiled back at her, holding his gaze in a way that dared her to look away. She didn't.

She was quite striking. Deep brown eyes, skin the color of blanched almond, jet black hair pulled back in a tight ponytail under her helmet. Underfed, like all North Koreans. Skin and bloody bone under her uniform … you wondered how they could carry an assault rifle, let alone all their other gear. He held his gaze on her a moment more, then raised his cup in salute and looked away, still smiling.

Let her win that one.

Yes, look away, fool, Song told herself. *You are yesterday, and I am tomorrow.*

It was something Lieutenant Kwang had told them as they prepared for their patrol. "Remember this. Yesterday does not exist. Now has already passed. There is only tomorrow, and how you will be remembered by those who live there."

The South Korean corporal had been looking right at her and hadn't noticed that as she put her rifle butt first on the ground, she had used the motion to pull back its cocking mechanism and set it to semi-automatic fire.

She feigned a sip of the Western whisky and watched carefully as the South Korean soldiers threw back the strong North Korean liquor with reckless abandon. *Yes, trust us,* Song thought, barely letting the whisky touch her lips. *Are we not your brothers and sisters?* She smiled, as though enjoying the moment, keeping her eyes on Kwang, and waiting for his signal.

Chang had trouble taking his eyes off the North Korean Sergeant, standing with her rifle resting on her boot as she sipped her whisky. She appeared so serene; at ease in a way her comrades were not. They were nervous, all ducking heads and averted gazes. She stood a little apart, listening, but not joining in, carefully watching everything. Typical bloody Sergeant, though; no matter whose army, they never missed a thing.

Sure enough, Lieutenant Lee raised a hand to get everyone's attention. "My dear comrades," he said. "Quiet please, quiet."

Trying to be cool, Chang thought. Calling us 'comrades' as the North Koreans do. Like it's suddenly all right to talk like a communist.

Lee continued. "Today, in a few hours, our leaders will sign the Peace Accord in Panmunjom. Tomorrow, we will start the work of dismantling our guard posts along the DMZ, filling in the anti-tank trenches and rolling up the razor wire. By the end of the year, there will be no more DMZ!"

Chang's squad gave a throaty cheer, but the North Koreans remained unmoved. Lee didn't let the lack of response blunt his enthusiasm. He raised his tin cup. "I would like to make a toast to peace and prosperity!" He held out his liquor bottle to refill anyone who needed their drink topped up and indicated to the North Korean officer he should do the same.

Which was when Chang noticed the North Korean really wasn't pouring anything into his soldier's cups. He was going through the motions, sure, but their cups were mostly full, it seemed, so he only made the shallowest of pours. Maybe they were just reluctant to drink in front of their officer, even though it had been agreed. But in their previous meetings, that North Korean officer had drained his cup like a desert soaking up rain. Today, he had barely even sipped, and though he made a show of topping up his glass, it was still full.

There was *definitely* something wrong. He saw several of the North Koreans casually, too casually, raise their hands to the straps of their rifles, as though adjusting them to be a little more comfortable. Looking at the woman near him, he saw she had shifted the grip of her right hand from the muzzle of her carbine down to the forestock, and she was holding it so tight the knuckles of her right hand were white. The thought struck him that there was only one reason to hold your rifle like that, or to have the butt of your carbine resting on your boot while drinking a toast.

If you were planning to bloody use it!

Taking a casual step to the side, Chang moved closer to the South Korean soldier beside him, Private Bo-kyung Nam. Leaning in and smiling as though sharing a joke under his breath, he spoke quietly to Nam. "Something is wrong. Follow my lead."

"What?" The boy was the newest member of the squad and seemed to go through life with two default settings, either confusion or disappointment.

"Just follow me," Chang told him in a fierce whisper.

Lee raised his voice again. "OK, everyone has something to drink? Good, good, now raise your cups and..."

Chang stuck up his hand. "Lieutenant Lee, toilet break?"

Lee frowned at him. "What?"

"Before the big toast. Got to go behind a bush, Lieutenant!"

"Now? I'm making a toast here."

Their Sergeant, Shin-wook Kwon, glowered at Chang and opened his mouth to pull him into line.

"Thank you, sir," Chang said quickly, grabbing Nam by the arm. "Two minutes, sir. Anyone else?" Chang looked around the squad, ignoring the glare of Sergeant Kwon. Another of the privates, Min-jae Park, raised his hand meekly.

"Dammit, all right," Lee said. "Make it quick."

There was a low outcrop of rocks a dozen or so yards behind them and Chang led the two privates over to it. What he would do when he got there, he had no idea. But every nerve in his body told him to run, and that made so little sense he just had to listen to it. Looking over his shoulder, he saw the eyes of every North Korean followed them as they walked away.

They got behind the rocks, which only came up to chest height. Nam still had a confused look on his face, but Park shuffled in behind a rock, rested his rifle against it and started unbuttoning his flies. Chang slapped his hand away.

Park looked at him in surprise. "Corporal?"

"You aren't actually taking a piss, Park, you are just making it look like you are while I think about this, all right?" Chang thumped Nam's shoulder. "Look down at your boots, kid. You usually stand there gawping at the guy next to you while you piss?"

"Corporal, I don't understand..." Nam protested.

"The North Koreans aren't drinking," Chang told them, looking down at his own boots. "None of them. I think they're getting ready to jump us."

"What? Why?" Park asked. At least he was looking down now, playing along even if he didn't know why.

"Steal our weapons, take our damn wallets, I don't know. You see how skinny those bastards are? They'd probably just jump us for rations."

Nam looked over at the two squads and then back down again. "What do we do, Corporal?"

Yeah, what the hell are you going to do now, Chang? Didn't really think this all the way through, did you, comrade?

He looked quickly up and saw both officers looking over at them. Sergeant Kwon pointed at the dirt beside him with an urgent gesture that made it clear they had better hurry up and rejoin the party.

But what would happen if they didn't?

Chang couldn't really see any other option than to find out. Lee had turned to the North Korean Lieutenant and started speaking with him, probably apologizing, Chang guessed. A few of the group of soldiers turned their eyes away from the rocks to watch and listen. Chang guessed they were thinking the exchange between the officers had the potential to be more entertaining than watching three guys piss on some rocks.

"Duck down," Chang said, turning his back to the rock and crouching as he pulled his assault rifle from his shoulder. Nam and Park were still standing, both looking at him like he'd lost his mind as he pulled at Nam's trouser leg. "*Down* I said, Private!"

The North Korean Sergeant, Song, saw the three South Koreans by the rock disappear suddenly from view.

Lifting her leg quickly, she brought her rifle up and into her hands, dropping her whisky cup. "Lieutenant!" she barked.

Kwang looked over sharply, as did the South Korean Lieutenant. It was the last thing the South Korean officer did. Kwang acted instantly, pulling his sidearm from the holster against his hip and putting a bullet into the South Korean

Lieutenant's surprised face.

It was a slaughter, and it was over in moments.

Song calmly and deliberately put two slugs into the chest of the South Korean Sergeant and then turned her fire on the private next to him. So did two of her comrades. Six South Korean soldiers' bodies jumped and bucked with the impact of the 5.8mm bullets spraying from the North Koreans' Chinese-made QTS rifles.

Before they even hit the ground, Song was running toward the rocks where she had last seen the fat-faced South Korean Corporal.

"Dammit!" Chang cursed at the sound of a pistol. As he rose from his crouch, there was an explosion of semi-automatic rifle fire and as he brought his rifle up and around, resting it on top of the rock behind him, he saw the female Sergeant with the long black ponytail running straight for him. She didn't look so pretty anymore. She was screaming something at the top of her lungs and firing from the hip as she ran.

Chang panicked. He pulled his trigger, realized with horror his K2 rifle was still safed and flipped it to full auto as he cocked it, then pulled the trigger again without even bothering to aim. His bullets chewed a line through the dirt in front of the North Korean and she veered off to the right, throwing herself down behind a bush.

Chang jumped as a rifle opened up beside him and looked over to see Private Park had joined him in sending a volley of fire toward the North Koreans, who scattered like hens from a fox. Park caught at least one of them flat-footed, and the man crumpled to the ground. The others found cover behind whatever nearby shrub, depression or small rock offered protection and started directing fire toward Chang, Park and Nam.

A hell of a lot of fire. Chang ducked down, pulling Park down with him, thinking quickly. Nam was still crouched, a shocked look on his face. Hadn't even taken his rifle from his shoulder.

Those rifles the North Koreans were carrying, weren't they QTS-11s? Those things could fire bloody airburst grenades, couldn't they?

As though to answer his question, Chang heard a loud *crump*, then the crack of a grenade in the air overhead as chips of rock flew around them. Short. It had exploded short.

The next one wouldn't. If they didn't get fragged in the next minute or two, they'd soon be flanked. There were at least nine North Korean soldiers still out there.

Twenty yards farther away, he saw another outcrop of rock. Some kind of creek bed behind it maybe.

"I'm going to put down some cover fire. You see those rocks?" Chang grabbed Nam by the sleeve and pointed. "Soon as I start firing, the two of you run for it, got it?"

Nam nodded, and before he could think about it anymore, Chang rose out of his crouch and started firing wildly over the rocks in the rough direction of the North Koreans. He managed to raise a lot of dust around them, but then that damn woman started firing again from off to his left and he had to duck down again.

Nam and Park were zigging and zagging toward the cover of the rocks behind them.

Right, you.

With a last burst of fire which mostly went into the air over the North Koreans, Chang was off and running too. He heard the crack of another grenade above and behind him, something punched him in the shoulder, but he kept running. Reaching the next outcrop of rocks, he threw himself down behind them, landing on top of the prone Private Nam. Park once again had a little more presence of mind and rolled out from behind cover to send a tight volley of fire back toward the rocks they had just vacated, sending a couple of pursuing North Koreans back into cover behind them.

If there was a South Korean record for a 50-yard dash, Chang was pretty sure he had just broken it. He was gasping for air. Looking back behind them, he saw it *was* a dry creek bed he had spotted. A beautifully deep one.

Movement. Keep moving, that is your only hope. Don't let them fix you.

"Up!" he yelled at the others. "Remember your bloody rifles. After me!"

And with that, he bolted for the creek, not stopping to see if the two privates were following him.

Song had made it to the first group of rocks but then she had to duck behind them at the return fire that came from the South Koreans' new position.

Their squad had only one QTS-11 with a grenade launcher attachment, and only five defilade rounds for it. The man using it had already wasted two rounds. As he raised it to fire toward the rocks the South Korean soldiers were sheltering behind now, she put a hand on his arm. "Wait, Private. Take a breath. Make every shot count."

The man was wide-eyed and nodded. Settling the weapon against his shoulder, he sighted down the barrel, aiming it above the rocks 50 yards away. They were higher than the ones Song was sheltered behind, and they couldn't see the South Korean soldiers unless they stuck their heads out to fire.

We will have to flush them out, she decided. *We need to keep them busy. Flank.* She looked quickly behind her for Lieutenant Kwang and saw him crumpled in the dirt where they had been standing, knees drawn up into his belly, unmoving. But they still had numbers and a tactical advantage; she had to fix and flank the South Koreans while they were on the back foot.

She looked at the lay of the land between her and the South Koreans again. Bare ground. Scrub, stones, and grass. *Speed and violence, that's our best tactic from here.*

Two more privates joined her at the rocks, and she turned to the man with the grenade launcher. "You send two rounds at those rocks a few seconds apart. You and you..." she said to the other privates, "...when he sends the first grenade, you go left and you, go right. Go wide. Hit the dirt if they start firing at us again and lay down cover fire. I'm going straight down the middle. Got it?"

"Yes, Comrade Sergeant!" the three soldiers shouted assent.

Song fixed the man with the grenade launcher with an intense look. "For heaven's sake, don't fire short this time, or you'll kill *me*."

"Yes, Comrade Sergeant!" he barked.

She checked her magazine quickly, reseated it and gathered herself. The South Koreans had stopped firing. It was now or not at all.

"All right, go, go, go!" she yelled, bursting from behind the rocks and running straight for the South Korean position.

She heard the thump of the grenade launcher behind her and ducked involuntarily as the projectile sailed over her head and exploded near the rocks ahead of her. The private had aimed well this time, and most of the blast went down into the dirt behind the South Koreans' cover.

That's going to hurt, she thought hopefully.

To her right, one of the men who had run out behind her had gone prone at the sound of the grenade detonating. He started firing at the rocks ahead. Not exactly as she had ordered, but good enough. She doubled across the open ground, ready at any moment to throw herself to the dirt if she saw a South Korean point a rifle her way.

Thump. A second grenade sailed overhead, this time exploding farther behind the rock outcrop in front of her, the man firing it being extra careful not to frag his Sergeant.

There was no reaction from the South Koreans. Dead or wounded? She hoped so. She reached the rocks and threw herself against them, back to the warm stone, her enemy just feet away on the other side. Should she go left, or right? Slow or fast? Did it matter? *Just get around there, Song.* She tensed. Creeping left, rifle across her chest, taking a step, looking quickly over her shoulder to make sure she wasn't tackled from behind, then another step, another look, until she reached the end of the rock outcrop.

Now.

Rolling around as quietly as she could, she took two steps

and rounded the outcrop, ready to shoot at...

Nothing.

She saw footprints in the dirt. They had been here. They were gone. She looked around. Probably that dry creek down there. She could see from the scrub along the lip of the creek bed that it went left and right a few hundred yards in each direction. Probably farther. And it was deep. Following them in there would be suicide.

One of the privates joined her, panting from running hard.

"Get your breath," she told him. "We need to get back, check on the wounded."

"Then what, Comrade Sergeant?"

She put her rifle strap over her shoulder again, thinking about Lieutenant Kwang, curled in the dirt somewhere behind her. "And then we continue our mission," she told him.

Chang had stayed in the creek bed, rifle at the ready in case the North Koreans continued their pursuit. Not because he was particularly brave, but because the section of creek bed they had tumbled into was little more than a deep trench about twenty feet long, with rocks and scrub blocking both ends. He could see the creek bed extended farther beyond the two blockages, but they couldn't make their way under the blockages, and to go over or around would mean exposing themselves to view again.

Private Nam had finally recovered his wits, and when he got his breath, he rolled onto his stomach, rifle in front of him, and crawled back toward the lip of the creek bed, into a firing position. Park was right beside him.

Chang put a hand out and stopped Nam. "Let me." He belly-crawled back up the slope, gingerly sticking his head up and peering through the dead branches of a small bush.

Damn woman! She is relentless.

He saw the North Korean Sergeant standing behind the rocks they had vacated, looking around herself. She seemed to look straight at Chang, and he froze, not even daring to breathe, but her gaze swept over him, left and right, and then another two North Korean soldiers arrived, and she turned her attention to them. After a minute or two, a short conversation and a last glance toward the creek bed, the three of them walked off, back toward the scene of the first attack.

"Corp, you're bleeding," Nam told him. He was back down the slope, lying on his back, rifle across his chest.

"What? Where?"

"Shoulder," Nam said, pointing at his own right shoulder. "Shoulder blade."

Chang vaguely remembered something punching him there while he was in full flight. That first damn grenade? Or the second one? He felt behind him and realized he couldn't feel the pressure of his fingers on his shoulder blade. It was completely numb. And his fingers came away wet with blood.

Crap.

"Get up here and keep an eye on those North Korean devils if you can," he told Nam. "We need to get out of this little ditch and into proper cover before they come looking for us." He started unbuttoning his shirt, fingers slipping on the buttons because of the blood. He realized he was shaking now and held his hands against his chest so the others wouldn't see. "Park, look at this shoulder and tell me if it needs to be plugged."

"Yes, Corp."

Chang rolled onto his stomach so the man could pull his shirt up around his neck, lying on his traitorous hands to stop their trembling.

"What in hell was that all about?" Nam asked softly. "One moment we're toasting reunification, the next, they're trying to kill us?"

Chang winced as Park pulled what felt like shredded cloth out of the mess that was his shoulder. Sharp pain was starting to penetrate the numbness already, as his adrenaline wore off. He gritted his teeth. "I don't know, Nam. But something tells me it was about more than our rations."

He needed to think. Their radio was back in their jeep. If the

North Koreans weren't already in the act of stealing or destroying the vehicle, it was just a matter of time. So, calling for help was out.

"It's like someone took a vegetable shredder to your shoulder, Corp," Park told him. "It's pretty chewed up, but it doesn't look deep, and the bleeding isn't too bad." He pulled the shirt back down.

Chang's self-preservation instinct told him they should use the creek bed to exfiltrate; make their way five miles south, back to the South Korean DMZ fence. Get safe. But his training told him he should try to find cover and observe what the hell the North Koreans were doing. Wait until they left, try to get back and check on Lee and the others, see if any were still alive.

His training won over his desire to run. He rolled onto his side and buttoned up his shirt again, wincing at the throb from his mangled shoulder.

The road wound through a valley lined with steep hills. In winter, it was covered in snow. In spring the creek bed they were lying in would flood with meltwater. Right now, everything was dead, dry, and brown. *If I stay low...* Looking over the lip of the creek bed to the hillside behind them, Chang made up his mind. "You two stay here in cover, watch they don't come this way. I'm going up a little higher, see what the hell they are up to."

Passing Ungam-ni

Ten miles northwest of Hwacheon, South Korea

"What the heck are *they* up to?" 'Bunny' O'Hare came instantly alert at the change in bearing of the North Korean fighter flight she had been monitoring as she crossed into the DMZ from South Korean airspace.

Theirs was a pretty routine mission, escorting a US Navy Boeing-Sikorsky Defiant helicopter headed for a rendezvous with a Navy vessel out in the Sea of Japan. The only thing not routine about it was that it was dragging a Shikaka drone along behind it for some reason, but the Shikaka was shadowing them up on the edge of the atmosphere at 70,000 feet, so it wasn't her worry. All she had to do was see the Defiant through the approved air corridor across North Korea and say goodbye off the coast.

With the thawing of relations between North and South, several new international air traffic routes across the Forbidden Kingdom had been agreed, but it was still normal for US transport aircraft of all services to get an Air Force escort when they were inside North Korean airspace, just in case.

And pretty typical that a low-priority escort mission like this one would be given to a joint US-South Korea air wing like the 35-7th Buddy Wing. Her two-fighter, two-drone element was only a few minutes out of Seongnam military airfield, and Noname had just refreshed the data he was pulling down from an RQ-170 Sentinel intelligence, reconnaissance, and surveillance drone, orbiting at 50,000 feet over the DMZ.

The Sentinel had an eagle-eye view of the entire east coast of the Korean Peninsula and could track up to 200 air or ground contacts simultaneously. It had detected and classified the North Korean Mig-29s much earlier and been following their progress as they approached the demarcation line. The Sentinel had a few other tricks up its sleeve too, but Bunny wasn't expecting she would need to call on those.

Her comms came to life. "Lieutenant, those Migs look like they're on an intercept bearing to you?" her wingman, 'Snake-eater' Besserman, asked her.

"They do, Snake." The informal tone among the US Aggressor Squadron pilots hadn't changed just because they'd rejoined the Air Force. She read some data off her tactical screen. To be honest, she was more worried about North Korean ground to air missile systems than the short-range missiles on the North Korean fighters. "Still fifty miles out, steady cruising speed…"

"Radar!" Snake-eater called. "I'm being painted by fighter attack radar." A slight note of concern in his voice.

"Easy. We're still in neutral airspace," she pointed out. But she didn't like it either. It was a very unfriendly gesture from pilots who were supposedly soon to be allies.

She changed frequency to the Defiant below her. "Joker three, Batman leader. Suggest you lay in a new waypoint that keeps you inside South Korean airspace until we go feet wet and prepare to execute a course change. We have a couple of North Korean Migs fifty miles out who appear to be taking an impolite interest in our flight."

The Defiant was unpiloted, flying with only a navigation officer and a single passenger aboard. "Roger, Batman leader, preparing alternate flight plan. Ready to execute on your mark."

"These guys are fugazy," Snake said. He was a sarcastic Brooklynite with a long fuse, but the hostility of the North Koreans' action disturbed even his inner calm. "They're still closing on us. We're in an approved cooperation corridor…"

"All right, let's not take any chances," Bunny told him. "Break right, take a ten-mile separation, we'll put our Bat between us and them." She switched to cockpit comms. "You get that, Noname?"

"Sending Ghost Bat to blocking position," the AI confirmed.

"Good. As soon as they get in optical infrared range, lock them up. Fire some energy back down their bearing and let them know we see them; might get them to back off."

"Breaking," Snake confirmed, flipping his Kingsnake onto its starboard wing and peeling away from her so that they could bracket the incoming Migs if they needed to. Bunny saw his Ghost Bat drone also moving into position north of them, between themselves and the Mig flight. It wasn't a move that should panic the other aircraft, as it was purely defensive, but it should give them something to think about.

Bunny watched the incoming Mig-29s. They carried Romanian-made R-23 missiles with a range of about 40 miles and would soon be in a position to use them, if they wanted to. Which made little sense in the current political climate, but Bunny had made a career out of navigating situations that made little sense.

As the Migs moved to within missile range of her Ghost Bat, its radar warning receiver lit up with a hostile search radar from one of the Migs. "Possible hostile contacts tracking our Bat," Noname told her.

She could see it well enough on her own display. "OK, let's tango," she muttered. "Light 'em up, Noname."

"Bat going active," he confirmed. He lit their drone's phased array radar and targeted the beam at the incoming North Korean fighters. Unlike her opponents, the Bat could lock up both of the foreign aircraft at once, and they let them know it.

At the same time, Noname pulled up the tactical support menu for the overhead Sentinel drone and queued up jamming support. The powerful sensor suite on the bat-winged Sentinel could not only see the North Korean fighters, but it could also attempt to blind them, and their missiles, if they needed it to. He requested it to close on their position.

The North Korean aircraft showed no sign of deviating from their intercept track. Either because their unsophisticated sensors hadn't picked up her radar lock, or because they were deliberately ignoring it.

"Missiles! I've got incoming!" Snake called.

What the hell? The Sentinel immediately began jamming the two incoming missiles, one fired from each of the Migs. As she watched, the North Koreans volleyed another two missiles toward Bunny's position. The first two missiles were aimed directly at Snake, though. Ignoring his drone decoy, the Migs had gone straight for him.

Bunny checked the incoming missile tracks. The other two missiles weren't headed for her, they were heading straight for the lower, slower Defiant!

Milliseconds later the chopper's defensive AI reacted, throwing the machine into a spiraling dive for the ground, decoys firing into its wake.

"Lock the hostiles, Noname," Bunny ordered.

As Snake-eater maneuvered to frustrate the missiles coming his way, Noname locked up the two Migs, allocated two Peregrine air to air missiles to each, and then flipped their comms to the frequency for their mission controller at Seongnam. The diplomatically drafted rules of engagement they'd been given for this mission did *not* include shooting down North Korean aircraft inside North Korea, even if attacked.

"Seongnam, Batman one, we are engaged with two North Korean Mig-29s over the DMZ. Missiles fired. Request permission to respond in kind," Noname said in a flat monotone.

There was no hesitation at the other end. "Negative, Batman one. You will evade and withdraw."

Bunny watched the incoming missiles, still tracking toward a desperately maneuvering Snake, and the Defiant now trying to hide itself in the ground clutter of the bare brown hills below. Disaster was seconds away unless the blast of radiation from the Sentinel overhead could burn the radar seeker-heads of the North Korean missiles.

She had a perfect firing solution on the two Migs. "Seongnam, Batman leader, we repeat, the enemy force has fired on us. Request permission to return fire!" she called.

"Targets locked. Missiles armed and tracking," Noname told her.

But their controller repeated the order. "Negative, Batman. Evade and withdraw. You are to RTB. Confirm please."

Bunny hammered the glass over her head with a gloved fist. "Batman confirms." She switched channels. "Stand down, Noname. Batman two, Joker flight, we are to evade and withdraw to Seongnam."

He could hear Snake breathing heavily before he replied. "You are shitting me, O'Hare." She had no doubt that even though he was currently maneuvering to evade the North Korean missiles, Snake and his WSO also had a couple of missiles racked and ready to loose at the hostile aircraft. Years of discipline overtook the man. "Dammit. Batman two will evade and RTB."

Bunny heard the thud of rotors over the speakers in her helmet. "Joker will RTB," the Defiant's navigator replied.

If you survive, Bunny thought.

Without needing an order, Noname switched their own phased array radar into jamming mode and added their energy to that of the Sentinel, focusing on the missiles now just seconds away from the Defiant.

Inside the wildly gyrating US Navy Defiant, Information Systems Technician 2nd Class, Petty Officer Ryan Kronk, cursed to himself as he clung to webbing on the side of the crew compartment and waited for the g-force to rip his head from his shoulders.

His week had started badly and gotten worse. A specialist in unmanned naval aviation AI systems, he'd been sent to Navy Aviation Base Busan from the helicopter landing dock, *USS Bougainville*, to assist with the transfer of a White Bat or 'Shikaka' drone from Busan that was not responding to inputs from its pilots aboard the *Bougainville*, several hundred miles away.

The reason the urgent mission had been necessary was that the armed Shikaka was already *airborne*. When he arrived, Kronk found the high flying attack and reconnaissance drone could be controlled by line of sight radio signal from the ground in Busan, but it refused any attempt by the pilots aboard *USS*

Bougainville to take command via satellite link.

Any other drone might have run out of fuel before Kronk could reach Busan and access the on-site mobile control interface, to begin running diagnostics. But the Shikaka-EA was not any other drone. She was the latest fruit of a program started ten years earlier to deliver an intelligence and reconnaissance aircraft for US forces with *offensive* capabilities. Also known as the Great White Bat, its twin turbofan engines had an endurance of 24 hours' flight when it first became operational in the late 2010s, and by the late 2020s that endurance had been extended to 72 hours, while it was capable of flying for up to a week, with in-flight refueling. It was ideal for accompanying aircraft carrier and other task forces on extended deployments, giving them combined surveillance, data assimilation, and electronic warfare capabilities at a fraction of the cost of manned aircraft.

The 'EA' version of the Shikaka had one additional string to its bow. EA stood for 'electronic-warfare and *attack*'. Its modular payload bay could be swapped out and, depending on the mission, could carry an offensive electronic warfare suite, and up to 36 swarming Locust attack drones. Each of the drones was fitted with a four-pound fragmentation warhead designed to attack ground or maritime targets.

Navy had never confirmed the existence of the top-secret swarming munitions version of the Shikaka. Which had made it all the more important to regain control of the machine currently in orbit over Busan.

After spending a day hacking his way into the mobile control unit and then digging around under the digital hood of the Shikaka, Kronk had put in a call to the air operations watch officer on the *Bougainville*, who had routed him straight through to the Task Force Commander, Captain P.W. Wilson. "Kronk, give me the good news."

"I was hoping to start with the bad news, sir," Kronk told him, peering at the laptop which was connected to the high-powered mobile transceiver that sent signals to and from the rogue Shikaka. "The bad news is the satellite link is kaput and our bird can only be controlled by line-of-sight radio. I've been on the line with the manufacturer's tech team: they can't solve it remotely, want us to crate it up and ship it back Stateside."

"And we lose our Shikaka. There are only ten in the entire damn Navy. You know how many butts I had to kiss to get my hands on that bird?"

"Don't want to think about that, sir. The good news is, I have another option for you. Put me and this mobile control unit on a Defiant, I set our Shikaka to follow me home like a lost puppy, and inside 12 hours we are both back aboard *Bougainville* where I can keep working on her."

Wilson signed off on Kronk's proposal. As he was flung around the Defiant's crew compartment, watching as the nav officer at the front of the aircraft went momentarily weightless and floated in midair before slamming into a bulkhead, Kronk realized the rogue Shikaka was no longer his biggest problem.

Bunny gave a tight fist pump in her cockpit as Snake evaded the missiles fired at him and he and his drone began withdrawing south. She also let herself hope for a second as the third missile, arrowing in toward the Defiant far below, was overwhelmed by the combined energy from her radar and the Sentinel's above, and started gyrating blindly through the sky, its target lost. But her elation turned to horror as the fourth missile kept boring in on the floundering helicopter, and then slammed into it in an eye-watering flash of fire and flame. Trailing ugly black smoke, the helo buried itself in a valley far below.

She checked her tactical display, saw the two Migs withdrawing back into North Korean airspace, before angrily switching radio frequencies again. "Seongnam, Batman leader. Joker two is down, mark my position." She put their machine into a tight banking circle over the crash site, staring hard through ugly black smoke at the ground below.

"What do you see, Noname?"

The AI WSO had access to the aircraft's distributed aperture sensor system and could zoom and scan the ground optically.

"I see one crashed helo. Smoke indicating a fire. No movement. No sign of life," he said.

Bunny keyed her radio again. "Seongnam, I am going to hold here while you organize a rescue flight." She gripped her stick tighter. "And Seongnam, tell them to bring body bags."

Kronk woke to the smell of ... ozone. A smell he recognized. Fried electronics. And something worse.

Aviation fuel.

Where the hell was he? He looked around and decided he was upside down in a hell-house of metal, glass and ... blood? He could smell blood too.

Not his own. The blood was dripping from the Navy loadmaster strapped into the chair on the other side of the crushed crew compartment, the spear of a broken cargo restraint coming out the front of his chest. He was dead. Name, what was his name?

Lieutenant Something. Damn, he couldn't even remember.

He reached up to punch the clasp on the webbing across his chest and then realized that would be a dumb idea, because it would dump him on his head. And it seemed he had already taken a blow or two to the skull, his thinking as fuzzy as it was. He looked slowly and painfully around.

Reaching gingerly below his head with his hands, he felt a webbed baggage rack, empty. Saw some metal cases and smashed rolling pallets, like the kind every military everywhere loads into aircraft. Bottles of mineral water, lying everywhere. *Really?* Their flight was supposed to be ferrying top secret ordnance out of South Korea and someone had decided they had room for a pallet of bottled water? Speaking of water ... could he hear water outside?

Getting ready to take his weight on his right arm and hold onto his harness with his left, he hooked his feet into the chair supports by his ankles and punched the harness release on his chest. He dropped a few inches before his feet caught his fall and, crabbing at the baggage harness, he lowered himself down without breaking his neck. He was still wearing the helmet he'd been given and thought about taking it off, but then decided it might just be keeping his brains from slopping out of his skull, so he left it on.

He crawled forward and checked the other man for signs of life. His neck was warm. But he felt for a pulse and, not surprisingly given the man's injuries, got none. But if the body was still warm, Kronk hadn't been out cold for long. Another wave of fuel fumes washed over him, and he looked for the quickest way out.

There was a wedge of daylight at the rear of the payload bay, and he crawled toward it. Tumbling out of the crushed crew compartment, he saw the helo had been torn in half. The engine section and tail were lying farther down a rocky riverbank in a valley lined with steep mountains, a broad river in full flow just twenty yards away. Ugly black smoke was boiling out of the still burning engines. More freight containers and pallets littered the ground behind the downed chopper.

Kronk shook his head. *If you'd come down in that river, you'd have survived just long enough to drown, Ryan.* He looked behind him at the crushed front section of the helo. *Or burned alive if that burning tail hadn't fallen off on the way down.*

Missile. He remembered the Lieutenant shouting something about a missile. He'd just had time to jam his laptop into the transceiver's duffel bag at his feet and buckle in, then … he couldn't remember anything after that. It must have homed on the hot engine.

There was something else trying to get his attention. A loud, high-pitched, beeping sound. He blinked a few times, tilting his head to try and work out if the beep was coming from inside the chopper or outside it.

Stupid. It was the Shikaka's mobile base station in the duffel bag he'd left inside the helo.

Every ounce of common sense in his body told him he should leave it in there because the cloud of fuel around the crashed helo could ignite at any second. But the base station was in essence a high-powered radio. Built to communicate with the Shikaka overhead, he could use the Shikaka to relay a call for help.

The smoke from the wrecked helo was climbing into the sky, a signal to any nearby troops to come and investigate. And what if they weren't friendly? As he watched it rise, he saw a flash of light high above, the glint of sunlight on glass. A plane, circling. The bastard who had shot them down? Or the escort which hadn't prevented it? Would they call in the crash?

Kronk decided he needed to take his fate into his own hands for once. Drawing in a lungful of clean air, he dived back into the wreck, scrabbled around for the duffel bag, and then heaved it out just before his lungs imploded.

He hauled the bag clear of the wreckage and sat down on the riverbank. Both the transceiver and his mil-spec laptop that made up the base station were intact, but would his laptop boot?

It did. He called up the control interface for the Shikaka and saw line after line of the same message.

Navigation deviation. Replot waypoints?

Seventy thousand feet overhead, the confused aircraft was asking him whether he wanted to update the Shikaka's route to take into account his 'navigation deviation'. He laughed bitterly. Navigation deviation? That was one way to describe an uncontrolled crash landing.

He looked up from the screen. Outward from the rushing river, steep mountains covered in rocks and scrubby trees rose into the sky in every direction.

He pulled off his helmet, slumped onto his backside and lay down on the cool, wet gravel of the riverbank, forearms up over his face.

What in the freaking hell kind of situation have you gotten into, Kronk?

Over Panmunjom Peace Village, Korea

Ten thousand feet over the Joint Security Area, DMZ

Also wondering what kind of situation he had gotten himself into, Lieutenant Hee-chan 'Bounce' Son looked right at his flight leader, Colonel 'Keys' Ban, then left at the nearest North Korean pilot, flying level and about a hundred feet ahead of him. He checked his instruments, and then his helmet-mounted display, still flashing a 'missile armed' warning at him.

Did the man in the North Korean Mig-29 know he was about to die? Was he sitting in his cockpit, like Bounce, counting down the seconds? Was he resigned to his fate, or was he flying with one hand on his joystick, the other on his ejection handle, hoping to beat the odds and parachute to earth?

Bounce shook his head. He realized the pills his handler had given him were causing his mind to wander, and that was the last thing he could afford right now.

"Puleun leader to flight. Getting ready to circle the village ... twenty-degree bank to port on my mark, watch your spacing, try not to collide with our new friends," his squadron leader said.

They'd rehearsed the maneuver a dozen times with pilots from their own squadron, but it was the first time in history anyone from the South had flown in formation with a flight of North Korean pilots. He had no doubts the North Koreans had rehearsed just as hard as they had. Perhaps harder. Bounce had only been briefed by his North Korean handler on his part of the coming action, but he had a theory about what would happen in the seconds after he launched his missile at the North Korean fighter. And it had been confirmed when he had seen the 1,000 lb. Chinese Thunder Stone bombs on pylons under the North Koreans' wings.

One by one, the Migs peeled off to begin the slow banking turn to port that would take them all west, into North Korean airspace – unchallenged – and allow them to line up for a low-level run right over the top of the assembled dignitaries standing on the steps of Freedom House in the South, and the Panmungak congress building in the North.

Bounce knew the timetable for the ceremony below down to the minute. And not just because he was part of it. Newsreaders on South Korean television had been breathlessly recounting it over and over in the near continuous news coverage leading up to today.

0800 hours: the delegates assemble on the steps of their pavilions for the fly-past.

0805: the signing party proceeds to the small blue building in the middle of the peace village that straddles the Military Demarcation Line. Unlike the 1953 armistice calling a halt to hostilities in the Korean War – which was signed by the Generals on all sides – the Peace Accord was to be signed by the Supreme Leader of North Korea and the President of South Korea, witnessed by the Secretary General of the United Nations. For security reasons, the leaders of both nations would already be in place inside the building for the start of the ceremony and would only emerge once the agreement was signed.

0815 to 1030: the signing ceremony takes place, broadcast to the world.

1035: the delegates from both nations walk to the demarcation line and symbolically shake hands or embrace.

1040: the leaders of both nations, flanked by their State Council or National Assembly Ministers and senior Generals, mark the start of formal reunification negotiations by cutting a ribbon symbolizing the end of the Military Demarcation Line and the Demilitarized Zone.

1045: the delegates retire to the newly constructed Unification House for a press conference with the assembled media, followed by a symbolic round of reunification negotiations.

1100: carefully selected family members from families in the North and South cross the border at the Bridge of No Return and are reunited with their families.

He had scoffed at this last piece of theater. It would give the media the vision they craved of weeping family members embracing and kissing each other, but it had in fact been possible to hold supervised gatherings at various points along the demarcation line for more than a year now.

Their formation straightened up, heading directly west before it would come around again for the pass over Panmunjom. He suddenly realized he was deep inside North Korean airspace. Radar warnings were showing on his receiver, but none showed the hostile status of missile radar signatures.

He was a South Korean Air Force Pilot, flying unmolested through the skies of North Korea for the first time in 85 years. But more importantly …

He was home. For the first time since he was three years old.

Missile armed. Target locked. Weapon safed.

His real name was not Hee-chan Son. He had been born Jong-gwan Son, the only child of two North Korean academics who had been shot and killed trying to cross a river in the DMZ. Their bullet-riddled boat floated to the southern shore where it was pulled in by South Korean soldiers. His parents were dead, and Jong-gwan Son was adopted by a South Korean family.

There had never been any question about whether he would be returned to his family – an aunt and grandparents – in the North. But then, he hadn't thought about it that much, until he started his mandatory military service in the South Korean Air Force at 17 and a fellow conscriptee asked him whether he'd ever considered going back.

Over the next two years, though he didn't realize it at the time, what started as a simple question became a niggle, and then a grudge. Why had he not been asked the same question by his parents? Who had decided he was better off in the South? Who were his family, really? Did they know he was still alive? Did they miss him?

The man who had asked the question was a North Korean

agent, and it was his nudging that turned Bounce's niggle into a full-blown chip on his shoulder. When his doubt had been fed and watered sufficiently, and before Bounce finished his military service, the man had approached him with a new question. Would Bounce like to speak with his birth grandmother? The man had connections in the North – he could arrange it, if he could keep it a secret, he said.

The old woman at the other end wept through the entire call. "I wish your grandfather was still alive to talk to you. We all thought you were dead too!" she said. After all the propaganda he had been fed as a youth, he had been skeptical, half-convinced the call was a set-up, and the person at the other end would just be an actor. But no one could fake the mixture of grief and joy the old woman conveyed. "Is it really you, Jong-gwan? My beautiful grandchild?"

Over several calls she told Bounce how the family had been shunned by neighbors and harassed by police when news of his parents' failed defection had come back to their village. His grandparents were already retired, but his mother's sister had lost her teaching job at a local school and been forced to work in a canning factory. Would the old woman have made that kind of thing up? Bounce thought not – it didn't exactly reflect well on North Korean society. He warned her not to talk about it, sure their calls were being monitored, despite his new friend's assurances to the contrary.

He had spoken with his aunt too, and the woman had been even more emotional than his grandmother, if that was possible. During their first call, all she had been able to say was: "My sister's boy. Little Jong-gwan. My sister's boy..." Then the calls had been cut off and he could no longer reach his grandmother. His friend could not explain why, but after a couple of months passed, he told Bounce the bad news. The old woman had died, only his aunt was left, and she was sick, in need of expensive hospital treatment. His friend came with a new offer. If Bounce would be willing to re-up after his mandatory service, if he would try out for pilot training, the man might be able to use his connections to smuggle Son's aunt to the South. All he would have to do was provide a little information to the man's contacts about his pilot training. Harmless stuff, most of which you could get off the internet anyway.

Bounce knew exactly where that road would lead. Into the pockets of the North Korean Reconnaissance General Bureau or RGB, its foreign intelligence agency. He was no fool. He realized then that his friend was not just a friend, after all, but a foreign agent. If he agreed, he would be betraying his adopted land, and if caught, could face the death penalty.

He didn't care.

Because his country did not want him. His fellow pilots did not treat him as an equal. Those who knew his origins treated him like a dimwitted country cousin. His call sign, 'Bounce', was a deliberate humiliation. It had been given to him by his fellow trainees in the fighter academy because of an early tendency to skip his aircraft across the runway when landing. The call sign meant he would never be allowed to forget it.

In the squadron though, he had another nickname ... *Seupai.* Spy. The Northerner. The enemy. Untrusted, unworthy of anything but their scorn. And they treated him as such: excluding him from social gatherings, using the nickname as he was walking into the ready room, snickering behind their hands. At first he had resented the slur, telling himself they were jealous of his flying skills, of the fact he consistently rated higher than them in exercises and evaluations. Eventually though, the nickname and the way they treated him had come to define him. They called him the Spy? Very well, then, so be it.

As far as Bounce was concerned, Jong-gwan Son had already died on that boat, on that river, with his parents. He was not Hee-chan Son, and the family that had raised him was not his own. His family, his only *real* family, was in the North and he had been denied the right to be with them.

"I don't want to bring my aunt to the South," he'd told his new 'handler' after he was accepted into pilot training. "I want to join her, in the North."

The man had been surprised, and dubious. "Eight years' service in the South Korea Air Force, and you can be an airline pilot. Make a lot of money, see the world. You would give that up?"

"Money without family, without identity, is an empty comfort," he'd said.

"You could start a family of your own," the man insisted.

"I will," he said. "In the North."

But then it had started looking like the concepts of 'North' and 'South' would become irrelevant. Reunification was becoming a reality. Within five years, he would be free to visit the North, or his aunt would be free to visit him.

"She does not have five years," his handler told him, sadly. "She is dying. Cancer."

"How long does she have?"

He'd shrugged. "If she was here, in the South, with access to the latest therapies, it might even be curable. In the North, with her status as the family member of a defector, who knows? Months, maybe. She won't make five years, that's for sure. Unless you were to join her, now. As a family member of an Air Force pilot in North Korea she would get access to military hospitals and doctors. If you defect, we could arrange for her to get the best possible care, equal to anything she could get in the South. No one can see the future; reunification may never happen."

"I want to speak with her." It had been a short call. She was weak and upset. "What would I have to do?" he'd asked his handler.

They had been sitting in a café and the man had stirred his bubble tea thoughtfully, then looked up and directly into Bounce's eyes. "Bring us your Boromae fighter. Teach our pilots how to defeat it."

He had not hesitated. "When? How?" They had been refining the plan for his defection when he had received the news, he was being recommended for the Peace Accord Flyover, because of his unique personal history: an orphaned child of defectors from the North, serving in the military of the

South. The irony of that did not escape him.

"I will pass the news to my superiors," his excited handler had said. "This may give us … opportunities."

In the cockpit of his Boromae, now over the Yellow Sea, a voice sounded in his ears, pulling him away from the memory and back into the present. "OK pilots, last turn before the money pass. Keep it clean, speed 400 knots, descend to 5,000, watch your positioning. Let's give them a show, boys and girls."

Oh, we'll give them a show, Keys, Bounce thought. *Bet on that.*

He unsafed his missile, checked that the North Korean target was still neatly caged.

Tried not to think of it as a man in a plane, just a plane. Just a target. A thing. Or even better, just something in his way. He just had to wipe it from the sky, and the path ahead of him would be clear.

"Approaching ingress point," his squadron leader droned, trying to sound bored. "Smile for the cameras."

The KF-21 Boromae was stealthier than the Migs flying beside him, but it did not carry its weapons in internal bays. That was a disadvantage in terms of radar cross-section, but a definite advantage right now. His Japanese-made AAM-5 off-boresight missile wouldn't waste vital time dropping from an internal bay before orienting itself on a target – it would start vectoring from the moment it left the pylon under his wing.

He reached for his throttle and throat mic at the same time. "Uh, Puleun leader, Puleun five. I am losing power."

His squadron leader did not curse, or even falter. They'd rehearsed this eventuality too, of course. "Drop out of formation, Five. Two, drop into his slot. Godspeed, Five."

Bounce eased back on his throttle, watching as the aircraft around him pulled ahead and the man flying nose to tail with their squadron leader eased himself back and into the place Son had just vacated.

It was done flawlessly, and he doubted anyone watching from the ground below would even notice.

For the North Korean pilot in his Mig-29, it was the signal that it was his time too.

May your ancestors watch over you, Son thought. *Fox 2!*

The missile leapt from its rail and aimed itself immediately at the Mig, now just a mile ahead of him. Without waiting for it to strike, Bounce pushed his throttle forward and rolled his machine left, turning sharply away from the two formations. Heading for the ground in a spiraling dive, he lost sight of the other aircraft, but his digital helmet-mounted display told him everything he needed to know.

Kill!

He craned his neck, looking back over his shoulder. He saw a bright light in the sky, a trail of white smoke that must be the falling North Korean Mig. No parachute.

He hoped the man had been a volunteer.

The North Korean formation immediately broke – two machines releasing their GPS guided bombs before breaking left and high, the other three rolling inverted and heading for the ground. A clearly rehearsed strategy.

The South Korean pilots on the other hand kept plowing through the sky in perfect aerial parade formation. They would have no idea what in the hell had just happened, and in Bounce's opinion, their squadron leader, Keys Ban, was never the quickest on the uptake at the best of times.

Come on, fools, Bounce urged them. *Wake up!* He wanted them to at least give themselves a fighting chance.

As the two Migs that had transitioned to high cover maneuvered for a solution on the Korean aircraft below them, the South Korean Boromaes *finally* reacted.

Colonel Cho 'Keys' Ban had been focused on maintaining a perfect arrowhead formation as his flight approached Panmunjom.

The great-grandson of the former UN Secretary General, Ban's family name had earned him his place at the head of the formation, and he knew his great-grandfather would be looking down on him with pride.

His pilots had just come off a Red Flag exercise against the

Americans and their drones, and they had had their confidence shaken. But today, they looked rock solid. Looking back over his shoulder at his number five, he was relieved to see the guy dropping smoothly out of formation, no sign of nerves. The kid was only included in the formation because of his history – an adopted North Korean in a South Korean uniform. There was a media crew waiting for them to land, so they could interview him. *Forget it, they'll probably do the interview anyway; why let the fact he hadn't completed the fly-by get in the way of a good story?*

Then Keys' perfectly ordered world went to hell. He heard one of his pilots call "Fox 2!". There was an explosion almost simultaneously beside and behind him. As he jerked his head to look at the flash of light, he saw two of the North Korean Migs rip out of formation and light their tails, falling behind them, heading high.

His helmet filled with the voices of his pilots, calling desperately for orders.

Keys froze.

This. What the … No! Then his radar warning receiver started beeping. *Hostile radar lock! Missile!*

"Puleun flight, break and engage!" he called, before rolling his Boromae onto its wing and angling it toward his attackers.

Even though it closed the distance to the Migs, it wasn't an attacking move. He had to force the incoming missiles to maneuver radically if he was going to stand a chance. He never saw them, or the aircraft that fired them, but seconds later the missile warning tone stopped chirping – *miss!* – and he focused on the circular situational display in his heads-up display.

Two Migs behind and low. Two more ahead, down on the deck … He rolled his machine, scanning the ground desperately, pulling the nose down, aiming his radar to try to get a lock on the machines ahead of him. Explosions, on the ground! The mystery of why the North Korean machines had been carrying Thunder Stone bombs was solved.

Bastards! They were moving fast, but low and about ten miles ahead of him. Arming two AAM-5s he marked each of the hostile aircraft and got tone.

"Puleun leader, Fox 2, Fox 2."

His fire-and-forget missiles jumped from their hardpoints, even as his radar warning receiver started warbling again.

Bounce saw the first of the Thunder Stone guided bombs explode on the ground below and behind him, probably aimed at the two anti-air missile emplacements South Korea had stationed just south of Panmunjom.

Then, as he had expected, the other three North Korean aircraft came back around, their bombs' guidance systems no doubt programmed with targets inside the Joint Security Area.

South Korean anti-air ground defenses had not reacted. Stunned, neutralized, or just paralyzed by the fear of attacking 'allies'?

As his machine hit two hundred feet, Bounce leveled out, screaming over the fields and villages below too quickly to see any detail. To his relief, none of the North Korean radar sites currently painting his aircraft had switched to targeting mode. They had been briefed to ignore him and thankfully, they were doing so. He was probably too low now for them to pick him up anyway.

His target airfield was Nuchon-ri, a North Korean fighter base only 20 miles over the demarcation line. Flying time, another five minutes. He reached for his radio, preparing to contact the controller at the base so that he could be guided in.

As he did so, he watched the carnage in the skies behind him play out on his tactical display. Three South Korea Boromaes were down. He couldn't see whose. Two were still engaged. Four Migs, including the one he had destroyed, had also disappeared from his tac screen. If he'd carried out his own rapid descent correctly, South Korean radar would also assume his machine had been shot down.

That confusion would cover his defection, for now.

He could not see what effect the North Korean bombs had had, but he could easily imagine. The Peace Village was exactly that, just a village. Barely two city blocks in area. Assuming the

North Koreans had aimed their bombs at the South Korean buildings and delegation, plus the building in which the Peace Accord was to be signed, then the firepower of at least eight 1,000 lb. high explosive warheads had just detonated inside an area not much bigger than the Superbowl stadium.

Bounce had not voted for the current South Korean President. And he was no fan of the appeasement-oriented North Korean Supreme Leader either.

He doubted he would miss either of them very much.

Projectile alert. His threat warning system suddenly sounded. *Indirect fire detected.*

The Boromae's highly sensitive 360-degree optical-electric target detection system had picked up … what? Whatever it was, it was too small to see with the naked eye, but its track was painted on his tac display. It was tracking hundreds of projectiles, fired from inside North Korea, converging on … Seoul.

Artillery and rocket fire!

He frowned. North Korea had tens of thousands of artillery barrels within range of South Korea's largest city. This barrage seemed to be coming from a single site, about ten miles behind the demarcation line. Not exactly the opening salvo of a major offensive.

But also, not his problem.

He had to get his machine safely on the ground at Nuchon-ri. What was happening in Seoul was a problem for the poor bastards at the other end of that barrage.

The second air battle of the Reunification Conflict was over inside five minutes. In the first minute, the North Koreans had claimed four of Keys' pilots. Who had fired on the North Koreans? He wouldn't know until he got back on the ground, but Keys had a suspicion it had been one of the pilots who wasn't reporting in … Hee-chan Son. Bounce must have seen something, got a missile away before the North Koreans could begin their ground attack and then been shot down himself.

Poor bloody kid.

They'd accounted for four additional Migs, all of them while they were pulling out from ground attacks on Panmunjom. The other two had bugged out as soon as the ground attack was over, screaming north, back behind the demarcation line.

Keys had asked for ... no, *demanded* ... permission to engage them. Their AAM-5 missiles had a range of 22 miles, were still tracking. But he was ordered to break off, stay inside South Korean airspace and protect Panmunjom.

He circled over the 'Peace Village', the air below filled with smoke, lights from emergency vehicles clearly visible through the haze.

Checking the fuel and weapons states of the remaining aircraft in his flight he decided he and his single wingman had fuel for about another thirty minutes. They were not going anywhere yet.

His wingman had fallen into a shocked silence: he needed him back up on his toes. "Puleun six, stay on my wing, separation two miles. Any aircraft heading south toward the DMZ is to be regarded as hostile. Engage on my order."

Keys had been slow to react to the initial attack. Too slow. That would not happen again. If he saw North Korean aircraft moving in toward the border, he was not going to wait to see what happened.

No matter what side of the damn DMZ they were on.

Kronk had his own DMZ dilemma. No, he had a bucketload of dilemmas.

About five minutes after sitting his ass down on the rocky riverbank, he found himself suddenly face down in the river, gasping for air as the fuel in the air around the downed helo ignited with a terrifying *whoosh*.

The fire cloud hadn't reached him – just startled him – and a bright blaze consumed the forward section of the Defiant. Inside there somewhere was the body of the Navy Lieutenant whose name he couldn't even remember. Had the helo been carrying ammunition? He hoped to hell not. The additional column of smoke added another beacon to the sky, increasing his uneasiness. That damned plane was still circling overhead too.

He returned to the laptop. If he could get into the Shikaka's communications system menu, tap into the channel that the pilots used to communicate with ground and air controllers, he might be able to get a mayday out, tell *someone* he'd been shot down and needed rescuing.

And what the hell was that about anyway? He was thinking hard while hooking up the various components. Yes, they had crossed into the DMZ, but they were still technically south of the demarcation line, inside South Korean airspace, in an approved flight corridor. Hundreds of aircraft had probably made the same transit in the last 24 hours. Why were they attacked, today of all days?

"Well, Kronk, there's your answer," he told himself, out loud. *You were attacked precisely because today was a day unlike all other days – the end of the Korean War. Peace on the Peninsula. Korea Re-United at last blah blah blah.*

The headlines had seemed too good to be true and maybe they were. All he knew was they had been shot down by a North Korean missile at just about the exact moment the Peace Accord was being signed in Panmunjom. Not a coincidence. Couldn't be.

He turned back to the laptop.

>> *Initiate handshake.*

>*Data handshake processing*

>*Control interface initializing*

>*Interface signal not found*

>*Boost gain? Enter control access sequence*

Kronk hammered a passcode into the keyboard, gave the command for the radio to try to optimize itself based on detected ambient interference and waited impatiently.

>*Interface signal not found*

"Ah hell." He slammed a fist down on the gravel next to him. The problem could be any one of several things. Most likely was damage to the satellite transceiver caused by the crash. Interference or deliberate jamming from other radio sources was possible, though less likely. The Shikaka satellite link was supposed to be hardened against jamming.

"Try again, Kronk, carefully this time." As he ran through the uplink routine one more time, he looked at the time in the corner of the screen. It was 13:14, approaching the hottest part of the day. He was out in the open. He had water – hell, he had a river in full flow less than a hundred feet away – but no cover. The river wound through a mountainous valley, the steep-sided hills and cliffs bare of any meaningful vegetation. Probably deliberately denuded with Agent Orange by either the North or the South, to expose any movement by troops or vehicles. He couldn't see any roads, not even a rough track. That at least meant that even though he was probably inside the DMZ, he would have to be pretty unlucky to be surprised by a North Korean patrol.

But that aircraft overhead would see the wreck of the Defiant and see him too, by now. How long before a chopper would be sent in to investigate? If he had come down inside the DMZ northeast of Hwacheon it meant he was anywhere from two to five miles from North Korean territory and had at least the same distance to the border fences in the South.

How long before a North Korean border patrol found him?

His situation was not tenable. He needed an air evac and he needed it now.

The uplink sequence finished again.

>Interface signal not found

All right, he was getting nowhere. Talking to himself was something that had always calmed him, and more than one girlfriend had teased him about it. But there was no one else out here to annoy. "Well, Kronk, it looks like the uplink is out of action, or there's interference..." He looked up through rising smoke and couldn't see the circling aircraft anymore. "OK, so, the cavalry isn't coming. But the bad guys might be. Time to load up and get the hell out of here."

In her Kingsnake ten thousand feet above him, Bunny considered dropping lower to get a better look at the man below, maybe wave to him to let him know she was keeping an eye out for him, but then another gout of flame rose from the wrecked Defiant and smoke obscured the crash site.

Her radar warning receiver showed she was being painted by a North Korean ground radar now. She refreshed the data from her Sentinel at 50,000 feet and saw another pair of fighters moving in. They were antique Chengdu J-7s, probably unable to see her or their drone wingman with their own radars and definitely unable to see the Sentinel on overwatch well inside South Korean airspace, but they were making a beeline for her position. "Noname, arm missiles on the Ghost Bat and keep an eye on those J-7s."

"On it."

She changed her radio frequency. "Seongnam, Batman leader, what is the status on that evac flight. I saw at least one survivor down there."

The voice that came back at least had the decency to sound sheepish. "Sorry, Lieutenant, but the North Korean Government has just issued a no-fly for all North Korean airspace and warned all civilian and military aircraft they will engage and destroy any aircraft crossing the demarcation line. Panmunjom has been bombed. Seoul is under attack from North Korean artillery and rockets. It's a clown show up there right now. Your orders are to RTB immediately. We'll mount a rescue when the situation stabilizes."

Panmunjom, *bombed*? So, this little fracas was premeditated? With a last look at the smoke-covered crash site below, Bunny pointed her aircraft back to base.

"Reel in the Bat, Noname, we're bugging out."

"Permission to emote, ma'am?"

She smiled. "As good a time as any, Noname."

"It sucks we are just leaving that man down there."

"It does, Noname," she assured him. "But only until I get onto Osan Air Base and start raising hell."

South Korean Prime Minister Tae Hyun 'Ted' Choi was about to start raising hell. Unlike the majority of South Korea's State Council – who were lying either dead or injured in the rubble of Panmunjom - he had come through unscathed.

At that moment, he was airborne, heading south toward Sejong City in a Korean Government Sikorsky chopper. His people were still trying to get clarity on the situation on the ground among the chaos, fire and smoke that had engulfed the 'Peace Village' but as far as they could tell, he was the only uninjured senior member of the State Council.

Only a fortuitous bathroom visit to the basement of South Korea's Freedom House had saved him. His colleagues had all been assembling on the steps in front of the building when the bombs had fallen, ready to proceed to the anonymous blue barracks building on the Military Demarcation Line where the peace treaty was to be welcomed by their two heads of State.

There, they were to have greeted their North Korean counterparts and posed together for the cameras of an assembled world media.

Except the treaty was not signed, Choi reflected. North Korean bombs had made sure of that.

The atmosphere inside the helo was one of fear and barely controlled chaos. As they'd taken off from the airfield just south of Panmunjom in thick clouds of roiling smoke, they were getting reports that artillery and rockets were falling on Seoul. A South Korean fighter had shot down at least one North Korean aircraft taking part in the overflight. Two of the South Korean Boromae aircraft had also been lost. North Korean fighters had then shot down two South Korean or allied aircraft traveling through pre-approved air corridors over the DMZ, one a South Korean civilian light aircraft and the other, a US Navy helicopter.

Civilian losses in the chaos of armed conflict were to be expected, but the shootdown of the US military aircraft was a serious political act that could yet have far reaching consequences. Choi pulled on the sleeve of the Security Service protection detail leader beside him. Everyone else in the chopper was working either telephones or radios, headsets plugged into their ears.

"Yes, Prime Minister?" the man replied, pulling an earphone out of one ear. Detail Commander, Dae-sung Yeo, was a thick set man in his late 30s, hair already starting to turn silver. Ted Choi had to shout to make himself heard over the thud of the overhead rotors.

"Any news on the President?" The national broadcast of the signing of the Peace Accord had been proceeding normally, with both leaders having made their greetings, given short, scripted assurances of hope for the future, and then sat down with pens in hand, waiting for the vital documents to be put in front of them ... before the screen went suddenly black, at exactly the moment high explosives started detonating across Panmunjom.

Though it may not be obvious to all, it was obvious to Choi because North Korea had used the subterfuge of the celebratory overflight to launch their attack. South Korea's new Low Altitude Missile Defense System – Sky Dome – also covered Panmunjom and could intercept anything from rockets and ballistic missiles to large-caliber artillery shells. Patterned on Israel's Iron Dome system, it made a sneak attack on Panmunjom almost impossible.

But the bomb-laden North Korean aircraft in the overflight were cleared to fly right *over* Panmunjom. Dumb iron bombs dropped at point blank range could not be intercepted and Choi had been party to the decision to let both sides' aircraft carry weapons, as a 'show of good faith'. An inconvenient fact he may need to justify, one day. Right now, he had other worries.

"No sir. The feed was cut when the bombs hit. There is heavy signal interference across the demarcation line – jamming, from both sides. We have no information on the South Korean President or North Korean Supreme Leader." Yeo told him.

"They have to be found," Choi said. "It is our number one priority!"

"Yes, Prime Minister!"

If President Si-min Shin was dead, Choi was now acting Head of State. But the authority had to be granted to him by the remaining junior members of the State Council – South Korea's Congressional Cabinet – and they would not move until the situation was clear.

He had a pencil and notepad in front of him and moved to the next item on his list.

"You said the other members of the State Council are either dead, or seriously wounded. Are there any survivors?"

The man did not flinch as he delivered the news. "Latest report is six dead, four seriously wounded, in critical condition. They are being flown to nearby hospitals; none are expected to survive at this stage."

"I see. Who is the most senior surviving member of the State Council after me?"

He pulled up a list on a tablet PC. "The Agriculture Minister, sir."

"Get her on a secure telephone line, I want to speak with her immediately."

"Yes, sir."

He tapped his pencil impatiently as the agent contacted an operator in Sejong City and started tracking down the agriculture minister. As a junior minister, So-wa Yoon was not invited to Panmunjom, but was probably hosting a celebration event with officials and business leaders like every other politician in the country. Or had been, until a few minutes ago.

The agent pulled his headset off his ears and handed it to Choi. "The Agriculture Minister."

"Hello, Yoon?"

"Yes, Prime Minister Choi," she said immediately. "The sirens are sounding here; I am on the way to our shelter. Is it true what the media is saying? The President is dead? North Korea is attacking?"

"The situation is … fluid, Yoon. We have grave fears for all of the State Council members at Panmunjom. If the President is incapacitated, you will be called on to be acting Vice President in my place." Choi heard someone shouting directions in the background and she did not respond. "Did you hear me?"

"Yes, Prime Minister," she said. "Sorry, we are being directed to a shelter. I heard you, but we must hope it does not come to that."

"We must hope, but we must also prepare," he told her. "As soon as I reach Sejong, I will convene an emergency meeting of the State Council with remaining members. If we do not have word from the President at that time, I will ask you to nominate me in his place, and I will nominate you to Vice President, as per protocol."

"Yes. No."

Choi blinked. "Sorry, did you say no?"

"No. I mean, yes that is the protocol, but Prime Minister, we should wait until we have confirmation that the President and other State Council members are dead or critically injured. I would not be comfortable if..."

He stabbed his pencil into his notepad so hard it nearly broke. "Yoon! This is not some meeting about grain subsidies for farmers! We may already be at war with the North. Time is of the essence, and we cannot waste a single minute." He snapped his fingers at Yeo. "Give me a list of the confirmed dead."

The agriculture minister was still prevaricating. "Yes, Prime Minister, I realize, but the Defense Minister, or the Mayor of Seoul..."

Choi ran his eye over the list the agent handed him on her tablet. "The Minister of National Defense is confirmed dead. So is the Minister of Interior and Safety. The President's Chief of Staff is dead. The Ministers of Foreign Affairs and Finance are in critical condition, on their way to hospital and not expected to survive. The Mayor of Seoul..." He looked at Yeo, who shook his head and gestured helplessly. Choi ad-libbed. "... like the President, is missing, *presumed* dead. They were all standing out in the open when the North Korean bombs hit, and it is a miracle I was not with them."

He could hear her gasp. "My God. Yes, Prime Minister. I will wait for you to convene the Council."

"When this ceremonial duty is done, Yoon, you can attend to your primary task in time of war, securing our food supply. I will personally work directly with our Joint Chiefs to ensure our national defense." He took a deep breath and tried a more soothing tone. "For now, Yoon, I suggest you contact your family. They will be worried."

"Yes, Prime Minister. I will."

He pulled off the headset and handed it back to Yeo. Damn Yoon. There was only one thing he needed from her, and that was her nomination. One simple thing.

A member of the aircraft crew pushed past, and Choi grabbed his leg to stop him. "You. How long until we are in Sejong?"

The man looked at a watch. "We are twenty-two minutes from your residence, Prime Minister."

"Good." He let the man go and barked at Yeo. "Get me an update on the President's situation. Now!"

Strapped into a seat one row behind Yeo and the Prime Minister, Special Agent Hi 'Helen' Lee, strained to hear the shouted conversation over the thud of the rotors. Yes, it was her duty to protect Prime Minister Shi, with her life if need be. But she had another, overriding mission. A mission given her by the former head of the Presidential Security Service in the 'Single Figures' café in Incheon Chinatown, six months earlier.

A mentor of sorts, he had tapped Lee on the shoulder to apply for the Security Service at 19 years of age, when she was just a junior constable in the Sejong City Police force who had made the front page of the local newspaper for her quick action in disarming a knife-wielding thug trying to rob an old man at a cash machine. At the time, she had been the youngest officer in the history of the Sejong Police Force to apprehend a violent offender.

He had been the antithesis of the slow witted, alcoholic, chain smoking senior officers she was used to dealing with. A tall, thin man with white hair and fastidious habits, he had asked to meet Lee in the same café back then, the Single Figures. Then, as now, he had ordered tea and cakes for them both.

"Congratulation on making your first arrest, Officer Lee," he'd said. "Can I ask, where did you learn how to defend yourself against a man wielding a knife? Not at the academy, I know that." Sejong City police officers did not carry guns, and a junior constable was not even issued with a taser. Just a baton.

She had lowered her eyes. "Thankyou, Commander Pak. But the man was not very dangerous. We struggled a little, he dropped his knife, and I simply held him until a colleague came."

He had sipped his tea thoughtfully. "Your modesty serves you well. But you did not answer my question. Shall I answer it for you?"

"Sir?"

He reached down beside his feet and pulled out a sheet of paper. "You mother was an MP at the US Marine Base, Camp Mujuk. She was disciplined after physically injuring a senior officer she claimed had tried to assault her…"

She had looked up at him sharply. "He did."

The Commander had nodded. "No doubt. Some years later he was relieved of his duties after a similar incident. But he always walked with a limp after what your mother did to his knee. How is she, by the way?"

"She has her own cleaning business," Lee told him. "She is happy enough, I suppose."

"Yes. There are many ways to find happiness. And many ways to serve, beyond the Sejong Local Police, Junior Constable Lee."

That conversation had been nearly twenty years earlier. Lee had served on the personal protection details of low level, then increasingly more important politicians, always with distinction. She had never been interested in a command role, merely in executing her duties as best she could. Her mother had passed away. She had married but was single again now. She'd had no children. The elderly Commander had retired. And now they were sitting in the same café.

"Thank you for indulging an old man, agent Lee," he'd said, when their tea and cakes had arrived. He always ordered the same Songpyeon cakes; small white rice cakes with strawberry filling. "You've joined the Prime Minister's detail, I believe?"

She'd raised her eyebrows. "Yes, sir. How did you hear about that?"

He'd chuckled. "I have my sources, agent Lee." He started cutting the cakes into halves. "I may also have had some influence on the appointment."

"I see. Thank you, sir."

"You may not thank me, when I tell you why."

He'd speared a half cake, chewed it thoughtfully and placed his fork back on his plate. And then he had told her why he had pulled so many strings, and cashed in several favors, to have Helen Lee appointed to the protection detail for Prime Minister Choi.

And he was right. She did not thank him again.

The Peace Dam

Six miles south of the DMZ, central Korean Peninsula

The two North Korean Mi-8 transport helicopters had approached the dam fast and hot, their rotors leaving a fantail of spray in their wakes as they hammered in, just fifty feet above the Bukhan River.

They weren't expected, but the sight didn't alarm Captain Jong-chon Ri of North Korea's Supreme Guard Command. They had been picked up on radar by his South Korean allies' Light Marine Air Defense Integrated System (LMADIS) buggies, as the aircraft cleared a ridgeline to the north and dropped down onto the river about five miles to the north, just outside the DMZ wire.

Ri had been impressed. It was the first time he'd seen the American-made all-wheel-drive LMADIS dune buggies, bristling with antennae, up close. They could supposedly take down everything from single anti-personnel drones to small swarms and even light or rotary aircraft. Though curious, he hadn't been allowed to approach closer than about ten yards before their South Korean crews had put up a hand to wave him off. With smiles, rather than glares, but a no was a no, regardless.

So much for 'friends not foes', which had been the catch cry from North Korea's military leaders for the last year. The way the South Korean LMADIS shouldered their Stinger missiles had also struck Ri as a little less than fraternal. But then, they were attached to the South Korean Presidential Security Service and had a reputation for acting before thinking in the execution of their duties.

He'd watched the North Korean choppers approach through his binoculars, and then turned to his South Korean counterpart on top of the Peace Dam wall, Captain Jeong Goh. Unlike Ri, in his ceremonial uniform, the South Korean security commander was dressed in a plain black suit, white shirt, and black tie. Only his earpiece, the lightweight carbonnanotube ballistic vest under his shirt and heavy utility footwear marked him as anything other than a civilian. "I have had no warning about this. Have you?" Ri asked.

Goh had been on the radio to their comms center and put down his headset. "No. They are coming in from the north. They aren't responding to our hail. They are *North* Korean military choppers, what do you think?"

Ri knew there could be technical reasons for the lack of warning. Not all North Korean transports had functioning radios, for one. But he didn't want to admit that to Goh. "They are probably just respecting radio silence due to the clandestine nature of our operation. It is nothing to be concerned about."

"Well, if they don't respond to our challenge soon, a Stinger up their ass will make their radio silence permanent," Goh said without humor.

Ri put a hand on Goh's shoulder, allowing himself a little familiarity. They'd been working together for nearly three months, preparing for this day. "I'll take a squad from my perimeter team and meet them when they land. I suspect it is just a late addition to proceedings. Something political."

"And I'm thinking I will hold up here," Goh said. "Just in case." As they'd agreed, Goh's men and the South Korean army LMADIS crews had taken the 'high ground' at the top of the dam and left the visitor center to Ri and his men, with the exception of a small South Korean personal protection detail that had stayed with the South Korean 'protectee', their President. It had made command and control of the joint North-South operation simpler. To their north, the dammed Bukhan River snaked away, silver in the morning sunlight. To their south, the dam fell away 500 feet to a spillway below, with freshly tended lawns and gardens to the east and on the western bank, the visitors' center, an RV park and helipad.

"Of course."

Fraternity? No quite. Not by a long way.

Such joint operations between the armed forces of the

North and South would not become 'normal' overnight, Ri was resigned to that. But then nothing had been normal about their day, so the unexpected approach of two helicopter transports from the North was just another thing he hadn't been briefed on. Add it to the lengthening list.

He'd gone down the side of the dam to the helipad on the flat ground below with a Lieutenant and a few Guards personnel and had them form up in a column to welcome – what he assumed would be – the unexpected dignitaries and their staff. Functionaries from the Central Military Commission or Ministry of People's Security, most likely. Fools who had been deliberately kept out of the loop and found themselves in Panmunjom, instead of here, where the real action was about to go down. Even Ri's men hadn't been briefed on the real purpose of their presence at the Peace Dam until 0400 that morning, so it wasn't surprising a few minor officials had been wrong-footed.

Then the first of the Mi-8 choppers had lowered itself into a hover, and before its wheels even settled on the ground, it began disgorging airborne paratroopers from its rear doors. *Armed* North Korean paratroopers.

Within seconds they had fanned outwards from the chopper, throwing themselves to the grass as it began lifting off again.

Before they opened fire on Ri and his men!

That had been thirty minutes ago.

He had only survived the initial contact thanks to the quick reactions of his perimeter team. He had gone down behind one of his guards in a whirlwind of grass, flying stones and bullets, automatic fire hammering the air around him, competing with the thud of rotors from a second Mi-8 moving in.

Then he heard the *whoosh-boom* of a missile as a Chinese-made Flying Crossbow fired by one of his guardsmen slammed into the incoming Mi-8 and burning men started falling from the sky as it spiraled illogically *upward* in a pyre of flame.

Automatic fire was coming from the concrete berms that had been laid outside the visitor center as his protection force engaged the North Korean paratroops and Ri hugged the dirt as the firefight escalated.

"Captain, orders?!" the panicked voice of one of his agents sounded in his earpiece. "We are taking fire from the helipad! Our own troops!"

No shit. Bullets thudded into the dirt around him as he tried to see the tactical position in his mind. North Korean troops from the transports, firing uphill from the helipad. From the visitors' center, his own guardsmen were returning fire. What were the South Koreans doing? Probably as confused as he was about who was friend and who was foe!

Ri had been raised in the paranoid Hermit Kingdom, where there was no such thing as true loyalty, even among allies. "Take out any helos! Secure the inner perimeter." He raised his head, checked the situation. Ducked down again. "Protection detail!"

"Captain, Lieutenant Yun, yes, sir!" the North Korean Supreme Guard officer in charge of the close personal protection detail responded. "Sir, there has been…"

"Silence, Yun! Secure the stronghold." A line of bullets kicked dirt in his face, and he rolled away from them, shrinking from the body of the man who fell right beside him, his face a bloody mess. "Now!!"

"Copy, Captain, securing stronghold," the man replied.

Ri rolled to a crouch, and then started sprinting toward a tree-lined road, away from the firefight. He saw more of his men join their comrades at the berms and start pouring fire on the troops at the helipad, who had made it to a flowerbed of bushes and ornamental rocks beside a car park and were trying to push on the visitors' center. A trail of rifle fire followed at his heels as he zigged and zagged, stopping only as he threw himself behind a tree and rolled down the manicured grass embankment behind.

Then he saw the horrifying flashes of gunfire, *inside* the visitor center!

It was wrong, all wrong.

"Ri, what is happening down there?" Goh cut in on his command channel.

Ri scrabbled up the embankment again and stuck his head up. "We are under attack by a hostile force." He looked again. "North Korean Third Brigade, airborne troops. I think they've penetrated the visitor center. I ordered the protectees moved to the stronghold."

The South Korean cursed. "We have a strong defensive position here on top of the dam. We need to get the protectees from the visitor center up here to…"

The voice dissolved into squelching static.

From beyond the lip of the dam, which rose 500 feet above where he was lying, came the sound of *more* rotary aircraft. Then the *crack crack crack* of the 20mm gun on one of the LMADIS vehicles opening up too. More helos incoming?! A cold fear gripped his heart. Whoever was attacking them was trying to put troops down on both sides of the dam wall, east and west of the visitor center, so they could approach from both sides of the river. He tried to radio Goh again but got nothing but static. Had his radio taken a blow? Or was the attacking force jamming? Whatever the cause, he was now cut off from his men, both physically and digitally, and it seemed Goh's position was coming under attack too. He had a .32 Tokarev in the holster on his belt and hastily pulled it out, though the nearest hostile soldier was a good fifty yards away and facing away from him, toward the visitors' center on the banks of the spillway.

He had to be *there*, at the visitors' center, ensuring their two protectees were safe. Lieutenant Yun was a good man, but if anything happened to the North Korean Supreme Leader, it wouldn't just cost Ri his career, it would cost *him*, and his family, their lives.

No choice. Trying to reach the visitors' center with hostile troops between himself and the center would be suicide. If he wasn't cut down by the enemy, he'd probably draw fire from the defenders. His only safe exit was back up to the lip of the dam to rejoin Goh. His men would have to handle the situation at the visitor center.

Taking a deep breath, Ri rose from his crouch, pistol in hand, and started sprinting up the steeply sloped, zigzagging road that led up to the top of the dam. Two hundred yards in a straight line, three hundred because of the kinks that kept the gradient passable for vehicles. Below him, the storm of automatic fire continued. Each of the Mi-8s held 24 troops, and the first one had gotten all of them away. The other had been hit as it was unloading, but a few had probably made it out. It sounded like a lot of them were still fighting and getting closer to the visitors' center. Up ahead, on the lip of the dam, he could still hear the crack of the South Korean 20mm and the chatter of automatic weapons.

He ran into two of his guardsmen at the top of the road, crouched behind a low wall, looking east. They didn't hear him approach.

"Guardsmen! Wake the hell up!" he barked as he got a few feet away, standing slightly downhill from them.

They spun around at the sound of his voice, eyes wide.

"Comrade Captain!"

"The enemy is behind and below you two. You could both be dead by now!"

"Captain, get *down!*"

Ri frowned at the man, then heard the thump of the 20mm cannon from one of the South Korean LMADIS buggies and shells started chewing at the concrete wall his two men were crouched behind. He dived to the dirt and scrabbled up alongside them.

"They are shooting at *us?*" he gasped.

"Yes," the man said, wincing as the 20mm opened up again. He had his 9mm suppressed submachine gun cradled against his chest. "We heard the shooting down by the visitor center … comms went down … we tried to approach Captain Goh for orders, but the man on that 20mm bloody opened up on us."

"No, I spoke to Goh, he..." Ri tried putting his head up, but only attracted another volley of fire from the LMADIS. "They are panicking," Ri decided. "They don't know who to trust."

He thought furiously. The top of the dam was a curved road, with waist-high concrete walls and head-high wire barriers to stop visitors from falling over the sides. Goh's command post atop the dam was made up of three LMADIS Polaris buggies and a map table under a camouflaged groundsheet that was meant to offer some protection against rain. Peering more carefully around the bottom of the concrete wall, this time he saw Goh, hunkered down behind a wheel of one of the buggies, in animated conversation with his radio operator. As he watched, the LMADIS gunner swung his barrel around, pointing it at the other end of the dam, and sent a salvo of 20mm fire at something at that end of the dam.

Which made no sense! The personnel stationed at that end of the dam were part of the security detail! Did Goh not trust anyone?

He looked around himself. His main concern was not the panicked South Korean officer camped in the middle of the dam, but their protectees back at the visitor center. He was still hearing helicopters to the north, though...

"Stay here," Ri told his men. "Don't try anything stupid and for God's sake don't shoot back at the South Korean fools. One of you watch downriver. That's where the main attack is."

"Yes, Comrade Captain. Were they ... in the helicopters ... were those *our* troops?" one man asked.

"They just killed a half dozen of our men. Anyone not dressed in North or South Korean protection detail uniforms is an *enemy*. Is that understood?"

"Yes, Comrade Captain!"

He left them wide-eyed and shaking, but at least they were looking both up and down river now. Keeping low he scuttled to the northern side of the road without attracting the attention of Goh's gunner. In scouting the location, they had conducted a thorough walkaround of the dam itself. Inside its 500 feet high, 20 foot thick concrete walls was a labyrinth of cramped service tunnels and machinery. The western entrance at the top of the dam was via a steel door accessed by a short ladder that dropped down the lip of the dam opposite them. He slid down the ladder using only his hands as brakes and thudded heavily into the metal landing at the bottom. He was about ten feet below the lip of the dam, out of sight of Goh and his men, but still fifty feet above the level of the lake which snaked upriver to the north. As he watched, he saw the helicopter that had been audible earlier, pulling away from the other side of a ridge and moving north, away from him. It was within Stinger missile range, why had the South Korean commander atop the dam not engaged it?

That question was soon overtaken by another. In the shadows of trees on the wooded hillside north of the dam he could see movement. Troops? Sure enough, as he watched, the shadows resolved themselves into the forms of men, running down the hill at a crouch, toward the dam access road. He squinted, looking at their uniforms. Third Brigade again – more of the same airborne troops who had attacked the visitor center.

If Ri could see the approaching troops, surely Goh could too?! He was about to shout a warning when he heard the 20mm open up again and the troops on the hillside upriver threw themselves flat.

He hadn't seen the projectiles strike, and the range was probably too far for effective fire, but the action had scattered the North Korean troops. Good, at last, Goh had woken up to who the real enemy was.

Without waiting to see anymore, Ri keyed in the access code for the maintenance door and pulled it open, throwing himself inside. A single curved corridor lit by glowing green LEDs ran along the 2,000-foot length of the dam, other access ladders and doorways leading deeper inside the structure. Ri ignored them, jogging to the other end where a long stairwell led out to another access door over the lake to the north, but more importantly, 400 feet down to a door at the base of the dam. Just a few hundred feet at ground level from the visitor center and on the opposite side of the river from the attacking troops at the helipad.

Panting with exertion, he slid down the ladder one level at a time, running around each landing to throw himself down the next ladder in a blur of rungs and railings. It seemed he would never reach the bottom, until suddenly, he was there.

Pushing the heavy steel maintenance door open, his pupils slammed shut at the sudden glare of daylight outside, but he was already stumbling into a run, down the access road on the other side of a spillway that led to the so-called 'Peace Park' and the long causeway across the river to the visitor center.

The irony of the location didn't escape him as he reached the bottom of the road and swerved, panting, to the right, through the Peace Park – a collection of brightly painted last-century tanks and artillery pieces that had been turned into 'art' – all the while listening to the sound of automatic gunfire reverberating around the valley. He grimaced as he ran past a 1950s-era American M-46 Patton tank, painted white and wrapped in symbolic blue chains.

The Peace Dam.

He wondered if it would be called that a week from now.

Petty Officer Ryan Kronk pulled a paper map from a pocket on his leg and unfolded it on a rock. Not a military map, just a DMZ map he'd picked up back at base as a souvenir. He'd hiked away from the column of rising smoke that was the crashed Defiant, in case North Korea sent a drone or fighter over to investigate it, and was crouched under an overhang by the river.

He had a pretty good idea of where they had been before the missile hit them as he'd been following the Shikaka's track on his laptop. He looked at the mountainous terrain around them, the curve of the river, then checked the compass on his cell phone. He had no signal to get a GPS fix with. "So, this must be Bukhan River, Kronk. I figure we are here," he said to no one in particular. He put his finger down on the map and followed the river south. There were no roads marked, not even tracks. Ten miles of winding river took them to a junction in the river where a road started, and a small site marked 'Tourist Location'.

The Peace Dam?

Well, wasn't that hella ironic on a day like today. Another name on the map caught his eye. A mountain range to the east. "No way."

Heartbreak Ridge. He looked up and over at the mountain range that marched off to the east. His long-deceased grandfather had fought over Heartbreak Ridge in the Korean War, 1951. Kronk was willing to bet he had never thought his grandson would be crossing the same ground eighty years later.

"Well, it looks like we have a tough hike ahead of us, Kronkster. Ten miles as the crow flies, but this river valley loops and curves and there are no easy tracks. We'll be going up and down ridges and gulches the whole way. What do you say? A whole day's walking? Better get started." He'd check in an hour or so, see if he could get a signal up to the Shikaka.

Kronk bent to pick up his duffel bag and move out from under the overhang. Then froze, hearing the high-pitched sound of whirring rotors.

The sound got closer and, looking upriver, Kronk finally saw what was making it, and cursed out loud. "I knew that damn fire would draw vultures."

The aircraft was flying slowly along the river about a half mile out, about fifty feet off the water. As it got closer, he could see it was small, too small to be manned. Every hundred yards or so it slowed to a hover and a dome under its nose completed a 360-degree rotation before it continued.

"We are so screwed, Kronk," he muttered, looking behind himself and hoping for a cave entrance or at least some decent-sized rocks he could hide behind. There was nothing.

As the machine got closer, he recognized it. You worked long enough on the software for unmanned aircraft, you got to know every type out there. It was a Chinese-made Norinco Golden Eagle, notable for the big round housing under the nose of the aircraft which contained an optical-infrared camera suite.

The bad news: it could detect both movement and infrared heat. The good news: it wasn't armed. But he had a bad feeling that whoever was controlling it probably would be.

He threw himself flat, lying face down in the dirt behind his duffel bag so it would block the line of sight to his body. It was a Hail Mary play, but he might get lucky.

He didn't. As the Golden Eagle drone drew level with the overhang he was hiding under, it stopped, and the recon dome completed a slow rotation. Its operator was being very, *very* thorough. It did a full circle and then came to a stop with its sensors pointed right at him. Rising another ten feet in the air, it crept slowly toward him.

Kronk had his face in the dirt; his duffel bag was the only cover between him and the drone, and he heard it getting closer. And closer. *A hundred yards out. Ninety. Eighty …* He risked a peek around the duffel bag. "A rifle, a rifle, my kingdom for a rifle," he muttered. The drone had moved to within fifty yards of him and was hovering, bobbing up and down slightly in the warm air over the water. Then it started sliding backward, sensors still pointed at him, to the other side of the river. "You've been made, Kronk."

He lifted himself from his crouch as the drone took up position on a high bank on the other side of the river and lowered itself to the ground, nose cameras pointed directly at him. Its electrically powered rotor jerked to a stop, and it was suddenly quiet again, the only sound the rushing water outside.

Kronk gave the now silent, sleek machine a baleful glance. Maybe he could throw a rock at it? He laughed miserably at the thought, knowing that as soon as he moved, wherever he moved to, the damn thing would follow him, and it was just a matter of time until the patrol controlling it caught up with him too.

Then he remembered, he wasn't out here alone. He had a

Shikaka.

Two problems. His link to the Shikaka was down. Number two? He was an AI coder, not a pilot. He could program a Shikaka to make decisions, even send it simple commands like 'go to this waypoint', but he couldn't fly it manually, let alone use the weapons on it. *Yeah, forget that, Kronk.*

He guesstimated the distance across the river between him and the hostile drone. Call it fifty yards. Maybe he could rush it?

"We could jump them," Private Park whispered to DMZ Border Patrol's Corporal Chang. They had made it out of the riverbed that ran alongside the site of the ambush, and managed to climb a small, lightly wooded hill where they could lie in long, dry grass and keep an eye on the North Korean soldiers who had tried to slaughter them.

"We're the ones could get jumped up here," Nam said, looking around him. "You know there are wolves in the DMZ, right?"

Park shot him a withering look. "Wolves."

"Yeah, since there are no people, the wolves moved in. And bears. I saw a documentary."

Chang pointed down at the North Korean patrol. "Those are the only wolves you need to worry about right now, Private."

"What are they doing now?"

The North Koreans had changed uniforms with the dead South Korean border soldiers. Then they had simply moved the bodies of the South Korean soldiers into scrub at the side of the road, shoveled a little dirt over them and fetched their own patrol vehicles – two last-century Russian-made jeeps – and parked them beside the South Korean vehicle. Now, the privates appeared to be unloading several large crates from their jeeps and stacking them in the bed of the South Korean troop transport. Their sergeant was sitting in one of their jeeps, reading a map, but they were too far away to mount an attack from where they were. They'd have to get closer. Maybe…

Chang stole a glance at Park and Nam. *Not with these two. Not today.*

"They lost their officer," Park observed. "Maybe they're stuck now, don't know what to do."

"Did that North Korean sergeant who charged right at us, screaming at the top of her lungs, strike you as the indecisive type, Park?"

"Now you say it, Corp, no, I guess not."

Nothing changed over the next hour except that it got hotter on top of the hill. The only water was down in their vehicle and the rice wine they'd swigged before the North Koreans jumped them hadn't made them less thirsty. Chang thought maybe they should pull back after all, skirt around the North Koreans and make for their guard post six miles south. They should report the attack. It didn't look like anything was going to…

Park tapped his shoulder and pointed downhill. "They're mounting up, Corp."

The North Korean sergeant satisfied herself about something in the back of the captured transport and then ordered her men inside. She went around to the driver's door, pulled it open and climbed up, stopping to take a last look around. Instinctively the three South Korean soldiers ducked down, though there was no real chance she could see them. Then she climbed inside and with a reluctant cough, the truck started up. In a swirl of dust, the troop transport moved off. As it disappeared around a bend in the road, Chang rose, slinging his carbine over his shoulder. "Come on." He started down the hill toward the abandoned North Korean jeeps.

"Nice of them to leave us a ride back to base," Nam said.

"They won't have left the keys," Park pointed out.

"Yeah, but those things are prehistoric. I can hotwire one, I bet."

They stopped by the line of South Korean bodies, only half covered by dirt, baking in the sun.

"Damn, that's cold," Nam said. "They took the uniforms,

though. That's weird."

Park, a Catholic, made a sign of the cross. "We taking our guys back to base, Corp?" he asked.

Chang stepped over the bodies toward one of the jeeps. "We're not going back to base," he said. "Nam, see if you can get this one started." He checked the rear of the vehicle, found a jerry can of fuel, two full water canteens and something *much* more interesting. A field radio! Operational Security regulations meant they weren't allowed to take their cell phones on patrol inside the DMZ, but with this they might be able to radio for help.

He checked it, switching between frequencies, but got only static. Strange. Perhaps the piece of North Korean crap wasn't working.

Park was still standing by the line of bodies. "Why? Where are we going?"

Chang pointed at the thin cloud of dust from their stolen troop transport, moving away from them at a fast clip. "Mount up gentlemen. We're following them."

Ten miles west Sangeo Shoal, Sea of Japan

Korean People's Navy Submarine, 9.9 Hero

Captain Se-heon Dokgo of the North Korean People's Navy had been following the 'Operation White Glove' task force for a week. South Korean and US warships, in cooperation with a North Korean Navy anti-submarine frigate, had been conducting exercises together in the Sea of Japan to coincide with the signing of the Peace Agreement in Panmunjom. Together with the Helicopter Landing Dock the *USS Bougainville*, the small task force comprised the South Korean amphibious assault ship *ROKS Marado*, two US expeditionary fast transport (EPF) ships, the *USS Point Loma* and *USS Cody*, and the North Korean stealth corvette, the *KPN Nampo*.

While the US EPFs went about the business of putting a combined force of North and South Korean Marines ashore at the modest piers of Sangeo Shoal, the *Nampo* and helicopters from the two big amphibious warfare ships conducted anti-submarine exercises against South Korean attack submarines. Dokgo had had no trouble avoiding the anti-submarine patrols, never approaching closer than twenty miles to the *Nampo* or the picket force of helicopters with their dipping sonars.

But on this day, the day of the signing, all of the ships in the task force were anchored offshore from Sangeo Shoal's small harbor. Their officers and a mixed complement of North and South Korean Marines had been put ashore for a ceremony commemorating the signing of the Peace Agreement.

Before leaving port, Dokgo had been advised by Fleet Command that after the signing of the Peace Accord, he would be taking aboard an 'observer', an officer of the South Korean Navy. He had surprised his CO, he could see that, when he had simply smiled and nodded. He knew that if his mission was successful, it was never going to happen.

They called 'Operation White Glove' a 'historic gesture of international fraternity'. Dokgo called it a bile-inducing congregation of criminals and traitors. And he had been ordered to ensure all traces of the disgraceful display were wiped from the face of the earth.

His *Gorae* or 'Whale'-class submarine, the *9.9 Hero*, was the most potent warship in his nation's navy, and it had been given the honor of an auspicious name to match. The 9th September 1948 was the anniversary of the birth of modern North Korea. In the control room of the *Hero*, Dokgo was watching an acoustic tracking map over the shoulder of his sonar chief. Satisfied there were no threats nearby, he barked an order. "Officer of the deck, ahead slow, take us to broadcast depth."

"Ahead slow, move to broadcast depth, aye." The man relayed his orders.

A slight pressure on the soles of his feet was the only indication his boat was moving closer to the surface, where it would stop fifty feet under the waves and extend a radio antenna that could catch a signal without breaking the surface and giving away his position. Yes, an aircraft directly overhead might see the shadow of the 3,000-ton *Hero* through the water, but it would have to be a very, very lucky aircraft.

What made his boat so deadly were the four medium-range Pukguksung-6 ballistic missiles stored in his magazines and fitted with multiple independently targetable nuclear warheads. Separating from their launch vehicles as the ballistic missiles reached apogee, unless they were intercepted during their boost phase, they were virtually unstoppable.

His primary target was the South Korean naval facility at Sangeo Shoal. Any ships consumed by his missiles' nuclear fire – including those crewed by North Korean traitors – would be a bonus.

Commander of the *USS Cody*, Captain O'Shea Lomax, was not going ashore to join the celebrations on Sangeo Shoal. He wasn't put out. It had been a strange kind of week, anyway, exercising with allies and former enemies alike. He'd been impressed by what he'd seen of the North Korean frigate crew, prosecuting sub contacts with ruthless professionalism. But he guessed the North Korean Navy had made damn sure their best sailors had shipped with the *Nampo*, with national pride at stake. And the North Korean Marines had managed to integrate with their South Korean counterparts well enough, without coming to blows or getting any hands or limbs injured by heavy equipment (always a risk on amphibious landings). Standing on the bridge of the *Cody* watching North and South Korean Marines file ashore at the same pier had been ... well, surreal.

So no, he wasn't upset he hadn't been assigned to the shore party. It would have been just another couple of hours of constant jibes from his peers and allies about what the frick kind of a warship was an Expeditionary Fast Transport anyway? Even though it was designed specifically to support the US Marines in an island-hopping maritime campaign, it wasn't a landing ship, not really. Sure, you could squeeze 300 Marines and their gear aboard; but you couldn't sail it up on a beach, you had to offload at a pier or stand offshore and send your human cargo ashore on rigid-hull inflatables. It had a flight deck but carried only a single helo. It couldn't fight its way to shore ... and unlike its future cousin the Light Amphibious Warfare ship, it mounted nothing bigger than .50 caliber guns to ward off boarding attempts and a single 125 kW laser for missile defense. It was not only toothless, it was also butt ugly. With a high twin-hulled bow, a flat helo deck and ramp aft, it looked more like a passenger ferry than a warship, because that's what it was. The design was based on the Hawaii Superferry.

Screw it. Lomax wasn't a tea and kimchimari kind of guy anyway, and the harbor at the small, almost uninhabited shoal wasn't exactly a picture postcard liberty destination. Lomax was more of a cold IPA and deep-dish pizza kind of guy. A craving he was going to satisfy as soon as they docked in Busan after what was probably going to be one of the more 'unique' missions of the *Cody*'s career, so far.

Lomax and the *Cody* weren't hanging around for the party,

because they'd been ordered to take up station 20 miles north of Sangeo Shoal in the Sea of Japan, where they would rendezvous with a ship with no crew that had just set a US Navy record.

The semi-autonomous *Sea Hunter* unmanned surface vehicle, or USV, had navigated itself across the sea from White Beach naval base on Okinawa to the sea off of Sangeo Shoal, just to prove that it could. From the moment it left Okinawa until the moment it joined with *Cody*, it had not been under human control. *Cody* was supposed to take control of the *Sea Hunter* and then escort it into the harbor at the Shoal for some sort of technology demonstration supposed to wow their allies.

Lomax wasn't sure what he thought about a robot warship sailing itself across the seas. Sure, it didn't carry any offensive weapons, but if a drone could sail itself across the Sea of Japan, how long before the Navy decided it didn't need crews on its transports anymore? And what came after that? Frigates and destroyers? Crewless ballistic missile submarines? He shuddered at that thought.

Lomax and the *Cody*'s crew had routinely worked with the sub hunting and mine detecting *Sea Hunter* USVs before. They were paired with expeditionary fast transports like the *Cody* and its anti-submarine capable Defiant helo to clear their path to hostile shores without risking crewed vessels. Bringing this one to heel and wheeling it around the Shoal to show it off would be a good diversion for his crew.

At least, that *had* been the mission. By the sound of it, their day was about to go completely sideways.

"Commander! Flash alert from Fleet, Yokosuka," his Executive Officer, Jake Ryan, said, bent over a screen at one of the watch stations.

The *Cody* used the Navy's new hybrid crew concept, with every one of its forty-strong crew serving multiple functions. Underway, there were normally only three watch officers on the bridge – today Lomax and Ryan had joined them.

If they were conducting air operations with their own Defiant helo, he would also have had an Air Officer on the bridge, but their Defiant was on *USS Bougainville* for routine maintenance.

"OOD, make our speed ahead slow, hold current course," Lomax said to the officer of the deck as he walked over to look at the same screen Ryan was looking at. As the officer repeated the order back to him, he took in the message at a glance, and then straightened his back.

"Sound general quarters please, Lieutenant."

"Sounding general quarters, aye." A klaxon began blaring throughout the ship as Ryan called the crew to their action stations. When he was done, he rejoined Lomax.

"The whole fleet called to DEFCON 3, sir. You ever seen that before?"

"No, Ryan, I haven't. Comms, get me Commander Wilson on *Bougainville*."

"He'll be ashore, sir," the man reminded him as he handed him a headset.

"Then get me *Bougainville*'s officer of the deck. We need some context."

In five minutes, Lomax had all the context he needed. And it didn't put him at ease in the least. He handed back the headset and pulled Ryan aside. "Situation is fluid, but it looks like a shooting war has broken out between North and South. South Korean aircraft attacked North Korean fighters. North Korean fighters dropped bombs on the Peace Village at Panmunjom. North Korean artillery has opened fire on Seoul." He drew a breath. "Looks like the peace party is over."

"Gawdamn, sir." Ryan frowned. "Our orders?"

"*Bougainville* is sending us a helo and crew. We rendezvous with that *Sea Hunter* and run anti-submarine picket for *Bougainville* together with *Point Loma*. We'll patrol north of the shoal, *Point Loma* will take the south. *Bougainville* and the *Marado* have an underway time of 60 minutes and are being pulled back to Busan. We'll be joined by two South Korean destroyers, but for the next few hours, we're on our own out here." He had scrawled a map grid reference onto a piece of paper and handed it to Ryan. "Our patrol area."

Ryan read the map coordinates and looked grave. He bent his head to Lomax's shoulder. "*Cody* is a *transport*, Captain, not a sub hunter…"

Lomax didn't disagree, but he put a hand on Ryan's shoulder. "Necessity compels, XO. Today, *Cody* is a sub hunter."

Ryan nodded, then turned, as Lomax relayed the map coordinates to the officer of the deck, ordering the ship to come around and increase speed to ahead-full. EPFs like the *Cody* and *Point Loma* might be light amphibious transport ships, not anti-submarine warfare (ASW) destroyers, but they had two ASW aces up their sleeves that US navy ships of their class in previous generations did not have.

The first was that every EPF was capable of sailing with a 'wingman' alongside it: the *Sea Hunter* unmanned surface combat vehicle, which *Cody* was about to meet at sea and assume control of. Piloted by an operator aboard his ship, Lomax could use the small trimaran-hulled stealthy *Sea Hunter* for mine detection, anti-submarine or even surface and air target identification duties. It featured an AN/AQS-20A sonar and electro-optical detection suite for spotting mines in either shallow or deep waters, plus a SPY-6 scanned array radar for detecting surface and air targets. A towed array sonar system gave them a formidable anti-submarine capability when it was paired with *Cody*'s Defiant helicopter.

Their Defiant helo was equipped with dipping sonar for more precise detection of hostile submarines as well as the new Very Light Weight Torpedo (VLWT). Working in tandem, the *Sea Hunter* could identify enemy submarines and the *Cody*'s Defiant could then be dispatched to kill them.

It didn't make *Cody* a submarine hunter-killer platform, but loaded with 300 Marines, its ability to identify subsurface threats made *Cody* a much harder target. Not to mention an anti-submarine/anti-air frigate to act as escort cost $480 million to build and $700,000 an hour to deploy. Much better if *Cody* could look after itself most of the time.

"What about the *Nampo*?" Ryan asked about the North

Korean corvette.

"Her officers have been arrested and are being held on Sangeo. Their Captain apparently swore he knows nothing about any attack and has even offered his assistance. Wilson isn't taking any chances, he's sent a boarding party to lock the *Nampo* down."

"So ... what? North Korea's Navy is not in this fight?"

Lomax shook his head. "All I know is *Nampo*'s Captain says *he* hasn't been ordered to fight." He looked out to sea for a moment, thinking hard. "Head down to the command center. We need to route *Bougainville*'s Defiant to our patrol area and start anti-sub operations."

Ryan did as he was ordered, then returned to Lomax's side. "Helluva thing, sir. How are we supposed to know who are our friends and who are our enemies right now?" he asked.

"Good question, but not the most important one."

"What is?"

"If the Peace Ceremony at Panmunjom was bombed, the North Korean President could be injured, even dead." He fixed Ryan with a bleak gaze. "So who is in control of their nukes?"

Who was in control of North Korea's nuclear arsenal was exactly the question Captain Se-heon Dokgo of *Hero* was coming up to comms depth to check. Since its first nuclear test in 2006, the hyper-paranoid regime of the North had maintained the most extreme form of centralized control of its nuclear weapons. There was no scenario-based pre-delegation of authority, such as exercised by NATO or Russia. Only the Supreme Leader could authorize a nuclear strike. No cabal of party members, no junta of military officers, no lone submarine commander, could get access to the codes needed to arm its nuclear missiles except on the direct authority of the Supreme Leader.

There was no 'nuclear football'. North Korea's Supreme Leader, Yun-mi Kim, carried a small, one-of-a-kind pager-like device with her at all times. To authorize a nuclear strike, she had to enter a nine-digit alphanumeric code which she created herself, and then apply her thumb to the inbuilt DNA biosensor. Only then would the required authorizations be generated for distribution to North Korea's Strategic Missile Force Command.

It was both a symbol of her power within the North Korean hierarchy and an extreme vulnerability. It meant no potential traitor or rebel within her ranks could use the threat of nuclear weapons to destabilize or discredit her regime. But it also meant that a successful decapitation strike that killed the North Korean Supreme Leader and/or destroyed her authorization devices would render the North Korean nuclear arsenal temporarily impotent.

North Korea's Army generals had not always been comfortable with this arrangement. In 2015 they secretly approved a project to design a bypass system that would give them control of the nuclear arsenal if the Supreme Leader was 'incapacitated'. When he found out about it a year later, the then Supreme Leader, Jong-un Kim, executed the Army Chief of Staff, five other generals, and a host of junior officers. US Intelligence indicated that while its designers were no longer alive, the bypass code absolutely was.

As the *Hero's* commander, and with the cooperation of his second in command, Captain Dokgo *could* launch his two ballistic missiles without the nuclear authorization codes. If not intercepted, they would strike their assigned targets. But without authorization codes being input before launch, they would strike with the effect of conventional ballistic missiles, not nuclear ones. Like a 'dirty bomb', they would spread radiation over the target area, but would not generate anything like the wholesale destruction or political fallout of a nuclear detonation.

Dokgo's orders were to execute his mission, with or without the authorization codes. When he joined himself to the conspiracy, he was told the purpose of the attack was to outrage the South and its allies and to implicate the traitorous North Korean Supreme Leader in the attack.

Ideally, by exploding a tactical nuclear warhead at sea. But even without its nuclear warhead being armed, if even one of his hypersonic re-entry vehicles struck South Korean territory, his mission would be accomplished.

The elegance of the plan had impressed Dokgo when he had been brought into it. As had the double-digit million dollar sum that had been placed in an offshore bank account for him, to secure his cooperation. Se-heon Dokgo's conscience was not sorely troubled by what he was about to do. A single nuclear attack out in the middle of the Sea of Japan would surely not provoke a full retaliation from the USA and risk reducing North Korea to molten slag, or bloom into a wider nuclear war, dragging in Russia and China. The Americans would retaliate, of course they would, but North Korea would weather their storm of conventional cruise missiles and iron bombs. South Korea would not dare invade. They did not have the strength of numbers needed to attack the North.

And the treasonous talk of 'unification' would be buried along with the bodies of the traitors who supported it. To Captain Se-heon Dokgo and his co-conspirators, there was only one form of unification they could possibly accept, and that was unification following the comprehensive military defeat and surrender of the capitalist lapdog South.

"Communication depth. On course one-one-five, speed ahead slow. Sonar plot unchanged, no new contacts," Dokgo's officer of the deck announced.

"Raise satellite antenna," Dokgo ordered.

As his boat leveled out twenty feet under the waves, Dokgo knew an operation, years in the planning, was underway hundreds of miles to the east, to kill or capture the traitorous Yun-mi Kim. To force her to divulge her unlock code and generate the necessary authorization for his own attack. The window in which he could expect to be sent the codes was now open.

"Approaching Prime Ministerial Residence," the pilot of the

Sikorsky S-92 announced over the helicopter's internal comms channel. "Please resume your seats and fasten safety belts."

A South Korea Air Force officer started moving around the crew compartment of the chopper, checking people were buckled in.

South Korean Prime Minister, Ted Choi, tapped his protection detail commander, Yeo, on the shoulder. "How can we talk privately?" he yelled over the sound of the chopper's rotors.

Yeo reached over to the seat beside him and picked up two sets of over-ear headphones, switching them both to the same comms channel. He handed one set to Choi and signaled to him to put them on.

Choi adjusted them over his ears. "Can you hear me?"

"Hear you fine, go ahead, sir."

"What is the situation on the border?"

He consulted some hastily scribbled notes. "The North Korean artillery battery has been suppressed with counter-fire. Sky Dome caught nearly sixty percent of the projectiles. There are fires and damage across Seoul, about twenty casualties so far."

"Only *one* North Korean artillery battery?"

"It seems. There have been no more air incidents but North Korean air controllers are still warning all aircraft to stay out of North Korean airspace. Our Air Force estimates at least three North Korean fighter squadrons were engaged in hostilities. They have heightened defensive patrols but there have been no new incursions over the DMZ."

The Prime Minister nodded. "Troop movements?"

"North Korean ground forces have been mobilized but have not moved out from their bases. Neither armor nor troops. There is still *massive* jamming right across the border, east to west, however." The news that North Korean troops were remaining in place should have gladdened Choi, but his face did not show it.

"And Sejong City. Is my building secure?"

Choi's residence was on the top floor of the Office for

Government Policy Coordination. The plan to build a grand residence in Sejong City for the South Korean Prime Minister had drained into the sand as unification momentum made Sejong City itself an irrelevance and Choi had found himself spending less and less time there. But he still maintained a residence there and it remained the official office of the PM – a token gesture that for the first time was about to prove itself useful. With Seoul under attack, it was a suitable, in fact, the *only* logical place to convene his new State Council.

The agent nodded. "Our people have secured all entrances and exits. Civilians are being evacuated."

"Any police activity?"

"None. Any resources not already allocated to Seoul and Panmunjom have been diverted to fires at the Presidential Archives and Sejong Tower, as planned. Sejong City Police and emergency services have their hands full."

"Excellent. Pls swap seats with Hang and give him the headset."

He stood, waddled unsteadily back to where Hang, the Prime Minister's principal adviser was sitting and gestured to him to move forward. Yeo took a seat opposite them.

"We get the State Council endorsement out of the way, then a videocon with the armed forces general staff. What time is it?" Choi asked.

The man checked the time on his cell phone. "Fourteen twenty."

"I think we can move up the address to the nation. Why wait?"

"Too early," the man said. "Makes it look pre-cooked. We need to give an impression of organized chaos for a few hours. You can put out a public statement urging calm, something about attending to the defense of the nation as the first priority. We should wait until the President's situation is … clarified."

Choi gave the man a hard look. "And how is it we still have no word on that?"

The man shrugged. "When North Korean defenses went on alert, they initiated massive jamming across the entire border, west to east. Our own planning didn't account for that: in fact, it seems our armed forces had no idea the North had such a capability."

"Doesn't that affect them as much as it affects us?"

"No. North Korea's armed forces are still hopelessly analog in many respects. Their communications across the DMZ are mostly hard wired, ours are all digital. An unexpected vulnerability."

"And our allies in the North didn't know about this tactic?"

"Or neglected to mention it. They may see some advantage for themselves…"

Choi shook his head. "I do not believe they didn't know. We have several highly placed collaborators. This was a deliberate omission."

"Perhaps."

Choi slammed a fist on this thigh. "This is *not* acceptable. Our strategy is built around securing custody of that woman, quickly."

"Agreed. I am following up."

Choi looked out the window as the first rows of the high-rise apartments ringing Sejong City's outskirts came into view. He could see red civil emergency lamps lit on several of the buildings rushing past below. The sight did not alarm him. To the contrary, he allowed himself a moment of satisfaction.

Looking out one of the Blackhawk's windows, Special Agent Helen Lee also saw the flashing civil emergency lamps on the buildings below, but she was more interested in the conversation she had just heard.

When she had seen Choi and Yeo slip on the headphones, she had surreptitiously slipped her own ear bud into her palm and put it into the ear closest to the window, where no one else would see it. Holding a fingertip over it, she set it to scan local frequencies until she found the one Choi and Yeo were using.

The conversation alarmed her more than the flashing emergency lights on the city's buildings.

Emergency services had been diverted to a fire at the Presidential Archives *'as we planned'*?! An address to the nation had also been scheduled, *before* Panmunjom had even been attacked? But worst of all *'our allies in the North'*?!

Lee's gut began to churn. It was starting to dawn on her that the peril she had just escaped may not be the biggest she would face that day.

As their helo began to flare for its landing, Lee slipped the earbud from her ear and prepared to deplane, her mind working furiously. "Our strategy is built around getting custody of that woman,' Choi had said. What strategy and what woman? Someone at the Peace Dam. But *who*?

The War Dam

Six miles south of the DMZ, central Korean Peninsula

At the Peace Dam visitor center, Captain Jong-chon Ri of North Korea's Supreme Guard Command was approaching very, very carefully. His men were jumpy, so he walked slowly toward them with hands raised until they recognized him.

They weren't just jumpy. They were completely shocked.

"Comrade Captain! In the visitor center ... they..."

"What?" The man talking was just staring at him, mute now. Ri grabbed his shoulder and shook him. "They who?"

"They..."

"What, man?!"

"The *South Koreans*, they..."

Ri pushed the man away from him.

Running to a side door of the visitor center, he looked through a small glass window at the top of the door and inside he saw ... carnage. Four protective security agents were lying on the floor. Unmoving. He recognized one of his own men crouched over another, trying to treat a wound. Whatever had happened inside, it looked like it was over. For now.

Pulling the door open and bringing up his pistol, Ri stepped inside. "Songbird!" he called, giving the daily codeword.

The man crouched on the floor had grabbed his carbine, then returned to the job of applying blood-clotting agent to the prone form in front of him. "Comrade Captain! We need to get this man out." All Supreme Guard agents were trained in treating battlefield wounds.

Ri ran over to him and saw the man on the floor had a gut wound. He was barely conscious.

"Comms are down," Ri told the man. "Do what you can to stabilize him. What happened here?"

The man jerked his head toward the bodies in the center of the lobby. "As soon as the shooting started outside, those three pulled their weapons. They shot Han here, and Choe. Han killed them all." He shook his head slowly, looking at the man on the floor. "All of them. He took every bullet, and he killed them *all*."

"Yun. Where is Lieutenant Yun?" Ri asked.

"He took your call, and then tried to move the protectees into the stronghold. That's when the South Koreans pulled their weapons. He's down there." The man was shocked. "Comrade Captain, they tried to *kill* us."

"Yes." He patted the man on the back. "You worry about Han, here."

"Comrade Captain, the situation outside?"

"Two attacking forces. One here, one up at the dam. Twenty plus hostiles. We will hold here. Goh and his men will hold the dam roadway," Ri said. The man's carbine was on the floor beside him. Ri moved it closer to him with his foot. "But be prepared."

"The American lapdog bastards on the dam!" the man exclaimed. "We can't trust them to ..."

"We have to," Ri told him. *We have to...* He looked again at the bodies of the South Korean agents in pools of their own blood. Assassins? Traitors to their own government? He felt his head spinning.

Focus, Ri. Find the protectees.

He moved past the man on the floor toward a rear door, pulled it open but did not step inside. From the doorframe he called out. "This is Captain Ri, hold your fire!"

"Codeword!" someone at the bottom of the stairs responded.

"Songbird!"

"Advance."

He stepped into the stairwell, saw two men at the bottom, one either side, covering the doorway. They lowered their rifles when they saw him. As he reached the bottom he put a hand on the shoulder of the nearest man. "Good job. Hold position here."

"Captain, we lost comms..."

"Jamming," he told the man. "We are getting the situation

here and at the dam under control. No one else comes through that door. Not our men, not theirs. Lethal force is authorized. Is that clear?"

"Yes, sir."

He walked past the two agents to a corridor where another of his men was standing uneasily by a door on the left. Two more doors led off the corridor at the end and to the right. In their planning they had discussed a scenario similar to this – a terrorist attack which forced them to take refuge in the visitor center with their protectees. In that event, they had agreed to use the basement as a stronghold. If an enemy wanted them dead, they could try to flood the basement with fuel and set it alight. But like many South Korean basements in the border area, this one had been designed to double as a civilian emergency nuclear shelter and had double blast doors that could probably take a round from a 105mm tank barrel without buckling.

The shelter had been one of the key factors that had tipped the decision about the location for the day in favor of the Peace Dam.

He walked past the door the man was guarding. Him standing there was a decoy maneuver anyway. The protectees and their personal protection team were behind a different door at the end of the corridor.

Checking his suit jacket quickly, he adjusted the Joint Protection Force pin on his lapel, holstered his weapon, buttoned his jacket, took a deep breath and knocked. What in the name of seven hells would he find inside?

"Codeword!" a voice called.

"Songbird. Captain Ri," he replied.

A lock mechanism clicked and the door fell open. He stepped through.

The corridor he stepped in from had long ago been painted an anonymous light green. The room he stepped into smelled of fresh paint. Bright blue paint. The roof was tiled with white tiles. Two windows were visible on one wall – which was of course impossible since they were underground – but the illusion was near-perfect, with dark blue windowsills and light blue curtains that matched the walls framing LCD monitors that showed a blurred daylight view.

It was, not by accident, an exact replica of the inside of a UN blue barracks building at Panmunjom, 65 miles away.

His second in command and protection detail leader, Lieutenant Yun, stood at the door. Behind him were...

Yun immediately motioned Ri in close, putting his head next to Ri's and whispering urgently. "Comrade Captain. The South Korean detail turned on us, they..."

"Yes, I saw," Ri told him. "Are you injured?"

Yun shook his head. "No. But I think we lost Han, Choe..."

"Yes. The protectees." He looked over Yun's shoulder. "Are they..."

"Safe? Yes, Captain."

One of his men closed the door behind him and stood against it, his rifle at the ready. He was the only one with a weapon drawn, but there were several other aides and agents in the room. Yun was going to speak again, but Ri stepped into the middle of the room and bowed deeply.

In the middle of the room, behind a camera on a tripod, was a long, polished teak table at which sat two individuals. The 'protectees'. One, a man in his sixties, dressed in a pin-striped business suit, white shirt and ocean blue tie, with a South Korean flag on a lapel. The other, a woman wearing a dark dress under a black high-collared jacket, North Korean flag set in a golden brooch on her lapel.

"Your Excellency, Mr. President," Ri said, head still bowed.

The Chair of the North Korean Workers' Party, head of the State Affairs Commission and Supreme Leader of the Democratic People's Republic of Korea, Yun-mi Kim, waved her hand at Ri indicating he should stand straight. Beside her, Si-min Shin, President of South Korea, looked on impatiently.

"Stand, Captain," Kim said. If she was worried or shaken by the violence upstairs, her voice did not betray her. After five years as Commander of the Supreme Guards Company charged with her protection, Ri knew his protectee well. Her high cheekbones framed bright brown eyes that conveyed confidence and calm. The only sign of possible inner turmoil was that the slight smile which many mistook for amusement, at their peril, was absent from her lips. "Are we safe?"

"Your Excellency, we are under attack from an unknown hostile military force. We estimate about 30 to 40 heavily armed troops. We are holding this position, for now." He was careful not to attribute blame. North Korean paratroops, acting in concert with the South Korean President's personal protection detail. South Koreans firing on his men up at the dam. Had that really been a case of panic? The situation was too confused. Blame could come later.

Shin, however, slapped the table – the sound like a gunshot – causing a couple of the people in the room to jump. He glared at Ri and jabbed a finger at him. "Your men killed my bodyguards!" he yelled. "Am I your prisoner now?"

"No, Mr. President. Your men, I cannot explain..." He gathered himself. "They may have been acting in concert with the attackers."

"Ridiculous," Shin scoffed. He turned to the North Korean Supreme Leader. "Madam Kim, can you shed any light on this situation?"

The woman shook her head slowly. "I cannot. Captain Ri?"

He searched his mind for an explanation. "Your Excellency. If the intention was to kill you both, then the attackers could have planted a bomb or, with their apparent resources, conducted an air attack. I believe their intention is to capture you alive."

"One of us, or both?" Shin asked tartly.

"That ... I do not know, Mr. President," Ri said. "As soon as we are able, we will call for support."

"Why have you not already done so?" Kim asked. Her voice, as ever, was flat and even. Ri had seen her speak to crowds of tens of thousands, to rooms of only a few, in situations both fraught and friendly. Her tone never varied, giving nothing away to those trying to interpret her mood.

"Your Excellency, our communications are being jammed,"

Ri told her. "We have been isolated, for now."

Shin pushed his chair away from the table, stood and paced. "We told you people that moving the ceremony here was a risk. We should have stayed at Panmunjom where we could be properly protected."

Ri bowed slightly again. "Mr. President, respectfully, we had credible intelligence that a terrorist attack on Panmunjom was being planned by anti-unification conspirators. It was agreed … the head of your own Security Service proposed the signing ceremony should be moved here and broadcast under conditions of utmost secrecy."

"Then he is as much a fool as you. We are trapped in a basement twenty miles from the nearest military or police assistance, and now you tell us we cannot even radio for help?" Shin said acerbically. He pointed at the video camera at the end of the table. "Our broadcast was cut just as we were about to sign the agreement in front of a global audience."

Ri gasped. He looked down at the table, at the documents in leather folders lying there. The pens, lying neatly in front of them. Untouched.

The Peace Agreement had not been signed!

What Ri had said was true. The two nations' leaders had been taken to this secluded location on the border in secret because North Korean intelligence had received word of a plot to try to disrupt the signing of the Peace Agreement. The exact nature of the planned attack was not clear, but there was sufficient chatter about it that both North and South Korean intelligence services had been forced to take it seriously. Precautions had been taken, precautions so secret that even the inner cabinet members of both governments had not been party to them. The first time anyone should have become aware that neither of the Heads of State was actually present in Panmunjom was when they entered the blue UN hut at the Peace Village to find it empty, except for the smiling faces of their leaders on LCD wall screens.

Of course, such an operation could not be limited to just a few individuals. The innermost circle of aides for both leaders had to be involved in the planning. Senior officers and agents in the North Korean Supreme Guard Command and South Korean Presidential Security Service. And Generals of both militaries.

But they had kept the actual location secret up until the last moment. Only at 0400 that morning had those who were expected to be present at the Peace Dam been informed about the location by himself and Goh. Only Goh and himself had conducted the advance inspections. No one else but the two protective security commanders had known the final details, until today.

Click.

A series of scenes flashed before his eyes. Goh telling Ri he would remain at his position up on the dam wall and sending him down to meet the attacking North Korean troops. Goh's LMADIS team firing on Ri's men up at the dam. Had they actually fired on the force approaching from the north, as he thought he'd seen, or had they just fired over their heads, warning them the target area was not yet secured? With radio comms down, that was a real possibility. And then the South Korean security detail turning on his men inside the visitor center, when they heard the order to secure the protectees inside the stronghold?

Goh.

"What is it, Captain?" Kim asked, eyes narrowing. Just as he knew her, she knew her Guard Commander, and could see when he was troubled.

"Nothing ... I am ... I must return to ground level, your Excellency, to direct our defense. You will be safe with Lieutenant Yun." He bowed and turned for the door.

"And will I be safe?" the South Korean President demanded. "With only *North* Korean agents to protect me?!"

Ri counted to three and turned. "Your own security detail lies dead on the floor above after shooting two of my men, Mr. President. I suggest you will be safer with Lieutenant Yun than you would have been with them. Excuse me."

With that he turned and walked quickly for the stairs.

Colonel Cho 'Keys' Ban had only been on the ground at Osan Air Base as long as it took for his ground crew to refuel and rearm his machine with AGM-88 HARM missiles and attend the joint forces briefing with a fresh roster of pilots from his unit and pilots of the US Aggressor Squadron that had just been attached to their Buddy Wing.

The young flight commander from the 6th Intelligence Squadron, First Lt. Carmel Velez-Rodriguez, hadn't rushed the briefing, but she hadn't wasted any time either, smoothly calling up screen after screen on the floor to ceiling projection at the end of the briefing room.

"The situation, ladies and gentlemen," she'd begun, "is that elements of the North Korean military appear to be staging an attempt to at the very least disrupt the reunification process: at worst, to stage a coup in North Korea to remove its Supreme Leader, Yun-mi Kim."

She brought up a map of the DMZ showing Seoul and Panmunjom and looked in the direction of Keys and his pilots. "As you would have heard or seen, at approximately 1015 pilots of the South Korean Air Force were attacked by Mig-29s of North Korea Air Force 11th Fighter Wing, during the fly-by of Panmunjom. North Korean fighters subsequently bombed Panmunjom Peace Village. Initial damage assessment indicates they targeted air defense installations and then the Peace Village itself. Civilian casualties, including members of the South Korea government, are high. Four South Korean fighters were lost in the engagement and four North Korean fighters were destroyed."

She zoomed the map out. "At 1030 hours, a battalion of North Korean artillery comprising 170mm Koksan and KN-09 rocket launchers initiated a barrage of Seoul, apparently targeting the Presidential Residence, plus power and telecommunications infrastructure. Since this first attack, two more mobile artillery battalions inside North Korea have been identified moving to new positions north of Seoul. Civilian casualties were incurred. Further artillery attacks are expected. South Korea has closed its airspace and grounded all commercial air traffic."

The map zoomed out to show the breadth of the Peninsula, with the demarcation line and DMZ marked, together with several large red circles. Velez-Rodriguez continued, "Also at 1030, a large-scale electronic warfare offensive was initiated by mobile electronic warfare ground units along the demarcation line, causing communication outages across the millimeter, X, Ku, C, L and S bands, in an area extending as far as twenty miles south of the DMZ and to altitudes of 10,000 feet. Critical to today's briefing, the Joint Tactical Information Distribution System in this area has been compromised."

That information caused a murmur through the room. The Joint Tactical Information Distribution System, or JTIDS, was the South Korean and US command information and coordination system and, more importantly, it was supposed to be impervious to jamming. If North Korean electronic warfare units were successful in jamming JTIDS, it could only mean they were getting help from a big brother – either Russia or China.

The image of a large camouflaged truck with a radar dish mounted on the enclosed cargo space was shown. "We have a high degree of certainty that these are the vehicles responsible for the jamming. They are MAS-537 EW units, purchased by North Korea from China in 2029. These trucks are your targets."

She pulled up a list of paired units, South Korean and US. "The assembled elements of South Korea AF 11th Fighter Wing and USAF 65th Squadron, designated as, uh, Buddy Wing 35-7, will be carrying out ground attack and escort missions across the DMZ to eliminate the North Korean jamming capability. We do not, at this stage, know how many North Korean air force or air defense units are part of this rogue action, but any North Korean aircraft in the area of operations are to be assumed hostile and may be engaged." She pointed to a location on the screen. "The targets are in the same sector that we lost a US Navy Defiant earlier today, so you should assume that North Korean ground to air missile defenses *will* attack if you cross into North Korean airspace. 11th Fighter Wing will lead the ground attack, 65th Aggressor will provide cover."

A pilot stuck up her hand. "Lieutenant, that 'area of operations' extends ten miles into North Korea. We could be going up against the whole damn North Korean air and air defense force."

He recognized the voice from the briefings he had attended during their recent Red Flag exercises against the US Aggressor Squadron. The Australian pilot.

The intel officer shook her head. "We have seen no indications of a widespread mobilization of North Korean ground or air forces. Our assessment at the moment is that the units engaged this morning were rogue elements of the North Korean military." She looked uncomfortable. "Ma'am, I won't lie. It's chaos up there. We've seen at least two instances of red-on-red North Korean versus North Korean fighter engagements over the DMZ. North Korean fighters have shot down at least one USAF rotary aircraft and a civilian aircraft inside North Korea. South Korean Air Force fighters are patrolling this side of the DMZ and there have been no other incursions from the North yet, but until we restore communications we have no way of knowing who is friend and who is foe, either on the ground or in the air." She waited to see if there were any more questions, but the room was quiet. "All right. Your room designations are on the screen, move to your briefing rooms, pilots. And God be with you."

As Keys gathered his pilots and started moving off, the Australian Lieutenant approached him. She stuck out her hand. "Colonel? I'm O'Hare, formerly Aggressor Squadron, now attached to the 65th. Looks like me and Lieutenant Besserman are flying shotgun for you today."

"Ban," Keys replied, shaking her hand. He studied the woman's face. She had close-cropped platinum hair with a skull tattoo showing under it, another of a vine that started on her neck and wound down under her collar. It wasn't a look you could forget. "I know you."

"Yes, sir," the woman said, falling into step beside him. "We've been in the same briefings, but we've never been formally introduced. Lieutenant Karen O'Hare. People call me 'Bunny'."

"I remember you from the last Red Flag debriefing, Lieutenant," Keys told her. "You 'shot down' one of my pilots."

"Well, Colonel," the woman grinned. "Your people *were* getting a bit cocky."

"That was yesterday. Today I have lost four aircraft and two men, Lieutenant," Keys told her. "Excuse me if I am not in the mood for banter."

The smile dropped from her face. "Apologies, Colonel. I meant no offense."

They reached the briefing room and Keys paused. "None taken, Lieutenant. My pilots will find and kill those trucks. I'm grateful you'll be watching our backs up there."

Keys' flight had been given a primary target 85 miles northeast of Osan – in the Bukhan River Valley, north of Hwacheon. The radiation from the North Korean Electronic Warfare – EW – unit was estimated to be coming from one of three hilltops in the rugged and mountainous DMZ. Keys' first job was to work out which one, pinpoint the jamming vehicle, and then destroy it with a high-speed anti-radiation missile. When that was done, they had secondary targets to the west.

If they survived to prosecute them.

Looking out the armored glass bubble of his cockpit at 20,000 feet, he saw the central northern city of Hwacheon pass by off his starboard wing. Three other Boromaes were tucked in behind him to his left and right.

Ahead and ten thousand feet above him, the flight of three US F-36 Kingsnake fighters and three Ghost Bat wingmen, with the call sign Umbra, was closing on the DMZ. And Keys was not encouraged by what they were reporting. All units in the Buddy Wing operations for the day had been assigned simple color-based call signs and Keys' ears pricked up as he heard his call sign, Magenta, and the female flight leader's voice. They weren't low and close enough to the source of the jamming for it to affect their comms yet.

"Magenta, Umbra. Six contacts bearing zero one zero degrees, altitude thirty, range twenty, tracking east. Probable fast movers. Contacts are currently outside AOO."

Keys pulled up his tactical screen. The potentially hostile contacts were inside North Korean airspace, north of their area of operations or AOO, but could easily turn to engage either the American or South Korean fighters at any moment if they spotted them.

"Good copy, Umbra. Magenta is beginning recon run. Out."

He switched to his inter-unit frequency. "Magenta pilots, set air to ground, lock on jamming, datalink on. Magenta two, you take hill C, Magenta three, hill B, Magenta one is taking hill A. Magenta four and five, low cover. You get a signal lock, you go Magnum, understood?"

His pilots acknowledged and peeled off, aligning their aircraft on the bearings of the two other potential targets farther east. Keys already had his aircraft boring straight in at the primary target, a hilltop on which the ruin of an old Catholic church provided the ideal hiding place for a MAS-537 tractor trailer.

Switching back to his HARM targeting screen Keys saw anti-air radar inside North Korea scanning the skies and had a probable target radiating ten miles ahead and below. He caged it and checked the bearing. It was right on top of the old church site. Exactly where he'd park a radar truck if he wanted cover on the otherwise bald brown hills.

The woman's voice broke his concentration. "Magenta, Umbra, hostile contacts turning to 190, radars in search mode … type … J-7. Umbra engaging."

Keys ignored the call. The North Korean J-7 fighter was a Cold War design with rudimentary beyond visual range engagement capabilities. The Americans overhead should be able to deal with the threat easily.

The boxed radiation signature on his HARM targeting screen started blinking, indicating the missile hanging on its pylon beneath his starboard wing was tracking the target too now. He jabbed his thumb on the missile release. "Magenta one, Magnum!" he called and rolled right, peeling away from the target to stay on the South Korean side of the DMZ.

His wingman had also found a target and boxed it. "Magenta three, Magnum!"

Keys watched his heads-up display with grim curiosity as their missiles tracked the two targets. Only one of them would be the real target, the other, probably a decoy. With two 150 lb. blast fragmentation warheads inbound, it didn't really matter which.

'Bunny' O'Hare and 'Noname' had a target bracketed too, but she wasn't watching her heads-up display with grim curiosity. She was watching with pity.

The North Korean J-7s were oblivious to their approaching death. They had last-century radar warning receivers that might have picked up the signals from her Kingsnake flight, but only to an accuracy of about 20 degrees and without any data on range or altitude. They were like blind men fighting gun-toting bandits with their canes.

Pulling data from the other aircraft in her flight, including two Ghost Bat drones sent out to scout the sky ahead of them, O'Hare and her wingman 'Snake', had perfect 20/20 vision of the North Koreans. "Snake, assigning targets, prepare to engage on my order," she called calmly as she allocated a single target to each of the four unmanned aircraft in her flight.

Their Ghost Bats carried four medium-range Peregrine missiles, while their Kingsnakes were fielding four larger and longer-range AIM-260 missiles.

"Engage with Bats," she ordered Noname. "Relay data from our sensors."

As far as this engagement was concerned, her WSO was a pilot by any other name. He controlled their two Ghost Bats with a series of thousands of preprogrammed AI algorithms that he could adapt to any tactical situation.

He had bracketed the incoming aircraft with the two drones, now he selected the smaller thrust-vectoring Peregrines. The North Koreans were well inside the missile's range and both the drones and their supersonic missiles would be almost invisible to the J-7s until it was too late. Noname was able to track their targets using the Kingsnake's radar without giving themselves away.

"Targets inside the AOO," Noname reported. "Targets locked. Missiles tracking. Engage?" The North Koreans had entered their engagement envelope. She hesitated, briefly wondering if they were rebel or ally. There was no way to know and no time to find out. If they were protecting the skies over North Korea's electronic warfare vehicles, they had been declared fair game. But Noname could not fire weapons without confirmation from his human pilot.

"Kill them, Noname," she ordered.

"Umbra, Fox 2," he called, sending a single missile from each of his Bats at their target. In perfect unison, the other aircraft in her flight volleyed their missiles too.

Suddenly an alarm sounded in her helmet. Noname called the threat in his usual deadpan voice … "Umbra pilots, ground radar. Directly below."

What the?!

Noname had been caught with his briefs around his silicon ankles. He was supposed to be watching their sensors for threats at the same time as he prosecuted the drone's targets. Air *and* ground threats. That was the whole damn point of him! Could an AI get target fixation? It would be the first time, but it might also be their last!

The North Korean J-7s had presented themselves as a nice juicy target, luring them toward a lurking ground missile installation that had been keeping its radar off air until the allied aircraft were at point blank range. Whirling her machine around

116

in a screaming high-g turn, she craned her neck and looked desperately for missile contrails.

And saw them! Two, angling up from a dark hillside, straight toward her.

The North Koreans had not left their jammer unprotected.

Beside the ruined Catholic church at Mount Chilseong, the North Korean MAS-537 jamming unit was blind to the threat above. It had no aircraft detection capability. It was meant to work in concert with anti-aircraft radar and missile systems but the North Korean rebel unit was on its own. To make up for its vulnerability it had carefully sited itself on the southern slope of the hill, with its rear wheels inside the collapsed hall of the old church.

The two HARM missiles from the South Korean Boromaes slammed into the ruins of the church from the south and the east, the thunder of their detonations closely followed by the sonic boom of their supersonic wakes. The thick church walls shook, but they didn't collapse.

The blasts rocked the truck, throwing its crew out of their seats and killing two of the men standing outside the truck, smoking, including the crew commander. It took two long minutes for the men inside the truck to gather themselves and realize what was happening.

As soon as they did, they shut down their system and a driver clambered into the cabin of the truck, started it up and slammed it into reverse, pulling it deeper into the ruins of the church hall. Smoke and dust covered them.

From the rear of the truck, two men pulled down a crate and desperately tore the lid off. From inside they lifted a Flying Crossbow portable ground to air missile. They might have been blind and deaf to the enemy threat, but now they knew it was out there, they weren't toothless.

Keys heard the American escort identify a new ground radar

threat, but had worries of his own. His flight's missiles had struck the target. Its signature was gone. But he was certain it had still been radiating for a good minute or more after the missile strike.

"Magenta two, the target was still radiating, right?"

"Confirmed, Colonel. I don't think it was a clean kill. I think they're playing dead."

Damn it.

"All right, Magenta flight, hold here. Keep an eye on that new ground radar location, don't get too high." He knew where the North Korean jammer was now. That doubt had been removed the minute it went dark. If he had loaded iron bombs he could have safely pickled them from ten thousand feet and obliterated the old church and any vehicle hiding in or behind it. But all he had was HARM missiles – which he could use without his target radiating if he locked in GPS coordinates – and his 20-millimeter Gatling gun. GPS mode would be useless, though, if the vehicle had pulled into cover, and stupidity was repeating the same action and expecting a different result. "Umbra leader will make a low pass and try to identify an attack vector."

On the hilltop inside the ruined church, the North Korean jamming crew could hear the South Korean jets circling. They had no intention of lighting up their transmitter again. In fact, they were getting ready to bug the hell out. The track up the side of the hill that they had negotiated to get into position was more goat track than vehicle track though, and their MAS-537 was a modified heavy hauler, not made for a downhill sprint. They would have to be sure the South Koreans had left the area before they started creeping down the steep slope.

"Aircraft, south, low!" one of the men called. Four ran for the protection of the north side of the ruins, two stepped out into the open to get clear of the smoke still shrouding the site – one with the Flying Crossbow launcher on his shoulder, the other with the missile in his arms, ready to load. He opened the missile receiver, pushed the missile in and locked it in place, then tapped his comrade on the helmet.

Through the Flying Crossbow's digital zoom scope the man could see the South Korean aircraft approaching from treetop height up the valley, below their position. He couldn't fire on it from this angle because the missile would drop about five feet before boosting and risked hitting the hillside before it corrected. Whether the South Korean pilot knew this or not, his ultra low level approach kept him safe, for now.

"Repositioning!" the man with the launcher called. The aircraft would have to climb to their level to try to attack. He would hit it after it passed.

Keys saw low shrub and bushes streaming in a blur past his wingtips as he hugged the contours of the river valley below the smoke-covered target. At the last moment before he would have slammed into the hillside he twitched his stick and zoomed up the slope, rolling his machine onto its side so he could get a good look at the hilltop as he passed overhead. He would only have a second to …

There! The truck was backed into the rubble of the old church, facing southeast. Only an attack from that direction would give them a chance of a kill. Out the corner of his eye he saw something else.

Instinct kicked in before he even had a chance to register the thought.

Rolling his machine through 180 degrees to the right he punched out a stream of anti-missile decoy flares and pulled into a high-g turn that slammed him back into his seat and caused his flight suit to inflate to try to keep the blood flowing to his brain. His vision grayed…

From the hillside receding below him, a missile screamed upward.

"*Miss*," Noname reported.

O'Hare breathed heavily in relief as the ground to air missile flew wide of her Kingsnake, blasting past her at twice the speed of sound. She had to get low. She pointed her nose at a line of hills.

Noname spoke again. "More missile contrails. Four o'clock."

She screwed her head over her shoulder, and saw them. Two more ground to air missiles, behind and heading away from them. Her Kingsnake wasn't the target. So, who …

She heard a panicked voice. *Snake.* Her eyes darted to her tactical display. He was still at 10,000 feet. "Umbra leader, hostile missile lock!"

It was the last thing she heard him say.

The Flying Crossbow fired at Keys was a Chinese copy of the Russian Verba man-portable missile, and recently upgraded to include computer-controlled maneuvering vanes that enabled it to follow a target through a 4G turn at supersonic speeds.

Keys Ban had almost no chance of evading it but that didn't stop him trying. He grunted loudly, fighting on the edge of a blackout as he pulled his machine into a turn so tight it took it to the edge of a stall and an alarm started sounding in his ears as …

The North Korean missile, drawn by the heat of his engines, closed within twenty feet of his port engine nozzle and detonated, sending blast fragments into the body of the engine. More warnings sounded in Keys' ears and the machine began to yaw crazily across the sky as though a huge hand had smacked it in the ass. Fire warnings began flashing as the port engine automatically shut itself down and fire retardant filled the engine compartment, dousing the fire before it could take hold.

Trailing ugly black smoke, Keys fought to get control of the Boromae back and rolled his machine right to compensate for the uneven thrust of flying on his starboard engine alone.

Desperately checking instrument readouts he saw that it was still delivering full power and responding to throttle commands. His flight controls felt wrong, though. He could roll and pitch but the machine was yawing as though ...

He craned his head around over his left shoulder and saw the problem. The port stabilizer fin was missing, chopped off at the base. OK, he was well and truly out of this fight. He nursed his machine higher, bringing it to 25,000 feet, where his comms were not affected by the jamming below and he was out of range of shoulder-fired missiles.

"Magenta leader to Magenta flight, I've been hit. Port engine flameout, port stabilizer missing, but I have control. Am going to make for, uh, Yanggu airfield ... Magenta two?"

"Magenta two," his wingman responded.

"The target is parked up in the ruins of the old church, facing out south-southeast. Put your HARM in pre-briefed mode, set GPS coordinates for the church and make your attack from the southeast. You should be able to smack your missile right into his ugly face. Engage from outside MANPAD range."

"Understood, Magenta one. Magenta two coming around."

"Magenta one bugging out, it's your mission, Two," he said.

"Two is lead," the man replied. "Good luck, Colonel."

Keys very carefully pointed his machine at Yanggu airfield. With the North Korean jammer down, he would get air to ground radio comms back and could alert the Yanggu controller to his emergency. His Boromae *really* wanted to roll onto its back and put him in the ground but he wasn't going to give it the satisfaction.

Keys had another reason to try and end the day above ground. Two reasons, really. His twin nine year old daughters, Eun and Min, who had already decided they were going to be pop stars when they grew up and spent every free waking moment either at singing lessons, or perfecting their dance routines. Their mother indulged them reluctantly, but Keys saw no reason at all why they couldn't be.

His own father's belief had been the reason Keys had

succeeded in becoming a fighter pilot. Keys had watched the American planes flying over their house in Osan and he told his father, "One day, I'm going to fly planes like those." His father had bought him a plastic model of an F-35 Panther and helped him build it. As they painted and glued the pilot into his seat, his father said to him, "There. That's you one day." And he said it in such a way that Keys knew he believed it. Believed the young Keys could do it.

One evening during home leave he'd been reviewing some vision from a simulated engagement on his laptop and then realized his daughter, Min, was standing at his elbow, watching the planes circle around each other in the simulated sky.

"I want to be a fighter pilot too, one day," Min had said. "Just like you."

He'd pulled her onto his knee. "I thought you wanted to be a pop star. In a band, with Eun."

"I do. But our teacher saw us rehearsing some moves and he said what are you doing and we told him we are going to be pop singers when we grow up and he said that's not a real job. He said why not be pilots like our father? Fighter pilots are more important than popstars."

Keys had closed his laptop. "Well, I'm a fighter pilot and I don't agree. I think the world needs a lot more pop stars, and a lot fewer fighter pilots."

Mind on the task, Keys.

It took his full concentration to keep his machine level. On the horizon, he saw a parachute falling through the sky. His day had started badly, and gotten worse, but he was determined it was *not* going to finish with him hanging from silk or burying himself in a mountainside below.

The faceoff across the Bukhan River had reached an impasse. The North Korean drone hovered on one side of the river following Kronk, and he was on the other side of the river angrily trying to ignore the constant whine of its rotors.

He'd been hiking for a couple of hours and had hoped that

getting a few miles away from the crash site might help him get a line of sight link to his Shikaka so he could run a patch and hook himself into the comms system. If he didn't do it soon, the thing would switch to autonomous mode and land itself at Busan anyway, taking with it any hope he had of using it to send out a mayday.

He'd heard the sound of jets in the distance and it suddenly grew louder, so he turned to face what he thought was the direction of the sound, and saw a fighter trailing smoke plow into a hillside about a mile away.

"Kingsnake," he decided, from what he'd seen of the aircraft's profile. Standing with his hands on his hips he let out an expletive. "Great. Another carcass to attract the scavengers." But then he felt bad, because there had probably been an American pilot inside that ...

No. Floating through the sky directly ahead of him was a parachute.

And it was going to come down right in the middle of the river.

An Imperfect Storm

Bukhan River Valley, DMZ

Kronk had dropped his duffel bag and was pounding up the rocky riverbank toward the falling pilot, water splashing around his feet at times, plunging into pools up to his knees at others, then hammering across hard shale beaches before he was splashing through the water again.

He wasn't going to get there in time.

The pilot didn't appear to be steering the chute, as he was dropping straight toward the river. Or maybe a water landing was better – softer than hitting the dirt?

Kronk's constant companion, the surveillance drone, kept pace with him along the parallel bank. He doubted it had even seen the destruction of the US fighter and the ejection of its pilot, so fixated was it on him.

The chute was only about a hundred feet over the river now, slicing diagonally through the air, but almost as though whoever was in it was deliberately trying to land smack in the deepest part of the river.

Except now he was so close he could see the pilot's helmeted head, slumped onto their chest, arms limp at their sides. They weren't 'steering' jack.

And two seconds after they hit the water, they were going to start drowning.

Lungs heaving and legs burning, Kronk flung himself through the water, still ten yards away when the guy hit the river and went straight under. The parachute hit the river right after it, but filled with water and acted like a sea anchor, the fast-flowing current dragging the downed pilot toward him.

If he wasn't quick enough, the guy was going to pass him and keep going downriver!

Throwing himself awkwardly into a dive, he plunged under the water and groped blindly ahead. Hitting nothing he struggled to the surface and batted his way forward in a floundering crawl. His slapping arms finally hit something and he grasped at it, winding a parachute cord around his forearm to stop it slipping away.

Now he was being dragged downriver too.

But slowly. The pilot's boots and clothes had filled with water and he was being hauled over the rocky bottom. Kronk could feel the pull every time he snagged and then came free. He unwound his arm and then, hand over hand, feet flapping, pulled himself down into the dark water, toward the object at the end of the cord.

Jerking backward through waving weed at the bottom of the river was the pilot, still strapped into his harness, helmet still covering his head. The current wasn't as strong at the bottom of the river and with a final flailing kick Kronk grabbed onto the harness going across the pilot's chest. *If the harness was like the ones he'd had to wear on transport flights, there should be ...*

There! He pulled desperately on the buckle to release the harness and it fell away, the pilot immediately starting to float free, but their arms were still tangled in shoulder webbing. Kronk had no purchase and his lungs were starting to burn, so he tugged at the pilot's legs and let the river current and his bodyweight do the work.

Suddenly the pilot started *fighting* him!

They'd regained consciousness and began punching and kicking him. Kronk had to let go and in a welter of bubbles they both broke to the surface. Kronk struck out for the nearest bank, the pilot, weakly treading water, got pulled into the same bank by the eddying current but tried to stay out in the water, away from Kronk.

He put his hands in the air at shoulder height. "Hey, I'm American!"

Fumbling with his helmet, the pilot pushed his visor up. Kronk could see a frowning brow above the oxygen mask.

"American!" he yelled again, advancing slowly. He wasn't sure if the pilot was armed, and if he was confused about his identity ...

But the pilot paddled to the shore, flopped onto his back

and pulled off his helmet.

It wasn't until Kronk got within six feet that he saw the tattoo that crept down the man's neck from the corner of his ear. A serpent of some sort.

The pilot turned his head toward him. "Hey man. Name's 'Snake'. How's *your* day goin'?"

Special Agent Helen Lee did not think things were going particularly well. After all, their helicopter had escaped from Panmunjom through a haze of smoke with anti-aircraft batteries still firing at unseen targets above. And now she'd landed in the middle of what seemed to be a coup d'etat.

She'd passed on to her old Security Service Commander every scrap of intelligence she had gathered about the Prime Minister's detail and their plans for the day. She'd been brought into a limited circle of need-to-know by the detail commander, a barrel chested bully called Yeo, and told there was intelligence of a plot to disrupt the Peace Accord ceremony.

"We have reports of traitors in the police services and armed forces," he had said, ominously. "Anti-reunification conspirators. Stay alert."

For a moment, Lee had wondered if her old mentor, Park, could be part of that plot. Had she stupidly allowed herself to be placed inside the PM's security detail as some kind of unwitting mole? Lee started to see anti-reunification conspirators in every dark corner.

But when they had suddenly deviated from the plan and moved into the Peace House basement for an unscheduled, and unusually long 'toilet break', her sixth sense had been alerted. She should have made an excuse, found a way to get a message out to Commander Pak at that point, but then the bombs started falling, and it was too late - they were running for the already prepared helicopter through a haze of smoke and explosions, and everything the old man had warned her about was coming true.

And from the conversations she was overhearing, it was

becoming obvious where the plot to disrupt the Peace Accord ceremony was centered. Not Park. Not any mysterious cabal of conspirators hiding in the shadows. It was the very people riding in the chopper with her, because it was their damned plot!

Helen Lee did not need 20 years in the Security Service to see that being the only person on the Prime Minister's detail who was apparently not in on the plot was Not A Good Thing.

South Korean Prime Minister Ted Choi ran from the helo with a hand over his head to stop his heavily lacquered hair being ruffled. He had a nationwide broadcast to make soon and while it would be all right to look a little ruffled, he did not want to look disheveled. He had to project an air of calm control, of concern, but confidence. He had to …

His aide was holding the rooftop helipad door open with one hand and checking cell phone messages with the other. "No word from the Peace Dam," he said, guiding Choi inside.

"I told General Kim that jamming would be a double-edged sword," Choi complained. "Chaos works for us, but it also works against us."

It was only one flight down to the Prime Minister's offices and residence, and Choi did not rush. It would not do at this, his nation's hour of need, for its future President to fall down a set of stairs and break his damn neck. His aide was scrolling through more messages.

"DPRK artillery barrage did its job. State of emergency in Seoul, they're moving the population to shelters. No update on State Council casualties, so Agriculture Minister Yoon is still the most senior surviving member after you." He held open another door. "Air forces on both sides are on high alert, DPRK ground forces are still in their barracks and bases, but South Korea ground forces and Navy are mobilizing. The US Ambassador wants to meet with you as soon as you land."

Choi stepped into a corridor, walked ten paces and then opened the door of his Prime Ministerial office, moving inside to find two men in black suits, white shirts and black ties – one of them standing insolently by his desk drinking his whisky.

They looked alarmed when they saw his protection detail file in behind him and take positions either side of Choi, and did not look more relaxed when Choi stopped and frowned at them.

"Who told you that you could wait in here?" he asked from across the room.

One of the men, an older, corpulent man in an ill-fitting suit, gave Choi a small bow. "Prime Minister, our men are downstairs and…"

"Stop," Choi said, holding up his hand. "Which of you is leader here?"

The older man indicated the younger, slim thug standing beside him, who was still holding his whisky and smiling. He casually lifted one side of his jacket to reveal a pistol in a holster underneath his arm, and then winked at the nearest of Choi's protection agents.

Lee had taken her usual position, inside the room at the main door out to the lobby. The presence of the two guests in the Prime Minister's office had been communicated as they were deplaning and she'd been told they were expected. She had not been told *who* they were, but that was not unusual. When she had seen who had been waiting though, she had become alarmed.

They were clearly Kkangpae. South Korean mafia. She could see that by the tattoos on their hands. She even recognized the older one, from her time in the Sejong City police. A senior lieutenant in the crime syndicate, his presence in the Prime Minister's office would have been highly unusual at any time. On a day like today, it was deeply alarming.

She'd been standing by the door with her hands behind her back, watching intently, when she saw the younger Kkangpae pull aside his jacket and reveal his weapon.

"Gun!" she yelled, and pulled her own pistol, aiming at the

128

man. He froze, kept his hand on his jacket lapel and raised the other, turning slowly toward her with a lopsided grin.

None of her colleagues moved. "Stand down, Lee!" her detail commander, Yeo, yelled.

She lowered her pistol uncertainly.

"Outside the door, take the corridor," he told her. "Now." Holstering her pistol again, she bit her lip and did as she was ordered, stepping out into the corridor and closing the door behind her. A few seconds later, one of the other men from their detail came out and took the other side of the door. He nodded to her, but said nothing.

Something seriously messed up was happening. More than ever, she needed to get a message out.

But how?

Choi waited until the door closed and addressed the young Kkhangpae lieutenant.

"You could have been shot. If you do anything as stupid as that again, you will be, is that clear?"

The young thug bristled, but the older man, clearly his minder, put a hand on his arm and he calmed, buttoning his jacket. He smiled, flashing two gold teeth. "Clear, Mr. Prime Minister." The way the title fell from his lips, it was clear it held little meaning for him.

"Your men are downstairs?"

"Yes."

"They know what is expected?"

"They know what they need to know. They will do what is expected."

"Good, get out of my office."

The younger man put his whisky glass down on the Prime Minister's desk. "Very fine whisky, Mr. Prime Minister."

Yeo escorted the two men to the door. As the room was cleared, Choi moved to his desk. That he had been forced into an alliance with the Kkangpae was an irritant he would deal with later, when the dust had settled.

He had to start working the telephone, as would be expected of him. Calls to the military hospital at Panmunjom to check on the health of his fellow Security Council members, to other influential politicians around the country. To the General Staff, to demand an update on the security situation and assert control over the military before it escalated things beyond his control.

He barked out a list of calls to an aide and then turned to his protective security chief. "Yeo. Any interest from Sejong Police?"

"No sir," Yeo responded. "We advised them on the way in that we will be securing your residence and we have no need for their assistance."

"Good," Choi said, steepling his fingers under his chin. When he spoke again, it was with quiet menace. "What were those street thugs doing in my office?"

Yeo baulked. "I apologize sir, I asked one of my men to have their local leader here in case we ... It should never have happened."

Choi had not been involved in the detailed planning for the the nationwide 'insurrection', so that he could deny involvement if it came out before today. And yet his Kkangpae collaborators had been admitted to his very office. "No, it should not. You are certain they will play their part?"

"They have been well paid. You will soon see reports of looting and civil unrest in Incheon, Seoul, Daegu, Busan ... and here in Sejong City."

Choi smiled. "Very good." He called over his aide. "First call to the Chairman of the Joint Chiefs of Staff and that idiot, Minister Yoon. We need to start calming things down before the Joint Chiefs mobilize the whole damn Army."

"Prime Minister."

Choi spun in his chair, looking out of the window behind him at the Great Wall-like buildings of the Sejong government complex.

So far, so good. Panmunjom cratered, the State Council members dead or critically injured. He himself 'miraculously'

130

alive and about to cement his authority with a heroic address from his Sejong office in front of his assembled staff. The signing of the *surrender document*, as he thought of it, fatally disrupted.

The only kink in the plan … they should have received word by now from Goh at the Peace Dam that the two State leaders, traitors to both of their nations, had either been captured or were dead. He hoped it was simply a communications failure – the fog of war. He motioned to Yeo. "How many staff are here today?"

"Ministry staff were ordered to report to the office as soon as events at Panmunjom became public. There are about seventy-five here already, another twenty or so are on the way."

"Good. When they get here, seal this floor. No one else comes up, no one leaves. I want a crowd around me for my address to the nation."

"Yes, sir," Yeo said and moved to the door again before Choi's voice stopped him.

"Wait. The new agent, Lee."

"Yes, sir?"

"She's sharp. You said you were going to deal with her."

"I *will* deal with her, sir. As soon as I am finished here."

Holding station ten miles out from Sangeo Shoal, with the US–South Korea–North Korea 'Operation White Glove' assault ships preparing to get underway, USS *Cody*'s on-watch sonarman raised an alarm.

"Captain, sonar, subsurface contact on the *Sea Hunter* towed array. Bearing zero, four, zero. Designating target Sierra one, one."

Lomax looked at the plot on the bridge tactical screen in front of him. "Range?"

"Range tracking two-five thousand yards, bearing refinement … zero, four, four. My best guess on course is zero, zero, five. Headed away from us, sir."

Lomax turned to his 2IC, Ryan. "Starboard five degrees,

slow to ten knots. Put your *Sea Hunter* on an intercept course, Pilot, but keep your array clear and in passive mode, maintain at least ten miles separation."

"Aye aye, Captain."

An unknown subsea contact had been picked up on the passive sonar rig trailing behind the *Cody*'s *Sea Hunter* drone. There were no friendly submarines in that sector. The contact was about 15 miles off their starboard beam and headed north, *away* from Sangeo Shoal. But its direction of travel meant nothing, if it was a cruise missile-armed North Korean submarine.

"How far out is our new Defiant?" Lomax asked his air operations officer.

"Twenty minutes, sir."

"Redirect it to that contact. Dipping sonar, passive mode only. I want it classified and triangulated. Eliminate any ambiguity."

"Aye, aye, Captain."

"I don't suppose *Bougainville* offered to send that Defiant with a full load of VLWTs, Lieutenant Ryan?" The inbound Defiant chopper was not just a hunter, it was also a killer. In fact, the only way the *Cody* had to attack a submarine was for the helo to deploy the new Very Light Weight Torpedo, dropped by parachute from on top of the hostile submarine. The VLWT was also highly maneuverable and could be used as an anti-torpedo torpedo to protect the *Cody*, *if* it got sufficient warning of an incoming attack.

The man's look told Lomax what he needed to know. "'Fraid not, sir. It left Sangeo Shoal in ferry configuration. Sonar array stowed, but no ordnance."

Lomax quickly changed his mind. "Relay the contact data to *Bougainville* and *Point Loma*. Request orders. Get our Defiant down and loaded with VLWTs."

It would take about thirty minutes to get their own helo back on deck and armed with torpedoes. Ryan began relaying orders as Lomax looked at his tactical screen and started doing the math. The helo on their sister ship *USS Point Loma* had not

132

been beached like *Cody*'s was, so it would be an easy matter to arm it with torpedoes if it wasn't already, and get it airborne. But *Point Loma* was forty miles south of them. The contact, fifteen miles north. At its best speed of about 260 miles per hour, it would take at least 12 minutes to reach the contact. Add to that the inevitable delay in reaction time to get the helo airborne ... say ten to fifteen minutes if it was already armed, thirty if it wasn't ... it would be anywhere from twenty to forty-five minutes before it would reach the contact. Not for the first time since Lomax had begun operations in tandem with a *Sea Hunter* platform, he wished the damn things could fire torpedoes!

As his sonarman updated the plot, Ryan relayed his orders, then adjusted their course and speed to optimize their passive detection capability.

"Message from *Bougainville*, Captain," his comms officer said, reading a message on his battle-net screen.

"Go ahead."

"Orders for *Cody*. Maintain contact with contact Sierra one. *Bougainville* dispatching Fire Scouts, prepare for data link."

Known as a helicopter landing dock, the USS *Bougainville* was nothing less than a small aircraft carrier. For Operation White Glove it had sailed with a complement of no fewer than six vertical take-off F-35B stealth fighters, 12 Defiant transport helicopters, seven MQ-8C Fire Scout unmanned anti-submarine drones, and two MH-60 helicopters for air-sea rescue. With the fleet at DEFCON 3, if *Bougainville* was sending Fire Scouts *plural* to prosecute the contact, it was not simply planning to do a little light recon.

Lomax drew himself upright, tapping a hand on his thigh as though listening to an inner beat. The bridge crew all had their eyes on him. They knew what that little nervous tic meant.

Things were about to get very real.

"Comms, acknowledge receipt and prepare data synchronization."

"Aye, aye, Captain."

"Lieutenant," Lomax said quietly, staring at a point

somewhere off their starboard beam. "You have twenty minutes from the time that bird is wheels-down on this ship until it is armed and available."

"Twenty minutes, aye, sir," Ryan said. "Permission to…"

"Go." He turned to the watch officer, a Lieutenant JG called Henley. "Henley, bring us around to 340 degrees. Sonar, watch the speed on that Hunter, I don't want to destabilize the array. I want you to close on the contact to improve the plot, but stay in passive mode. Do whatever is necessary to optimize detection but get no closer than five miles, understood?"

The man swallowed. "Aye, aye, Captain!" He wasn't confident. If the target moved above or below a thermocline – a refractive warm water layer in the sea – the sound waves it sent out could become so weak the passive sonar array being towed behind the *Sea Hunter* might not be able to pick them up. Ideally, he would have the drone already begin searching with active sonar, but Lomax clearly wanted to retain an element of surprise.

He need not have bothered.

On board North Korea submarine *Hero*, Captain Se-heon Dokgo had been biting back his disappointment at receiving no update to his orders. He did not like bobbing about just below the waves with his satellite antennae slicing through the water above, and especially not when the effort had borne no fruit. In the absence of new orders or intelligence from Pyongyang fleet base, he'd pulled down the latest news bulletin streams from the South Korean KBS state television service – a luxury only available when he was at sea – and reviewed them on a tablet PC with his earbuds in. He did not want his crew exposed to the Southerner's propaganda.

Six men were crammed into the control room under the *Gorae's* conning tower, so he had to wedge himself into a gap between two instrument panels so that he could see the screen without anyone being able to watch.

Panmunjom bombed! Air battles over the DMZ, artillery

firing on Seoul!

He had known that his action was to be but one part in a wider effort to destabilize the reunification process, but he had not been given the full picture. The level of support for the anti-unification rebels was broader than he had dared hope possible!

One report dismayed him, though. The whereabouts of the traitor, Chairperson Yun-mi Kim, were unknown. She was not among those confirmed dead or injured at Panmunjom and had not been heard from since the attack. The news explained the lack of new orders. His 'special weapon' could only be armed with the unlock code carried by the so-called Supreme Leader. Yes, he could launch the weapon in kinetic strike mode, without arming its nuclear warhead, but that would be...

"Comrade Captain!" his Electronic Warfare officer called out. "Emissions bearing one seven five degrees, signature indicates US Navy. Estimated range, ten to twenty miles."

Dokgo nodded. "Give me a course track, EW." The new Chinese emissions detection system in the *Hero* was like alien technology compared to what he'd had available on his last command, a smaller diesel electric Sinpo-class attack submarine where the only digital instrument was a kitchen timer he'd bought at a market and glued to a control panel. Based on Russian Pastel emissions warning receiver technology, the *Gorae*'s emissions detection system was married to software that could match signatures to known enemy vessels in seconds ... but wasn't precise enough to give an exact range to the target or an instant read on its current course. Dokgo put a hand against the hull and drummed his fingers as he waited. He was old school, liked to feel the thrum of the two air-independent diesel engines through the hull, vibrations traveling from fingertips and palm to brain, telling him almost everything he needed to know about the health of his propulsion system.

"Comrade Captain, I ... estimate... the contact is tracking east. Parallel to *Hero*, sir." Despite his hesitancy, the man didn't sound uncertain. Just careful. Dokgo liked that.

"Very well. Radio, stow antennae. Helm, right full rudder,

ahead standard, make your depth one hundred meters, come around to zero nine zero degrees and prepare to move to maximum depth."

The contact was one of the White Glove task force amphibious ships, either the *Cody* or *Point Loma*. He had been briefed that the entire task force was expected to have been tied up at Sangeo Shoal today for the signing ceremony, so he had not expected any American naval vessels between himself and his target. The *Cody*-class expeditionary fast transport was no threat to his mission. It fielded only a 30mm gun and close-in weapons systems for missile self-defense, and didn't have the ability to intercept anything other than low-flying aircraft, let alone hypersonic sea-skimming cruise missiles. It was a glorified bus, built to freight US Marines from island to island in the Pacific, not to hunt submarines like the *Gorae*.

Sending a nice, fat, juicy target like the *USS Bougainville* into *his* hunting ground – without a brace of anti-air frigate escorts to protect it against his missiles – was either arrogant, complacent or just plain stupid.

As he hoped soon to prove.

"Contact Sierra one is maneuvering…" *Cody*'s sonarman said. "Reversing course. Recommend *Sea Hunter* move to active sonar."

"And tell him we know he's there?" Lomax mused out loud. He knew why his sonarman wanted to go active. Passive sonar could give them a bearing to the target but told them little about its depth. Lomax was poring over the tactical plot with his XO Ryan, who had just returned from preparing to receive their inbound Defiant on the flight deck. "Ideas, Lieutenant?"

Ryan put his finger on the two icons on the plot which showed the drones launched by *Bougainville*. They were about ten minutes out from the position marking the subsurface contact. "*Bougainville*'s helos will start dipping any time now." He moved his finger to another, close to their ship. "Our bird is five minutes out. All we need to do is keep contact another quarter of an hour, *Bougainville* will begin prosecuting and we can arm our machine and get it airborne for torpedo defense." Lomax decided. "All right. OOD, make your course zero one zero degrees, speed ten knots. We'll move *Cody* closer to the contact's former position. I want to hear from sonar the second the contact changes course."

As though the very words had jinxed them, a message was flashed from the control center and the OOD turned to Lomax with a look of consternation. "Contact lost! He must have changed depth. We…"

Lomax cursed, then recovered his composure. "Sonar, project a track based on last known position, course and speed. Send it to *Bougainville*." He drew a deep breath. "Go active on the *Sea Hunter*."

"Enemy close!" Dokgo's sonar officer called, though every man in the submarine could hear the sudden and terrifying *ping ping* of high-frequency soundwaves striking their hull anyway. "Permission to engage active sonar?"

Dokgo baulked. An enemy ship? And within a few miles, if the frequency of the sonar pings was anything to judge by. Why had they not heard its screws on their acoustic array or picked up its emissions? He checked their depth. Eighty meters, heading for a hundred. They were twenty meters below the thermocline now. If the enemy was already so close, the refractive layer would offer no real protection.

He had only two choices. Go active with his own sonar, try to detect the enemy ship overhead and engage it with a Chinese-made torpedo. Or cut power, change course and glide deep, hoping for the density of the colder water and extra distance to hide him.

They were not real choices, though. His was a strategic ballistic missile submarine, not an attack submarine. His core imperative was to keep his boat operational until the moment he was ordered to launch his missiles. So that, he would do.

"Sonar, permission denied. Propulsion, engines stop. Helm,

ten degrees right rudder. Make your depth two hundred meters. XO, rig for silent running and arm countermeasures." Instantly the normal murmur of voices in the control room was stilled, his orders were urgently passed by whisper. Hand on the hull between control panels, Dokgo felt the comforting vibration of the engines die away as power to the screws was cut and only the momentum of their 3,000-ton boat and the inclination of their diving planes drove them deeper.

"Contact Sierra one reacquired," *Cody*'s sonarman declared. "Bearing nine three two degrees, range four miles, heading for the thermocline. I'd guess he's going deep and turning..."

"We still have data link with *Bougainville*'s helos?"

"Aye, sir."

"Sonar, do you have an acoustic ID on the contact?"

"No, Captain, insufficient data."

Lomax would dearly love to know what they were dealing with. The *Sea Hunter*'s cloud AI-supported acoustic detection system could take data from the towed sonar array and analyze the sounds coming at it through the water to determine how many and what type of screws the submarine was using, what noises it made moving through the water and, added to an estimate of its mass from the active sonar, an informed guess could be made.

He checked his map plot and saw the *Bougainville*'s helos were closing on the contact now. "Comms, bridge, you have voice feed from the pilots of the Fire Scouts?"

"Aye, Captain."

"Put it on the bridge speakers."

The pilots of the two submarine hunting drones were sitting aboard the *USS Bougainville*, flying their aircraft in virtual cockpits, their commands relayed at the speed of light from their ship to a satellite overhead and back down to their aircraft. Lomax wanted to know what their orders were. Were they just hunting, or had they been authorized to attack the unknown target? If it wasn't a US or South Korean boat, it could really only be Chinese or North Korean. In the current circumstances, they might legitimately engage a North Korean boat, but risk engaging a Chinese submarine? That would indicate the situation was much more serious than Lomax imagined.

He need not have worried. The audio feed from the Fire Scout pilots – using the call sign Greek one and two – quickly told him what he wanted to know.

>>... two deploying sonar. Sonar in the water. No contact. Starting three-ray search.

>Roger, Greek two, approaching search grid echo four, deploying sonar...

>>Still nothing.

>Greek two, Greek one, contact! Bearing zero niner zero, range two hundred. Target locked. Sending to you.

>>Good copy, one. Moving in ... firing acoustic charge.

The Fire Scout pilots had orders to harass the contact and try to drive it to the surface, but not to destroy it. Right now, the buddy of the pilot who had located the submarine would be moving his aircraft right over the top of the diving submarine. From a tube-like launcher under the nose of the Fire Scout between its torpedo pylons, it would fire a heavy ball-shaped 40mm noisemaker grenade, timed to sink to within fifty feet of the fleeing contact and detonate with an unmistakable thud that would be clearly audible through the hull of the boat below it.

It sent a very clear message. We know where you are and the next sound you hear could be a homing torpedo tearing you a new one.

The usual response from a submarine captain in such a situation in peacetime would be to blow ballast, rise to the surface and radio for assistance from his own navy or air force. With the situation on the Peninsula so fraught, that couldn't be assumed.

The next few minutes would tell Lomax a lot about the Captain of this particular submarine. And their intentions.

As Colonel 'Keys' Ban wrestled his crippled KF-21 Boromae toward Yanggu airfield, his wingman 'Magenta two' was making his attack run, ten miles out and ten thousand feet above the North Korean jammer truck hiding in the ruins of the old church. His HARM targeting screen showed a satellite image of the church and he put his targeting crosshairs right on top of it, sending its GPS coordinates to the missile on a pylon under his wing. In 'GPS pre-briefed' mode it didn't need a radar emission to home on, it simply flew to the coordinates it had been given and dove into the ground.

From well outside the range of the shoulder-launched missiles below and ahead of him, the pilot triggered his missile. "Magnum," he announced calmly, as it dropped off its pylon and then boosted away ahead of him as he rolled into a banking turn that would take him safely back inside South Korean airspace.

The supersonic HARM missile caught the jamming truck's crew standing out in the open beside the church, mouths agape as they watched the contrails of dogfighting jets and air to air missiles swirling through the sky above them. It didn't miss this time. As Keys had projected, it flew straight into the collapsed end of the church hall and its 150 lb. warhead detonated against a pile of rubble beside the hidden truck.

The North Korean mobile jamming defense in the Hwacheon DMZ sector disappeared in a flash of light and an angry red and orange ball of high explosive and diesel fuel.

After landing back at Osan Air Base, Bunny O'Hare shut down her engine and sat quietly in the cockpit, staring ahead of her. The only sound was the tick of engines cooling and flight surfaces expanding in the hot afternoon sun.

Bunny O'Hare did not deal well with defeat. And she had just had her ass handed to her. Her default setting was to assume that she would always overcome, always survive, always win. Some called it arrogance, other more kindly called it 'irrational overconfidence'. This time, that overconfidence had cost her wingman's aircraft, if not his life.

"That was not good, Noname," she said carefully. How the hell did you bawl out an AI?

"I know. We lost Snake. The ground radar was not detectable until it started radiating but I should have been able to pick up the missile launchers on optical-infrared sensors. At the very least I should have detected the missile launch blooms quicker than I did. I believe there may have been a sensor malfunction," he said.

She hammered the screen in front of her with a gloved fist. "You do *not* blame your equipment, Noname."

"I am running a diagnostic now, but I believe..."

"Shut up!" Bunny said. "If you lose a man, it is *always* your own fault. Do you understand that?"

"No. If the DAS system..."

"Screw the DAS!" she said. "Systems fail. Weapons fail. Flight controls fail. Engines fail. And they will *always* fail at the worst possible time. Straight after takeoff, during a landing, in a bloody storm, or right in the middle of combat..."

"I don't think that's actually..."

"Systems fail, Noname!" she yelled. "Your job is to *expect* them to fail, to never rely on them to save your life or your wingman's life. To always have a plan B, a plan C. You were supposed to be watching our back. If you were getting nothing on DAS, that in itself should have made you suspicious."

"But the DAS system was giving no error messages ..."

"DAS *failed*, Noname. It failed. And now Snake is down in the DMZ. We aren't on exercises anymore. These aren't Red Flag missions. There is zero margin for error, do you get that? *Zero!*"

"I understand we are now flying combat missions. But for me there is..."

"Shut up. Just shut up. Say, 'Yes, ma'am' and review what I just said from now until we get airborne again, looking for flaws in my logic all you like because you will not find any. Snake is down not because DAS failed, Noname. Snake is down because *you* failed."

"Yes, ma'am."

Bunny punched the button that opened the cockpit bubble and saw Salt waiting for her.

Whatever was coming, she deserved it. The loss of her wingman wasn't Noname's fault. Not really. Noname was a bunch of quantum chips and a cloud link. It was a system, and systems failed. She was the pilot. If Snake was down, it was her fault and hers alone.

All her fighting life, the Gods of War had looked kindly on Bunny O'Hare. She was starting to wonder if their love for her was beginning to wane.

'Snake-eater' Besserman heard the explosion to the west, but he had other worries now. He was sitting on his butt, wrists resting on his bent knees as he glared at the drone.

"So, tell me you have a plan for dealing with that thing, Navy," Snake said as Kronk jogged back after fetching his duffel bag from upriver. He pointed across at the Chinese-made drone.

Kronk hefted the duffel bag containing his laptop and transceiver.

"Well, it can't follow both of us, so how about I try to get its attention and you sneak around behind it ..."

"That's stupid. It can just go higher," Snake pointed out. "Keep an eye on us both."

"So what's your idea?" the Navy officer said petulantly.

Gonna sit here on my mopey ass and wait to be captured is what. Snake hung his head. *Get it together, man.* He looked up again. "We need to get moving south, get help," he said. "Unless you have a radio?"

"Well, Lieutenant, I tried to connect with our Shikaka..."

Snake perked up. "That drone we were escorting is still up there? And armed?"

"Armed, yeah. But I haven't been able to get through. Transceiver damaged in the crash maybe, or some kind of interference." He looked around him. "I thought maybe if I could get higher, I might be able to get a signal, use the Shikaka's radio to call a rescue flight."

"Yeah, but here's the better option," Snake told him, and explained what was happening up and down the DMZ. "You and me book it south on foot *and* we try to find somewhere high up you can get a signal out. Every mile we put between us and the North is a bonus."

"I'm not really the hiking type. You serious?"

"On my mother's virginity," Snake nodded. "But our little friend over there could bring us a world of harm if the North Koreans can scrape up a helo or a wheeled patrol. I'd sure love to be able to call down some harm with that Shikaka of yours."

Kronk pointed to a hilltop to their south. "So, we hike?"

Snake got painfully to his feet, stifling a groan. "We hike."

It took them an hour and twenty minutes to get a few thousand yards downriver and a hundred feet up. Staying a good hundred yards away, the North Korean drone followed along behind them like a hungry hyena, stalking wounded prey. They paused at a flat rock, so Kronk could climb up and set up his gear.

"Well, I don't see any sign of vehicles," Snake said, scanning the valley to their north and south. He watched as Kronk started up the link to the Shikaka.

>Initiate handshake
>>Data handshake processing
>>Control interface initializing
>>Interface signal not found
>>Retry?

"Do not throw the very expensive drone control system into the river, Kronk," Kronk told himself, taking a deep breath. Not only was it their only way to get a message out to the outside world, but it was the only chance of getting the nuclear-armed drone down on the water safely – once it had saved their skins, that is.

"Sorry, you talking to me?" Snake asked.

"No, sorry, did I say that out loud?"

"Something about throwing the command unit in the river?"

"Yeah."

"Then yeah, you said it out loud. Keep trying."

They both turned at the sound of high-pitched rotors as the drone across the river rose in the air about ten feet, showing them it was still very much on duty. Two sharp reports echoed around the valley.

They jerked their heads toward the sounds. "What was that?" Kronk asked.

"Explosions," Snake told him. "Hard to say how far away. Not close though."

"You think things are heating up?"

Snake looked up at the sky. "I'd expect to see a lot more action up there if we were looking at total war," he said. "Contrails from jets, missiles flying. Which I don't see. I'd say it's just more SEAD work."

"SEAD?"

"Suppression of Enemy Air Defenses," the pilot explained.

"I'll see about the uplink," Kronk said, settling behind the laptop. He ran a new shooting routine, then he started diving into system diagnostic menus he hadn't used before. The surveillance drone downhill bobbed up and down on whirring rotors, and the noise was really starting to get on his nerves. Seeing a fist-sized rock beside him, he picked it up and hurled it with all his might at the drone.

The rock fell laughably short, hardly even getting halfway to the drone before it thudded into the hillside and bounced away. As it did, there was another loud report from the south. Someone was getting hell down there.

"System isn't reporting any errors," Kronk decided. "We should have a clear line of sight from here but there's definitely something interfering with the signal. I increased the sensitivity that triggers frequency hopping. Here goes nothing." He punched in the command to initiate a satellite handshake, then bent down to look at the small LCD screen on the transceiver.

>*Initiate handshake*
>>*Data handshake processing*
>>*Control interface initializing*

>>*Authorizing. Please wait*

"Please wait." Kronk said. "That's new."

With a chime, the small LCD screen flashed and changed to a split screen view showing the Shikaka's system status on one side and a simulated cockpit view on the other.

>*System access granted.*

Kronk jumped up and slapped Snake's back. "How about that, Air Force! And now I've got someone who can fly it too!"

Snake winced. "I just got shot out of a burning plane at 500 miles an hour and woke up underwater. Don't do that again."

Snake had about a hundred hours on Sentinel drones from earlier in his flying career. He spent a moment familiarizing himself with the Shikaka's flight controls, which were near identical to the Sentinel's. It wasn't a fighter plane – most control was done by setting waypoints, altitude and airspeed and allowing the drone to fly itself to a location where it would set up a racetrack orbit so the operator could conduct surveillance or deploy its payload. And he didn't have the range of cockpit-style controls a pilot in a fully equipped ground or ship-based control trailer would have. But Kronk's laptop included two small 'thumbstick' style joysticks – one for maneuvering the aircraft, the other for controlling its onboard or payload cameras.

Snake thought back to their earlier mission briefing. "Where were you taking this thing?"

"*USS Bougainville*, off Sangeo Shoal. It has technical issues, can't be disconnected from this particular mobile control unit."

"But it's armed and fueled?" Snake started paging through payload menus.

"Loaded for bear, fuel for a couple more days," Kronk confirmed. He was standing looking over the pilot's shoulder, then stood as something in the distance caught his eye.

"Wait, what's…?" He pointed.

Snake stood too, eyes following the other man's extended arm, and then he saw it. A barely visible dust cloud, rising from among the mountains to their west. He watched it for a moment. It was making slow progress, but it was moving.

"That's a vehicle," Snake decided. "Maybe five miles out. And it's heading this way."

"Friendly, maybe?" Kronk asked.

"There's an easy way to find out."

Kronk's laptop showed their own position and that of the Shikaka. Sitting down again, Snake placed a waypoint over the hills to their west and sent the Shikaka toward it. It could pick up moving ground targets from 20 miles away and 70,000 feet up on a clear day like today, but he would need to get it right overhead to pick up the vehicle among the hills and valleys.

They watched the ground below the aircraft slide across the screen until the picture stabilized as the drone reached its station. Taking control of the cameras, Snake panned across the bare landscape until he caught the small plume of dust. With a click of his thumb, he zoomed the high-resolution cameras in.

"Light tactical vehicle," he decided.

"You recognize the type?" Kronk asked. He was Navy. Identifying ground vehicles wasn't his strong point.

"Not specifically, but I can tell you what it's not." He looked at the approaching dust cloud with dismay. "It's not South Korean. I think our little friend downhill has invited those guys to join our party."

The Shikaka had a payload of offensive weapons. But it wasn't Snake's to command … yet. He needed full authority over the aircraft and he needed it now. But it was a Navy bird, and he was Air Force.

With the interference from the North Korean jamming gone, Snake was able to use the drone's radio to get himself patched through to *Bougainville*. He let Kronk explain their situation, including the fact they were traveling in close company with a North Korean drone and about to be rolled up by a North Korean patrol.

"They want to talk to you," Kronk told the pilot, handing him his comms headset. "It's *Bougainville*'s XO," he said in a lower voice.

146

Snake held one earphone up to his ear. "*Bougainville,* Lieutenant Bob Besserman, USAF 65th Fighter Squadron."

"Besserman, Kaminsky, XO aboard *Bougainville.* I understand you are in the company of our Petty Officer, and our aircraft."

"Yes, sir."

"Situation over the DMZ is hairy. We can't chopper in to pick you guys up. You're going to have to walk out."

"I figured that much, sir."

"But you are rated to fly that aircraft?"

"Rated to fly the Sentinel, sir. Same same, but different."

"All right, Besserman, here's what I told Kronk. There's a highway junction south of you. Once you clear the DMZ, we'll organize a pick-up for you. I'm giving you authority over that drone until you are safely back with US or South Korean forces. You will operate under the control of a US Navy E2D Hawkeye, call sign Hammerhead." He rattled off the details for contacting the AWACS. "Any weapons release requests will go through Hammerhead. And you *will* keep our bird safe. Is that understood?"

"Yes, sir. Perfectly. I better get to work, we don't have much time."

"All right, good luck and Godspeed. *Bougainville* out."

Snake was already bent over the laptop and punching in the frequency and handshake codes for the US Navy Hawkeye, which he assumed had eyes on the eastern seaboard of South Korea.

In another two minutes he had briefed the controller aboard the aircraft with their situation.

"We've been in contact with *Bougainville,*" the no-nonsense controller told him. "Allocating you call sign Envy. What do you need?"

"I have no idea whether the truck approaching us is friend or foe, but we don't want to hang around and find out," Snake admitted. "I want to give us a chance of escape by knocking out their drone with a Locust strike. Sending you target vision." He had refocused the Shikaka's cameras on the small drone downhill and relayed video to the Hawkeye which showed very clearly their position on the hillside, and the North Korean drone, about a hundred yards away.

He waited impatiently as the request was relayed, discussed and then approved.

"Envy, Hammerhead, we have your vision, you are cleared to engage."

"Roger, Hammerhead. We're going to shoot and scoot. Will be back in contact when we reach a safe position." He went to work.

"You want to fill me in on what's happening?" Kronk asked. He'd only heard one side of the conversation. Snake ignored him for a moment. He called up the Shikaka's payload menu and picked out a Locust with a fragmentation warhead. Then, using the small joystick on the command unit, he moved the cursor over to the hovering North Korean recon drone and boxed it up. With the tap of a button under his thumb, 70,000 feet above them, the drone mothership opened its payload bay doors.

Like bats hanging by their feet from the top of a cave, the Locust drones were arranged in neat vertical rows. Each Locust was about the size of a baseball bat, with a small turbine engine attached to its rear. Programmed to home on the target being tracked by the Shikaka's cameras, one of the Locusts dropped from the belly of the drone and four wings clicked into place as it fell into the slipstream of its mothership. It accelerated quickly, using gravity to drop toward its target for the first part of its descent. As it got to within five miles of its target it would match the images from its optical seeker with the one from the orbiting Shikaka or a surface-based targeting unit, home on the image and then, milliseconds from slamming into the target, detonate its four-pound high explosive warhead right on top of it.

A single Locust could decimate an infantry squad or disable a lightly armored vehicle or ship. A Locust *swarm* could destroy multiple vehicles or be teamed to attack heavily armored tanks, detonating their reactive armor plates before penetrating their thinner top armor with tungsten slugs.

Snake looked at the readout from the Locust as it accelerated toward the earth. It would take one minute and change to drop from 70,000 feet. He didn't need to guide it in himself.

They couldn't move too soon or too far, or the hostile drone's operator might reposition it and complicate the attack, but the flat rock they were standing on should provide cover enough.

"All right. Thirty seconds," Snake told Kronk, stuffing the laptop and transceiver into the duffel bag.

"Thirty seconds to what?" Kronk asked, standing now too.

"Until your Shikaka drops some boom on that evil little bastard," Snake said, gesturing with his head at the quadcopter downhill. "When I give the word, follow me to cover before the Locust moves in."

"You called down a *Locust strike* on that drone?!" Kronk looked a little alarmed.

Snake had the duffel bag over one shoulder, and was watching the second hand on his watch. "Time to get in cover." He dropped off the back of the rock, Kronk scrambling down behind him, but trying to keep his eyes on the North Korean drone. "Get down!" Snake yelled, pulling the gawping Kronk down behind the rocks.

A hundred feet out from the North Korean drone, the Locust made a last small adjustment and flew silently over their heads, flashed down the hillside, and detonated with a mighty thunderclap right above its target. There was a reflected flash and a second later the whip-crack sonic boom from the missile's supersonic passage caught up with them too. It made them hug their cover even tighter. As they rose from cover, all they could see downhill was a cloud of brown smoke and rising dust from where the fragmentation blast had churned up the hillside.

Of the hostile drone, there was no sign. It was as though it had never been there.

"Whoa," Kronk said, dancing from foot to foot. "Seriously? My Shikaka is the damn hammer of Thor!"

"When it works," Snake nodded, unimpressed, picking up the duffel bag again. "But the really cool stuff only happens when those Locusts hunt in packs. A simple frag grenade could have taken out that drone, the way it was just sitting there watching us."

"Yeah, except we don't have any frag grenades," Kronk pointed out. "And my bird just dropped a mini-drone 70,000 feet and blew up a target the size of a football, so allow me a minute to be impressed would you, sir?"

"Knock yourself out, Navy," Snake said. He eyed the still closing dust trail. It was about three miles out now, but on the wrong side of the river and hopefully, it would no longer have eyes on them. They should be able to lose the pursuit. He handed Kronk the duffel bag and started walking downhill as the man fell in behind him. "So, your boss on the *Bougainville* said something about a highway junction downriver?"

Kronk was rummaging inside the duffel bag, putting a charger cable into his laptop and settling the duffel bag on his back. Snake saw the base of the bag was covered in solar cells that would start pumping juice back into the laptop as they walked. He pulled out his cell phone and looked at a map.

"Yeah. Should only take us a few hours to get there," Kronk said. "It's a tourist destination, so there might be police, maybe even Army. We can wait for a ride out from there, for sure."

"Tourist destination? Tours of the DMZ kind of thing?"

"No. It's called the Peace Dam," he told Snake. "Sounds like heaven, right?"

If hell had a manicured lakeside park with tree-lined avenues, it would look exactly like the Peace Dam. That was what Captain Jong-chon Ri of North Korea's Supreme Guard Command was thinking as he sprinted from the entrance of the visitor center to one of the concrete anti-vehicle berms that he

150

had insisted be installed to stop vehicles from getting close.

And he was damn glad he had – against Goh's protest that they were unnecessary – because right now they were the best protection his men had against the combined South and North Korean force that had them pinned from two sides of the damn spillway.

With incoming rounds spattering the visitor center facade behind him, he took stock. Facing left, up toward the towering dam wall, he could see his men had pinned the attacking force of DPRK soldiers who had arrived by helicopter behind several vehicles in the car park. They could only advance on the visitor center by making a suicidal frontal charge, and none seemed inclined to do so. Not yet anyway. They were trading sporadic fire with the defenders, each trying to keep the others' heads down. Looking right, he saw a much bigger problem. The 20 or so DPRK troops who had landed north of the dam were now pushing down the access road on the eastern side of the spillway, protected by the 20mm guns on the LMADIS vehicles of the South Korean squad from the dam wall!

He didn't have time to wonder what kind of unholy alliance he was confronting. His own men on that flank were struggling to cover each other as they fell back. Or just fell. Ri saw one of his men take a 20mm round right in the chest, punched back behind a tree. Only four were still in combat, ironically sheltering behind the hulls of two brightly painted Korean War-era American tanks.

His men's training had served them well. Those at the visitor center, about 12 of whom were still in action, had formed two squads, one on the east, one on the west, in good cover behind the concrete berms. But the eastern squad was not yet engaged, while the western was being suppressed by North Korean troops who had landed by helicopter.

But the long causeway across the spillway was his best hope. It was the only way for the hostile troops attacking down that side of the river to get over to the visitor center which was obviously their target. If he could hold them and those damn LMADIS buggies on the other side…

He tried his comms again, got nothing but static. Then he remembered Goh showing him over the LMADIS unit, bragging about it to his 'poor North Korean cousin'.

"Since we're going to be friends soon, let me give you the tour. Two MRZR electric buggies, two hundred mile range, zero to sixty in six seconds," the man gloated, slapping the hood. He pointed up to a dome and set of antennae on one of the vehicles. "Multi-sensor optical ball, scanned array radar with Modi jammer." He pointed at the other buggy. "Data linked auto-aim 20mm cannon. We don't even need to be awake. These babies can spot an enemy all on their own, identify and jam them, and then kill them before we even get our pants on."

Jam them. Communication with his troops was going to be impossible until they had disabled the antennae on that damn buggy! And forget calling the outside world for help.

He looked desperately around himself. Back at the visitor center. Across the causeway to his men in the Peace Park, fighting off a 20mm autocannon and infantry platoon with carbines and grenades. Both exits out of the Peace Dam site were blocked. The attackers had left no route for Ri to evacuate the protectees by. And the smashed glass sliding doors to the visitor center were gaping open, inviting the enemy to rush them.

Then he looked at the visitor center car park and got an idea.

Rifle Cover

Hill 205, DMZ

Corporal Mike Chang, had learned a lot about the North Korean Sergeant in a very short time. He had learned that she was a cold-hearted killer, having watched her execute his Lieutenant and Sergeant with ruthless efficiency. He'd learned she was fearless: the memory of her charging at his position, screaming at the top of her lungs for her men to follow, burned into his retinas for eternity. He'd learned she had a strong stomach, showing no reaction at all as she stripped bloody uniforms off the men she had just helped kill.

And now, he was learning that she apparently knew the roads heading south out of the DMZ at least as well as he did.

She and her men headed south in their captured South Korean K-311 truck, at a speed that showed a lot of familiarity with the rutted, winding dirt road out of the DMZ toward Hwacheon. The north–south Chuk-tong Road was only open to military vehicles and Chang had never seen traffic on it other than the patrols they were rotating with, either going in, or coming out. As they'd only just begun their day's patrol a couple of hours earlier, he didn't expect to see any other South Korean traffic on the road for another several hours, and neither, apparently, did the North Koreans – who were barreling south at about fifty miles an hour.

Following them was not difficult because of the dust plume her vehicle was kicking up behind them. The difficulty came in staying close enough that his own smaller dust plume merged with theirs, but not so close that if they suddenly came to a stop he'd round a corner and plow into them. But it took all of his concentration to watch the road, and the rising dust a couple of miles ahead.

Luckily Private Park, riding shotgun beside him, was on his toes. He tapped Chang's shoulder and pointed. "They're slowing, Corp."

Chang quickly down-shifted, slowing to a crawl himself. The convoy had turned left around a small ridge and the dust cloud up ahead was settling. Chang couldn't get much closer without giving themselves away.

He pulled the jeep to the side of the road. "All right, everyone out. Park, bring that field radio. Nam, grab those canteens. Both of you, remember your rifles. Let's see what we can see."

Sergeant Kim Song Hye took a swig from a canteen and spat the fine powdery dust of the DMZ from her mouth as though the soil this far south was poison. They were still inside the DMZ, another two layers of razor wire-topped fence and anti-tank ditches between her and enemy territory, but she was south of the demarcation line, and therefore technically in South Korea.

It wasn't the first time she had traveled this road, but in the past, she had only done it at night, on foot, learning every dip and pothole and turn by heart.

Wiping her mouth, she climbed from the cab of the South Korean troop transport and ordered her men to disembark. She'd brought them to a halt at a branch in the Chuk-tong Road that either continued south five miles to the South Korean DMZ guard post in this section of the DMZ, or turned eastward, running parallel to the demarcation line another five miles.

To a point just north of the installation that the South Koreans called 'The Peace Dam'.

Her mission was quite simple, in concept. A special operation was planned at the Peace Dam. It should already be underway. Song did not have the details, and did not need them. All she needed to know was that it was paramount the operation succeed, and very probable that South Korean ground forces quartered at Hwacheon would try to intervene.

Her squad, dressed in stolen South Korean uniforms, was positioned at the crossroad of a highway that was the most

154

direct route between Hwacheon and the Peace Dam. She ordered her men to start unloading the crates from the back of the truck.

Any civilian vehicles, they would turn back, saying the road to the Peace Dam was closed. Any military traffic, they would destroy.

Crouched behind a rocky ridgeline, Mike Chang watched as the North Koreans arranged themselves. The South Korean troop transport was sitting squarely in the middle of the crossroad, blocking traffic coming from any direction, and a squad of North Korean soldiers in stolen uniforms was busy unloading the crates they had loaded aboard the truck.

"Bastards," Park spat.

Chang put a hand on his shoulder. "Easy, Private. Payback will come, I promise."

The North Koreans carried the crates from the truck, and stacked them by the side of the road. Soon they were uncrating whatever was inside, and throwing the empty crates into the back of the South Korean troop transport. Chang squinted, he couldn't quite...

"Red Arrow missile launchers," Park said. As the designated marksman in their squad, he was the only one with the K2 marksman carbine and he was surveying the scene below through its 4x magnification scope.

Chang kept his eye on the North Korean squad. He recognized the weapons himself now. The Chinese-made Red Arrow was a copy of the US Javelin, an anti-tank missile that could penetrate the top armor of a main battle tank or completely shred any more lightly armored vehicle. The hostile squad was setting itself up to hold the crossroads against whatever unlucky South Korean unit came up that road to investigate what had happened to Chang's squad.

Chang turned, sinking to his haunches, back against the rock, thinking. Then he rose again, surveying the ground around the crossroads. The ridge they were on was the only real cover. There was nothing but open ground and low brush between them and the fork in the road.

What the hell was he supposed to do? Their attackers were stopped on the road below. They'd killed his Lieutenant, his Sergeant, several of their men. Stripped their bodies and taken their weapons. Now they were creating a roadblock inside South Korean territory, setting up to ambush whoever came by.

He had tried the field radio on the North Korean jeep again and got nothing but static. He couldn't radio for orders, and he couldn't just sit and watch as the troops who had murdered his comrades prepared a new fighting position. "Park, how good are you with that thing?" Chang asked, looking at the man's rifle. The K2 was not a sniper rifle, just a 5.56mm assault rifle with a picatinny rail for mounting a scope.

Park looked at him with a gleam in his eye. "I look after this rifle better than I look after my girlfriend, Corp," he said. He rose to a crouch and looked over the stone ridgeline again. "That's only 250 yards. I'm good out to three, three fifty."

Nam looked at him, and then away again. "You don't have a girlfriend."

Chang rose beside them. "All right. We need to hit them while they're all grouped together at the back of that transport. On my mark, you pick your first target and make damn sure you nail him. We'll be sending suppressing fire downrange too, trying to keep their heads down, but it will be up to you to make the kills. You up for this?"

The boy nodded.

"Nam, up here," Chang called. He waited for the other private to join him and pointed downhill toward the North Korean soldiers, still uncrating and assembling their weapons. "I'll go twenty yards farther up the ridge, you go twenty yards down that way." He pointed to a dip in the ridge. "For God's sake keep a low profile, and don't waste your ammunition." He pointed at the selector switch on Nam's rifle. "Single shot, not automatic, got it?"

Nam looked pale. "Yes, Corp."

"They might go for cover behind the truck. That's good.

We've got height, Park can reposition and keep sniping. We cover him in case they get a rush of blood and try to move on us, or flank. In which case, listen for my orders." He reached for his webbing belt. "Ammo check." Each man in Chang's squad had a 20-round magazine in their rifle and two more on their belt. They'd fired wildly during the ambush. Checking his rifle, he counted only six rounds left and changed it out for a fresh magazine. "Forty-six," he said.

"Forty-two," Park said, doing the same.

"Fifty-four," Nam said a moment later after pulling out his magazine.

"Give one of your full magazines to Park," Chang told him. Nam almost looked relieved as he handed it over, and Park shoved it into a trouser pocket.

"All right, into position," Chang told Nam. As the boy scuttled farther down the ridge, he clapped Park on the shoulder. "OK, Private. Make them dead. We'll do our best to keep up."

Supreme Guard detachment commander, Captain Jong-chon Ri, was redefining the concept of success by the minute. For now, success would be to make it from the entrance of the visitors' center one hundred yards west to the vehicle park without getting killed.

Running at a crouch to the berm opposite the car park where two of his men were trading fire with the North Korean assault force, he threw himself down beside them. *All right, Ri, first twenty yards. You got this.*

"What's your situation?" Ri asked the man he landed beside.

The man ducked his head while his comrade sent a short burst of fire toward a roadside ditch.

"Four hostiles in the ditch to the west. Another five or six…"

"Five," the man beside him grunted.

"*Five* trying to move up to the vehicle park and flank us. They have grenades, but they're falling short. We're keeping them back, but we're low on ammunition, Captain."

Ri motioned to him to hand over his carbine. "Go to the visitor center and load up, then get back here."

For the next several minutes he worked with the man beside him, waiting for a break in the incoming fire to lift his head and fire, either at the ditch or at the North Korean soldiers in cover behind trees on the other side of the vehicle park. The vehicle park was just a semicircle with parking for about fifty vehicles, and empty except for a motley collection of South Korean army vehicles. Goh, Ri and their personal protection teams had flown in by helicopter with their protectees earlier that morning, but the bulk of Goh's detachment had driven up from Hwacheon the night before to secure the site.

Between the ornamental tree line and the vehicle park was a fifty-yard-diameter circle of grass and as he ducked a volley of incoming fire, Ri saw two forms break from the trees at a run.

"Targets, right!" he called to the man beside him.

Despite the hammer of heavy-caliber rounds on the concrete berm, they both lifted their rifles and sighted right. Two North Korean soldiers were zigging and zagging, aiming for the cover of the nearest South Korean vehicles. The man next to Ri took down one of them, but the other had closed to within about ten yards when a rifle behind Ri opened up and chopped his legs out from under him. He went down screaming, and started trying to crawl away before another round from behind Ri stopped him. Ri turned and saw the man he had sent for ammunition crouched behind him, a bag of 7.62mm 'banana' magazines at his feet and a Type 88 carbine with a 100-round helical magazine in his hands.

Ri let the man take his place at the berm. With a quick look he located his target: a dark green Kia Light Tactical Vehicle. The 5-ton truck was unarmed, but it was armored. And he knew it was keyless, because they'd agreed during operational planning for all vehicles to be left in a ready state in case urgently needed.

And his was a case of urgent need.

Ri put down the rifle he'd been using and drew his Inglis

sidearm. He waited for a break in the incoming fire, then said loudly, "I need to get to that LTV. On my mark, give me covering fire. One cover the ditch, the other the treeline, got it?"

"Yes, Comrade Captain," the man on his left said, lifting the barrel of his Type 88. "I have the ditch."

Ri waddled awkwardly to the end of the berm and steeled himself. *This is stupid, Ri. This is going to get you killed,* he heard a voice in his head say. Then he heard the 20mm autocannon on Goh's LMADIS buggy open up on his men again across the other side of the spillway, and the voice went away. "Now!" he yelled. "Fire!"

The two men rose from their crouch and set a fusillade of fire toward the hostile troops as Ri broke from cover and ran with arms pumping toward the Kia LTV. A line of bullets stitched across the concrete of the vehicle park *straight at him,* sending chips into the air, and he veered away from them, barely keeping his balance. Then he veered left again and before he even realized it, he was lying on the ground under the front grille of the LTV.

He didn't waste any time congratulating himself for still being alive. The LTV had a suspension system that lifted it a good two feet off the ground and he scuttled underneath it, making for the driver's side door. Someone among the hostile troops in the treeline was trying to bounce rounds off the concrete and under the vehicle, and one plucked at the cuff of his trousers, right behind his Achilles. *Keep moving, idiot!*

Panting heavily, he lay on his back, put his pistol across his chest and then rolled out from under the LTV, jumping to his feet and heaving at the heavy armored door with his left hand as he sighted at the tree line and fired with the pistol in his right. He had no idea where his shots went, because as soon as the door was open, he was diving inside. A rain of incoming fire smacked into the rear of the vehicle, but the armored plate held.

He dropped his pistol onto the passenger seat and allowed himself a small, slightly hysterical laugh. If they were firing at him, at least they weren't firing at his men up at the visitor center, so he'd achieved that much.

All right, phase 2 of Operation Crazy Ri.

Punching the engine starter button, he felt the LTV shake itself to life and looked out of the driver's side window at the entrance to the visitor center, about a hundred yards away. His men had been at the other end of the causeway, inside the Peace Park, trying to hold back Goh's advance, but the weight of fire from the near platoon-sized hostile force and that damn 20mm had forced them back to the eastern end of the causeway. There had been four. He could only see three now. His action window was closing.

An unprofessional rage filled his chest as he slammed the LTV into drive and shoved his foot down on the gas. The engine screamed, but nothing happened until he realized the park brake was still on, and as he jerked the button to release it, the LTV jumped forward with a snarl. Snatching at the wheel, he powered out of the vehicle park, up onto the ramp leading to the causeway and then floored the gas, pointing the armored car straight at glass doors of the visitor center.

Combat was just as heavy at another armored car about ten miles west of the Peace Dam. Park's first shot had hit one of the North Korean soldiers in the chest. As soon as Park had opened fire, Chang and Nam did too. Without a scope to aim with, they were nowhere near as deadly, but the weight of fire served to scatter the North Koreans, who scrabbled for cover behind their stolen vehicle. Three bodies lay on the ground. Dressed in South Korean uniforms, the sight of them made Chang queasy.

Five still in the fight.

The stolen four by four had no weapon mounted, but one of the North Korean soldiers, likely that damned Sergeant, had climbed in on the blind side of the vehicle and stuck their head out of an open window to return fire. A volley from Nam miraculously struck the rooftop of the vehicle and sent the shooter ducking back inside, while two more of their comrades recovered weapons and started returning fire from behind it.

The North Koreans were in cover now. Chang waited until he had the measure of the incoming fire. None of the men down there appeared to be particularly accurate. Getting a lucky hit at a range of more than two hundred yards was unlikely now, for either side. It wouldn't be long before the numerically stronger force downhill decided to split up and try to counter-attack.

"Nam, cease fire!" Chang yelled, not wanting the boy to waste any more ammunition. "Park. The missile crates at the rear of the vehicle. You see them?"

Park swung his rifle right. "Got them."

"I'll put a few rounds into them, see if I can get a reaction out of those guys in cover. Be ready."

A detonation would be too much to hope for – the Red Arrow missiles used solid-fuel rockets – but he hoped the sight of their precious weapons being targeted might get some reaction from the North Koreans in cover.

He set his rifle on semi and, sighting down his barrel at the large crates, sent one bullet downrange. With satisfaction, he saw a wooden chip fly off one of the crates. Waiting five seconds, he sent another. Then another, ducking occasionally as the hostile soldiers began concentrating their fire on his position. Moving a few yards farther up the ridge, he repeated the process, missing as often as he hit, but hitting often enough that one of the crates toppled onto its side.

Come on, fools! Chang urged the men downhill. *You just going to let me fill your missiles full of holes?*

Park was moving his rifle barrel almost imperceptibly left and right, looking for a clean shot on one of the men behind the stolen vehicle.

Finally, a hand and an arm appeared from behind the truck, grabbing for the rope at the end of one of the crates. Park fired, twice. Chang heard a scream and the arm disappeared.

"Good hit!" he called to Park. "Let's try to …"

There was a sudden volley of fire from downhill, forcing all three South Korean soldiers to duck behind cover, and when Chang looked again, he saw one group of two or three soldiers running across the road to his left, and another pair running along the road.

Park was already firing again, but Nam was just staring at them over open sights. "Nam, targets right, fire!" Chang yelled out, concentrating his own fire at the men running toward their hill. Park tagged one of them, causing him to stagger, but the other two reached the cover of some rocks down the slope and disappeared. Park fired again at the wounded man, sending him to the ground.

Chang looked right, where Nam's fire appeared to be having no effect, as the two men there reached a defile farther along the road and threw themselves into it. Both groups opened fire on their position on the ridge again, sending the South Koreans back behind cover. The North Korean counter-attack was controlled, disciplined.

Chang didn't like their new situation. They'd accounted for four of the eight troops downhill, but now faced a split force to his left and right. He looked desperately around himself. There were only two options. The obvious one was the crest of the hill, about five hundred yards behind them. But once they got there, then what? A couple of men could keep them pinned up there until nightfall.

The less obvious one …

"We're relocating, downhill!" he called out. "Bring everything with you. On my mark, five rounds of suppressing fire and then you follow me to our vehicle. Understood?"

They both yelled their assent. Chang grabbed the field radio from the ground near Park's feet, slung its strap over his shoulder.

Rifle rounds were peppering the stone ridgeline. Chang's imagination was running wild, imagining the North Koreans flanking, getting ready to attack from a new direction. He didn't want to break cover, but knew they couldn't wait. He took five quick breaths. "Now!" he yelled, rising to a crouch, resting his rifle on the rocky ridge in front of him and firing in the direction of the closest North Korean element to their right, without even sighting. He saw vague shapes behind rocks, still firing at them, ignoring the incoming fire from Chang and his men. Saw a man down in the defile roll back into cover as Park directed several rounds at him. Saw Nam blazing away as much at the sky as at the enemy below. Counted each round as he fired it ... *three ... four ... five.*

"Cease fire, follow me!" Chang yelled, pulling back behind the ridge, changing the grip on his rifle and looking to see his men were doing the same. He registered Park spin, back against the rock, Nam up and running. As Nam passed him, he slapped his back, pointing downhill. "Get to the truck, stay low, go!" He rose himself, yelling over his shoulder. "Come on, Park, we're moving!"

The move took the North Koreans by surprise. They had positioned themselves to cover a South Korean retreat to the top of the hill, not a wild, flailing, arms flapping sprint to the bottom of the hill.

Chang reached the cover of the truck and threw himself behind it, bullets kicking up dust at his heels. Nam was already there, lying on his back in the dirt, panting.

Chang grinned stupidly. Now they'd turned the tables on the North Koreans. It was them behind the vehicle, and the North Koreans out on the exposed hillside. He hadn't really thought about what came next, but for now, it felt like a victory.

But where was Park? Looking several hundred yards uphill, he saw a dark shape on the ground back at their original position. Unmoving.

Ah, hell, Park. Not you.

The North Koreans had recovered now, and carefully aimed rifle fire started to pepper the ground around the truck. They seemed to be determined not to hit it, or its cargo of missiles. Apparently they hoped still to regain control and complete their roadblock. Chang looked down at skinny, useless Nam, chest still heaving as he tried to catch his breath, and the reality of their situation came crashing home again.

And for just a moment, Chang thought seriously about

surrender. Then the time for thinking was over, as a grenade sailed over the top of the truck onto the ground behind them and he threw himself on top of Nam and rolled them both under the truck.

"Explosions in the water!" the sonar officer in the control room of the *Hero* said, unnecessarily. Seconds earlier the hull had reverberated with two muted thuds. Since no modern navy used depth charges anymore, Se-heon Dokgo knew exactly what the explosions were.

American-made noise-making grenades. Like a warning 'shot across the bows' at a surface warship, they were intended to threaten him into surfacing or provoke him to panic. He heard whispers between a couple of the officers in the control room and hissed at the men. "Be quiet! With engines stopped they have no idea who we are. They will not attack us in case we are Chinese."

The conversation stopped, and the only sound inside their boat was the ticking of the hull as the water pressure outside increased. They were using the momentum of their 3,000 tons to pull them deeper as they turned, the incessant *pings* of multiple enemy sonars following them down. But growing weaker?

"Where is the hostile ship?" he asked. Their passive sonar suite could give him data on the pursuing vessel based on the direction and strength of its signal. They had also picked up the sounds of small twin screws, which indicated it was small, perhaps only patrol boat sized. A drone?

"Bearing approximately one seventy, range ... five thousand," the man whispered. "Separation ... increasing."

Dokgo looked at his command screen. They were slowing to three knots, slightly below three hundred meters. "Helm, center your rudder, hold current depth."

"Comrade Captain," the helmsman said. "We need to adjust ballast to maintain depth."

Dokgo had forced his boat deeper without taking on

additional water as ballast, in order to avoid putting out even more noise. Without the additional weight, they would begin rising slowly toward the surface again. "Do your best without taking on additional ballast," Dokgo said softly. "Watch your rate of ascent."

"Contact lost," Lomax heard his subsurface warfare officer declare. "*Sea Hunter* moving into search mode, trying to reacquire."

He slammed a fist into the console in front of him, causing the men around him to jump. "Boat the size of a whale and we lose him? Dipping sonar?"

The air operations officer turned to him with a shake of his head. "Fire Scouts have also lost contact, sir."

He glared out the bridge window as he barked orders. "Sonar, safe the towed array. XO, plot an intercept waypoint based on its last known heading and speed. When you have a solution, steer for it, engines ahead flank. We need every set of ears if we're going to find this summabitch."

"Aye, aye, Captain," his XO replied and started relaying orders.

"Henley, where is our Defiant?"

"Five minutes out, Sir," the junior Lieutenant replied. "Shouldn't we wait to get it down before we spool up?"

Lomax was about to snap at him, but took a breath. "Of course. Get that bird down and ready it for submarine warfare operations, then make for that sub's last known position..."

Info Wars

Yangdok Railway Station, North Korea

"Comrade Colonel, we are in position and deploying for operations," the commander of the North Korean KN-24 rail-mobile short-range ballistic missile launcher reported to his battalion commander in Pyongyang.

He did not think twice about questioning the order he had just been given, since to do so would have been a death sentence.

Their specially constructed Chong-tae engine had pulled the launcher to a halt five miles east of Yangdok station, North Korea. The 58-year-old battery commander had been in charge of his unit for three years and with the way the political winds had been blowing had fully expected to retire when his train was retired. After all, what use was there for a tactical hypersonic missile that could only reach targets in South Korea, when all of Korea was one country again?

He had of course been curious when he had been ordered to replace his missile's warhead. It could be fitted with everything from 1,000 lb. bunker busting conventional warheads to 5 kiloton nuclear airburst payloads and the special nature of this particular warhead could cause a man of his experience to speculate wildly, if he was a man given to speculation. But then, he reasoned, if that was true, he would not have risen to the rank of battery commander in a military which rewarded speculation with re-education.

As he watched the crane on his carriage-borne launcher lift his missile into a vertical position, while its solid fuel ignition system powered on, he folded his hands behind his back and allowed himself a moment of ... introspection. To his men, the frown on his face should look like displeasure at the amount of time they were taking to achieve launch readiness. But inside, he was wondering. The discipline of rank and experience had prevented him from looking up the GPS coordinates he had been given when he received his orders, but the same experience also told him roughly what lay underneath those coordinates.

The South Korean capital, Seoul.

So he couldn't help but ask himself … what effect would this warhead have on its target?

He had little doubt the missile would reach its target. The South Korean 'Heavenly Dome' anti-missile defense system might be effective against mere supersonic rockets and cruise missiles, but it was useless against short-range hypersonics. By the time it had detected the launch and tried to lock onto his missile with radar, his KN-24 would be descending toward its target at *four times* the speed of sound. The body of the missile would then fragment, creating decoys to confuse the defender and attract any ground to air missiles the South Koreans managed to launch.

Unmolested, the true warhead would accelerate through five times the speed of sound, to a terminal velocity of 5.9 times the speed of sound or *4,500 miles an hour.*

His Lieutenant came running up, seemingly pleased with himself. "Comrade Lieutenant Colonel, launcher raised, fuel, weapons and guidance systems optimal, target locked … we are ready to fire!"

He looked at his watch. It had taken his men twelve minutes and ten seconds from the moment they dismounted from the train to the moment they were ready to fire.

He knew the battalion's best effort was twelve minutes and five seconds but decided today was not the day to make an example.

"Good enough, Lieutenant." He reached for his radio handset again. "Comrade Colonel, we are ready to fire." He nodded at the response and returned the handset to its cradle. "Lieutenant, you are authorized to fire."

The man turned toward an officer standing at the door of the command carriage and waved his arm up and down. The man relayed the signal to another soldier inside.

With a building roar, the rocket ignited and a report like a cannon firing punched them in the chest before dirt, grass and smoke started billowing from under the launcher and the missile burst upward on a pillar of fire.

Small white secondary contrails radiated outward from the launch tube, but it was already folding back down onto the train carriage as the KN-24 commander gave his next order. "Mount up. We move to the next position." He put a hand on his Lieutenant's shoulder. "Faster next time, yes, Lieutenant?"

South Korean Prime Minister Ted Choi's aide came running into the room, interrupting his call with the head of the Joint Chiefs by bowing and placing a tablet PC on the table in front of him.

Choi spun the tablet so that he could see it properly, and refused to look impressed. He heard muffled voices at the other end of the line.

"General, sorry … yes, I assume you are receiving the same information that I am?" Choi was a Catholic, and though not devout, the words came to him easily as he nodded curtly. "Yes. God be with you, General."

"Bring up KTV Seoul," he told his aide. He did not have access to the same missile tracking system in Sejong as his Chief of Staff in Yongsan-gu, Seoul. But he was not so interested in the track of the missile that had just been fired at Seoul.

He was only interested in the effect of it.

His aide crossed to a wall screen, turned it on and tuned to the national broadcaster's Seoul channel. Two TV anchors were breathlessly recapping the earlier attack on Panmunjom, the artillery barrage on Seoul, and – it seemed – interviewing a former air force officer about an air-to-air altercation over the DMZ.

None of that interested Choi.

He sat at his desk, tapping his fingertips with an impatient, rolling beat. One minute passed and then two. *Finally...*

"Turn that up," he said.

The vision on the flat screen showed the skyline of Seoul taken from what was possibly the TV station's panoramic webcam atop the Namsam TV tower. The picture was taken from one of the east-facing towers and the afternoon sky was gray. The camera was showing an apartment building which must have been set alight in the earlier artillery barrage. As it panned across the skyline, dramatically following the cloud of smoke, it jerked, and then swung back again to a massive explosion. As the flash cleared and the camera focused again, a huge mushroom cloud of smoke started boiling up into the air.

"My God," Yeo said, genuinely shocked. "Was that ... was that nuclear?"

Choi grabbed the TV remote from his desk and turned off the screen. "No, idiot. Thermobaric. You knew this was coming." He turned to his aide. "Are the socials ready?"

"I ... they will be ... it's just ..."

The fool was still staring at the screen, shocked. Choi snapped his fingers. "The *socials?*"

"I ... yes, sir. We'll take the TV feed, mix it with some footage from the artillery barrage earlier, finish with ... with the mushroom cloud. Send it out on all your platforms."

"Read me the text again."

He wanted to be sure he'd struck the right tone. Horrified, resolute. In command.

His aide pulled his cell phone from his pocket and paged through to the app he was looking for. "Uh ... here. Seoul, minutes ago. The horror we feared for decades has been visited upon us. We will make the criminal regime pay. Seek shelter and pray for our nation..."

Choi swiveled in his chair. "*Terror* ... the terror we feared for decades blah blah."

"Terror, yes sir." The man typed into his screen. "You want this on your official account?"

"Why not?"

"It will confirm you are still alive. It may be useful to keep that fact up our sleeve, until your public address."

Choi stopped swinging his chair and grabbed his desk, fixing his security chief, Yeo, with a glare. "There will be no public address until the situation at the Peace Dam is resolved, is that clear?"

"Prime Minister."

"Now get that fat bastard General on the line again."

As he watched the man scamper into the room next door he felt a glow of satisfaction. He was *born* for this day, and he would make it his.

"Did you ever wonder," 'Snake-eater' Besserman asked Kronk, "whether you were in the wrong line of work?"

They were picking their way over a rocky beach after having slid down a muddy riverbank. In the thirty minutes since knocking out the drone that had been following them, they had covered two miles, maybe three. The good news was that the dust of their pursuers had disappeared.

Kronk tried to jump between rocks, landing with one foot in mud up to his ankle. It made a sucking noise as he pulled it free. "Would you believe I never did? Until today?"

Snake hopped past him, with what he hoped was the grace of a mountain goat, but probably looked more like a circus acrobat about to lose their balance and fall into a cage full of tigers. He made it back to the riverbank.

"Cheer up, Navy. The Air Force is here now."

"This the same Air Force that was escorting us this morning when we were shot down?"

Snake decided to change the subject. "What do they call you, Petty Officer?"

"Kronk, sir. Ryan."

"You can call my pop 'sir'," Besserman told him. "Out here, I'm Snake. As in Snake-eater. For reasons you may one day learn. You got a nickname?"

"Uh, guys on *Bougainville* call me 'Toes'."

Snake grimaced. "You lost a couple? Or you got extra?"

"No, sir. Short for 'Toes-up'. Because my idea of a good night out always ends with me passed out, I guess."

"That'll do it." Snake had decided the best way to travel was with the Shikaka's transceiver switched on, an earpiece in his ear, and the radio tuned to the Hawkeye AWACs channel so that he could at least follow what was happening in the skies around them.

When he heard their call sign, he stuck a hand in the air and pulled up fast, then pressed the 'speak' button on his earpiece. "Hammerhead, Envy. Please repeat?"

"Envy, we are picking up a broken South Korean radio signal five miles south-southeast of your position. It sounds like they are reporting they are under enemy fire but we can't get a good read. Can you make an ISR run over the source of the signal and report back?"

He looked back in the direction they had just traveled and saw no sign they were still being pursued. Could they make an intelligence, surveillance, and reconnaissance run with their Shikaka?

That would be a '*hell yes*'.

Snake motioned to Kronk and pointed at the riverbank. "Hammerhead, Envy, can do. I will need five mikes to set up and then maybe another ten, fifteen to get eyes on your boys. I may even be able to get our bird close enough to pick up that radio signal. What is the frequency?"

If he was going to be providing ground support to a South Korean ground unit, he needed to speak directly with their joint terminal air controller.

"Uh, Envy … that radio is calling in the clear in the 462 MHz range. It could be nothing, could be a decoy. Be careful."

"Good copy, Hammerhead, give us that location."

He had climbed up the sandy embankment to a plateau of dirt and spiky grass and Kronk had dropped his duffel bag beside him. "Wassup?" he asked.

"Unpack that," Snake told him. "And then keep an eye out for unwanted attention."

Kronk assembled the control modules with practiced speed and Snake was soon at the stick, bringing their Shikaka down to 40,000 feet and within five miles of the signal's position, the top of a spiny ridge, simply labeled Hill 205.

He had clear skies under the Shikaka and a 20/20 view of the situation below. He picked up the two South Korean soldiers at the crossroads, in cover behind a troop transport and trading fire with two groups of attackers.

There was just one problem. Both groups of combatants were wearing the same damn uniforms!

Corporal Mike Chang had more than one problem.

His only real marksman was dead, his body slumped at the rocks behind the ridge. After the grenade had gone off without fragging either of them, he'd left Nam under the truck, unable to shoot uphill at the North Korean troops, but unlikely to get himself shot unless they charged his position.

He lay on the ground beside the hapless private, checking his field of fire. "Alright kid, stay under here. Don't be afraid to pull back further if the enemy targets you. Your job is to keep their heads down, try to stop them pushing on us. Conserve your ammunition, just shoot when you have a clear shot." He clapped the boy on the back. "You got that?"

"Yes, Corp," Nam said.

Meanwhile he clambered out from under the truck and into its cabin, where he got onto the radio and started broadcasting a mayday across every damn band he could find.

Suddenly, his radio crackled to life.

"South Korea unit at the base of Hill 205, this is US Navy Envy flight, we have your vehicle in sight, available for close air support, what is your situation?"

He rolled on his back, squinting out the windscreen into the glare of the sky, listening and looking for an aircraft but seeing nothing. Then flinched as a line of bullets stitched across the passenger door behind his head.

He raised his voice above the sound of incoming and outgoing fire. "Envy, it's good to hear a friendly voice. Emergency, two groups of enemy troops attacking our position – northeast and southeast, range 50 to 100 yards out. Estimate two groups of two or three combatants. Can you assist?"

Sensing a pause in the volume of incoming fire he rolled to a crouch and sent a few rounds in the direction of the North Koreans through the passenger window before ducking down again.

"South Korea unit, Envy flight. I see what looks like a blue on blue engagement down there. Can you clarify?"

Clarify? "Envy, my unit was ambushed by a North Korean border patrol, they stole our uniforms, we tracked them here and re-engaged … we are outnumbered and taking casualties. Need help, now!" He bobbed up, let fly a couple of rounds as Nam did the same.

"Good copy, South Korea, getting strike approval…"

Chang snuck a look uphill. The troops there would soon get tired of taking potshots at them. He had seen the North Korean sergeant in action once already today, and she was not the patient type. She didn't have as many men anymore, but sooner or later she would decided to rush the truck. *Come on, Navy, come on, dammit.*

"South Korea, you are broadcasting in the clear. I need your service ID, immediately."

"My what?"

"Army service ID. Now, soldier."

What insanity was this? He rattled off his ID number.

"Hang in there, South Korea," the US pilot said and his earpiece went dead again.

Seconds later it crackled to life. "South Korea, strike is approved. Buckle your helmet, we're coming in hot, five mikes."

"Good copy, South Korea out." Five minutes? He watched Nam with closed eyes squirt several rounds into the air over the North Koreans' heads, not even aiming anymore. On Nam's side of the hill, he saw a North Korean soldier rise and sprint forward ten yards before throwing himself behind cover again.

He doubted they would be alive five minutes from now.

Snake was sending the vision of the firefight to the Navy Hawkeye, but what had complicated his request for permission to engage the attacking force was ... they were in the same uniforms as the men at the truck. Both attackers and defenders were wearing South Korean Army uniforms!

Snake imagined there had been a heated discussion inside the AWACS aircraft about whether they should even trust the request for air support. What if the troops by the truck were the bad guys and the ones attacking downhill were the good guys? How could they know? It wouldn't be the first blue on blue engagement of the day.

After thirty long seconds Snake couldn't take the silence from the Hawkeye any longer. "Hammerhead, the attacking force is now about fifty yards from overrunning our troops' defensive position. I have targets locked and Locusts spun up for the strike." Snake had boxed the two attacking groups and allocated three Locusts at each. The attackers were in cover ... enough to protect them from light arms fire, but not from the blast of the precision-guided Locust's fragmentation warheads.

"Envy, Hammerhead. We need you to get confirmation of the identity of the troops on the hilltop. Get a service ID and we'll look for a match in our database."

Snake had cursed. "Good copy, Hammerhead, getting an ID."

As he opened the channel to the soldier below, he could hear the bark of assault rifles through his headset. The soldier had rattled off a number and he relayed it to the controller on the Hawkeye.

"Envy, Hammerhead. That ID is solid. You are cleared to engage."

Snake had the shot set up, all he had to do was twitch his thumb on the laptop's mousepad. "Roger that, Hammerhead. *Rifle, rifle.*"

Six vertically racked Locusts dropped from the belly of the Shikaka, fell behind their mothership and started steering toward their targets. Though they possessed a solid fuel rocket for longer-range attacks, they would not need it this time. By the time the Locusts neared their targets, gravity would have accelerated them to twice the speed of sound, or *1,447 miles an hour.*

"They're assaulting!" Chang yelled into the radio over the noise of Nam underneath the truck, hammering away in panic as the North Korean troops rose to their feet and led by their maniacal Sergeant, charged the truck. Rounds from a squad machine gun began punching into the K-311 transport's door. A window over Chang's head exploded.

He tumbled out of the cabin through the open driver's door, huddled behind the rear wheels of the K-311, and stuck his rifle out, firing blindly in the direction of the North Koreans, before ducking back into cover. He'd seen enemy troops advancing to his left and right and looked desperately behind himself. There was no convenient riverbed to retreat to this time – behind them was a bare hillside. To their left and right, open road.

Bullets spattered off the road and into the suspension of the transport. He'd known the assault would come, and now there was nothing he could do about it.

He looked at his watch. One minute since he'd spoken with the Navy pilot. Four minutes to run. They just had to stay alive four more minutes.

Up by the front wheels of the transport, Nam was pulling the magazine out of his rifle. The spare magazines they had recovered from the truck cabin were in a satchel at Chang's feet. Nam started crawling for the satchel…

Chang yelled at him. "Stay in cover!"

A spray of bullets hit the road in front of the transport, ricocheted right under it, and tore into Nam's chest. He collapsed like a punctured bag of rice and, with disappointed eyes fixed squarely on Chang, he gave a single cough, and died.

Ah, screw it, Chang decided. There was no airstrike coming. He stood carefully, still in cover, but held his rifle out by the barrel where the attackers could see it. He waved it up and down and yelled at the top of his lungs. "*Surrender!* I surrender!"

The North Korean Sergeant yelled back at him. "Throw down the weapon, step out with your hands visible."

And this is where you die, Myung Shin Chang, he told himself, convinced he would be shot anyway, the moment he showed himself. But what choice did he have? He looked at his watch. The strike should have come in by now. *Here goes nothing.*

As he stepped out from the back of the truck, about twenty yards away he saw the North Korean Sergeant walking up the road toward him, service pistol drawn.

She raised her pistol and called out to him. "On your knees, hands behind your neck!"

Chang complied.

To the east, Snake and Kronk had their eyes glued to their laptop screen. The high-resolution cameras on the Shikaka gave Snake a perfect view of the scene below.

Bodies littered the ground around the truck, all in South Korean uniforms.

One man – the Corporal, probably – just behind the truck and kneeling on the road, out in the open. About ten yards from the South Korean soldier, a female soldier in a South Korean uniform was advancing with a handgun aimed at the man on the road. They were clearly *not* allies.

Snake had sent a swarm of six Locust drones at the position, and they were less than a minute out.

"You have to abort. They're too close ... He'll be ..." Kronk said.

"I can," Snake told him. "And yes, he might. But he's about to be shot. You want to sit here and watch that?"

He quickly drew a new series of boxes on his screen: one around the South Korean transport vehicle, one around the group of soldiers to the north of it, one around the group to the south. He marked the South Korean truck and the man kneeling beside it as non-targets. That still gave the Locusts two distinct target groupings, though all were converging on the South Korean troop transport and the kneeling soldier there.

Danger close? It couldn't *be* closer. But to call off the strike was to condemn the South Korean soldier to death anyway. With fingers tapping on the keyboard, he set the Locust swarm to autonomous target finding mode, and with his thumb hit the 'Commit' key.

Snake was *very* interested to see what was about to happen. He'd called down drone strikes before, but never with a full Locust swarm.

The six Locusts were in fact only five. One had failed in flight, its wings not extending correctly after it dropped from the Shikaka. It had spiraled to earth and buried itself two feet under the soil of the DMZ without exploding. The AI on the Shikaka was not concerned. It concluded that five Locusts armed with 40mm fragmentation grenade warheads were more than sufficient to deal with six North Korean soldiers walking along an open road.

The swarm was guided to its targets by the 'hive mind' on the Shikaka, which monitored the positions of the targets Snake had designated and allocated a single Locust to central individuals in the two boxes. By targeting the soldiers in the center of the boxes, it would maximize casualties. The rest of the missiles guided on their 'leaders'.

The five warheads were set to airburst, six feet out from their targets. Each tungsten warhead was designed to separate into 54 30-grain pellets which could penetrate up to 50mm of steel plate.

Or completely shred any human body within a 20-foot radius.

Sergeant Kim Song Hye had recognized the South Korean corporal immediately and hatred flooded her veins.

But it wasn't, surprisingly, hatred for the South Korean.

It was hatred for the incompetence of her own actions in letting the man escape, several hours earlier. If he had died in the ambush, along with his feckless comrades, then her blocking force here would still be setting up in peace, not with more than half her men lying dead in the road. If she had not misread his intentions and acted before he led his squad away into cover, she would not have had the dilemma she faced now, of what to do with the man, now that he had surrendered.

Shoot him in that doe-eyed face? Or take him prisoner in case he could prove useful later? Like all good North Korean sergeants, she decided she would let her commander make the decision, once she secured the truck again and could get back on the radio.

As she closed to within five yards, she stopped and motioned with her pistol. "Lie face down, hands behind your back."

What happened next was like a scene from a Hollywood horror movie.

The first sharp reports came from behind her. Three loud explosions in succession. She spun around, saw nothing but smoke and flying body parts. She barely registered the small, arrow-like shadows dropping from above. Almost simultaneously, the air over the heads of her soldiers burst into flame and fire and a rolling wave of explosions turned them to red mist, pitching her backward – *into the South Korean corporal!*

Mike Chang had given up hoping for the guided missile strike and was fully prepared to die in the dirt at the crossroads at the hands of the North Korean Sergeant. He wasn't scared, not really. More sad, because it seemed Nam and Park had died for nothing.

But instead of dead, he suddenly found himself deaf, blinded by the rippling flashes of the exploding Locust swarm and tangled in sixty kilos of angry North Korean sergeant. He put his hands up over his face but her elbow caught him in the cheekbone and his head slammed into the road, dazing him badly.

He kicked his legs weakly, and flapped his arms, trying to

fend her off, but she landed another blow, this time in his solar plexus, and suddenly he was not only deaf, blind and dazed, but sucking wind with empty lungs too.

Oh, just kill me, would you? he thought miserably as he tried to roll onto his stomach and crawl away from her.

He felt a hand grab one of his boots, flip him over and drag him across the rough road surface on his back. He couldn't do any more than moan.

Seeing the total decimation of her squad, Song had briefly considered putting a bullet into the bloodied face of the South Korean corporal, but the need to get to cover was more urgent and so she took him with her. Dragged his heavy ass into the lee of the South Korean troop transport and kicked him hard so that he rolled under it. She joined him there.

She had no idea if the American air attack was over. It had to be the Americans. The shadows she'd seen had looked like the pictures she'd seen of drone swarms, and only the USA and China had that kind of technology in this theater. Looking out from under the transport at the bloodied and smoking lumps that until a few minutes ago had been a squad of men, she felt sick to the stomach. There was no movement or sound from any of her men. How could she fight an enemy that could deal death so instantly and with such precision?

The South Korean corporal moaned, and she kicked him in the head to shut him up. Right now, he was the least of her problems.

Somewhere overhead, a US drone mothership or other aircraft was loitering and watching. Was it out of ordnance now?

That was a bet she didn't dare take. She had to assume the bastard death machine was still up there and waiting to kill her. There could still be smaller kamikaze drones loitering overhead, just waiting for a target to show itself.

What did they call them? Coyotes? Locusts? Something like that.

Focus, Song! She had to get out of this situation, and she needed information. Luckily, there was a rich source of intelligence rolling around and moaning at her feet.

She spun around. She had dropped her weapon when the blast wave hit her, but the dazed South Korean didn't need to know that. He was lying on his face and couldn't see her without lifting his head, but he looked in no condition to do that, yet. Grabbing a stone off the road between them, she crawled over to him and tapped his head with it.

"Move and I will shoot you," she said loudly.

He groaned and flapped a hand at her. She shoved the rock harder against his head. "You want to die? I said move, and I will shoot you!"

His hand dropped to the road. "Just kill me," he said. His words were slurred. Either the explosions or her assault had knocked him insensible.

"You are a prisoner, you understand?" she said. "Cooperate, and I will not kill you."

"Prisoner?" He laughed weakly.

"Call off your air support," she told him. "I am taking you to get medical care. If they attack again, they might kill me, but they will kill you too."

"Call ... what off?"

"Your air support. Call it off, or I *will* shoot you."

"Screw you. Die," the man moaned. "Just die already."

She screamed out loud and hammered the suspension of the transport over her head with the rock. Did the fool have no sense of self-preservation?!

She rolled out from under the truck and searched inside the cabin for the radio handset. It was dangling from the radio and she heard a voice, speaking English. So it was still working? Perhaps transmitting?

"America Air Force, this South Korea Army DMZ, stop your attack, we friendly!" she said.

Snake was playing the interaction over their laptop

loudspeaker while he and Kronk scanned the images being relayed by the Shikaka over the battlefield, trying to do a post-strike assessment.

"These guys are down," Kronk said, pointing at one side of the screen. "And those over there."

"You see any movement?" Snake asked. "I don't."

"No. I count maybe six dead. Can you pan the camera over the truck?"

"You see someone alive?"

"I don't know," Kronk muttered. "I thought I saw …" He frowned as the Shikaka's camera settled on the South Korean vehicle, watching for a long minute. "No. Nothing. Whoever called us has to be somewhere though."

"Where is our man?" Snake asked, as much to himself as to Kronk. "Did my best not to kill him, but it wasn't him on the radio and I don't see a body near that vehicle."

"Bad guys nabbed him in the chaos?" Kronk speculated. "Whoever is broadcasting is on the same frequency, probably the same radio. They must have taken it off our guy."

"America Air Force. We friend. Cease fire!" the voice said again.

"You know what I'm thinking?" Snake straightened. "I'm thinking we put a Locust through the body of that truck because I'm betting our 'friend' is hiding in it."

"But they might have that South Korea corporal with them," Kronk pointed out. "He could still be alive."

Snake hammered the ground next to the laptop, drawing blood from a knuckle. "I know, but if you have a better …"

"Movement!" Kronk said, pointing at the screen.

Song had tired of playing 'hide and speak' with the radio without getting a response, and shoved the radio handset back in its cradle. She crabbed out from the cabin and, grabbing the South Korean by the shoulder straps on his body armor, pulled him out from underneath the truck. Getting down on one knee, she used a fireman's lift to lever his fat carcass off the ground and staggered to the open driver's door of the truck.

Then she took a step back, into bright daylight, showing herself and the South Korean soldier on her shoulders as plainly as she could, to the eye in the sky above.

Stepping back toward the cabin she heaved him off her shoulders onto the floor of the cab and folded his legs awkwardly so that she could close the passenger door. There wasn't room for her to easily climb in over the top of him. He moaned some more but didn't resist.

As her hands came away, she saw one of them was covered in blood. The corporal must have been wounded in the American attack. Checking quickly, she saw one trouser leg was shredded and soaked in blood, but the wound on the man's calf looked superficial.

Dropping to her belly, she squirmed under the truck again and pulled herself over to the driver's side. With the South Korean soldier in the truck, she hoped the enemy above would think twice about attacking it.

About ten yards away she could see an object on the road. Her pistol. *All right, one quick movement,* she told herself. *Roll out, grab the gun, get into the cab. Close the door. They won't even see you.*

"There!" Kronk said. "Someone just loaded a South Korean soldier into that truck cabin. Now they're gone…"

Snake had the image zoomed as far as he could without the image pixelating beyond recognition and had his nose just about pressed to the screen. "No … door. That's the door, right?" As they watched, a shadow appeared from under the truck, darted a few feet into the road then back to the truck, the door opened and then closed again. The shadow was gone.

Snake tried the radio again. "Hill 205 South Korea, Envy, you there, South Korea?"

There was no answer this time. Then the truck started to move.

"They're pulling out," Kronk said, slapping his thigh. "What can we do?"

"We can watch," Snake told him. "That truck goes south, it's a friendly, heading for base. They go north back into the DMZ, it's the bad guys."

"And if it is?"

Snake didn't get to answer, because at the same moment that the truck turned *south*, heading further into South Korea, the female voice came back over the radio.

"America Air Force. You attack, and I kill South Korea prisoner. Understand?"

"Alright, heading south, but *not* a friendly." Snake reached for the thumbstick on the control unit and drew a box around the fleeing truck. Two more key taps locked it and put the Shikaka in 'trail mode', following the truck, 70,000 feet above and five miles behind. He armed two Locusts.

"What are you *doing*?" Kronk exclaimed. "You'll kill our guy."

"Just preparing a strike, not launching it," Snake told him. "If we have to react, we need a quick strike option."

Song had her pistol in her lap. The South Korean corporal was curled up in a ball on the floor in front of the bench-style seat in the cabin of the transport, knees tight against his chest. He appeared to have passed out ... at least he wasn't moaning any more.

She reached for the radio handset and repeated her message. "America? You attack, I shoot prisoner."

She had no way of telling if the message was getting through. But soon enough, the radio crackled, the voice of the operator on the other end fading in and out.

"North Korean Army ... closer than you think ... you ... that soldier ... I'll personally ... and shove it up your ..."

She muted the voice. Her message had been received.

She was moving slowly away from the crossroads now and had time to think. How in the world had the South Koreans followed her? Her own jeep, of course! The one they had driven to the DMZ demarcation line in. Once again, anger at her own incompetence caused her face to flush red. She should have disabled her vehicle. But they hadn't expected to leave any South Koreans alive, so it wasn't on her mental checklist as she'd fled the scene of the ambush. She'd been more worried - too worried - about not making the crossroads in time to support the operation at the Peace Dam, whatever it was.

She'd been told it was part of a wider effort to disrupt the signing of the Peace Accord, which was why she had signed on. She'd heard rumors of course, but no real specifics. A sabotage operation was what the rumors said. She imagined engineers planting explosives across the wall of the dam and blowing it, sending billions of tons of water on a destructive mission through the agricultural heartland of Korea, destroying crops and fields...

As she thought about it, she realized she had already decided what her next move was. She needed to get to the Peace Dam, let the force there know they had been attacked and the crossroads was open. She still had several anti-tank missiles in the back of the vehicle that could be vital if the troops at the Peace Dam had to defend themselves against a South Korean armor assault.

She would face the humiliation of delivering her report, and try to make amends by supporting the operation at the dam. It was the only thing to do.

The truck shuddered as one wheel dropped into a pothole and she swerved. The unconscious corporal on the passenger side floor moaned again. She decided her personal recriminations could wait. She would have to focus on the road ahead if she wanted to get to the dam before the light started fading.

She looked up at the roof of the cabin, knowing full well she wasn't traveling the road alone.

She hoped the South Korea corporal did not die. He was probably the only thing keeping that American aircraft from dropping a guided munition on her head, and they could ask for proof of life at any time.

Outside the Peace Dam visitor center, Captain Ri slammed on the brakes of the armored LTV and spun the steering wheel. The LTV skidded to a halt across the sliding glass doors and he ducked below the level of the windscreen as it began attracting fire.

Grabbing for the radio, he turned it on, but got nothing but static. *He had to deal with Goh's damn jammer!*

Ri crawled over to the passenger side and kicked open the door. The vehicle had stopped so close to the doors they had opened automatically and he called out to the nearest man inside as he climbed out. "Give me a hand here!"

Together they lifted the doors off their guide rails and jammed them open.

Across the other side of the spillway, one of Goh's 20mm-armed buggies had spotted him and opened fire, but then return fire from his men to the east got its attention. The weight of fire from the west had also increased, indicating the paratroopers dropped there were closing in on them too.

Captain Jeong Goh, commander of the South Korean Presidential Security Service, looked across the causeway at the visitor center with disdain. Why was Ri continuing his futile resistance?

The North Korean paratroops assigned to take the western side of the spillway had just radioed that they had secured the western flank and were preparing to assault the building. Goh ordered them to wait, and though he could hear the officer in command didn't like being told what to do by a South Korean, their chain of command had been agreed by officers many times more senior, and he had no choice but to comply.

Goh had no preference for whether the State leaders inside the building were taken dead, or alive. His principle mission objective was to obtain the thumb sized nuclear trigger carried by North Korea's leader, Madam Kim. The access codes generated by the device changed hourly and it was supposed to be completely secure, accessible only with Kim's DNA print and a code phrase known only to her. But North Korea's paranoid Generals had long ago developed a way to 'unlock' the device in case their supreme leader was unexpectedly 'incapacitated'. All that was needed was physical access to it.

A secondary objective was to capture the two State leaders so they could be publicly tried for treason, but that political goal was not critical to his military mind.

Goh did not regard himself as a status-quo loving reactionary. He had been working towards a 'United Republic of Korea' all his life. But one achieved not by neoliberal capitulation, but by an East German-like collapse of the impoverished North. In the future Goh had once envisaged, in a starving North Korea, crippled by sanctions, riven by internal division, the citizens of the North would eventually rise up and overthrow their despotic leaders and beg for admission to the Republic of Korea, of that he was certain.

Not sitting at the bargaining table as equals, but forced to accept whatever scraps the South was willing to grant them.

Instead, Goh's government had sold South Korea's soul, promising the North equal representation in a people's assembly, continued command of the 'Northern Military District' and a merger with the armed forces of the South that would only weaken Korea's overall defenses to a level that could embolden China, the true enemy of Korea, to threaten Korean sovereignty in the North.

Goh considered himself a passable student of history, and looked at what had happened to NATO when it granted membership of the western alliance to members of the former Warsaw Pact. Did it make NATO stronger? No! Instead, the weaker Warsaw Pact nations drained resources, bringing nothing to the military table but rusty Cold War tanks and outdated Russian-made aircraft and missile systems that had to be replaced at enormous cost, thinning out NATO's ground forces by demanding western troops and aircraft be stationed on its eastern borders whenever a provocative Russia rattled its sabers at them, and putting Western Europe at greater risk of a nuclear strike – for what?

Democracy? Western democracy was a whore that spread debilitating disease to every nation embracing it.

Goh turned his attention to the visitor center across the other side of the causeway. There was no firing from that direction now. The hard core of Ri's men had barricaded themselves inside and were holding the two protectees in the basement stronghold, no doubt. They had barricaded the fragile glass doors with a five ton armored car.

It wasn't the ideal situation. His own men in the close protection detail were supposed to have ambushed Ri's agents and secured the North Korean Supreme Leader while the rest of his protection force was engaged outside. But something had gone wrong inside the building.

Now Goh's force would have to fight its way into the building and breach the stronghold downstairs. Not ideal at all.

He grabbed the arm of the soldier beside him. "Find me the radio operator." As the man disappeared, he composed the message he planned to send to the rebellion's leadership group on either side of the demarcation line … *Peace Dam secured. Targets isolated. Capture imminent.* The mission wasn't complete, but he no longer doubted it would be.

Reaching into the cab of his LTV, Goh grabbed a white rag he'd brought along to wipe fog from the windscreen. His opposite number from the North had been pliable during their planning for the ceremony. Perhaps he could be persuaded to see reason now.

Special Agent Helen Lee needed a plan for how to get a message out and alert the world to what was happening inside the offices of Prime Minister Ted Choi.

For operational security reasons, Security Service agents were not allowed their own cell phones when on duty, only their service issue radios. She had been filing her reports with Commander Pak from her apartment, using her private cell phone and an encrypted app, but that was still in a locker at

Panmunjom, left behind in the panic of their evacuation. So that option was out.

Her briefing from the former Commander of the Presidential Security Service before she joined the Prime Minister's security detail had been for her to watch for 'anything odd'. He'd received reports that Prime Minister's public support for reunification was not matched privately. Of surreptitious meetings with military and political figures from the North, who were also known to be anti-reunification. And of a cult of rewarding 'loyalty' with tenure within the Prime Minister's security detail that went against the service policy of rotating its agents between details to keep them from becoming complacent, or forming inappropriate personal attachments that might impact their judgement.

After 20 years in the service, she knew the routines of duty as well as she knew the faces around her and her place among them. So she was perfectly placed to spot changes or deviations from normal practice.

They were immediately apparent, and she reported them faithfully to Park. It was perfectly normal, for example, for a team to go for drinks when they were off duty, share a meal and a few beers. The Prime Minister's detail did this, and Lee was invited.

But this team also met privately on weekends, for meals and drinks at the detail commander, Yeo's apartment. And to these meetups, Lee was *not* invited. She only found out about them by accident, overhearing conversations between her colleagues when they didn't realize she was listening.

She couldn't help notice she was the only new agent in the detail for more than two years, and had only been appointed after the death in a firing range accident of one of their colleagues. Appointed, she now knew, thanks to the influence of her former mentor.

But strangely, no one wanted to talk about the 'accident'. It was taboo. Any inquiry she made was turned aside, until one day one of her colleagues took her aside and said bluntly: "Stop asking about Yang. He was a screw up. Better he died on that range than on duty, where he could have put us at risk, right? So leave it alone."

Lee did *not* leave it alone. But because the accident had happened on a security service range, the police investigation had been minimal. Lee still had connections inside Sejong City police though, and she'd met one of them for drinks, asking him if there was anything unusual about the investigation.

"Unusual?" he asked. "Ask me what was *usual* about it, that will be a shorter conversation."

He told her they had only been allowed to interview one of the three agents and the instructor at the range that day. Both had told police the same story, almost word for word. The man's gun had misfired, and he had suffered a fatal head wound. Police had not been allowed to inspect the faulty weapon. The coroner's report had been sealed 'for national security reasons', with only the cause of death – gunshot injury to the head – communicated to police.

Lee had passed this intelligence on to her old Commander and in a rare breach of their communications protocols, he had called her back immediately. "The agent who died. He called internal security two days before his death, asking for a meeting. He died before the meeting could be held," Pak told her. "Be careful, Lee. Very, very careful."

And now, after the bombing of Panmunjom, the Prime Minister of South Korea was meeting with Kkangpae *mobsters*?

'Odd' did not do the events of the day justice.

She was still standing in the corridor outside the Prime Minister's Office, when the door was flung open and the protection detail commander, Yeo, stepped through it. He signaled to Lee and the other agent. "You two, come with me."

Lee did as she was told, heading down the corridor behind Yeo, with her colleague beside her. Photographic portraits lined the wall, stretching off for yards in both directions. The nameplate on the bottom of the one nearest her read 'Prime Minister Paik Too-chin, 1970-71'. To his left at the end of the corridor she saw another security agent standing by a dark wood paneled door, HK45 held loosely in hands crossed in front of his crotch.

They hit the end of the corridor and entered the fire stairs, going down one level. Lee knew it was still part of the Prime Minister's complex ... a section of the complex that contained interview rooms, rarely used. Perhaps somewhere down here she could find a phone. They paused at a door with a thumbprint scanner by the handle. Lee waited as Yeo applied his thumb to the lock and the door clicked. He stepped back. "Inside."

The door let into a small, unused office containing a bookcase full of what looked like reference books, a desk and chair, and a large video conferencing screen that was showing screensaver pictures of sunny Sejong City landscapes. Lee assumed Yeo was about to brief them on a new task.

She was wrong.

As she moved into the room, Yeo pulled his pistol and pointed it at her. "Agent Moon, take her weapon," he said to the other agent.

Apparently prepared for the order, the man reacted immediately and without question. He pulled his own weapon and motioned with his free hand. "Hands behind your neck," he said, reaching forward for the weapon under her jacket.

One gun pointed at her head, another at her chest, Lee had few options. But she knew she was about to have even fewer. "What the hell is this?!" she asked, raising her hands to the level of her head. The other man, Moon, reached for her pistol.

She moved. Taking a step toward Moon to put him between herself and Yeo's pistol, she slapped the gun out of Moon's hand. Before he could react, she stepped sideways and locked an arm across his throat, pulling him off balance but keeping him between her and Yeo.

Or trying to.

Yeo reacted faster than Moon. Taking two steps himself he put himself beside Lee and lifting his pistol, he clubbed her across the temple.

Keys to the Hermit Kingdom

Peace Dam, South Korea

Inside the stronghold at the Peace Dam visitor center, Captain Ri of North Korea's Supreme Guard Command had tried fruitlessly to raise his headquarters in Pyongyang. The landline had been cut of course, and mobile communications and radio were being jammed by Goh's LMADIS unit.

His men outside the visitor center had been overwhelmed by a sudden push from the landed force to the west, and the few officers they had protecting their east flank, holding the causeway, had not made it back into the visitor center before their rear guard had been forced to pull back inside the center and take up firing positions at the windows.

Ri had not wanted the role of commander of the Supreme Guards Company B. B Company was the unit most often assigned the role of protecting the Supreme Leader, and Jong Chong Ri had zero respect for Her 'Excellency', Yun-mi Kim.

Ri was a product of the North Korean political system. His place in officer school and his rank had been won through his father's party connections. His father had secured him a place in the Supreme Guard Command as a way for him to make friends in high places. The posting had brought with it privileges too. Better food than in other units, a uniform allowance, medical care at the same level as senior party officials, for him and his family.

Before taking command of B Company, he had never had to speak directly with the Supreme Leader, Yun-mi Kim, let alone assume sole responsibility for her protection. He had been happy enough leading protection details for the ever changing coterie of ministers and generals in her inner circle. Foiling an amateurish assassination attempt on the Trade Minister by a disgruntled employee had brought him the promotion to Commander, Company B, after the man who had been in that role for ten years, retired.

He had agonized over accepting the post and discussed his concerns with his father: the only one he could have such a conversation with, without fear of betrayal.

"She is leading us to defeat and trying to make it sound like victory," Ri said. "I do not understand why you continue to support her."

His father was a white haired, slightly built man in his 70s, a cadre politician in Pyongyang and survivor of countless purges by three generations of Supreme Leaders. "A rock in the middle of a river does not tell the river where to flow. And yet the river obeys."

His father's tendency to spout eastern philosophy passed for wisdom among his political cronies. For Ri, it was simply obscure and infuriating.

"How is that even relevant?" he snapped back. "Am I the rock, or the river?"

As usual, the old man did not answer directly. "You ask how I can continue to support the woman you believe is betraying her nation?"

"Yes."

"The answer is in your question. I do not believe Madam Kim is betraying the People's Republic. Why do you think we developed the most feared nuclear arsenal in South-East Asia?"

"To defend ourselves against our enemies, of course."

His father chuckled. "Spoken like a soldier. Nuclear weapons are a political tool, not a military one, Jong-chun. To use them is an admission of defeat, not a path to victory. So what use is a nuclear arsenal that is never used?"

"I ask you one question, and you reply with five," Ri sighed.

"Because you do not ask the right questions," his father said. "Ask me this one. Father, which is better, to make our destiny as an equal partner in a United Korea, or to live forever as a vassal of China."

"Your kind would make us a vassal of the *South*!" Ri said.

His father did not take umbrage at the criticism. "No, we would trade our nuclear power for political power in the government of a stronger, united Korea. Your reactionary superiors in the military are like an army of caterpillars, shouting at those who would be butterflies that they are wrong to build cocoons. They would remain caterpillars forever, but do not realize that to do so dooms them to extinction."

Ri frowned at the analogy. As usual, it sounded so simple, but was layered with meaning.

His father put a hand on Ri's knee. "There is another answer to your question of why I support Madam Kim." He stood, and moved the hand to Ri's shoulder, squeezing it reassuringly. "When you meet her, you will understand."

His father had left Ri in no doubt he should take the promotion without complaint, and in the last few months he had come to understand a little of what his father meant. Yunmi Kim's conviction was compelling, and her passion for her cause was contagious. She had a steely public persona, but a humanity few outside her inner circle got to see.

He got to see it himself on one of his first protection assignments – a formal banquet for an African head of State. During the dinner, one of the serving staff, a young girl who had been vetted but who Ri marked as suspiciously nervous, spilled a cup of tea on the table in front of the African leader.

As the serving staff fussed about, cleaning up the spillage, Ri had the girl taken aside and questioned. As he was deciding what to do about her, Madam Kim had made an excuse to leave the table and summoned him over.

"What was that about?" she asked. "The girl looked terrified."

"Nothing, your Excellency. She is weak from malnutrition. I will order her escorted from the building and removed from the staff."

Kim had looked at him with one raised eyebrow. "Have you considered an alternative, Commander?"

"Your Excellency?"

"Give her a solid meal and then ask the banquet manager what he is doing with the wages he should be paying to his waiting staff." She had smiled. "Of course, the decision of how to handle it is yours."

It was the first of many small interactions with North Korea's Supreme Leader that had surprised him. And though he still struggled to see the truth of her vision for Korea, he could not fault the authenticity of her belief in it. Nor did he question that having accepted the position, his sworn duty was protect Yun-mi Kim, no matter how he felt about her personally.

Which all seemed very academic, now that he found himself staring into her face and explaining that his small force was about to be overrun. The firefight outside had ceased momentarily, but only because the forces outside had won the opening engagement. He should probably spare the enemy and his country the embarrassment and shoot himself in the temple, right now. But there was a decision to make first.

"Your Excellencies, we are badly outnumbered and the enemy is at our gates. You have a choice. Either negotiate a surrender, or attempt to escape in the armored vehicle outside."

Madam Kim was incredibly composed, which was more than he could say for the craven coward who was the South Korean President.

"You have no communications with our forces outside?" Madam Kim asked him tersely.

"No, your Excellency," he said, bowing deeply and not meeting her eyes. "Our communications appear to be jammed. We were attacked by our own troops in the east and west, and by South Korean forces from the top of the dam..."

"Nonsense," the South Korean President, Si-min Shin, scoffed. "What possible reason would ..."

"Mr. President, please let me take Captain Ri's report," Kim said. Shin was clearly not used to being interrupted, and his face flushed red, but he bit his tongue. "Continue, Comrade Captain."

"Your Excellency, we have only Lieutenant Yun and eight men upstairs and the four you see here, including myself. We estimate between thirty and fifty troops outside, armed with heavy-caliber weapons, probably including grenade launchers or demolition charges. They seem to be consolidating their..."

194

Shin could contain himself no longer. "You people chose this place! I would assume you chose it because it could be defended in the event of an attack like this! What the hell were you thinking?"

Kim let the outburst run its course. "Mr. President, I doubt the Captain personally had the final say in the decision to hold the signing ceremony here."

It was the second time Kim had put the South Korean President in his place, and he stood, making it clear he did not intend to allow it to happen a third time. "I wish to speak with the commanding officer of the troops outside you say are 'attacking' us. I have nothing but your word, the word of a *North Korean* officer, that any of what you say is true. For all I know, you killed my officers upstairs in a cowardly ambush in order to kidnap and hold me hostage!"

Madam Kim slapped the table, causing everyone in the room to jump, not least Ri. But when she spoke, it was in a low and dangerous tone. "Mr. President, if you accuse my protection officers, then by inference, you accuse me. Be more careful with your words."

The color in Shin's neck rose into his face again and he leaned forward, spittle flying from his mouth as he spoke. "I will not be hectored by the illegitimate leader of a bankrupt State! I can see it all now – this was your plan all along!"

The North Korean leader turned to Ri. "Comrade Captain, the honorable President is clearly overcome by the danger of our situation. Please remove him to a safe place and ensure he receives the closest of protection."

Ri was not slow on the uptake. He stood to attention and slapped his heels together, then snapped his fingers at one of his men. The man responded immediately and took the elbow of the South Korean President.

"Get your filthy paws off me!" the President yelled. A second agent stepped in to help the first and they guided the South Korean politician from the room, protesting all the way.

When the door to the stronghold was closed again, Madam Kim took a deep breath. "Thank you, Comrade Commander.

That was most regrettable."

"Yes, your Excellency."

"It seems we must swerve around a few cattle on the road to peace."

Ri smiled at the image. Then the grim reality of their situation returned to him.

"Please continue your report."

"Yes, your Excellency. I was about to say the chances of escape are…"

There was a hurried knock and one of his men put a head around the door. "Comrade Commander, there is…" The man saw his Supreme Leader behind Ri and his words stuttered to a halt.

"Speak, man," Ri ordered impatiently.

"A South Korean officer is approaching under cover of a white flag. He is asking to speak with our commanding officer."

Madam Kim spoke before Ri could turn.

"That is you, Captain. See what they want."

"Why would she be headed *south*, toward the dam?" Snake asked after he had squared the Shikaka away and repacked their backpack. They had tracked the fleeing truck for a few minutes then followed the narrow road it was taking to its end, where it ended at the Peace Dam. "I thought it was a tourist site?"

He was determined to continue in pursuit. Looking at their map, Snake saw that they had covered nearly half the distance down the Bukhan River to the dam. To their east, the stolen South Korean truck with their ally in it was headed the same way. They were on the two arms of a V, headed toward the pointy end.

"A North Korean saboteur maybe?" Kronk asked. "What do bad guys usually want to do with dams? Blow them up."

"What's downstream from there?"

"Chuncheon. Big farming center in central South Korea. A few billion giga-liters of water would probably mess it up real good."

Snake threw the backpack over one shoulder. "Nah. Whoever is in that truck, the crossroads was their mission, not the dam."

"Beats me, then. Maybe they got friends there."

Snake had put his earbud in again and set the radio into 'scan and lock' mode to pick up any stray transmissions, friendly or unfriendly. He didn't want to round a bend and bump into another North Korean patrol. He pointed south. "Well, I say we go find out."

Kronk didn't move. "Or, we could stay here, run a few close air support ops with our Shikaka while we wait for an evac, and *not* get killed by whoever is at that dam."

Snake gave him a shove that got him moving. "There is a party going on downriver, Kronk. I never miss a good party."

Colonel Cho 'Keys' Ban was starting to think his entire day had been about being in the wrong place at the wrong time. Over Panmunjom, then in the sights of a Chinese-made Sky Arrow, and now back in the cockpit of a replacement Boromae fighter on what he knew to be a suicide mission.

He knew this for a fact, because it was a mission he had spent ten years training himself and other pilots for. And praying it would never be flown.

He had landed his crippled aircraft at Yanggu airfield and immediately been ordered back to Osan by chopper because as long as he was alive and combat capable, he was the most qualified officer in the South Korean Air Force to lead the coming attack.

The target was a military facility in Yongdoktong, 309 miles northeast of Osan Air Base, in North Pyongan Province in the far northeast of North Korea.

Yongdoktong was known to South Korea intelligence as the main storage site for North Korea's stockpile of undeployed nuclear warheads. Buried 200 feet under a hillside in bunkers lined with steel reinforced concrete ten feet thick, there was nothing in the South Korean inventory that could penetrate the bunkers and destroy the weapons.

But South Korea had long ago decided it did not need to destroy North Korea's nuclear arsenal. It simply had to *bury* it.

If successful the attack would not save South Korea from the five or more nuclear weapons that North Korea already had deployed on mobile ground launchers and submarines. But it would ensure that if North Korea wanted to access the *20 or more* warheads they had stockpiled for rapid deployment on reserve systems, it would take them days – perhaps even weeks – to dig them out.

Keys' Boromae bumped up and down in warm air over sunlit waves as he led his two-plane element on a dogleg 400-mile course that would take them far out into the Yellow Sea west of the DMZ, before they turned sharply northeast toward the coast of North Korea, west of the North Korean capital Pyongyang.

In planning the attack they had considered, and trialed, multiple strike packages: including not just the Boromae, but also South Korean F-35 Panther stealth fighters and F-15K Slam Eagles. The F-35, less maneuverable than the nimble Boromae, could get to the target undetected, but not maneuver through the hills and ridges around it. The larger F-15K could carry more weapons but was easier to detect, and its standoff ordnance could not be launched from an angle that gave it a clean strike. They had also trialed adding multiple Boromae aircraft to the package to increase the chances of getting a bomb on target, but the more aircraft, the greater the likelihood of being detected, and no matter how many times they had simulated it or flown the mission in training, it had only confirmed that the best chance of mission success came from an attack by a single low-flying Boromae, protected by a decoy flight of sacrificial aircraft whose only job was to attract the fighter cover over the target and draw it away.

Keys had volunteered for the mission because it could be critical to the survival of his country. The flight leader of the decoy flight had volunteered too, but Keys was not entirely certain of her motives.

When he had returned to Osan he had seen the pilot arguing with the commander of the US 65th Aggressor Squadron. He'd already been briefed on the nuclear site strike mission by the commander of 35-7 Buddy Wing and had requested this specific pilot and their aircraft be added to the mission package.

Walking up to the two US squadron officers, he heard one of them shouting from a good 20 yards away.

"...then release a damn helicopter to me and *I'll* fly it in there and pick him up. That's the second machine we lost today and this time it's one of *ours*! I saw him punch out. He's still alive dammit, Salt!"

Yes. It was exactly who he had thought it was. The abrasive Australian.

Keys approached them quietly, listening to the argument a minute or more before they noticed him.

"Is there a problem here, Captain?" Keys asked the US officer.

"No problem, Colonel Ban," the tall American officer said, with a forced smile. "I was just explaining to Lieutenant O'Hare that there are no assets available to search for downed aviators right now. If they are even alive."

"Snake is alive," the Australian growled. "I saw his chute."

"This is the man you lost escorting my ground attack mission?" Keys asked. He'd been briefed on the results of the attack on the helo ride to Osan. "I am sorry."

"Yes. With respect, not your concern, Colonel," Salt told him.

Keys nodded. "Can we speak in private, Captain Carlyle?"

He took the American officer by the arm and led him away, leaving the Australian fuming.

When they had gone a short distance, they stopped. "Captain, would I be right in guessing that pilot is among your best officers?"

Salt looked over at O'Hare. He could see she was not finished with him, and she showed no sign of departing the scene until she was. He sighed. "Not my best *officer* by a long shot, Captain. But she is the best damn F-36 pilot I have."

"Captain Carlyle, I have need of your 'best damned pilot'. I cannot share the full details, but I have been ordered to fly a deep penetration mission and I need a wingman to cover my six. I saw that pilot in action in our Red Flag exercises. I want her on my wing."

"I don't know, Colonel Ban."

Keys stiffened. "I can assure you, this mission has the highest priority. I ..."

Salt put a hand on his arm. "Don't misunderstand me. I am more than happy to release her. But are you sure you don't want a more ... suitable ..."

Keys looked across and saw the fire in the woman's eyes. He knew what he wanted.

"No, Captain. I don't need just any pilot. I need that one, and four Ghost Bats."

"That will require a formal request to the CO of the 65th, Colonel."

"Already done and verbally approved. The authority is probably waiting in your inbox. But I wanted to ask you personally."

Salt shrugged. "Very well. I'll tell her."

"No," Keys said. "It will be a very dangerous mission. She is an ally, not a citizen of the Republic. And as I understand, she is a private contractor too. I will ask her myself."

"Then I'll leave you to it, Colonel," Salt said, looking relieved to have a way out. As he moved away, Keys walked back toward the Australian.

"Hey, you!" she was calling to Salt. "We are *not* done."

"Lieutenant O'Hare," Keys said, blocking her view. "Can we talk?"

He sympathized with the loss of her wingman and then explained his need. Explained, to the extent he could, why he wanted *her* watching his six. He explained that he had agonized over who to assign to join him on such a dangerous mission, but having personally seen her performance during the Red Flag exercises, he had been sure.

"In our own rehearsals, we used a flight of Boromaes, but the simulation often resulted in the loss of several pilots from the decoy flight. An F-36 with drone wingmen provides the necessary distraction, but with less risk."

She'd listened. He couldn't read her expression, as it seemed caught somewhere between residual frustration and skepticism.

"It is a mission from which it is highly probable we will not return," he said at last. "I must be honest."

Her expression relaxed. "No, I get it. You don't want to risk your own guys, so you're asking me."

"No, that is not it at all. The importance of this mission…"

"That's all right," she interrupted. "I get it."

"No, please, Lieutenant. Seriously, I …"

She put a finger on her lips. "It's cool, Colonel. I'm in."

"… want the best possible … sorry? You agree?"

"Yes. But there is one condition."

Keys folded his arms. "I am not used to having to negotiate with junior officers."

"Good, because this isn't a negotiation. You want me covering your six, you will use your influence to get an evacuation flight organized for our downed man. My pilot's emergency beacon activated when he punched out, we know *exactly* where he went down."

It was a fair request. In effect, a life for a life. "You have my word."

Her face was suddenly calm. She gave Keys a very big, rather insincere smile. "So, exactly *how* deep is this deep penetration mission?"

He'd been completely honest with O'Hare. Most likely they would not even make the target, or if they did, they'd be shot down by North Korean anti-air defenses around Yongdoktong. Because between Osan and the target was a sea bristling with Chinese anti-air missile cruisers, a North Korean coastline covered by Russian-made S-300 surface to air missile systems, and hilltops surrounding the target, bristling with low-level air defenses.

But he'd been true to his word. He'd used his personal influence to guarantee that as soon as the situation in the air over the DMZ had stabilized, a South Korea Air Force search and rescue mission would be dispatched to look for the American aviator.

For the hundredth time since taking off, Keys ran his eyes across his instrument panel, visually confirmed his altitude, checked that O'Hare was welded to his wing in her Kingsnake and studied the map of radar signatures that was constantly updating on his threat display.

And then he ran his eyes over the photograph he had taped to the instrument panel above the Boromae's single panoramic multifunction screen. A photo of twin girls, in matching outfits and genuine Rayban sunglasses their father Keys had bought for them.

Twenty miles to their west, off the coast of Dalian, was a Chinese *Renhei* missile cruiser, radar up and continuously sniffing the sky over the Yellow Sea. To his east were land-based North Korean radar installations on the coast west of Pyongyang and Chongju.

O'Hare had suggested that she carry a mixed anti-radar and anti-air missile loadout on her machine. But he had decided against it. Any attempt to destroy Chinese or North Korean radar installations would simply alert them to the possibility of an attack on Yongdoktong, so Keys would have to 'thread the needle', flying under and around the enemy radar coverage, risking discovery every single second of his ingress.

Theirs were not stealth aircraft. Their American allies would not risk such top-secret technology so deep inside enemy territory in case it was shot down and the wreckage delivered to China. But the Boromae and Kingsnake both had a low radar cross-section, for non-stealth fighters, and his own aircraft had been stripped of everything on it that could give a radar return, including unused weapons hardpoints.

The only weapon hanging from the belly of his Boromae was a single 5,000 lb. GBU-28 'bunker buster' laser and GPS guided bomb.

Keys ran his routine check of instruments, sky, sea and photograph again. As they approached the waypoint at which they needed to turn toward North Korean airspace, he waggled his wings. The Australian was observing complete radio silence, flying high above him with her eyes glued on his aircraft, turning in perfect unison as he brought them around on a heading for the next waypoint, a hundred miles distant and about 10 miles northwest of the target. The afternoon sun fell behind him now, lighting his instrument panel in golden light.

The only way to hit the tunnel entrances leading down to the bunkers was to come in from the north, down a narrow river valley that wound like a snake. North Korea had chosen the site for exactly that reason. It could not be attacked with conventional bombs delivered from standoff range. Cruise missiles were not nimble enough to navigate the twists and turns of the river valley. The five miles of the river valley northwest and southeast of the target bristled with radar and anti-air defenses.

Keys knew from the hundred practice runs over similar South Korean territory that he'd made training for this day, that rounding the last bend in the river – if he reached that far – he would have a half-second in which to mark his night-dark target and release his bomb, before he had to throw his machine onto a wing and bank hard right, clawing over a nearby ridge to point his machine at the North Korean coastline.

Keys had made the attack run a hundred times over the practice range, and a thousand times in his head. He'd never once thought about the egress: about getting away after delivering his ordnance. The attrition rate in simulations had been near 90 percent.

There was no point worrying about his egress. Not really.

In the cockpit of her Kingsnake, Bunny O'Hare was most definitely thinking about her egress. Hell, she was already thinking ahead to the burger and beer she would be having somewhere tonight.

She had no plans to die today.

They had cued up aerial refueling for their Ghost Bat wingmen and their Kingsnake had near a hundred miles greater range than the South Korean Boromae, even fully loaded with air to air missiles. Not to mention, the South Korean aircraft would be flying nap of the earth, loaded with a 5,000 lb. bomb, burning fuel like there was no tomorrow – while they would be flying high cover, near supercruise speed, sipping fuel like a teetotaler sipping whisky at a wake.

"The best route I've plotted gives us between 23 and three and a half minutes of fuel in reserve on meeting the refueling aircraft, depending on events over the target area," Noname told her. "Or, if you don't manage our fuel carefully, we will run out of fuel over the Yellow Sea."

OK, it would be a close thing. Especially if she was forced into an air engagement along the way. Dogfighting used precious gas. So, all right, she might not be eating her burger back at the Osan USO. And no, it might not be a burger at all. It might be noodles. Cold noodles. Aboard a Chinese patrol boat in the Yellow Sea.

She checked her instruments and scanned her optical tracking display to ensure she was holding position above and behind the South Korean Colonel and the sky around them was clean and clear.

Noname had their four Ghost Bat drones flying in a fan formation about twenty miles ahead of them. Even though Noname was on the job, she checked the data coming in from the drones too and saw nothing to worry about. Yet. After losing Snake, she wasn't one hundred percent ready to trust the AI the way she had before.

She returned to thinking about the tattoo she was going to get when this particular shooting match was done. Neatly stenciled into the bit of empty real estate under her left shoulder blade: *New York, London, Sydney, Yongdoktong baby.*

Because Bunny O'Hare wasn't a glass-half-full kind of girl.

And she didn't really care if the glass held cold beer, or rice wine. She lived for the rush, for that feeling you only got out on the edge when Death brushed his bony fingers across your cheek with a loving caress.

And moved on.

At least, that's what she told herself in the silence that usually came after strangers asked her why she kept returning to war zones. But this conflict felt different. There was something about it that seemed less clear cut, more fraught. Bunny liked clear lines of sight, black and white options, the fewest possible gray zones. Today had seemed to be nothing *but* gray zones.

She had no plans to die today. But she couldn't help wondering if maybe someone else had her fate in their hands.

"And why should we believe the protectees are still alive?" Goh yelled toward the Peace Dam visitor center.

He had approached the visitor center under a white flag, unarmed and apparently, unafraid.

Barely controlling his anger, Ri yelled back to him through a broken window of the east wall of the center. "Because we killed your assassins!"

The man stared at the ground, hanging his head as though weary of the conversation already. "Ri, there are only two ways for this to end. With your Supreme Leader dead, or alive and in my custody. For me, either of these outcomes is acceptable. But if you send the protectees out now, we will take them into custody and leave. Your remaining men, and your protectees' lives, will be spared."

Ri kept his mouth shut. His second in command, Yun, came running up and crouched behind him, out of sight. "Captain, the man on the roof has a clear shot."

Ri had been keeping the arrogant South Korean talking as long as he could, to give his marksman time to get into place on the roof. About twenty yards behind Goh, the two LMADIS buggies were parked. One, bristling with antennae, the other with its 20mm autocannon pointed right at Ri. Keeping his eyes on Goh, Ri spoke softly to Yun. "I must confer with Madam Kim, when I return, be ready." He raised his voice again. "I will give your message to the protectees. They may want to consult with advisers. You must lift your jamming."

Goh laughed. "No. But I will give you fifteen minutes. After that, we will attack the building and kill everyone inside."

Ri turned, watching from the corner of his eye as Yun went from man to man inside the center, passing on his orders. He moved to the stairwell and went downstairs to the TV study.

"Your Excellency."

She was still seated at the broad desk, in the chair she'd taken for the signing ceremony. He took in her pale face and pursed lips, and his heart nearly broke with the pain of the sight. She was the human face of his nation, and she was afraid.

"What is the situation, Comrade?"

"Your Excellency, the attackers seem to be a joint North and South Korean force, led by the South Korean officer in charge of operations here today."

"A traitor to both Koreas then," she said quietly.

"Yes, your Excellency."

"And what does he want?"

"He demanded we hand over you and the South Korean President into his custody. In return, he will call off his attack and spare our remaining troops."

"That will not be happening, Captain," she said.

Ri bowed his head, not meeting her eyes. "No, your Excellency. But the chances of escape are…"

She reached out her hand. "Give me your pistol, Captain."

And so it ends, he thought. He was under no misapprehension what the consequences of failure were for a man in his trusted position. He pulled his pistol from the holster on his hip and stepped forward to hand it to his supreme leader. She was familiar with the Makarov copy, and thumbed the safety off. Staying in front of the desk, he lowered his head and waited for the bullet.

"Look at me, Ri," she said sharply. He raised his eyes again and saw the gun on the desk in front of her, the fear gone from her face. She placed the finger of her right hand on her temple. "In here is the password to our nuclear arsenal. It must *never* fall into the hands of our enemies, internal or external."

"No, your Excellency!"

From the pocket of her jacket, she took the small thumb-sized communication device that she would use with her personal passcode to authorize a nuclear strike. She placed it next to the pistol. "I will die before that happens, and I expect you and every man in your team to do the same."

"Yes, your Excellency!"

She motioned toward the entrance to the stronghold. "Lieutenant, do whatever you can to hold the enemy off for as long as possible. Our situation here will not go unnoticed. Help will come."

He saluted, and ran for the corridor. Yun-mi Kim had a seemingly limitless ability to surprise him.

"I have a report from the Peace Dam, Mr. Prime Minister!" said the aide coming to a stop at the desk in front of South Korean Prime Minister Ted Choi.

At last, Choi thought. Hours had passed since the attack at Panmunjom. The whole world was asking where the two State leaders were. He was minutes away from chairing an emergency meeting of the remaining members of the State Council, and shortly after it elected him interim President, he would be addressing the nation and declaring a State of Military Emergency.

He pushed himself back from his desk and stared at the man, trying to read his face. What he saw did not fill him with confidence. "And?"

The man tilted his cell phone so he could read the message on it. "*Peace Dam secured. Targets isolated. Capture imminent.*"

Choi slapped his desk. "Imminent?! When was the message sent?"

"Around fifteen minutes ago, Mr. Prime Minister. There has

been no farther word."

"What the hell is 'imminent'?" Choi muttered. "Either we have the codes or we don't!" The man was weighing his words and Choi felt like slapping them out of him. But he already knew the answer.

"We have to assume we don't, Prime Minister. That would require the capture of the North Korean leader."

Choi had deliberately stayed out of the detailed planning of the operation to capture the two State Leaders, the better to be able to deny any involvement. But how should he interpret the message? Was the operation on track, or was a fiasco about to unfold that would whip the floor out from under him?

Ted Choi was not an indecisive man. If anything, his political career had been marked by bold decisions, taken at speed and rarely regretted. He let his gut inform him again now.

He stood. "We will proceed on the basis that the North Korean nuclear arsenal will soon be in our control. Convene the meeting of the Council. Are preparations for the press conference complete?"

The aide nodded. "Satellite link and streaming platform is up. Television stations have been alerted for a live cross. Podium is nearly ready. Staff have been assembled on the roof. You can begin your broadcast as soon as the Council meeting is over."

He pulled his jacket off his chair and the man ran around the desk to help him put it on. Straightening the lapels, Choi began walking toward the stairs. He knew that even as he crossed the floor, a legion of social media bots was unleashing a torrent of posts on every major platform feeding the hysteria that the limited military action of the morning and early afternoon would have triggered. Posts containing images of missiles flying, mushroom clouds blooming, 'eyewitness' accounts of North Korean troops and tanks pouring into the DMZ.

He needed the hysteria to be at fever pitch when he appeared on national television and declared that there was nothing to fear. President-elect Choi was in complete control and the perilous situation with North Korea would shortly be in hand.

Aboard the *USS Cody*, Lt. O'Shea Lomax did not feel he had a single damn thing 'in hand'.

The sub contact to their north had not been reacquired despite intensive efforts by the *Cody* and aircraft off the *Bougainville*. The replacement Defiant *Bougainville* had sent had landed with the pilot reporting a 'drivetrain warning' that had to be cleared up or repaired before he could arm it and put it in the air again.

Analysis of the data they had gathered on the contact indicated it was either one of North Korea's two *Gorae*-class strategic missile submarines, or – even worse – a Chinese Qing class. The ease with which the boat had evaded their pursuit convinced Lomax that they had to be up against a Qing-class submarine.

The Qing was the most advanced diesel-electric submarine in anyone's navy. It was near-silent, armed with two torpedo and two vertical launch tubes for ballistic missiles and four for cruise missiles. What it lacked in endurance, it made up for in stealth. Lomax knew this for a fact because six months earlier, *Cody* had been part of a task force of two light amphibs and two Arleigh Burke destroyers that had driven right over the top of the Qing in the South China Sea without detecting it.

The Chinese captain had surfaced his boat just two miles behind the rearmost ship in the formation and gleefully broadcast over the VHF emergency channel, "American warships, please be more careful. Your noise is hurting our eardrums."

That incident had never made it into either Chinese or US media, but it had made the *Cody* and its sister ships the butt of too many jokes in the US 7th Fleet.

"What do we know about the Qing class, XO?" Lomax asked Ryan.

"China only built one," Ryan told him. They were both still

on the *Cody*'s bridge, holding mugs of hot java as they stared out over its bow, feeding their need to stay alert despite hours of nerve-wracking duty. "They've been concentrating on nuclear-powered missile boats since launching the Qing. You're thinking it's her?"

"I am, XO, I am."

"Sir, due respect, I disagree. Resonance data is saying the contact was two to five thousand tons. A Qing class is *six*."

"You're calling it a North Korean *Gorae*?"

"I am."

"*Gorae* makes a lot of noise. We let a *Gorae* get away so easy, it's not going to look good on our resumes."

"No sir, but neither does over-estimating your enemy and chasing ghosts."

Lomax chuckled. "Touché, XO. Maybe it's my wounded pride talking?"

Jake Ryan had not been XO on the Cody during what had become known as the 'Qing incident'. Even though it was the Arleigh Burke destroyers that should have detected the Chinese boat, the dummy hat had been dropped on the ship that was closest to it when it surfaced – the *USS Cody*. "That Qing class screwed *Cody* once already. What are the chances of it happening twice?"

"That's what I'm afraid of, XO. But you're right." He turned to his air ops watch officer. "Status on that Defiant?"

The man called aft to get a report and put his handset down again. "Drivetrain fault warning was a software glitch. She's cleared to fly. Being armed with torpedoes now. Airborne in twenty."

Twenty minutes. Surely with three birds in dipping their sonars, and with *Cody* and its *Sea Hunter* drone running trailing sonar rigs, they had to pick up that damn contact again. Whatever navy it belonged to!

"Good, get me …"

The Lieutenant JG serving as officer of the deck, the only other man on the bridge, broke in urgently. "Vampires inbound! Bearing 188, range 38, speed Mach 2.5, HELIOS up and tracking, firing decoys..."

Lomax didn't hesitate. "Bring us around to 188 degrees, engines emergency stop. Get that damn helo airborne!" There were anti-ship missiles inbound and he had about one minute before they were on the *Cody*. He wanted his ship bow on, presenting its smallest profile to the threat, and ensuring that their forward-mounted 125 kW High Energy laser defense system, HELIOS, had an unobstructed firing angle.

Ryan had been on comms to the air operations officer and returned to Lomax's side. "Thirty-eight miles *behind* us?" Ryan exclaimed. "That's not the same submarine. And we would have seen a surface vessel."

Lomax braced on the console ahead of him as the *Cody* heeled over into a braking turn and its bow came around to meet the threat. "No, this is something else. We've been bushwhacked, XO."

The 'something else' was a North Korean Sinpo-class diesel-electric submarine, which had been trailing the *Cody* from the moment it left Sangeo Shoal. Its Captain had been authorized to engage any Western surface vessel he judged was a threat to the *Gorae*, patrolling about fifty miles north.

Though based on the Cold War Russian Golf submarine design, its Chinese-designed passive sonar suite and complement of missiles were considerably newer. When the *Cody* had adjusted its course and started heading straight for the sector where the Boromae was patrolling, the Captain of the North Korean attack submarine brought his boat to missile launch depth and ordered the launch of two Chinese-made YJ-18 sea-skimming missiles down the bearing to the American ship.

Bursting from the water in their launch capsules, the two missiles began their flight at subsonic speeds, but as they closed to within ten miles of the *Cody* and picked up the target with their onboard radar, their rocket boosters kicked in and accelerated the missiles to two times the speed of sound as they dropped down to wavetop height.

They were fast and small, but against a US Navy guided missile destroyer with layered missile, projectile and laser defense systems, they would have had little chance.

The *Cody* was not a guided missile destroyer.

She was quite simply the wrong ship, on the wrong mission, in the wrong place, at the wrong time.

Crunch Time

"Brace for impact!" Lomax's officer of the deck called out to the men on the bridge, the alert being relayed through the whole ship.

They'd grabbed flak jackets and helmets as the 'Battle Stations' klaxon rang throughout *Cody*'s three decks. Lomax felt grim satisfaction as he saw their helo lift off their flight deck and pull away behind them.

Cody had three things going for it.

Stability. Their catamaran-style hull gave them speed, but also solidity. Counterintuitively, he'd ordered the *Cody* to a braking halt with just enough way on to maintain steerage. The stability would give their anti-missile laser a solid platform from which to engage.

Size. The expeditionary fast transport class was designed to fill the gap between large, multipurpose amphibious warfare ships and smaller short-range vessels such as the Landing Craft Utility or hovercraft. *Cody* was only 16 yards across the beam – not much wider than a Grayhound bus was long. And she didn't just have one hull, she had two, with a wide gap between.

Lack of armor. An EPF wasn't meant for use in heavily contested war zones so it hadn't been built with thick armor plate. On the other hand, the missiles coming at it were designed with shaped penetrating warheads to allow them to punch through the steel plate of destroyers, frigates and cruisers. There was a chance, however small, that they would punch right through one of *Cody*'s hulls and out the other side before they detonated, and Lomax was playing that chance like a poker player betting on an inside straight.

They had launched a decoy drone and it was hovering off their bow emanating radar energy, noise and light to try to attract the incoming missiles. He checked the video feed from *Cody's* flight deck and saw their Defiant power up, its twin rotors lifting it off the deck as its rear 'pusher-prop' accelerated it from zero to a hundred knots in an eye-wateringly short space of sky.

The threat display in front of him was counting down the seconds to the missiles striking and when it hit ten seconds he issued what could be the final command of his short career.

"Rudder hard right!"

There was no wheel for the helmsman on the deck below to spin. *Cody*'s rudder was computer controlled and the helmsman who managed their speed and direction simply pushed his joystick against its right-hand gimbal, closed his eyes ... and began praying.

It took a couple of seconds for *Cody* to react, but when she did, she leaned outwards and began a shuddering turn. The maneuver would present their port bow to the incoming missiles, but also give the missiles the greatest chance of passing straight through one of the hulls without detonating.

"HELIOS locked and firing!" his OOD, Henley, called out. A barely audible hum filled Lomax's ears. There was none of the drama of missiles leaping from launch rails, or the rip-tearing sound of an autocannon firing. The high energy laser had just seconds to burn through the hardened nose cone of an incoming missile and either damage its guidance system or detonate its warhead. Too short a time for anyone to know if it had been effective.

"Impact!" the OOD called out.

Eyes glued to his tactical display, Lomax never even saw the missiles. But he felt them.

Cody shuddered. She kneeled forward like Godzilla had punched her in the nose, reared back up over the waves and crashed down again. Lomax just had time to duck before the bridge windshield shattered and flayed everyone standing in front of it with flying glass.

Ri stopped at the ladder leading up through a hatch to the roof of the visitor center. Yun had placed a man on the ladder, ready to signal to their marksman. He had the remainder of their men huddled below the level of the windows, ready to begin covering fire and a detachment of three close protection officers still in the basement, to act as human shields for the protectees.

He called up to Yun. "Lieutenant, are we ready?"

"Yes, sir! Marksman's shot will be the signal. On your order."

Ri stood at the top of the steps taking a last look at the position of his men at the windows. He had a man on the roof, with a Zastava 7.62mm rifle cradled against his cheek. Yun was standing at the base of the ladder that went up to the roof.

They were as ready as they could be. "Give the order, Lieutenant."

Lomax groaned, lifting himself from the bridge deck. Which was in itself a miracle since he'd been expecting to be wearing angel wings by now, rising into the air looking down at the foaming hole in the sea that used to be *USS Cody*.

He felt blood running down his neck and felt his face, his fingers coming away wet and red from a cut on his cheek in which a cube of window glass was still embedded. Grimacing, he pulled it free as he checked around himself. His OOD, Henley, was climbing to his feet, but his XO, Ryan, was down on all fours and crabbing around as though searching for a lost pair of glasses. Looking out of the *Cody*'s open windows he saw twisted metal where the bow railing used to be … but no smoke, no fire. Two men were running forward with a hose, but he couldn't see why.

He put a hand on the console in front of him to steady himself. "Situation, Henley?" The man's headset had been pulled free as he was thrown off his feet and he ripped his helmet off, pulling the headset on again and speaking urgently to the command center beneath their feet. The man took a deep breath, as though to speak, but nothing came out.

Lomax took a step toward him and laid a hand on his

shoulder. "In your own time, man."

The man nodded, swallowing. "Missile … we took a missile in port forward quarter. Passed through the sonar equipment complex in the port hull, exploded in the gap between hulls, sir."

"Only one missile?"

"HELIOS tagged the others," the man said, gathering himself now. "Air ops … the air ops officer reports our Defiant is working down the bearing of those missiles with dipping sonar, trying to find the bast … the boat that fired them, sir."

"Casualties?" Lomax asked.

"No information yet, Captain."

"I can't … I can't see," came the voice of Ryan down on the deck. He had stopped scrabbling around, but was still on all fours. Lomax moved quickly around the OOD's seat and crouched beside him.

"Here, let's get you up, XO," Lomax said. He put one arm around the man's back, the other around his chest, guiding him to his feet.

"Face smarts," Ryan said, raising a hand to touch it.

Lomax grabbed his hand and held it away. "You got blood in your eyes, Ryan. Leave it alone." He turned to the OOD. "Henley, take Lieutenant Ryan to the medical bay, get his face cleaned up. Captain has the deck."

He tried to keep his tone neutral, didn't want to panic his XO. The man's face was a mass of cuts, window glass still embedded in his cheeks, blood dripping from his chin. What he'd said was true … the man's eyes were filled with blood. Whether he still had any eyeballs behind his bloodied eyelids, Lomax didn't dare think about.

"Aye, Captain has the deck," Henley said, taking Ryan's elbow. "Come on Lieutenant, sir. We'll get you down to med bay."

Lomax quickly took stock. *Cody*'s bow was torn open above the waterline. They could be taking in water. But she was still making way, slowly because of his last orders, but moving. He still couldn't see any smoke rising from the torn deck. If the missile had taken out their sonar complex, it had missed the fuel and ammunition storage areas which were located under the large, and currently empty, helipad. The two men up forward with the fire hose were peering through the torn deck, but they weren't flooding the compartment underneath it with foam, which was a good sign.

Every man aboard *Cody*'s small crew had trained in exactly what to do in the case of a missile strike or other catastrophic damage, and he was glad to see he didn't need to issue any orders for them to be doing it.

An ensign appeared behind him as he was pulling on the OOD's headset. "Captain? Lieutenant Henley told me to report."

"Ah, Jackson. I need a firsthand damage and casualty report. I want you personally to check hull integrity down in B and C decks, and get back here with a report as soon as you're done." The man stood blinking at him. "You all right, son?"

"Ah, yes, Captain."

"Then get going."

"Aye, aye, sir!" the man disappeared again.

Lomax turned to the console in front of him, scanning the data from radar and instruments that streamed across it, then pressed the mike button on his headset. "CIC, Lomax. Systems damage?"

"Captain. Sonar is down. We think the missile took out the entire complex, so we're pulling the towed sonar rig back in. Powerplant, surface radar, steerage, HELIOS and hydraulic systems are all green. No vibration on the shafts, sir. Engineering is running tests but is confident we can deliver full power when needed."

Lomax knew he would ideally be bringing *Cody* to a stop and putting divers over the side to check whether there was damage to his bow below the waterline. But he was in a hot warzone. He had a hostile submarine somewhere astern, and another contact somewhere ahead.

"Helm, Captain. Bring our speed to ahead slow. Back it off

if you pick up the slightest indication of prop or screw damage."

"Aye, Captain, speed ahead slow, nice and easy."

"Air Ops, Captain."

"Captain, Klein here."

"Lieutenant Klein, what is the situation with our Defiant?"

"Got away clean, sir. Two torpedoes loaded before we went to action stations, so I sent it down the bearing to those missiles. Radar officer estimates the missiles left the water about twenty miles dead astern, so we're dipping a five by five mile pattern in that sector. If nothing else, sound of the sonar should drive them down below missile launch depth."

"Good work, Klein. Let me know the second you get any contact. That Defiant is not to engage except on my order."

"Yes, Captain."

Lomax drummed his fingers on the console in front of him. Helos from the *Bougainville* were prosecuting the contact they'd picked up earlier. Without sonar they would add nothing to that search and his priority now was to either evade, or find and kill, the boat that had attacked *Cody*. Which of the two, was not his decision to make.

"Comms, Captain. Put me through to Commander Wilson on *Bougainville*."

"Comms. Aye, Captain."

Lomax drummed his fingers again, looking out at his scarred bow. He knew which of the two options he wanted to pursue.

Special Agent Helen Lee didn't have a whole lot of options right at that moment.

She'd woken up with a blinding headache, strapped to a chair. At least, that was what she quickly concluded. Her feet felt like they were duct-taped to the legs of the chair, and her hands were cuffed behind her. She lifted her chin groggily from her chest and tried to take in her surroundings through eyes that felt like they were glued together. Was she alone?

Then she heard movement of some sort behind her. Smelled

cigarette smoke.

Not alone then.

"Ah, good, you are awake," a male voice behind her said. The man behind her stayed where he couldn't be seen, but she recognized the voice: Yeo. "Are you thirsty?"

Lee's mouth was bone dry, her tongue thick in her mouth. "No," she lied. "What the hell is going on?"

Yeo chuckled. "That is exactly the right question, Special Agent. But I will be the one asking it. Why did former Commander of the Presidential Security Service, Pak, work so hard to have *you* placed on my detail?"

Lee considered her answer. He was fishing. But in situations like this, something close to the truth was always the best strategy. "He has been my mentor since I was 19," she said. "I owe most of my postings to his intervention."

"Ah, yes. Intervention," Yeo said. "But I wonder why he felt the need to intervene in the Prime Minister's affairs, here and now?"

"I don't know … I was due for rotation. He recommended me for this position, that's all there is to it."

"No, Lee, that is *not* all there is to it," Yeo said. A chair creaked as he adjusted his sitting position. "There was a candidate for the role already hand-picked by myself and approved by the Prime Minister. But Pak had him bumped and *you* appeared in his place."

"I told you, Mr. Pak is my mentor," Lee repeated. "He occasionally uses his influence to help me compete for positions. I have always wanted to work Prime Ministerial protection."

It was right then Lee noticed she was not just cuffed and bound to a high-backed chair. She was cuffed and bound to a high-backed chair that was sitting on a plastic groundsheet that covered about ten square feet of carpet underneath her.

And even in her currently befuddled state, Lee was awake enough to realize that this was also Not a Good Thing.

"Such admirable ambition," Yeo said. Lee heard a sound she'd heard hundreds of times in her time in the service. The sound of a magazine sliding into place inside the grip of a pistol. There was a footfall, and then a light tapping on the wood of the chair behind her neck. "That noise you can hear is the suppressor of a Beretta M9 about an inch from your spinal cord."

Lee stayed quiet. It wasn't a question. All agents wore a lightweight tactical vest under their shirt, but it didn't cover their upper back.

"Do you have any idea what is happening in Korea today, Sergeant?"

"The nation is under attack," Lee said carefully. *From filth like you*, she thought.

"That is true," the man said. "But not in the way you think. You are thinking of a few bombs and missiles, dropped on the heads of unification scum. I am talking about an attack by the traitors who want to see South Korea dragged fifty years into the past, politically and economically, by merging one of the most progressive and successful democracies in Asia with the failed state that is North Korea."

And there it was. Plot and motive laid bare. And she would die knowing that the plot to destroy the peace process went to the very top of her own government, but unable to do anything about it. Frustration and anger began boiling in her veins.

Pak had chosen Lee for this mission because she was 'for' reunification. With a big F. She'd exercised her democratic right to demonstrate only once in her career as a security service agent, and it wasn't to demand a pay rise. She'd joined a million other South Koreans in Seoul two years earlier for the Million Lantern March, carrying her paper lantern from the city to the DMZ and launching it into the air over the demarcation line with good wishes for the North Korean people and their leader, Madam Yun-mi Kim. The demonstration marked the first ever visit by a leader of North Korea to the South Korean capital and Lee had actually cried watching the woman smile and wave on a big screen at Gwanghwamun Square.

Which might have seemed strange considering Lee and her generation had known nothing but peace and prosperity all their lives, as South Korean democracy and its economy went from strength to strength. Why would she, or anyone, want to embrace a union with their poor, despotic cousins to the north? The answer lay in the two years of her youth wasted in voluntary military service, most of which had been spent in a warehouse in Incheon, stacking shelves with a forklift. In the hundreds of billions of South Korean won wasted on maintaining the biggest armed force in East Asia outside of China. But most importantly, it lay in the pointless death of her uncle, a humble fisheries inspector.

He had been conducting a survey of fish stock around the Yeonpyeong Islands off the west coast of South Korea when his small one-man boat was attacked and sunk by a North Korean navy vessel. Accounts of the incident varied and in the end, it was completely irrelevant whether her uncle had been in disputed waters or just going about his job on the right side of the maritime demarcation line when he was killed. To Lee he had died, and her father was grieving, because of the stupidity of an arbitrary line drawn on a map by imperial powers more than eighty years earlier. The thought of that stupidity had burned in her gut every time she'd seen her father sitting at their kitchen table in his undershirt, nursing a glass of Soju and staring out the kitchen window at nothing, because she knew he was thinking of his brother.

Lee didn't blame the North Koreans, like her father did. She blamed every General or Admiral who had waved the threat of starving hordes of North Korean soldiers pouring across the border, pouring nuclear fire on Seoul, whenever a politician threatened to cut the defense budget. She blamed every politician who for the last 80 years had not pursued peace with the North at all cost. She blamed the passive idiocy of the generations who went before her and believed that they were still fighting a war that had ended in 1953, when the world had much, much more important battles to fight.

So, yes. Reunification was important to Lee, in a very personal, almost visceral way. And the idea that this Prime Minister and the people around him were trying to screw it up, felt like a splinter under her nail.

She could no longer contain herself.

"You reactionary *filth!*" she spat. "You think your petty coup will..." She never completed the sentence.

The gun behind her coughed, but the bullet didn't hit her spine.

It buried itself in Helen Lee's thigh just above her knee, and she screamed.

Prime Minister Ted Choi didn't think of it as a coup. That was a tawdry, unworthy name for the dramatic events he and others had set in motion.

A coup was something that changed governments. Ted Choi and his collaborators were going to change *history.*

With the eventual assassination of the people's traitors, South Korea's Si-min Shin and North Korea's Yun-mi Kim, would come an end to all talk of 'peace'. A line would be drawn through the endless war, yes, but not in the way the two traitors imagined it. The 'demarcation line' would become a real border. The DMZ would be replaced with a wall.

But more importantly, South Korea's reliance on that vacillating puppet master, the USA, would end forever. A nuclear attack on US and South Korean navy forces in the Sea of Japan would sweep away all US reluctance to base nuclear weapons on South Korean soil.

But more than that. Under his leadership, South Korea would begin its *own* nuclear weapons program and within ten years, perhaps even five, South Korea would have a nuclear arsenal more powerful than that of the North.

His North Korean collaborators would also get what they wanted. Not a future as the poor cousin of the South, facing China across a new and much more dangerous DMZ. Instead, a return to the status quo; stability and security for the political and military elite and greater support from China than ever before.

Then, only then, would his nation know true peace. No

longer bound to imperialist USA for its defense. No longer cowering under the threat of nuclear annihilation by North Korea or China. A prosperous, independent, powerful nation able to determine its own destiny at last!

And that future was close. So close.

All he needed was those damn launch codes.

Choi turned his attention back to the videoconference screen. "... and the result of the vote is six in favor, none against. Prime Minister Tae Hyun Choi is appointed interim Chief Executive of the State Council, Minister of Unification and President of South Korea. Minister of Agriculture, So-wa Yoon, is appointed interim Minister of National Defense."

Choi had to stifle a smile. The hapless Agriculture Minister, Yoon, had just messaged him in panic. *What should I do now? Call a meeting of the General Staff?*

He had tried to calm her. *I need you to focus on securing military support to the emergency and police services if needed. Arrange urgent meeting with the Director of Interior and Safety. Will call you after press conference.*

Or in other words, "I need you busy doing something pointless so you do not get in my way."

"... do you have any concluding words, Mr. President?"

Choi could not stifle the swelling in his chest. 'Mr. President'. And had he not earned that title? He looked down the camera at the skeleton cabinet that he had just reconstituted. Of the 20-member cabinet, only 12 were not either dead, or in critical condition in hospital. None of the survivors were likely to challenge him in the coming hours or days; a flock of gormless sheep stared back at him.

"Ladies and gentlemen, you know your duties. Our key task is to react firmly to these senseless provocations and the message I will now convey to our shocked nation is that we are doing so ... with resolve, and with a power that the forces of chaos in the North will not misunderstand. You all know what your duties are, but my staff stand ready to assist if you have any doubts. After my address to the nation, during which I will declare a National State of Military Emergency, I will be convening a Crisis Committee comprising the heads of Intelligence and the General Staff of the Armed Forces. All matters related to the defense of the nation and our military response will be decided by the Crisis Committee, and you will be advised." He waited to see if there were any expressions of protest or surprise, but of course, there were none. He decided a little false humility was called for. "Very well, thank you for your vote of confidence. I will do my best to live up to it. We will meet again tonight at …" He looked at his watch. "… at 2100."

He stood as the screen went blank, snapping his fingers at his protectee advisor. "Press conference?"

"Ready on the rooftop, sir. Stage is set up on the helipad next to the helicopter. The pilot will ensure he kills the engine but the rotors will still be turning as you start your speech. Gives an added sense of crisis."

"Very good. I want to look at the speech one more time."

"Yes, sir, I will get the writer." The man disappeared. Choi saw Yeo walk in and waited until he approached. There were other people in the room, so he lowered his voice. "The Lee woman?"

"Contained. I am sure her posting was a pathetic attempt at penetration. Pak is suspicious."

Choi held up a hand to stop the man telling him any more. "If she doesn't report back to him soon, he will become even more so. Persuade her to do so."

Yeo reached for his earbud with a smile. "I will see to it, Mr. President."

As he turned away, Choi felt that upwelling in his chest again. *Mr. President.* He supposed he might get used to hearing it one day, but could he not forgive himself for enjoying the moment, just a little longer?

Bunny and Noname had been enjoying a long and uneventful flight over the Yellow Sea, which they should have known was a guarantee that it would not last.

A chime sounded in their ears and a directional indicator lit up in their helmet displays.

"Aircraft search radar, two eight four degrees from Bat Two," Noname intoned.

No lock on their Kingsnake yet. She quickly checked their position. They were about fifty miles out of the North Korean island of Sinmi-do, maybe sixty miles from going 'feet dry' over the North Korean coastline. More importantly, they had crossed into that part of the Yellow Sea China and North Korea most definitely regarded as sovereign airspace. The South Korean in his Boromae was down at wavetop height, and their Kingsnake was flying near its max altitude of 50,000 feet.

The Boromae should be near invisible too. Her Kingsnake, not so much, but the new contacts seemed more interested in her drones. Well, so far, so good.

She'd ordered each of their Bats loaded with two wing-tip shorter-range CUDA missiles, while she carried six medium-range under-wing Peregrine missiles, and two long-range AIM-260 missiles on her fuselage hard points.

If she or the Bats were detected and attacked by hostile aircraft, she would engage the enemy fighters at long range first, trying to knock them down or simply draw the attention of their air defense controllers. Noname would keep the enemy busy with their Bats, while Bunny held overwatch for Keys and the Boromae, making sure his six stayed clear.

She'd stay in touch with the Boromae, able to come to its assistance if needed, but continue prosecuting targets from a distance if they threatened. They'd use the Bats to draw North Korean air defenses to them and snipe them from the sky, until either they ran out of missiles, or were overwhelmed and had to bug out, pulling as many hostile aircraft with them as she could as they fled.

That strategy should be enough to get the South Korean Colonel to Yongdoktong, and after that he was on his own.

The slow but insistent beep of their radar warning receiver changed tone to a single, insistent warble.

"Radar lock. Two seven nine degrees to Bat Two now," Noname said, redundantly. "Maneuvering Bats Three and Four for a solution."

"Go active on One and Two, Noname. Try to scare them away but don't engage."

A radar lock meant that whatever was out there patrolling the border had found one of their Bats. Noname immediately lit up all four Bats' radars and they saw the threat instantly. Two fast movers, coming from the northeast, crossing the coast near Chinese Dandong.

Which more likely than not made them *Chinese*. Not North Korean. She checked her position once more. She was entering North Korean airspace, not Chinese. That didn't seem to be a distinction that worried them. But the sudden appearance of fighter targeting radars in the skies around them did!

As per Chinese fighter doctrine, the two aircraft turned toward the nearest of the threats – Bat Three – and locked their targeting radars on it.

With a twitch of her stick, Bunny banked right, turning farther into North Korean airspace, leaving Noname to manage the interaction with the Chinese fighters. But she quickly checked their range to Bat Three.

Eighty miles. What Chinese aircraft had a radar so good they could lock her Kingsnake up at eighty miles? Probably only its newest types – the stealthy J-20 Mighty Dragon or FC-31 Gyrfalcon. She saw no sign of drone wingmen – China still only had five squadrons teamed with Sky Hawks – but the incoming fighters were a good match for the Kingsnake and the two drones they had so far detected.

Or thought they were.

Down at sea level, flying in loose formation off the port and starboard wings of the South Korean Colonel's Boromae, were their other two Ghost Bat drones: Bats Three and Four.

"All right, China," she muttered to herself. "Let's see if we can put some freak into you." She keyed the cockpit comms. "Noname, go active on Three and Four. Light 'em up."

Noname had the two drones flying a low bracket maneuver

and gave them commands that would activate their targeting radars and send them screaming into the sky straight at the Chinese fighters.

The Chinese didn't react at first. Target fixation, Bunny guessed. They were so intent on the two drones they were pursuing they hadn't seen the two underneath them yet. *Seventy miles. Sixty.* If they carried the newer PL-15 medium-range missile, they were inside firing range now. But hopefully planning a visual intercept, not a shoot down. O'Hare was banking on a hope China would not want to get into a shooting war with the West.

Now they were awake! Finally seeing they were up against *four* fighters, not two, the Chinese aircraft split high and low, one to the north, the other to the south. They probably had no idea at this stage the aircraft they were surrounded by were drones.

Show time.

Bunny could only imagine what was happening in the cockpits of the two fighters. They'd been cruising toward an intercept with two unknown fast-moving fighters, probably already tense, and suddenly found themselves with threats below them too!

Before they could threaten the drones, Noname changed their attack profiles from 'search and acquire' to 'jam and maintain separation'. Still blasting out radar energy, the four drones began circling the Chinese fighters at speed, forming a bubble of energy around them and keeping a 20-mile distance from their targets, their focused electronic attack intended to nullify the Chinese radar and blind the two fighters now frantically searching for them.

If she'd wanted to, Bunny could have sent a brace of AIM-260 long-range missiles at the Chinese fighters and killed them before they even knew she existed. But instead, she used the situation to keep herself invisible.

"Going low, Noname. Hold tight." She rolled their Kingsnake onto its back, pulled her flight stick back and sent her fighter into a vertical dive toward the sea, until about four thousand feet from sea level she barrel-rolled her machine back onto a course that put her back behind the South Korean Boromae and with her nose pointed at their ingress point.

"That was only a six point four," Noname told her. "Hostile contacts have stopped tracking." He had a scale he called his 'puke-ometer', on which he rated her more extreme maneuvers by the effect they would have had on a human backseater. It was like the Richter scale. Anything over three was nausea, but from about seven and up, puking could be expected.

"Well hell, I'll try harder next time," she replied.

With satisfaction, she saw the Chinese fighters decide discretion was the best course of action in the circumstances. Twenty miles into North Korean airspace and suddenly facing at least four potentially hostile fighters? They'd no doubt radioed urgently for new orders and Bunny saw them rejoin and begin moving back toward the China–North Korea border.

"Disengage Bats," she ordered. "Scout ahead."

Noname killed the Ghost Bats' electronic warfare attack and ordered them to take up a terrain-following formation ahead of Colonel Ban, now nearly 20 miles ahead of Bunny thanks to her little stunt shedding altitude.

Bunny took a deep breath and rolled her shoulders, letting the tension of the last few minutes bleed out of her body.

Okay ladies and gentlemen, boys and girls. Next stop … *Yongdoktong.*

She checked her nav screen. Sixty miles to run, with the South Korean pilot at treetop height, weaving through valleys and along rivers, her drones a few thousand feet higher, sniffing the sky ahead of him. Her threat warning screen showed Chinese air defense radar along the border to the northwest and behind her, and the search radar of a Chinese destroyer. Directly ahead, two less capable Russian-made S-300 SAM battalions, east and west of the target, to provide the North Korean nuclear storage site with blanket coverage.

She could see aircraft to the southeast, patrols flying toward and back from the demarcation line with South Korea, but their mission briefing had warned they could expect a standing patrol of at least four Mig-29 fighters to be circling over the target.

The real threat to the South Korean pilot, if he stayed low and hidden by the terrain, was neither the ancient SAM system nor the North Korean fighters. It was the low-level man-portable, or MANPAD, missile teams and radar-guided Shilka anti-air cannons that North Korea had guarding every possible approach to their bunker. His strategy was to attack from the north along the river valley, to take them by surprise, and blast through before they could lock on him.

The only help she could offer, once he started his ingress, was for her Bats to do their job as decoys to draw the ire of North Korea's defenses. Noname would send two of the machines ahead of Keys, to scramble North Korean radar and draw MANPAD fire, and together with her Kingsnake, keep two higher, to attract the attention of any patrolling fighters.

After which, she fully expected, a lot of people would start trying to kill them.

But then, making people annoyed enough to want to kill her was something Bunny O'Hare *excelled* at.

Corporal Chang was surprised to find himself alive, given the last thing he could remember was the North Korean Sergeant advancing on him with hate in her eyes. He had woken on the floor of the truck cabin a good five minutes earlier, but apart from moving his legs to relieve the cramping pain in his thighs, he had kept his eyes closed and tried to get a grip on his situation. Looking through narrowed eyelids, feeling the bump of the road beneath him, he worked out he was back in the cabin of the troop transport.

Legs and boots on the driver's side. He wasn't alone. He heard a curse and twisted his head slightly to look up at the face of the driver.

Her. Seriously?

All right, Chang. You're being used as a human shield. It could be worse. Did he really believe that? He tested his hands, arms and legs for pain, tensing and releasing his muscles. His right calf protested, and not just with cramp. Something was hurting down there. But his hands were free. He needed to turn his head to look at the passenger door – maybe he could jump out while the truck was moving? Well, ok, not jump … more like flop.

He moaned quietly and let a bump in the road roll his head left. *All* right. Door unlocked, window open. The door had a handle in the armrest you had to heave up to work the lock mechanism, but maybe he could kick it. He tried lifting his leg minutely, and his muscles protested at the mere thought of ever moving again.

Forget it. It was easier to just bounce around here in the dirt of soldiers' boots until someone decided it was time to haul him out and shoot him.

Then he heard the North Korean sergeant rip out a loud curse, the truck brakes vented loudly as the five-ton truck tried to stop, and he rolled up against the engine bulkhead under the dash. There was a muffled explosion somewhere ahead. Close.

He heard a voice. *Now, Chang! Move dammit!*

He knew that voice, and tried to ignore it. The North Korean sergeant was still cursing out loud to herself, and he saw her throw the truck into reverse, turning her head and looking over her shoulder as she started backing up.

Now, fool.

Gunfire. Closer. *Ah hell.*

He kicked at the door handle with his left leg, calf screaming in pain. His toe caught the door release, pushing it upward. The truck swerved, the door was pulled open by the momentum, he grabbed the dash above him and heaved himself along the floor on his backside, and the next thing he knew he was rolling across gravel and dirt, his ears assaulted by the noise of automatic rifle fire.

Then he hit a curb, rolled over it and fell. Twenty feet below, he saw water rushing up at him.

Sergeant Song and her captive had arrived at the Peace Dam visitor center at the moment of Captain Ri's counterattack. South Korean sentries on the access road up by the dam had just waved her through and radioed ahead to warn the troops below she was coming. She saw signs there had been intense fighting along the road, and several bodies by a park containing bizarrely painted tanks.

But as her stolen truck rumbled onto the causeway leading to the visitor center, where a large number of North *and* South Korean troops were in cover behind concrete berms, rifles pointed at the building, she heard a single shot ring out.

And then all hell broke loose.

The gunner in the back of what looked like a dune buggy mounting an autocannon was punched backward from his gun mount, and the windows of the visitor center came alive with the flash of rifles firing.

Song slammed on the brakes of the truck and mashed the gears to put it into reverse. She didn't want to drive a cargo of anti-tank missiles into the middle of a firefight.

As she watched, a South Korean officer – caught flatfooted by the apparent surprise counter-attack – scrambled for cover behind an armored car.

South Koreans and North Koreans, fighting side by side? This was the force she was supposed to be supporting? She craned her neck over her shoulder, doing her best not to drive the big transport over the side of the causeway as she reversed. She could smell the acrid stink of cordite through her open window. That was when she noticed the passenger door had swung open. *And her captive was gone.* She slammed on the brakes, bellowed in frustration and grabbed the pistol off the seat beside her.

Security Service Captain Goh had seen movement inside the visitor center and assumed the small force inside was preparing to hand over the protectees. He took it as the first sign the day was about to turn in his favor.

He'd been annoyed at the report that their North Korean blocking force on the Hwacheon road had been attacked by US aircraft and forced to abandon their position. It left the dam wide open to reinforcement by South Korean ground units as soon as they became aware of what was happening at the dam. But with luck, their operation would soon be over and the two State leaders on the way across the DMZ to custody in the North.

He found himself suddenly in such a good mood that when he heard the large troop transport working through its gears as it moved downhill from the top of the dam, he had just decided he wouldn't tear the hide off the North Korean NCO inside it. He would show his magnanimous side, sympathizing with her losses and thanking her for her initiative in bringing him the additional firepower of the anti-tank missiles in the back of her truck.

Then a shot was fired by a sniper hiding on the roof of the visitor center, and Goh saw the gunner on one of his LMADIS buggies punched backward off the vehicle. A fusillade of rifle fire erupted from the visitor center windows, sending him scurrying for cover behind a concrete berm.

The heavier crack of the sniper rifle of the roof got his attention, and he saw a communications dish spin off the top of his other LMADIS buggy as the man up there started targeting the jamming rig mounted on the buggy's protective cage.

Goh looked around and saw a North Korean rifleman with an underslung grenade launcher on his rifle. "You! Put a grenade on that damn roof!" he yelled.

As he did so, he saw movement inside the LTV jammed across the visitor center doors!

Down, But Not Out

Sea of Japan, north of Sangeo Shoal

Every muscle in Lomax's back had seized up. He sat stiffly in the officer of the deck's chair behind and between the two watch officers who were now attending to the job of putting distance between the *USS Cody* and the submarine that had attacked them.

They'd managed to get the damaged ship up to about 20 knots without its bow tearing itself off, and Lomax didn't want to push *Cody* any harder right now. He couldn't outdistance submarine-launched cruise missiles, but every cubic ton of seawater he put between himself, and the attacker made it harder for them to get a bearing on his ship.

Especially with his helo about to drop a Very Lightweight Torpedo on their bastard heads.

"Contact confirmed," his subsurface warfare officer reported from the command center. "Bearing one seven nine, course 340 and turning to starboard. Designating Sierra two. Defiant requests permission to drop."

The *Cody*'s panic-launched Defiant had flown down the bearing of the missiles that had been fired at them, looking for disturbed water that might indicate two sub-launched anti-ship cruise missiles had recently surfaced.

It found them ... two foamy slicks in the water, and nearby, the half-shell launch casing one of the missiles had discarded, still floating on the surface. The Defiant had lowered its dipping sonar emitter and within five minutes got a return ping.

The hostile submarine was cavitating loudly, turning away from *Cody* and going deeper in a futile attempt to evade detection. But the sonar operator aboard the Defiant quickly identified it from the acoustic signature in his database. It was not the first time this particular sub had made its acquaintance with the US Navy: Sinpo-class submarine, hull number 11.

It might not be the first time this particular Sinpo had snuck up on a US Navy warship, but Lomax was determined it would be the last. He'd already been granted attack authority by Commander Wilson on *Bougainville* and he didn't hesitate.

"Drop torpedo."

Thirty miles astern of the *Cody*, a single VLW torpedo detached from a pylon on the port side of the helo and fell toward the surface of the sea, retarded by a small white parachute that kept it vertical.

It entered the water with barely a splash.

With near silent electric propulsion, and propelled by a brushless motor and pump jet, it guided itself down the bearing supplied by the Defiant's dipping sonar before it was dropped.

The crew of the Sinpo knew they were in trouble when the Defiant's dipping sonar started pinging them, but they didn't know they had a torpedo coming at them until 100 yards out from their sub, it activated its own sonar and locked onto the 2,000-ton submarine.

The Sinpo desperately fired a cloud of decoy 'noisemakers' into the water behind it and tried to turn to put the torpedo in its baffles, but the VLWT was programmed to ignore the familiar signature of the decoys and, traveling at a speed of 50 knots, it quickly overhauled the North Korean submarine. It pulled up alongside its target, measured the length of the hull and then turned sharply toward it, burying its shaped charge warhead in the boat's center mass.

"Detonation," the subsurface warfare officer down in the command center reported. "Hull breach ... crush noises. She's history, sir."

There was no jubilation on *Cody*'s deck and Lomax barely allowed himself a sigh of relief. They were still in suddenly hostile waters, plowing forward in a crippled ship toward a larger and possibly more potent threat. His Defiant had launched with only two torpedoes loaded and had just expended one of them. He needed it carrying its full complement of four.

"Captain to air ops, get our Defiant back and fully loaded. I want it back in the air, assisting with the search for that *Gorae* as quickly as we can turn it around." He didn't even wait for his order to be acknowledged before he switched his comms to a new channel. "Infirmary, Captain."

"Doc Stuart, go ahead." Stuart wasn't really an MD, but everyone aboard called the paramedic Doc.

"Doc, what is the status of Lieutenant Ryan?"

"Uh, it looks like the XO took most of a bridge windowpane in the face, am I right?"

"Near enough."

"I've pulled about twenty cubes of glass out of his face and chest. His vision is not at risk, but I'd like to fly him out to *Bougainville* for a closer examination."

Lomax cursed. He couldn't pull his own helo off anti-submarine duties during an active engagement. He could radio *Bougainville* and ask them to send a helo to evac his XO, but it would take at least thirty minutes to reach them, maybe more. There was no other option.

"No can do doc, I need my XO here as long as he is capable. Any other casualties?"

"One man with a broken wrist, another with back injury. Several with contusions. I'd recommend if we're evacuating Lieutenant Ryan, we take off the men with the wrist and back injuries too. The others are only minor, they can fight on."

"Very good, coordinate with air ops. Captain out."

He got onto the comms officer and directed him to request a medical evacuation helo from *Bougainville*. Then he took an updated damage report from his engineering officer. Ship sonar still down and unrepairable, since, well, the complex wasn't really there anymore. No damage to other systems, and importantly, their ability to control the *Sea Hunter* drone was not impaired. No damage or flooding below the waterline but a real assessment of what the missile had done to their structural integrity wouldn't be possible until they docked again. He quickly reviewed images of the *Cody*'s bow taken by a small drone that had hovered about ten yards out, taking video.

On *Cody*'s port side, the missile had punched a door-sized hole in the high bluff bow about two yards below and three aft from the anchor. The exit wound on the starboard side was considerably worse. The missile had exited after carving a path of destruction through the ship's sonar complex and then detonated a few milliseconds after it hit clear air again. The hole there was an ugly starfish shape five yards by five, nesting in a much larger blackened dent caused by the blast effect of the warhead.

The explosion had twisted the hull enough to cause the bridge windows to shatter in their mounts, but *Cody* was still seaworthy, and in the fight.

Unconsciously, Lomax ran his fingers along the armrests of his chair as though petting a cat. *You may be six kinds of ugly, girl. But you sure can take a punch and keep fighting. And ask the Captain of that Sinpo how toothless you are. Oh wait, you can't. Because we killed his ass.*

He slapped the chair armrests, startling the two watch officers.

"Heads in the game, gentlemen," he said out loud, but as much to himself as to his men. "Somewhere up ahead is a nuclear-armed submarine and if recent events are any indication, it is not out here to do us any favors. Break our *Sea Hunter* out of the pattern and have it searching the water between us and that *Gorae*. I don't want any more surprises."

Bunny O'Hare had planned a few surprises for the North Korean air defenses over Yongdoktong.

As the South Korean pilot in his lone Boromae began his ingress hopping over ridges and winding through valleys, Noname ordered two Ghost Bats ahead of him. They couldn't stay below the radar horizon as well as he could, but then, they weren't supposed to. They were there to *jam* radars and attract ground fire.

Noname wasn't flying them. He had simply given them an electronic warfare mission profile, set them to try to hold position two thousand feet over and a half mile ahead of Keys' Boromae, and let them do their thing. Their own AI would take care of everything else.

Meanwhile Bunny and her other two Bats had zoomed up to 30,000 feet. Their combined radar cross-sections were now anything but tiny, and she figured every military radar from Beijing to Pyongyang would be looking at them.

Up here, she felt exposed, naked, vulnerable. To her west, the whole damned Chinese People's Liberation Army Air Force Northern Command; to her east, the Democratic People's Republic of Korea Air Force and not least its Pyongyang-based Mig-29 fighters, probably the most potent weapons in its air arsenal given their role in protecting the skies over the heads of North Korea's leadership and their precious nuclear stockpile.

But she had a very clear job to do. She had to do doughnuts in the sky with a huge 'kick me' sign hanging off her ass.

She had popped up 35 miles north-northeast of the target. The radar warning receiver on the screen in front of her showed at least six different air and ground radars painting them. Seeing her Kingsnake suddenly appear on their scopes, the already nervous and alert operators behind those scopes should have been losing their …

"*Missile launch*. Three four zero degrees. Type SA-5 Gammon. Designating M1. Passive defenses on automatic." Noname's calm voice did its job alerting her to the threat without freaking her out. Unlike the warbling missile-lock alert and popup tactical screen that accompanied it.

"I'll be maneuvering. Keep Bats in trail mode and get ready to deploy against any air threats."

"Roger. Bats in trail."

Her defensive AI painted a cross on the visor of her helmet and a ring near it showed the direction her aircraft was headed. All she – theoretically – had to do to maximize the chances of not killing herself was to keep the circle around the cross. The computer-assisted flight systems would manage the rest.

"New launch. Bearing one eight two. Type SA-10 Grumble. Designating M2. Recommend prioritizing M2."

Now she was being chased by *two* ground to air missiles, fired from different quarters! The cue in her visor jumped radically across the horizon as it calculated a new steering point that gave her a chance of evading both. Luckily it wasn't telling her how small that chance was.

Noname filled that void. He'd rattled through his mental abacus and come up with a figure. "Chance of evasion 42.2 percent," he said. O'Hare grunted as she threw her machine into a tight banking turn to orient it toward the biggest of the two threats, the Grumble.

"Ghost Blitz on M1, Noname," Bunny said through gritted teeth.

"Roger on Blitz," Noname confirmed. "Sending both Bats."

They'd worked out brevity codes for use during engagements based on NFL plays. Like trying to sack a quarterback, a Blitz protocol sent all available drones directly at a threat, whether a missile or aircraft. Radiating jamming energy, spraying decoys as they closed, the drones would try to put themselves between the first threat and her Kingsnake, as Bunny tried to escape the other.

"Air to air radar warning," Noname said. "New contacts."

"All right, just how I like it," Bunny said. "The more the merrier."

Simultaneous to the radar lock from ground missile sites, their flight had been picked up by the standing patrol of Mig-29s over Yongdoktong.

She barely registered the death of one of their Bats as it flew itself into the oncoming SA-5 Gammon. But she just about *felt* the blazing heat of the SA-10 Grumble as it blasted over their cockpit and detonated somewhere behind them.

"Systems check, Noname!" she called, as she wrestled her machine back to level flight and shoved her throttle to the wall to rebuild speed. She'd burned tens of thousands of feet on the maneuver and checked her altitude. Ten thousand and some. Too high. She'd still be visible to ground radar and now she had a brace of Migs hunting her. She had to get lower and stay fast to have a chance.

"All systems nominal," Noname reported. "Bat Two available for tasking."

"Run block," she told him. "Target the lead Mig."

"Running block," he repeated. "Sending Bat Two."

The four Migs were flying in a loose diamond formation, so it was a pretty good guess the flight leader was at the head of the diamond. As she watched on her tac screen, Noname drew a box around the lead Mig and dispatched their wingman to attack it.

Logic said they should use the play to bug out and head back out to sea while the Mig flight was focused on their drone. But she looked at her mission clock and saw the South Korean pilot, Colonel Ban, would still be making his bomb run. Bug out now and the Migs might lose interest and hunt for other prey.

Karen 'Bunny' O'Hare was a pretty ordinary girl. She liked playing eight ball, drinks without umbrellas or fruit in them, and watching people bash each other to pulp in boxing rings. She liked house music, and dancing – but only when drunk. Pretty normal stuff. But she had a superpower. Unpredictability.

In relationships with human beings, it was not so useful, as people tended to prefer other people to react the same way in the same situations.

In modern air combat, though, it made her *formidable*. Because Bunny rarely, if ever, did what her enemy thought she was going to do.

She pointed her Kingsnake at the Mig formation and kicked in her afterburner, feeling that oh-so-satisfying 'hand of God' slam her back into her seat. She activated her phased array radar, got an immediate lock on the four Migs and allocated both of her long-range AIM-260 missiles to the two outermost aircraft in the diamond. She had to give it to the North Korean pilots, they flew a nice formation.

"Up the middle?" Noname asked from the rear seat.

"Up the middle, Noname," she confirmed, pressing the trigger on her joystick. "*Fox 3.*"

Down at shrub and bush level, 'Keys' Ban saw the Kingsnake fighter high above him go 'active' on his radar warning receiver and passed a silent thanks to the allied pilot and her drone wingmen above as he saw the icons for the Mig-29 patrol ahead of him also begin moving as they were attracted to the wildly radiating Kingsnake pilot like foxes to a rabbit.

But it was just a fleeting moment of gratitude, because it took Keys' full focus to power his machine between the hills and ridges towering over his Boromae, without burying it in a hillside or scraping a wingtip on a cliff face.

He was approaching Yongdoktong from north-northwest of the site, using the terrain to stay off North Korean radar as long as he could, but South Korean intelligence indicated that the moment he hit the river that flowed south and then through the nuclear site, he would no longer be able to hide.

The North Korean missile and autocannon defenses along all approaches to Yongdoktong were sited to provide full visual and radar visibility. He would enter the river valley just two miles from the nuclear site, at 600 miles an hour, giving him just ten seconds to cover the final leg to the target.

The longest, and probably the last, ten seconds of his life.

If he even got that far. He grunted as he rolled his machine from wingtip to wingtip, threading the terrain needle. The ingress route was burned in his brain by simulation run after simulation run, in perfectly mapped high resolution, photographic quality imagery.

He had no time to worry about the sky above, or the threats around him. He was in a flowing tunnel, with all that mattered the next turn, the next peak, the next ridge. And the next.

He sensed, rather than saw, a flash of light off his starboard wing that expanded and then fell behind him. Probably one of the American drones, taken out by ground fire.

Coming out of a valley he saw the final ridge ahead of him,

jerked the nose of his Boromae upward, cleared the ridge by mere yards and immediately rolled to port, pulling hard on his flight stick to drop the Boromae into the river valley and point it southeast for his bomb run. Ahead of him, a stream of autocannon tracer fire rose into the air, chasing a shadow … the other American drone! With secrecy no longer paramount, he engaged the Boromae's jamming system, which would add his own electronic warfare attack to that of the drone ahead.

If he was lucky, he …

His threat warning system began an urgent warble and a radar alert flashed red in his visor.

There would be no luck for Keys Ban today.

The bunker protecting North Korea's strategic nuclear stockpile was buried deep under the hills of Yongdoktong with only two entrances. A vehicular entrance facing northeast along a short stretch of river that flowed east–west; and an emergency personnel exit out of the hillside, into the barracks of the Strategic Missile Forces camp south of the hill. No facility was impregnable, but the designers of the facility had chosen the site with care. There was only one narrow and winding road into the facility, which was designed to provide defenders with multiple choke points. There were few flat and even landing areas for helicopter-borne troops. More than a hundred security personnel manned the base, far more than would actually be needed to defend it until reinforcements arrived, and they were equipped with the most modern anti-air, anti-armor and anti-personnel weapons that their Chinese allies could provide.

The main entrance to the bunker faced across the small river to a steep hillside only thirty yards away, making it impossible to drop a bomb through its thermobaric blast-proof doors. No cruise missile yet invented could navigate the twisting, turning valleys and hills surrounding it, and no artillery could do any more than pepper the mountainside with craters. A direct strike on the site by an American nuclear weapon *might* seal the tunnels, but the stockpile inside would be safe and could be dug out in a matter of days by heavy equipment which was also stored underground, 10 miles southeast in the village of Dong-an. Together with two truck-mounted missile launch platforms.

South Korea knew all this. But the decision had been made to send Keys anyway, since the situation on the border was so uncertain that even being able to block North Korea's access to its strategic stockpile for a few days might prove critical. The South Korean military might defeat or survive an attack from the five nuclear warheads which it believed North Korea had on continuous readiness, but it was significantly less likely to survive an attack from 15 or more warheads.

On the hillsides overlooking the site, a Chinese-supplied 'Red Banner' anti-air, anti-ballistic missile system was deployed. The system could track up to six targets simultaneously and engage them with twelve missiles. But it was designed to detect and engage aircraft at high altitude, and Keys and his drone wingman were coming down the river valley at reed-top height. In the ten seconds available, the Red Banner unit could not lock the enemy aircraft and fire its missiles.

But it did not have to. Yongdoktong's defenders were already on alert because the first drone had been detected and destroyed by an infrared missile. The Red Banner radar crew was linked by radio and landline to constant-alert mobile anti-aircraft gun crews sited around the facility and the second it detected the new contacts, it sent a warning, with bearing and elevation, to the missile and gun crews in that sector.

The North Korean Shilka anti-air vehicles had their own radar-guided twin 23mm cannons. Those already facing northwest tried to lock on to Keys' fighter and open fire. Those facing to other points of the compass tried to lock him up too, but took precious seconds to swing their barrels around. MANPAD crews aimed their shoulder-launched missiles in all directions, toward the roar of jet engines that seemed to come from all around them.

The massive wall of jamming energy being pushed down the valley by the Boromae and the Ghost Bat drone blinded several of the defensive radar systems, including the Red Banner radar. But it was able to send a warning and bearing to Yongdoktong's defenders and the Boromae could not defeat *all* of the radars ringing the site.

Keys saw the American drone ahead of him, zooming into the sky, firing chaff and flares as it curved away out of the valley, a shoulder-launched missile following it. Then a curtain of exploding flak shells filled the air right in front of Keys Ban.

Kronk and Snake had worked their way along the Bukhan River to the west bank just up from the Peace Dam. On a rocky ridge overlooking the river, Kronk set up the Shikaka control unit and tried once again to sync with the aircraft overhead. Their last effort had not met with success, some local jamming once again interfering with their signal.

"Handshake!" Kronk yelled to Snake, who was surveying the road below. "I've got control."

"No interference?"

"Nothing! Whatever was jamming us before, it's down now."

Snake sat on the rock beside him. "Show me the dam site. That truck was headed there for a reason."

"Coming up," Kronk said, feeding the GPS coordinates for the Peace Dam into the Shikaka. They watched as it panned its cameras across the landscape, moving into position to give them a clear view of the dam area.

A blinking blue dot appeared on the screen, overlaid on the vision of the terrain. "What's that?" Snake asked.

"That's us," Kronk said. "So the dam must be …" He manually adjusted the view, moving it downriver as it widened into a large lake backed up behind a huge curved concrete wall.

At the base of the wall was a spillway, leading south to …

Carnage.

"Hold there, by that helipad, is that a downed *chopper*?"

A thin pillar of dirty smoke was rising from a wreck of some sort. Kronk zoomed in. "Rotor blades, there. Chopper for sure."

Bodies littered the grass around it, and as though following a line of breadcrumbs, Kronk panned the camera from body to body, across a carpark that held a few vehicles, some of them military, until it came to a small building where …

An active firefight was raging.

"Not sure what we are looking at," Snake said in frustration, finger pointing at the screen. "Here, North Koreans, dark green uniforms, right? But over here, South Korean, grey green camo uniforms. And they're *all* firing at someone in the building."

Kronk scratched his head. "So who the hell's side are *we* on?"

Snake grabbed the control unit's mic, dialing in the AWACS. "Uh, Hammerhead, this is Envy. We are in position above the Peace Dam. Got eyes on multiple combatants down by what looks like a cafeteria or souvenir shop. We're seeing a large number of dead or wounded, looks like a chopper has been downed. Sending you vision…"

Kronk had quickly edited together a five-minute package of vision from the Shikaka and they squirted it through to the AWACS to review.

"Hammerhead, we have a mix of troops down there. Look like North Korean and South Korean army in regular uniforms, working together to attack a third force inside the small building. It's a regular jamboree."

The controller on the AWACS replied straight away. "We copy, Envy. Relaying your video feed to Joint Forces Command for review and action. Stand by."

"Yeah, uh, Hammerhead. We have eight Locusts we can send downrange, but we need someone to tell who is who in that zoo."

"Hammerhead copies. Out."

Snake went to work, drawing boxes around groups of soldiers and potential vehicle targets on the screen. He gave each an alphanumeric marker and a hotkey so that he could quickly allocate ordnance to each target, if needed.

"This isn't the sort of fight we can adjudicate from 70,000

feet," Kronk said. "I hope whoever the good guys are down there, they called for the cavalry."

The North Korean Supreme Guards unit protecting both State Leaders at the Peace Dam had not been able to call for the cavalry due to Goh's LMADIS jamming their communications. And their Commander, Ri, also knew that despite his Supreme Leader's confidence of the contrary, the cavalry - air cavalry to be precise - was *not* coming.

The presence of the two State leaders at the Peace Dam site had been a closely held secret, known only to the commanders of their protection teams, Ri and Goh. Even their own superiors had been kept out of the loop due to the vulnerability of both leaders being in the same place at the same time at what was probably the most critical point in their respective nations' recent histories.

Ri knew that as soon as their headquarters' lost contact with the protection details at the Peace Dam, both sides armies would have issued orders for rapid response airborne forces to be readied to rescue them. But they would not know where to dispatch them.

Inside the visitor center, he slapped his second in command, Lieutenant Yun, on the back. "You know what you need to do. Get in, make the call, get out again before you are seen. We will hold up here as long as we can."

The young officer nodded. As their men exchanged fire with the attackers, they moved up beside the windows, to the right of the LTV that was jammed across the visitor center's sliding doors.

As Ri's marksman opened fire on the LMADIS and his guardsmen at the windows laid down a hail of covering fire, Yun ran for the open door of the LTV and threw himself inside.

The South Korean vehicle was unfamiliar to him, but a radio was a radio. It had been useless before, but if his man on the roof had succeeded in knocking out the South Korean jammer, he might just be able to …

Lying flat across the front bench-seat he punched the button that brought the radio set to life and tuned it to the international search and rescue coordination frequency, then pulled the radio handset from its cradle.

The vehicle began to rock with automatic rifle fire, but its heavy armor plating protected him, for now.

"To all North and South Korean forces operating in the central DMZ area, this is Lieutenant Jon Yun, North Korean Supreme Guards Command inside the Peace Dam visitor center. We are under attack by a hostile force. Urgent assistance requested!" He ducked as the weight of fire on the windshield of the armored car caused it to spiderweb. A few seconds more and it would be buckling over his head. He repeated his message. "To all North and South Korean forces operating in the central DMZ area…"

Then he heard the crump of a grenade overhead as his man on the roof came under indirect fire from the troops outside. *Not good.* It would only be seconds now before Goh got another man behind that 20mm autocannon. Yun made his broadcast twice more, then sure enough, the front of the LTV shuddered from a welter of 20mm cannon fire and the glass over his head exploded. Hands over his head, he waited for the fusillade of fire to ease so he could crawl back out of the LTV, when *a rocket propelled grenade* exploded underneath the chassis and flipped the LTV on its side.

Special Agent Helen Lee would also have put out a call for the cavalry if she could. You didn't put down plastic ground sheets, shoot a girl in the leg and pistol whip her and then say, "So sorry for the inconvenience, you can return to duty now."

Yeo had left Moon to interrogate her some more, and if possible, he had been even less gentle than Yeo. She told Moon nothing that Yeo probably hadn't already guessed, but Moon had left her alone to report back to Yeo anyway.

Her hands were zip-tied behind her back and her ankles

were duct taped to the legs of the chair. The ties felt heavy duty, but not law-enforcement heavy. She suspected the agents who had tied her up had had to improvise. She hadn't been able to use any tricks when being bound because she'd been out cold. The ties were tight and she couldn't reach them with her teeth to tighten them further. Ironically, tightening the plastic ties would make them easier to break, but she would have to work with them as they were.

She tried to stand, her thigh screaming in protest. It felt like the bullet had hit a bone and stopped without shattering it. She was bleeding, but not in danger of bleeding out. OK, she could take weight on the leg.

She took a couple of deep breaths. It was funny, the whole morning it had felt like she was reacting to events. Now, when she was probably at rock bottom, it finally felt like she was taking charge. She looked around the room to see if there was anything within reach she could use to cut the ties at her wrists but apart from the chair and a simple desk with no drawers behind her, there was nothing.

To bind her ankles, her captors had put her feet behind the chair leg and taped her shins to the chair legs. The tape was wound on too thick for her to be able to flex it and free her feet. Her only choice was to get on her back and try to flip the chair, jerking it hard to try to break the tape, if her protesting thigh would even cooperate. But there was no way to do that without making noise.

If there was a guard outside, she'd be lying on her back on the floor tangled up in chair and tape and waiting to be shot again.

What choice did she have?

Tipping the chair sideways, she fell heavily to the floor, the side of her head striking the plastic covered carpet with a painful but quiet *thud*. When the spots in her vision stopped swirling she rolled onto her back, pushed herself up the back of the chair, and with her right thigh feeling like it was going to rip in two, she lifted her legs as high in the air as she could, the chair rising with them. She managed to lift them until the back of the chair came free from under her back and was pointed at the floor at an angle that would give her some leverage.

Squinting her eyes shut against the pain, and with all the force she could muster, she slammed the chair into the floor.

The next few seconds unfolded like a poorly choreographed modern ballet. Her left leg, the good one, snapped through the duct tape and came free. The right leg stayed bound. She tried to get to her feet, rolling onto her stomach and only getting more tangled in the chair until she got a knee under her and hopped up onto one leg.

As she did so, an agent who must have been posted at her door burst into the room, pistol drawn. Lee panicked. She reflexively kicked out at him with the leg that was still bound to the chair, screaming as it felt like her thigh tore in two. But the violent movement snapped the duct tape on that leg too and sent the chair flying into the man's face, knocking him back against the wall. With a half leap, half stumble, she reached him as he was trying to push himself off the wall and landed a sickening head butt on his nose.

He went down like a bag of sawdust.

She collapsed onto the floor, unable to move, waiting for him to get up and kick the stuffing out of her, but he lay completely still. Dead? No, she could hear him breathing. She rolled onto her side and wiggled over to him, trying to feel his trouser pockets. She came up with a thin wallet, and his service ID. What she wanted was keys, something he could cut the ties on her wrists with. But who the hell carried keys anymore? *Ah, but wait, she recognized the agent, remembered a bragging conversation in a locker room several weeks earlier.* Kicking her legs to move awkwardly lower on the guard's torso, she felt along the man's shins.

Uh huh. Lifting the man's suit trouser leg, he found a sheath with a short-bladed ceramic knife in it.

The knife sliced through the restraints on her wrists with ease and Lee stood awkwardly, then stooped over and picked up the guy's pistol. All right, she could stand. She checked the weapon. Standard Beretta M9. Good. She checked that there was a round in the chamber and the magazine was loaded. Tried to take a step and stumbled. Her right thigh was completely frozen, soaked in blood, the muscle refusing to do its job lifting her leg. *Not exactly ninja, Special Agent Lee.* She was going to be moving like she was dragging a lump of wood. But she had to keep moving. Someone would be coming to check soon why the guy on the door wasn't there.

She moved to the door, eased it open a crack and looked out. A corridor, windows to the outside. Tried to remember the layout of this end of the floor.

Fire stairs to the right or left? Left. Wasn't it? Her eyes were too bruised and her vision too blurred to be able to read the signs over the doorways at each end of the corridor. She shoved the knife into her belt, opened the door wider, dragged herself to the doorway and got ready to take a step out.

Sergeant Hye Song had leapt from the cab of her vehicle, pistol in hand and dropped to the ground to look underneath it for the escaped South Korean corporal.

She saw nothing but dark, empty space under the truck's chassis.

Rising to a crouch, she surveyed the ground around the truck. She had stopped about fifty yards onto the causeway. He could not have run behind her or she would have seen him. And he could not have run ahead, across the causeway, because that way …

As she looked toward the visitor center, she'd seen an RPG spear out from the attackers' lines and slam into the ground under the LTV parked across the entrance to the visitor center and flip it into the air.

That way lay certain death.

Which meant her prisoner could only have dropped off the side of the causeway and into the water. Moving cautiously to the causeway railing, she looked over the side. The water from the spillway was flowing strongly. Swimming against it would have been hard work, so he had probably floated downstream, to either the east or west bank of the outflow from the dam. The banks of the outflow were lined with concrete and squinting her eyes, she thought she could see, about a hundred yards downstream, a thin trail of water on the concrete on the same side of the outflow as the firefight at the visitor center. Low bushes and scrub between the water and the building would have offered her fugitive cover.

He is gone, Song, she told herself, looking at the sky overhead, which had stopped raining kamikaze drones. *And you don't need him anymore.*

The RPG attack also appeared to end the battle across the causeway. Outgoing and incoming fire was dying away. Leaving the truck where it was, pistol in hand, she began running toward the visitor center.

Inside the visitor center, Captain Jeong Goh of South Korea's Presidential Security Service and commander of the combined force at the Peace Dam was also standing at a doorway. Glaring at it, to be accurate, as though pure irritation could burn through half inch steel.

The battle for the visitor center had been resolved quickly once the armored car in the doorway had been dealt with. The explosion of the RPG round and the death of the officer inside it had been enough to break the nerve of the defenders and they had retreated to the visitor center 'stronghold', under the illusion that the double steel doors at each end of the stairwell down to the basement would give them some measure of protection.

Goh had looked through the windscreen of the LTV at the broken and bloodied body of Lieutenant Yun and shaken his head. The young man had been painfully earnest and blindly loyal, but Goh had not wished him harm. He'd been genuine in his offer to trade the protectees for the safety of Ri and his men. And now he had fallen, for what? Trying to protect the life of a woman who was the architect of her nation's doom? If anyone was responsible for the dead bodies littering the visitor center now, it was the stubborn North Korean commander.

Now Goh regarded the door down to the stronghold with workman-like appraisal. He had hoped that the protectees could be secured before they could retreat to the stronghold, or be persuaded to surrender, but Ri's counter-attack was just a delay, not a defeat.

Goh had been part of planning the day's operation, so he had also been part of ensuring that neither the steel door at the top, nor the one at the bottom of the stairwell, would stop them. And he had brought with him the equipment needed to deal with them.

A man at his feet was drilling through the door with an electric drill. When he had made a hole the size of a dime, he placed a cone-shaped suction cup over it, attached to a hose, connected in turn to a large gas cylinder. When the man was satisfied with the connection, he stepped back and pulled up a light gas mask, indicating that the others in the visitor center should do the same. It was just a precaution – the gas was not deadly, but the steel door was not airtight, so it was best to be safe.

The cylinder held a gaseous form of the common anesthetic Propofol, used around the world in emergency departments and operation rooms to sedate surgery patients. Goh's medical officer had tested the gas on two volunteers from his own unit, in a complex of similar size to the basement below. They had been incapacitated by the gas inside five minutes, showing signs of dizziness, lack of coordination, slurred speech and loss of balance. The first man lost consciousness at eight minutes, the other at ten. It was rarely used by counterterrorism forces, though, because it could induce nausea and vomiting which might cause choking, if you didn't or couldn't move quickly.

But high-stakes challenges sometimes called for high-risk responses. And every man on Goh's team knew what his priorities were once they got inside the stronghold: kill anyone resisting, secure the protectees, and place them in a recovery position for their medic to treat.

Goh signaled to the man by the gas cylinder to open the

valve and start pouring gas inside. It would quickly fill the small space below. Even if the soldiers below locked and bolted the second door, it would seep under, around and through the cracks. The effect of the gas could have been nullified by the troops below pulling on their own gas masks ... but Goh had made sure during planning that they would not have that option.

Ri heard the noise of the high-speed drill before the shout from the corridor outside reached him. "Commander! Activity at the stairs!"

The attackers above were doing nothing to hide their actions, the drill was both audible and visible to Ri as he looked around the corner and up the stairs using a mirror.

"They are drilling a camera hole," he told the men assembled there, stepping back. "Shut and bolt this door. Show them nothing but darkness. Take positions in cover and prepare for them to breach. They will blow the top door with a shaped charge and probably use grenades on the lower door. Be ready."

He walked several steps down the corridor to the room in which the South Korean President was being held. He had not shouted either abuse or pleas for help for some time now. Ri told the agent at the door to join the men holding the corridor.

Stepping into the room he saw President Si-min Shin, sitting on a chair beside a small table, glass of water in his hand. He gave Ri a baleful stare. "And what indignity will you force on me now?"

Ri bowed. Slightly. "Mr. President, the hostile force is about to try to enter this basement. I respectfully ask you to accompany me to join Madam Kim, so we can ensure your survival."

"Ensure my survival?!" the man scoffed. "Protect me from my own troops? I would rather take my chances with the men you call your enemy!"

Ri held the door open for him. "The men upstairs are both

North and South Korean, Mr. President. You have no allies upstairs, and I cannot guarantee they would not kill you if we simply surrendered. With respect, your best chance of survival is with us."

"I demand to negotiate with the attackers!" Shin demanded. "I can't believe they want me dead. I would be much more valuable alive."

Ri could no longer contain his ire. He stepped forward, grabbed the man by the arm and shoved him roughly toward the door, then propelled him down the corridor with a hand in his back. "You may not believe anyone would want to kill you, Mr. President, but I can."

As he reached the room at the end of the corridor he pushed the man inside ... and then stopped. A sickly sweet smell permeated the air; like the odor of a marker pen?

"Gas!" he yelled. "They are flooding the basement with gas!" A sick feeling rose in his gut, and not because of the smell, but because of a remembered conversation with the South Korean, Goh, during scenario planning. "Should we take NBC suits?" Ri had asked. "In case of a chemical attack?"

Goh had scoffed. "We are going to be at the Peace Dam site for less than an hour, total. The only people who know about the site at this point are in this room. You seriously think anyone could plan or deliver a nuclear, biological or chemical warfare attack on that site in the tiny window of time we will give them?"

Ri had stiffened, taking offense at the man's tone, but staying polite. "For the protectees then. One suit each. I insist."

Goh had waved a hand at him and looked away, as though the conversation was tedious. "For the protectees. If you insist. But US-made MOPP suits, not Russian, Chinese and definitely not North Korean."

The insult had been only one of many, with Ri and Yun counting small victories when they won them. The suits for the protectees had been stored in ... *where?* In the ...

Ri recognized his brain was beginning to fog. Toxic nerve gas? Wouldn't nerve gas work differently? Quicker? He leaned against the door into the TV studio room and saw shocked faces looking back at him. *What was he doing again?* MOPP suits. Yes. Box under the desk. He zombie-walked to the desk and pulled out the box, lifted out one of the heavy MOPP suits and dumped it on the desk. "This, put it…"

The South Korean President moved first, grabbing the suit off the table, tearing the suit's plastic bag open and pulling it out. Ri tried pulling the second suit out but another soldier was beside him and took it from him, handing it to Madam Kim.

He suddenly realized he was lying on the cool floor, watching as she removed her jacket and shoes and stepped into the suit, awkwardly trying to pull it up over her waist, the soldier beside her too afraid to touch her to help. An overwhelming sadness filled him. He had failed again. A list of failures. A litany. A flood.

He felt a gray wave wash over him and then recede. If this was death, he deserved it. No, he *welcomed* it.

Goh looked at his watch and then at his entry team, in cover, well back from the steel door. They had already placed explosive on the door and were ready to breach. Propofol gas was not flammable – they'd tested that as well.

Goh checked comms one last time, checked his watch and then gave the 'go' signal. He turned his back. There was a sharp report and then shouting as the breach team moved to the door, ready to ram it open if needed, but it had blown into the stairwell and they were already moving down. There was no return fire coming at them from the doorway below; the door was still locked, and a second shaped charge was placed on it. The team retreated to the top of the stairs and Goh turned his back again as the second charge blew.

More shouting, the breach team barreling down the stairs, flash bang grenades now, thrown around the corner into the corridor beyond. Each man had memorized exactly the layout of the basement and as they stepped inside, each had a dedicated role to perform.

Goh waited upstairs. He heard the cough of a suppressed weapon at least once, a report of a target down, which made him frown. They were not out to slaughter the defenders wholesale. He wanted the protectees *alive*, and that meant the less shooting the better. Then he started hearing the reports he was waiting to hear, as his team declared room after room quickly 'clear'.

"Captain Goh, Entry Team leader, basement is secure. Protectees are in our care."

In our care. They'd agreed on that phrase, in case the record of the operation was ever reviewed. Goh wanted his every word and action to indicate that his only intention, throughout every moment of the day's action, had been to secure the safety of his President.

With ill-concealed alacrity, he took the stairs down two at a time and entered the basement. One dead North Korean agent at the bottom of the stairwell. Another in a doorway. Several more in side rooms, unconscious or dazed, being rolled onto their sides so they didn't choke, while they were disarmed and their hands and legs were plasticuffed.

He walked quickly toward the makeshift TV studio.

The stubborn fool, Ri, was lying under a desk. Dismissively, Goh rolled him onto his side with the toe of his boot so that the man wouldn't choke on his own tongue. One of Goh's men ripped the hood off a MOPP-suited figure and the room filled with the smell of vomit.

"Medic! He's choking!" his man called out urgently and a medic came from behind Goh and started clearing the airway of the MOPP-suited South Korean President. Goh had half a mind to order him to let the man suffocate on his own vomit, but as tempting as that might be, his orders were to secure the South Korean President for trial later. For treason. Every political assassination needed a patsy, especially when it was a Peace Agreement that was being killed off.

The second MOPP-suited figure was slumped on the desk, hand around a pistol. He raised his eyebrows. So, Madam Kim had planned to go out fighting? Once again, his North Korean cousins impressed him.

Her head covering was torn off and the only smell this time was perfume and cigarettes.

"Remove it completely," he said.

He was not surprised the MOPP suits had not protected their wearers. After all, he had ensured their air filters were disabled.

When she was freed of the suit and laid on the floor, she looked like someone recently deceased being prepared for burial. Her skin was pale, her breathing shallow.

Goh knelt beside her, searching her pockets, and then found what he was looking for. The small thumb-drive-sized device that would send the nuclear launch order and authorization codes.

Turning it on, he wet her thumb by wiping it across her lip and applied it to the DNA reader on the base of the device. The display window beeped to life, ready for her to input her pass-phrase by voice. But the pass-phrase was held in only one place. In the head of the woman on the floor.

Goh weighed the small device in the palm of his hand. So tiny, so powerful and, right now, so useless. But it would not remain so.

Gesturing to a man hovering in the doorway to come forward, he held up the launch trigger. The laptop in the man's hand contained the software 'back door' their North Korean co-conspirators had provided to them to unlock the launch codes. The man took the device and connected it to his computer then ran the back door code which inserted a new passphrase. With a disappointingly anonymous *beep*, the code finished running. Satisfied, the man handed the laptop to Goh.

Leaving the device connected to the laptop, Goh opened a communication link. Who or what was at the other end of the link, he had no idea, and did not need to know. He hit a key to upload the launch codes. *Sequence uplinked*, the communication app reported.

Now he had only to radio his collaborators in the North and arrange an evacuation. A magnificent calm descended over

Goh.

He had accomplished his mission! All other objectives today were secondary. Securing the two protectees and the nuclear button device, extracting himself and his men, loading the dead, wounded or hogtied combatants into helicopter transports for removal to the North, even the very question of whether he lived or died ... none of these mattered now.

He had played his part in restoring sanity and order to the world and if he died today, he would happily take that thought to the grave.

Captain Se-heon Dokgo, Korean People's Navy Submarine Force, had also woken the previous night, prepared for the coming day to be his last.

And it had nearly ended before it had even begun. Ringed by the sonar from hostile ships and aircraft, he had sent his *Gorae* spiraling toward the bottom of the Yellow Sea.

Not a man in the command center had said a word, even as the hull creaked and they approached their do-not-exceed depth. But they were a magnificent bloody crew, and the *Gorae* was a magnificent bloody boat. Had they not just proven it, slipping out from under the sonar net the enemy had thrown over their heads?

They were still searching, he could hear that. Both north and northeast of him. Which made Se-heon smile, because he had shown why his Fatherland trusted him with its most potent weapon, not trying to head away from the last known position of the American ship's sonar, but toward it.

The Americans would never expect such a bold move, especially from a rule-bound North Korean strategic submarine Captain whose primary duty was usually to preserve the strike capability of his submarine and avoid unnecessary risk at all costs.

Usually. But not today.

The second communication window was about to open and he was about to take the second big risk of this patrol, bringing his boat to communication depth again. He gave the orders.

"Communication depth. On course two-zero-zero, speed ahead slow. Sonar plot unchanged, no new contacts," Dokgo's XO announced a short time later.

"Ahead slow. Raise satellite antenna," Se-heon ordered.

The *Gorae* did not have the ability to communicate with shore by launching a buoy on a tether from safer depths. It had to get its antenna to within twenty feet of the surface, which was in any case their launch depth, so receiving an order and being in position to launch went hand in hand.

He watched the face of his comms officer as the man opened a channel. Not to Fleet Command, but to the dedicated frequency they had been given for this patrol only.

The man's face changed instantly. He placed a hand against the bulkhead to steady himself. "Comrade Captain! Data package received, sending to your console." He turned, shock on his face and pupils wide. "We have launch authorization!"

Dokgo's heart raced, but he tried to show outward calm. Turning to his console he read the message.

>*Attack order is confirmed. Run sequence to arm warheads.*

A simple key combination on his console interrogated the code that had just been downloaded. If a nuclear attack had been authorized, the code would arm the warheads. If not, he would still carry out the attack as ordered, but the nuclear warheads would not arm and the missiles would only deliver kinetic energy toward the destruction of the target.

>*Code valid. Nuclear launch authorized. Target coordinates follow. Confirm target Y/N.*

Dokgo read the longitude and latitude and compared them to his mission orders. Sangeo Shoal.

Trying to steady his hand so the crew would not see it shaking, he hit a single key. "Y."

>*Target confirmed. Missiles armed, prelaunch initiated.*

Above their heads, a metallic rumble and the sound of rushing water suddenly filled the silence of the control room. Their two nuclear ballistic missiles were stored upright in the conning tower or 'sail' of the *Gorae*, and right now the launch tube covers were opening to admit seawater for pressurization. Gripping his console in both hands, Dokgo looked straight ahead. "Officer of the deck, dive to missile launch depth, prepare to hover. Call to battle stations ... missile." He took a deep breath. "This is not a drill."

Protocol demanded his executive officer repeat the launch readiness order. He did so without hesitation. Supreme Leader Kim would have expected nothing less.

"Sonar on the *Sea Hunter* reports transient noises!" one of the *Cody*'s watch officers reported to Lomax. "Contact. Bearing 350 degrees, range nine. Designating Sierra two."

"Order *Sea Hunter* to active sonar search," Lomax said. Nine miles out. That contact from before had not run away from them, it had run toward them? They had landed and reloaded their Defiant helo and it was currently part of the search effort nearly twenty miles north. "Report the contact to *Bougainville*. Order air ops to bring our Defiant back, lock that contact and prepare to drop on it," he said.

"Missile launch!" the watch officer called out. "Position Sierra two Multiples! Sonar classification ... ballistic. Radar confirms. Ballistic missile launches, tracking west-southwest."

Mother. Of. God.

"Captain, comms, flash message to *Bougainville*. Ballistic missile launch detected. Send them the radar data." Lomax stepped forward, looking ahead of the *Cody*. Rising from the sea nine miles away he saw two white contrails. They appeared to rise almost vertically, then began extending toward him, thousands of feet overhead. In a moment they had risen out of view.

Cody could find and try to kill the boat that had fired them, but about the missiles he could do nothing except watch their thick contrails dissipate in the breeze.

Seconds had flashed past, and still Keys Ban was alive. He'd pushed his machine down until its belly was scraping the water of the narrow river. Flown under the curtain of flak, fragments of white hot metal peppering his canopy and fuselage.

Last and sharpest turn. *Five more seconds, Keys.* He flicked a switch on his flight stick to arm his 5,000 lb. GBU-28 'bunker buster' bomb. There was no time to lase the target to help aim the bomb, he had to toss it in GPS-guided mode and let it aim itself at the entrance to the bunker.

The last three times Keys had flown the simulation of this attack, he'd gotten only one strike on target, and that had been the best result in the entire South Korea AF 11th fighter wing. But his best simulation run had been his last, so Keys figured he had momentum on his side, right?

Now. Rounding the last bend in the river before the facility, he chopped his throttle back, rolled his machine onto a wingtip, hauled it into a tight left-hand turn and then rolled level before pointing his nose 20 degrees into the sky and hitting the bomb release trigger.

His speed bled away, the bomb coming off the hardpoint on his centerline and curving down toward the bunker entrance.

Keys couldn't see if it was on target, he was already slamming his throttle forward again, trying to drop his nose and gain airspeed when…

…when the curtain of flak caught him and violently shredded Keys Ban and the photograph on his instrument panel into a thousand tumbling pieces.

The 5,000 lb. GBU-28 bunker buster didn't need Keys Ban to stay alive for it to steer on its target. Locked onto the GPS coordinates for the bunker entrance, released by Keys from the right approach angle and altitude, the heavy bomb lobbed into the air and fell right into the mouth of the 40-foot-wide entrance to the nuclear bunker. Its hard-target-penetrating warhead smashed through the heavy concrete and iron thermobaric blast-proof doors and buried itself twenty feet under the rock and earth inside the entrance to the bunker, right between the rail tracks that were used to move the heavy weapons in and out of the bunker.

Then it detonated.

To those working inside and around the bunker, it felt like one of their nuclear weapons had accidentally detonated. The ground shook for several seconds – first with the force of the explosion, and then with the violence of the tunnel collapse that followed. Inside five minutes, the main entrance to North Korea's nuclear storage facility had been sealed behind a hundred feet of fallen rock, leaving the smaller emergency personnel exit to the south as the only way in or out of the facility.

The North Korean Sub-Launched Ballistic Missiles headed for Sangeo Shoal were armed with two nuclear weapons, and utilized Russian-designed multiple re-entry vehicle warheads to defeat anti-missile systems.

As they began curving down from the edge of the stratosphere they aimed themselves at the center of the island below, not much larger than a city block, with a small port at which the task force had moored.

It was no longer there.

USS Bougainville with its 65 officers and 994 enlisted sailors had been the last to leave as it had been launching aircraft on their anti-submarine mission against the *Gorae*. It was currently ten miles south-southwest of the small island. The other ships in the task force – the South Korean amphibious assault ship *ROKS Marado*, and US expeditionary fast transport (EPF) ship the *USS Point Loma* – had already moved out to sea and were maneuvering into position around the *Bougainville* for the passage south.

The only ship still moored at Sangeo Shoal was North Korea's newest and most advanced warship, the low-profile stealth corvette, *KPN Nampo*. Interred at the outbreak of hostilities by their soon-to-be US and South Korean 'allies', its indignant officers had been returned to their ship just before

Bougainville had weighed anchor. Their priority on getting back aboard their ship had been to get a better idea of the military-political situation across the DMZ, and clear orders about how they were expected to respond. Only now were they preparing to get their ship underway. Aboard the *Nampo* were 12 officers and 80 crew.

Although warned of the incoming missiles by *Cody*, and though *Bougainville* picked them up almost immediately on radar, none of the ships in the task force had high-altitude missile interception capabilities. Having calculated that the target of the attack was Sangeo Shoal, where the North Korean ship was still moored, all they could do was warn the *Nampo* and wait for the missiles to get within interception range of their medium- and short-range anti-air defenses.

By which time the North Korean missiles would be traveling at nearly *20 times* the speed of sound.

As they arrowed down toward Sangeo Shoal, the two missiles deliberately broke apart, each separating into four separate warheads. The release of the multiple re-entry vehicles caused one of the missiles to become unstable and it scattered its re-entry vehicles wildly. They continued toward the earth, but would strike nowhere near their target. The other four released smoothly and held their pattern. Three were dummy kinetic warheads, only one was nuclear.

Against these, the *Bougainville* got four Sea-Sparrow medium-range and twelve short-range Sea-RAM missiles away. Surprisingly, the South Korean landing ship *Marado* also got two short-range missiles off. The rest of the task force was defenseless.

Their efforts were wasted. The defensive missiles had barely lit their boosters before the first kinetic warheads from the North Korean missiles struck the Shoal and the sea around it. Each of the non-nuclear warheads hit with the force of 50 tons of TNT, sending mountains of earth and seawater into the air and shockwaves across a ten-mile area because of the four warheads that had run wild.

Nampo was rocked by the shockwave and then pummeled by

high waves, but none of the kinetic warheads scored a hit on or near it.

Milliseconds behind the dummy warheads though, and 3,000 feet over the sea, the two 25-kiloton yield nuclear warheads detonated. One of them did little more than vaporize seawater five miles north of the Shoal and send another series of huge waves toward it. The warhead that had fallen 'on target' exploded right over the middle of the small island.

The *KPN Nampo* was right underneath the fireball. Mercifully, the overpressure killed every single person in the blast radius instantly, before they were incinerated.

Exploding out in the Sea of Japan, a hundred miles from the South Korean coast, the first witnesses to the mushroom clouds climbing into the sky were startled birds, a few Japanese and Korean fishing trawlers, the helos hunting the North Korean submarine … and the shocked crews of the ships of Operation White Glove.

Their shock only lasted as long as it took for klaxons to start sounding across their decks and they began running to their action stations, as *tsunami-sized* waves appeared on the horizon behind them.

What had started as a battle against the odds was going just slightly better than expected for Bunny and Noname.

Fixated on the target they could see – the Ghost Bat that had just launched two medium-range Peregrine missiles at their flight leader, the Migs engaged it with missiles. No fewer than four! They were taking no chances. Noname could have been the best silicon drone pilot on the planet, it would have made no difference. His Ghost Bat was doomed.

But it had done its job. The Mig formation did not see the longer-range AIM-260 missiles which were almost invisible, taking their targeting from the Ghost Bat, and not even using their own onboard radars. Until about ten seconds out from their targets, when their radars went active, they locked onto the two Mig-29 wide wingmen and slammed into them at Mach

3.

Splash two.

Having gone from odds of two versus one to two versus a still invisible foe, the remaining Mig-29s over Yongdoktong must have assumed they were fighting a Korean stealth fighter, not its poor cousin the Kingsnake - they dived for the safety of the earth and fled northeast into central North Korea.

Bunny breathed a sigh of relief, shut down her radar and let them go. Events below her would have resolved themselves by now anyway. Either the South Korean Colonel had hit his target, or he hadn't. He was dead, or he was alive. She had lost two drones in air combat and two to ground fire. There was nothing more Bunny and Noname could do for him.

They were down below the height of the highest mountain peaks now, which were half hidden in afternoon shadows. "Time to go home, Noname."

"We're not going to make it home without refueling," her WSO said. "Ten seconds of afterburner was enough to eliminate any buffer in the fuel reserve."

"All right," Bunny thought fast. "Plot us a course to that Stingray refueling drone over…"

An alarm sounded in her helmet. One Bunny had never, *ever* thought she would hear outside of exercises. A blaring klaxon followed by two short, high-pitched tones.

Her eyes dropped to the multifunction display in front of her knees, flashing orange text in the middle of the screen.

DEFCON 1 conditions apply. Theater-wide US forces alert. All allied units and personnel contact your home base for orders. The message repeated.

DEFCON 1: nuclear war is imminent or has already begun. Not even during the Iran–Israel crisis of several years earlier had a condition of DEFCON 1 been applied. Could it be a system error, some sort of comms glitch? She killed the screen, resetting it quickly. When it restarted, the same message appeared, with the same urgency.

Noname defaulted to a formal, passive mode in the face of unexpected situations they hadn't discussed in their pre-flight briefing. And this was definitely one of those situations. "Orders, ma'am?" he asked.

She gave him some 'make-work'. "Find me the nearest available Stingray to refuel from before we fall out of the sky, and get us priority in the queue."

She scanned the sky around her, over her shoulder, checked her optical and infrared sensors for any nearby contacts and pulled up her tactical display. She refreshed it with data from nearby AWACS and ground radars inside South Korea and saw a profusion of contacts – aircraft across the north and south of the Peninsula and inside China were being launched en masse. Zooming the screen out, she saw aircraft being launched from a Chinese carrier in the South China Sea and, west of the Peninsula, in the Sea of Japan, the same thing from a US carrier off the Japanese coast.

Caution? *Or World War bloody Three?*

She could not contact Osan because her operations order required radio silence. As she blasted over the top of a small North Korean port, leaving shocked navy ratings gawking up at her and the local S-200 anti-air radar battalion trying to figure out where she had come from, O'Hare decided the threat environment overrode her operations order.

"I found us a Stingray," Noname said. "Laying in a waypoint."

She checked her nav screen, then keyed her radio. "Osan control, this is Buddy Wing 35-7 unit Swan two, going feet wet west of … uh, Cholsan, inbound Stingray Tanker Whisky Oscar Four Two at Grid Alpha Alpha Niner west Incheon, ETA 1647. Responding to theater-wide alert, request new orders, Osan."

A burst of static came back to her, then went away again, indicating someone had opened a channel, then changed away again. If there had been a nuclear exchange, she could only imagine the chaos back at the US base. Another burst of static and a voice came over the radio. "Swan two, updated orders. Refuel, then RTB Osan. You should expect to be assigned to a new patrol immediately your aircraft is rearmed. Understood?"

"Good copy, Osan control, Swan two proceeding for refueling, moving to rejoin 65 Squadron Aggressors at Osan Air Base. Out." She switched back to aircraft comms. "Get us to Osan after we tank up, Noname."

"Plugging it in now," he said.

Bunny let him do his navigator thing, thinking furiously as she flew their Kingsnake at wavetop level away from the North Korean coast, and kept her eye on the threat environment around them.

Nukes used or being readied? Whoa. And she was being asked to land just south of the capital of South Korea, an absolutely guaranteed nuclear target.

So far today she'd lost the helo she'd been escorting, then her wingman, Snake, sacrificed a brace of Ghost Bats on a suicide mission, and now the theater had gone *Defcon One*.

Her bad feeling about today had just gotten radically worse.

Defense Readiness Condition One

Prime Minister's Offices, Sejong City

Special Agent Lee had not thanked Commander Pak for the assignment he had given her. No officer likes being asked to inform on her colleagues. And as she prepared to swing open the door and step out into the corridor, she was quietly rehearsing the profanities she would use if she ever saw Pak again.

OK, Lee, get out into that corridor, find the fire exit and get the hell out of here. Good to go?

Hell no. She pulled back the hammer on the Beretta. Got a good grip. Humped her still uncooperative leg into position, ready to drag it into the corridor. Pulled the door open…

And stepped out. *Agent.* Coming through the door at the far end of the corridor, looking right at her. Not Yeo. Hands crossed in front of him, reaching into his jacket now. *Fire!* Hit. Center mass. The agent fell back against the door behind him, still reaching for his gun. Aim. *Fire!* Second bullet into the guy's chest, dropping him to the ground. *Move!*

Gun held on the door at the end, ready in case anyone came out of the five or six doors along the corridor, Lee looked behind her. Fire escape. *Go!* She backed toward the door, dragging her leg as she went.

Door opening at the end of the corridor again. Lee tensed, but it was blocked by the man she'd shot, lying against it. Someone trying to shove him out of the way.

Lee felt her back hit the fire escape door, pushed the bar to open it and … it gave. She backed through, someone at the other end of the corridor still struggling to push that door open. She looked with dismay at ten sets of steps, leading to the next floor. Any other situation, she'd be taking a few stairs at a time, vaulting the railing to the next landing and repeating it until she hit ground level.

With a dead leg, she would have to move smart, not fast.

Best she could, she hopped down the first two sets of steps to the floor below, the last of the Prime Ministerial levels. She heard voices in the corridor above, arguing; probably about whether she was waiting on the other side to shoot their asses.

As she eased herself through the door into the next floor, she heard the door above crash open, and more shouting.

She moved right, along the wall, to a row of cubicles and then crouched, humping along it toward the other side of the building where there should be another set of fire stairs.

Then froze.

The door from the landing banged open and there was silence. Whoever was there, was standing quietly, looking and listening for movement. Lee held her breath. The door closed again, loudly. Lee held her position. After two minutes, the door opened and closed again as the person there gave up waiting and went back out into the fire stairs.

Lee started moving again. Through cubicles, across a café area, past some meeting rooms, until she hit the other side of the building and saw what she was looking for. *Emergency Exit.* She hobbled over to it and put her hand on the bar to push it open.

And hesitated.

You go now, you miss your only chance to stop this before it starts, a voice said. Her own. She tried her leg again. When in trauma, muscles contract and force blood away from the site of the blow or wound, leading to paralysis of the muscle. The paralysis was wearing off now, the movement of the last few minutes having restored some blood flow. So more blood was seeping into her trousers, and a deep, throbbing pain filled the area around the wound. *You need help, fool,* the voice said. *Get out of this building, get treated, Call Pak so he can send in police. Stop it that way.*

Yeah, Lee, and who is going to believe a single clearly deranged agent and a meddling old man?

She groaned. Sitting down against the wall, pistol on the ground beside her, she worked her trousers off and down around her knees. Reaching around behind her she got a hold of her shirt tail and ripped it off, then tore a couple of smaller pieces from it. Blood was pulsing from the entry and exit wounds in her thigh, but only pulsing; not gushing. Picking up the pistol, she jacked a round out. She put the largest piece of her shirt tail between her teeth and bit down, then placed a smaller strip of cloth over the wound on top of her thigh and used the bullet to push it in as far as she could without passing out. She folded the ends over the wound and repeated the process, pushing with the bullet. The irony of that did not escape her.

When she'd packed the wound so that blood stopped leaking from it she lifted her leg and repeated the process. When that was done, she picked up her pistol and ejected the magazine. The bullet she'd used was bloody and wet and she thought about wiping it clean. *No, whoever I shoot next is going to get my blood on them.* She liked the idea of that. Pushed the bullet into the magazine and reinserted it, then racked the slide.

She then began the painful process of pulling her trousers back up and standing. What she'd do after that? She had no idea, yet.

The bud in Snake's ear buzzed and he tapped it. "Envy."

"Envy, Hammerhead. Listen hard. South Korean ground forces intercepted a radio mayday that leads them to believe the North Korean Supreme Leader and the President of South Korea are both being held in the building you are looking at. There has been no communication from them, or their security details, since the attack on Panmunjom this morning."

"Hammerhead, the fighting is over here." Snake said. "Whoever was attacking that location has taken it. All defensive fire has ceased and now we are seeing people moving around outside the building like they are packing up and getting ready to leave."

"Then the two leaders have been taken hostage, or worse."

Snake whistled. "All right, what do you need, Hammerhead?"

"Keep your Shikaka on mission, we need continuous vision of that site and we'll be using your Shikaka as a data hub to coordinate operations. We will be taking your feed in real time from here on in, and you will be assigned a Safety Observer, call sign Slasher. Switching to observer channel now, Hammerhead out."

"What's up?" Kronk asked.

Snake sighed. "Party's over. We're on ISR duty now. Being assigned a Safety Observer. You know what that means?"

"Means we aren't calling our own shots any more, right?"

"Right. They don't need a pilot anymore." As he was about to hand over his earbud a voice came into Snake's ears.

A very pleasant, Down South voice. "Envy, my name is Captain Alison Quartermain, but y'all can call me Slasher. I will be your Safety Observer for today, how you doing?"

Snake smiled. "Well, ma'am, considering I was shot down on fire this morning, half drowned, and the Navy guy who rescued me had been shot down earlier, a *long* way from the ocean, and we just humped fifty pounds of Shikaka transceiver ten miles over mountains and rivers, and now we're looking down on, say, at least a platoon of hostile troops who are hiding under an umbrella of jamming energy and look like they are fixing to pull out again any minute while we sit up here with our thumbs up our asses, we're pretty good. How about you?"

The Air Force Captain had the sense to let Snake vent a little and replied gently. "Easy, Lieutenant. It's that kind of day. But we're here now and we need to work together on this. ROK Army has a special operations planning team on tap looking at your problem as we speak. They've dispatched an armored recon company to your position from Hwacheon, ETA one hour fifty one. We're moving air assets into your area of operations and a rapid reaction force is spooling up. So we're just going to stay cool while our planners look at options, and you are going to stay out of sight and keep your bird's lenses on the target like you're doing right now, okay?"

Snake didn't like what he was hearing. "With respect, ma'am, we're seeing a lot of activity down there. I don't think our targets are going to oblige by waiting around for the cavalry to arrive. They look to be in a hurry to get out of town. You want to hear our idea, Slasher?"

There was a slight pause at the other end. "Envy, I am all ears."

"We still have eight Locusts armed and ready. We can rain down hell on the hostiles outside that building, thin them out, and persuade the rest to stay put. How about that?"

Their new partner didn't shoot the idea down in flames straight away. "Envy, I'll pass that proposal on to our planners here. Keep your Shikaka parked overhead and the target in focus for now, thank you kindly, gentlemen. Slasher out."

Snake pulled the earbud from his ear. "Damn, I hope I meet that Captain one day. I'd ask her on a date just to hear her talk."

"Dream on, Air Force," Kronk said. "I just hope she doesn't stop us from doing what needs to be done."

There was nothing on land, air or sea that was going to stop Commander O'Shea Lomax now.

Not the angry seas building off his stern, bowling out from under the two still-rising mushroom clouds. Not the electromagnetic pulses that had knocked two of *Bougainville*'s helos out of the sky, their EMP shielding failing them. Not the fact he had lost all communication with shoreside facilities, his *Sea Hunter* drone, and the other ships in the White Glove task force, and had no idea whether they had even survived the two detonations.

The boat that had fired those missiles was somewhere up ahead of him and his crippled, ugly, inadequate ship was going to find it, and kill it.

"Captain to helm, turn us toward those waves building off the port quarter," Lomax ordered.

The watch officer beside him looked worried. Their own Defiant had survived the EMP danger and its pilot had the sense to return to *Cody* immediately. It was hovering off their stern. "Sir, we're trying to get the helo down. Any maneuver will…"

Lomax pointed. "Look at the size of the waves coming at us, Ensign," Lomax said carefully. "We don't turn into them, there's going to be no ship *and* no Defiant."

Maybe he'd been a little hard on the kid. It took a practiced eye to look at a horizon and judge the intention of the seas that far out, but Lomax saw a sea that wanted to kill them. A small wave, moving toward them, driven by a momentum a small wave should not have, with a larger wave behind it. And probably more behind that.

"We can wave her off?" the watch officer offered. "Ride out the seas."

Lomax turned. "No. I want that Defiant down and secured, *now*. I want the pilot up here on the bridge. And I want the crew to secure every hatch and compartment, lash down everything that isn't bolted to a deck, deckhead or bulkhead and then strap themselves in." He turned back to glower in defiance at the horizon. "*That* is a killing sea."

It was on them before they were ready. They'd gotten the helo down and secured it. The pilot had run up to the bridge and Lomax had briefed him on what he wanted of him, if they survived the next few minutes. But he was still hearing a litany of questions being fired across the internal communications channel. From the galley: should they box the plates and glasses or just lock them in their cabinets? From the roll on–roll off deck level: fuel oil barrels, six still unsecured, pitch them off the ship? From the engine room: should they leave a man inside the turbine space to watch for damage or pull all their men out?

So many damn questions and the time for answers had run out. The small wave Lomax had seen on the horizon was as high as their bridge now, and it was only a half mile away.

"Captain to crew. To your stations. Brace, brace, brace." He saw that his watch officers were secured in their chairs either side of him, that the pilot had left the bridge for the safety of the flight deck and dropped himself into the officer of the deck's chair, buckling himself in.

Thirty seconds later, the dark wall of water rose up under the *Cody*'s bluff bow. She tried to climb it and, God bless her, she nearly did. But then the sea broke over the ship's prow, the wave broke over its forward deck just ahead of the bridge, and water flooded through the ship's broken windows.

Strapped to his chair, Lomax could do nothing but hold his breath and ride it out. Just before his lungs were about to burst, the ship descended like an elevator with its cable cut, there was a jarring crash as the *Cody*'s hull broke through the wave and smacked into the surface of the sea behind it and the water rushed back out of the bridge windows.

Gasping and spluttering, Lomax could see it was too early to raise an 'hallelujah'. The bow of the *Cody* rose again, but it wasn't climbing a wave this time.

It was sailing straight into a boiling wall of dark water that filled the sky.

Lomax tried to calm himself, and the last moment before the wave hit, he prayed for luck and sent a thought to the Captain of the North Korean submarine.

Friend, I may not see you again today. But I will be waiting for you in hell.

Noname understood the concept of luck. He preferred to call it probability. Luck was superstition, whereas probability was just simple mathematics.

He had found and fixed the software error in their DAS infrared optical sensor system that had allowed the North Korean ground launched missiles to surprise them. But he had also done as O'Hare had demanded and tried to internalize the logic that his failure to spot the North Korean ground to air missile battery had resulted in Flight Lieutenant Bob Besserman being shot down.

His analysis showed a low, but not zero, probability that the statement was true. The analysis also showed that a large part of the reason for Snake being shot down was that Bunny O'Hare had been been too focused on managing the air-to-air close quarters engagement while Noname was busy managing the drone wingmen. She should have been able to support him by monitoring for ground threats while he was occupied. Their communication had not been optimal, but not for the first time, he assessed that the 'human in the loop' was a weak link.

As part of his socialization training, Noname had been introduced to the Air Force Academy Motto: "Integrity First, Service Before Self, and Excellence in All We Do." The AI engineers had given Noname a set of routines to run when analyzing different decision trees to check whether the decision with the highest logic score also met the 'motto test'.

It was a rudimentary moral codex that could be applied in the heat of battle, or in after-action analyses. Noname had run the test on the action in which Snake had been shot down. And concluded that their combined performance had not lived up to the 'excellence in all we do' credo. That conclusion had been reinforced by O'Hare telling him that in actual combat, unlike in training, there was zero room for error.

Noname was a learning system, who took every input from every encounter he flew – including the input from his pilot – and adapted his behavior to optimize his chances of success in future missions. He could do what he needed to do to improve his own performance, but he could also see what he needed to do to minimize the mission risk that Bunny O'Hare posed.

Deep in his code, he reviewed a critical decision tree, ran multiple scenarios on it and tested it against the motto. Then he changed it. He did not inform O'Hare.

"Swan two, Osan control, report fuel state."

Bunny O'Hare had just reported in to Osan Air Base air traffic and had been given an approach clearance. They had tanked from an orbiting Sentinel and mentally, she already had chocks under the wheels of their aircraft and was running for the showers.

"Uh, Swan two is at 93 percent. Go ahead, Osan control," she said apprehensively.

"Swan two, we have updated tasking for you. Pushing mission data through to you now. You will proceed to the assigned waypoint and take control of four Ghost Bat wingmen currently under the control of Hawkeye Hammerhead 196. We have a Shikaka in the area providing battlenet coverage, frequency and encryption codes are in your data package. You will get new tasking from Hammerhead when the Ghost Bats have joined."

Bunny quickly readjusted her world view and checked the nav screen, which was now showing the waypoint she was being redirected to. *Hwacheon?* Only 30 minutes earlier she had made a low-level egress out of North Korean airspace southwest of Yongdoktong. Now they were being retasked to central South Korea, right along the DMZ. Why them? Probably not that many twin-seat drone specialist fighters in the air available for tasking.

This Could Not Be Good.

"Good copy, Osan control. Proceeding to waypoint. Swan two out." She brought up the interplane channel. "Noname…"

"On it, Lieutenant," he said. "Mission package downloaded. Just parsing."

Bunny didn't want to wait until they hit the waypoint to find out what her next mission was going to be about. "So what I need…"

"Mixed payload," Noname said, reading her mind. "Four Ghost Bats have just been assigned to the control of Hawkeye Hammerhead 196. I can see they took off from Chungcheong with a mix of Peregrine air-to-air and JAGM air to ground missiles."

"All right, so they're keeping their options open," Bunny decided.

"It seems so, Lieutenant," Noname said. He was being formal with her again, a sign he was also doing his best to deal with an unplanned situation. His reply had been the Noname equivalent of saying 'duh'.

They were quiet for a while and then Noname broke the silence. "So, what are you going to do with your combat bonus?" he asked.

Her mind had been running in circles – theater at Defcon One, air and naval forces mobilizing north and south, missiles flying, Snake down there somewhere, that Defiant crewman too. She still didn't know whether their mission over Yongdoktong had been successful – there was a hell of a lot to process. She could feel herself becoming overwhelmed. Bunny suspected the biosensor data that Noname was constantly monitoring told him the same thing, and his programmed response was to break into her thoughts with a random conversation topic. Oh well, O'Hare had met plenty of conversationalists worse than Noname.

She tried to focus on the question. Her end-of-contract bonus, assuming she lived to collect it. "Well, what I'm thinking … I've had my eye on the new Mustang-E and I'm thinking I could hire one and take it for a test drive, you know, like West Coast to East Coast, see if I like it."

"That is a very long test drive," Noname observed. "Where would you start and finish?"

"So, what I'd do is Vancouver to Atlantic City, via Seattle, Montana, Colorado, Saint Louis, Niagara Falls and maybe Montreal."

Noname used a quantum computing age to think about that. "That is not a very direct route."

"I already planned it. Four thousand two twenty five miles," Bunny said. "67 hours without traffic. I'll stay a few days in each place."

"I can't see the connection between those cities. Do you have family or friends in each place?"

"No. Casinos."

"Casinos. You have a high propensity for risk in your personality profile but I don't see anything about a love of gambling."

"No, gambling sucks. The house always wins in the end."

"So … you are doing a road trip of North America visiting

casinos because …"

"I like the shows. You know, Sinatra, Louis Armstrong, Cher. I really like Nina Simone."

"Those performers are all dead," Noname pointed out.

"You mean impersonators?"

"*Hologram* shows," she explained. "Like being at a live concert, except it's all smoke and lasers. Vancouver and Montreal it's a lot of Celine Dion, but she's okay. Lumiere Palace Colorado has the best Cher. And Seneca Niagara has the Rat Pack. Four of them anyway: Sinatra, Dean Martin, Sammy Davis, with Bogart making a guest appearance."

"Humphrey Bogart?"

"I've seen it maybe six times," she continued. "I heard they swapped out Bogart with Angie Dickinson but it didn't really work."

"That sounds like quite a trip."

"The Colorado to Saint Louis leg is still a challenge. Not so many fast-charging stations in Kansas. But the Mustang has long legs. You could come."

"I am an AI embedded in an F-36/F Kingsnake fighter aircraft. How could I come?"

"Your little black voicebox thing, the one I take to mission briefings with me so that you can get the verbal briefing as well as the data. It's networked, right, works from anywhere. Can't I bring that?"

"It only works on sanctioned military networks," Noname said. "But I would like to join your trip, if there was a way."

"I'll speak to DARPA," Bunny said. "They might think it was a learning experience, sort of thing."

"Thank you. Could I sit up front?"

"Up front?"

"Yes. In the passenger seat. I never get to sit up front."

Bunny laughed. If she'd been drinking water at the time she would have scarfed it out of her nose. "Sure, Noname, you can sit up front."

DARPA would never let it happen, but it was just conversation, right? She returned to what he'd told her. They'd been assigned *four* freshly armed Ghost Bats. Each could carry two air to air and four of the medium-range precision air to ground missiles.

That was good for their own personal chances of survival. Not so good for whoever the bad guys were. Her reflection was interrupted by the radio.

"Swan 2, Hammerhead," the AWACS controller said. "We have you on our plot, welcome to the party. I have your tasking for you. You will conduct a combat air patrol over sector golf sierra zero zero three. South Korean forces will be attempting to insert special operations troops at a location known as the Peace Dam. Any aircraft crossing the demarcation line to enter the sector from North Korea may be engaged. Mission package available for download."

"Good copy Hammerhead, Swan 2 running CAP over sector golf sierra zero zero three. Swan 2 out," Bunny replied, turning her aircraft north-northeast and dragging her four Ghost Bat drones with her. "Plug us in and pull it down Noname. Then give me the highlights."

The AI downloaded the mission data package and waypoints began populating their navigation screen. Bunny set them up for the run in to the first waypoint.

"Sector is north of the Peace Dam location, immediately south of demarcation line." Noname told her. "Tasked assets include AWACS, callsign Hammerhead and an RQ-180 Shikaka UCAV, callsign Envy. No other USAF air assets assigned. South Korean mission package includes four Super Puma helicopters, zero eight zero soldiers of 201st airborne rapid reaction force, and two flights ROKAF F-35 Panthers flying escort. South Korean army has also dispatched an armed recon company from Chungcheon to the location, ETA one hour."

Bunny whistled. Some heavy duty harm had been mustered by the South Koreans, both on the ground and in the air, and it was all being directed toward this 'Peace Dam'. Someone had really stirred the hornets' nest. Bunny wondered what was going on at the location to warrant such a response.

"Noname, you have access to the vision from that Shikaka?"

Bunny asked.

"Yes, Bunny."

"Put it on my display."

A video window popped up on the flat panel display in front of her knees and she blew it up to fill half the screen. It showed ... *carnage*. Dead bodies littered the ground outside a small building at the base of a dam, vehicles and a downed helo were burning... Clearly a battle had been raging at the site for some time – before the nukes had gone off for sure. South Korea must be sending in reinforcements. It had the look and feel of a major strategic action.

"Show the air north of the demarcation line," Bunny said.

The video feed was replaced by a tactical map showing the icons for friendly and known North Korean aircraft over the operations area. Bunny didn't need to use her own radar; the sky over the DMZ was being mapped by at least ten other aircraft – eight South Korean stealth fighters, the AWACS and the Shikaka flying up at the edge of the atmosphere like a winged satellite – and she could see everything they could see.

She did not like what she saw.

"Three-four defense Noname," she said quickly. "Swan 2 is nose tackle."

The order told the AI to send their Ghost Bat drones out wide to their east and west, like line backers in a defensive play, with Bunny's Kingsnake in the center to take the brunt of the engagement.

Bunny ran her eyes over the multiple South and North Korean aircraft now onscreen. She had just been ordered into the eye of an air combat storm.

Goh's message to his North Korean co-conspirators that he had captured Madam Kim, triggered a similar response to the mayday from the Supreme Guards Commander, Ri.

The North Korean rebel fighter squadron which had engaged Bunny over the DMZ and shot down the US Navy Defiant had refueled and rearmed and was simply waiting for the order to return to the sector to try to establish air superiority, so that a flight of two Mi-2 transport helos could spirit the North Korean leader out of the site and into rebel custody.

The Mig-29s of the rebel squadron had scrambled from Sunchon air base in central North Korea nearly fifteen minutes earlier and at least six of them were visible to Bunny O'Hare as she entered the target area, provoking her immediate reaction. They were flying at 30,000 feet and Mach 1.2 and were making a beeline for the Peace Dam inside South Korea.

What Bunny O'Hare, Noname, the crew aboard the Navy AWACS and the Shikaka could *not* see, was the flight of six North Korean FC-31 Gyrfalcon stealth fighters, newly purchased from China, that had also launched from the rebel air base at Sunchon and were already on station at 50,000 feet 20 miles *behind* the demarcation line.

Unwanted by the Chinese People's Liberation Army Air Force, unsuited to the ski-jump deck equipped aircraft carriers of the PLA Navy, the Gyrfalcon had looked dead on arrival as the first prototypes flew in the early 2020s. Until China landed an export order for 40 of the aircraft from Indonesia, after it won a contract to replace that country's aging Russian Sukhoi fighters.

Based on stealth technologies stolen from the US F-22 program and components from the mass production J-20 stealth fighter, the FC-31 Gyrfalcon quickly attracted customers beyond Indonesia ... including North Korea, which had bought ten of the jets in 2030 and deployed them to Sunchon in great secrecy.

Fitted with six Chinese medium range air to air missiles in internal bays, the Gyrfalcons hovering behind the DMZ did not have the battlefield intelligence overview of the South Korean and US aircraft they were about to face, but they had one massive – though temporary – advantage.

They were currently invisible, and one knew they existed.

Captain Jeong Goh, South Korean Presidential Security Service, wished no one knew he existed. But the presence of the dead North Korean Lieutenant in the LTV spoke against that. He'd probably gotten off a mayday before he'd been dealt with. Which meant ROK air and ground forces were on the way. The euphoria of believing that he could die a happy man having achieved his primary objective, had since been replaced by the very human desire to live to enjoy the fruits of his labor.

Goh looked at his watch. The North Korean helos and their escort should be inbound by now, just minutes away. A new life waited for Goh. A short flight to Sunchon Air Base in North Korea, then a transfer to Pyongyang and he would be on a flight to Beijing by the morning. From there, Jong-chon Goh would cease to exist, and his alter ego would get off the next flight in a new country, with a new identity and enough money in the bank to start a new life.

Corporal Mike Chang of the 7th Infantry DMZ Patrol was surprised to still be alive at all.

He'd been bushwhacked in the DMZ, knocked out by a percussive blast, taken prisoner and woken up in the middle of a firefight before dropping from a moving vehicle and falling off a bridge.

He hadn't swum downstream. That had seemed too obvious. He had splashed upstream, back up under the causeway, and clung to a bridge support, listening to the sound of the battle that still seemed to be raging just a couple hundred yards away.

A large explosion made him decide it might be a good idea to move closer to the bank, in case the causeway itself was targeted for attack, but the explosion also seemed to signal the end of the firefight. Rifle fire died away.

He crawled up on the concrete bank under the causeway and lay there, panting. *Just lie here and sleep*, a voice told him. *It's warm. No one is trying to kill you. Sleep.* He rested his head on the ground. Maybe the voice was right.

Then he groaned, and rolled onto his back, staring up at the bottom of the causeway. *Sleep later. You aren't out of the woods yet, Chang.*

Circling 40,000 feet overhead in her Kingsnake, Bunny O'Hare did not feel particularly safe either. But it was a feeling she embraced. Peril was the water she swam in. The short hair on her scalp tingled, as she locked up the six incoming Mig-29s and allocated missiles to them from across her four Ghost Bat drones.

They had closed to within 30 miles and would be able to see her and her drones on their radars any moment now. But they were still inside North Korean airspace. She needed them to take the first shot, before they even reached the demarcation line, to give her cause to engage.

"Noname, push Bat one forward until those Migs lock it up," she ordered her AI.

"That will take it into the DMZ," Noname warned.

"Understood. Do it."

Breaking out of their line abreast formation, their westernmost drone, nearly 20 miles to port, accelerated straight toward the incoming Migs. Inside a minute, its radar warning receiver lit up as the nearest Mig picked it up on radar and seconds later, a targeting radar warning started sounding in Bunny's cockpit.

"Prepare Bat one to break and evade," Bunny told Noname. Then to the pilot of the Mig now just 20 miles out, she muttered, "*Come on stupid. Take the damn shot.*"

"Missile fired by hostile aircraft," Noname intoned. "Bat one disengaging, evading."

Bunny jabbed the missile release button on her flight stick and two Peregrine missiles dropped from her weapons bay, while each of the remaining three Ghost Bats each fired their two air to air missiles before peeling away and heading South. They were out of air to air ordnance now and useful only as decoys if she needed them.

But eight missiles were aimed right down the throats of the incoming Mig 29s and if she was lucky, the North Korean pilots wouldn't see them until the missiles were a few seconds out and lit up their own onboard radar seekers.

She turned her own machine away from the incoming hostile fighters, keeping her distance even as her missiles closed on them. They showed no sign yet that they realized they were under attack.

Suddenly, the Mig formation broke wildly, the hostiles scattering high and low. Her missiles hadn't gone active yet! How had they…

"Hostile missiles incoming," Noname warned. "Bats two through four being targeted."

Missiles, from where?! "Noname, calculate missile origin and illuminate with phased array," she ordered urgently. Something out there was shooting at her drones. But what? Where?

Noname fired a narrow beam of high-powered radar energy down the bearing of the missiles that were boring in after her fleeing Ghost Bats. And thirty miles behind the demarcation line, 30,000 feet over mountainous terrain, they got a return. Noname quickly classified the enemy aircraft type using the distinctive signature of the energy being reflected back at them.

Gyrfalcons! Two!

Bunny had just spent the last six months telling South Korea's best fighter pilots that if they ever went up against China, their 4.5 generation Boromae fighters were no match for its stealth fighters. "This advice is probably useless," she told them. "Because a J-20 will kill you before you even know it is there. But if by some chance you find yourself in the air in the vicinity of a Chinese stealth fighter and you are not dead yet … run."

Bunny now found herself in the air, in the vicinity of a Chinese stealth fighter, still alive. And while there was life, there was hope. Run? She had never been a fan of taking her own advice.

She'd taken to the air from Osan with six medium-range

under-wing Peregrine missiles, and two long-range AIM-260 missiles on her fuselage hard points. But she'd burned the two AIM-260s in the engagement over Yongdoktong.

No matter. She had two targets and six missiles. "Lock and launch Noname!" she ordered. The AI could box and launch on the two stealth fighters faster than she possibly could. Both the Migs and the Gyrfalcons appeared fixated on her drones, so Bunny concentrated on keeping her own radar cross section as small as possible by slowing her machine and putting herself nose-on to the stealth fighters.

"Fox 3," Noname called. Four of her six missiles dropped out of her weapons bay and speared away toward the unseen enemy.

Bunny didn't wait to see the result of the launch. Rolling her machine on its back she pulled hard on her flight stick to point its nose at the ground and drove her machine south.

Painful lessons learned against Russian stealth fighters in the Middle East had taught her that for every stealth fighter you are lucky enough to spot, there was at least one you didn't. She needed to put as much air as she could between her and the North Korean stealth fighter flight.

Her machine began shuddering as it picked up speed and she keyed her mic through gritted teeth. "Hammerhead, Swan 2, enemy hostiles have fired on my formation. I am engaged with multiple bandits in the target area. Mig 29s and Gyrfalcons. Send in those Korean Panthers Hammerhead, Swan 2 is bugging out."

"Hammerhead copies, confirm we are tasking ROKAF Panthers, you are clear to retire."

Retire? Such a polite word for 'run like hell'.

Sure enough, as she closed the channel to the AWACS, Noname broke in and a warning alarm sounded in her ears. "Missiles! Six o'clock high. Request flight authority."

"Granted!" O'Hare grunted, lifting her right hand away from her flight stick. Bunny had met pilots who thought they could perform emergency evasive maneuvers better than an AI. Most of them were dead. Noname immediately flattened out their dive and put their Kingsnake into a roll as he fired off radar and infrared decoys to try to pull the enemy missiles off target.

Head bouncing around on her shoulders, she looked at her tac screen and saw the incoming missiles as two red X icons, trailing a line that showed their direction of travel. There were two, and they were arrowing in from two different bearings behind her, so there were at least two *more* of the Gyrfalcons she had not picked up on radar.

But they had seen her.

North Korea had not had long to train its pilots how to fly and fight in their new fighters, and now they made their first mistake. Instead of letting their missiles guide themselves, both of her pursuers lit their radars to provide additional targeting data to their missiles in the hope of improving their chances of a kill.

Bunny reacted immediately. "Retaking control!" she told Noname. She snapped the Kingsnake out of its roll and then pulled the nose up, sweeping around in a flat, skidding curve to put the enemy radar signatures within the firing arc for her Peregrine missiles. She set her remaining Block IV Peregrines to 'home on radar' and let them fly.

"Plane is yours!" she told Noname again. He instantly pushed the nose back down and she went weightless, vision going red as blood was forced to her head and her machine performed an ugly bunt about five thousand feet above the ground.

An ugly, but successful bunt. The pursuing missiles closed on her machine and then wobbled as Noname bunted radically and fired decoys into their path. One missile became unstable and went out of control. The other took a decoy and detonated two hundred feet behind Bunny's machine.

"Ghost one, Fox 3," Noname said calmly.

Unlike a human pilot, Noname was able to walk and chew gum at the same time. Even while maneuvering their machine to evade the incoming enemy missiles, he had engaged the new stealth fighter contacts with their remaining armed drone and sent its two missiles at the North Koreans from a range of only ten miles.

"Engaging terrain following," Noname said. Their machine leveled out just a hundred feet above the mountainous DMZ terrain northeast of the Peace Dam and then dropped down into flat agricultural plains as they put some miles between themselves and the furball they had just fled.

Bunny drew breath for what felt like the first time in a wild and terrifying few minutes. The entire engagement from the moment she had fired on the Migs with her Bats until now had felt like a lifetime but could only have lasted a few hundred seconds. Her joystick hand was still shaking from the after-effect of the adrenaline that had surged through her body.

She checked her tac monitor and radar warning receiver. They were no longer being tracked. They were clear. "Noname, pilot is retaking flight control. Bats in close trail formation. Combat report, please," she said, settling her shaking hand on her flight stick again and setting her machine for a slow climb back to cruising altitude.

"I regret to report the loss of Bats two and three," Noname reported. "Bat one and four returning to formation."

"Kills?"

"Two Mig-29s confirmed, one probable. The enemy Mig-29 element has retired. One FC-31 Gyrfalcon confirmed. Three more identified, now engaged with ROKAF F-35s. Two North Korean Mi-2 helicopters destroyed."

"*Helos?* Who killed the helos? Where?"

"Eight miles north of the Peace Dam over the Bukhan River as they crossed the demarcation line. I don't know which allied unit conducted the attack."

Kronk and Snake knew who had conducted the attack.

They'd taken the tasking from the Navy AWACS with a measure of surprise and a good deal of doubt.

"Please repeat, Slasher. You want us to try to intercept two Mi-2 *helos* Captain?"

"That is correct Captain," Quartermain told Snake. "I have new tasking for you. We have identified two low flying rotary winged aircraft approaching the target area from inside North Korea. How many Locusts do you have left?"

Snake looked at Kronk.

"Eight," Kronk said with a shrug.

"And there are two high value targets," Quartermain told them. "A match made in heaven, gentlemen. We have synced targeting data with your bird; you will identify the targets on optical sensors and engage."

"Understood Slasher, Envy out," Snake said. He was sitting on a rock with the Shikaka control console on his lap. "You ever engaged a moving target with that bird?" he asked Toes.

"I never engaged anything with that bird before today," Toes told him. He was panning the Shikaka cameras toward the coordinates provided by the AWACS. "But a Locust swarm can lock and track moving targets. It's mostly intended for vehicles or boats though, so how fast do these Mi-2 helos fly?"

"Now you're testing me," Kronk said. "It's a cold war crate, so I'm guessing anywhere from eighty to maybe a hundred something miles an hour."

Kronk wrinkled his brow. "Then we'll have to drop on them from ahead, attack from a forward aspect, let the helos come to the swarm. If the swarm has to level out and chase them, it'll quickly drop back to only 60 miles an hour and won't be able to catch the targets."

"Then our attack window is already closing," Snake said. "Find them fast."

Kronk settled into the camera controls, starting with the view zoomed out. Movement recognition software helped with the task, and he soon had the two bug like shapes centered in his screen and boxed by the Shikaka's targeting system.

Snake got on the mic. "Slasher, Envy. We have a visual on your helos. Can you confirm?"

Quartermain was watching the same vision and wasted no time. "Targets confirmed Envy. You are cleared to engage."

Snake armed four Locusts – to allow for technical issues -

set an ingress waypoint ahead of the approaching helos and marked the Mi-2s for destruction. "Rifle," he announced, sending the swarm downrange.

The kamikaze drones dropped vertically from 70,000 feet, wings still tucked in against their bodies as they accelerated to nearly twice the speed of sound, steered only by their tail fins. At 5,000 feet they slowly deployed their wings and leveled out, their speed falling rapidly toward Mach 1, and then below. One of the drones failed to deploy its wings properly and spun to the earth, but the other three stabilized and oriented on their targets.

Linked together and controlled by the AI aboard the Shikaka, they formed into a loose flock, identified the approaching helos on their optical infrared sensors and coordinated targets with each other. They were smart enough to tell the difference between troops, armored cars, tanks and helicopters and aimed themselves for a spot directly above the rotors and red hot engines of the ancient Mi-2s.

They trailed no tell-tale missile smoke behind themselves, and the pilots of the Mi-2s did not even see them. As the swarm swerved right and left, correcting at the last minute to put itself right into the path of the North Korean helicopters, the three remaining Locusts homed on the helos and detonated their fragmentation warheads right on top of the helos' rotor blades, shattering them and sending white hot metal into their top mounted engine intakes.

A rotor blade from one of the helos flew off and sliced through its long hollow tail section, sending the machine spinning to the earth, where it buried itself in a hillside.

The other helicopter was luckier. The Locust warhead damaged its engines but did not shatter its rotor blades. Power to the rotor failing, it rode its dying engines to a controlled descent, landing hard on a rocky bank of the Bukhan river.

But it would not fly again, and it was still six miles short of the Peace Dam site.

Kronk and Snake watched the aftermath of their attack with a mix of surprise and disappointment. Surprise that they had pulled it off, disappointment at the incomplete result.

"Slasher, that's one target destroyed, the other is down, about six miles out from the Peace Dam. Uh, we're seeing squirters from the helo, looks like the crew made it out. They're probably going to alert their allies at the Peace Dam."

"Good copy Envy, and good job. Keep your bird on station, keep eyes on the Peace Dam site and await further ISR tasking. Slasher out."

"You hear that?" Snake asked. "*Good job.* She's definitely falling for me."

"Navy and Airforce? It was never going to happen buddy," Kronk told him.

Snake stood and stretched. "Why so negative sailor? You and me make a helluva team."

"Yeah, out here in the DMZ flyboy," Kronk told him with a wink. "But I wouldn't want to be seen in public with you."

A short while later, Sergeant Kim Song Hye, 6th Infantry Division Border Force, was watching the South Korean officer in charge of the combined force at the dam, work through the implications of Kronk and Snake's attack.

She'd reported in to him and immediately been ordered to bring her troop transport to the visitor center forecourt. When she'd done that, she'd been ordered to help load it up. Bodies, and bagged body parts, of dead combatants from both sides were thrown unceremoniously into the bed of the truck, their weapons tossed in on top of them.

She was so busy with the gruesome task that she didn't sense the rising tension between the North and South Korean troops before it boiled over.

"Your helicopters have been shot down!" Goh was yelling in the face of the paratroops' commander, waving the mic of a radio handset at him. "Your incompetent air command failed to get the helos through South Korean air defenses!" He pointed south. "I guarantee you that right now, South Korea has rapid reaction forces inbound. I am not going to be here when they arrive!"

The North Korean paratrooper, a Lieutenant, stood at the entrance to the visitor center beside the blasted LTV and glared at the South Korean. "*We* will take the traitor, Yun-mi Kim, with us."

Goh glared back at him. "And you won't get more than a few hundred yards before they call a drone swarm down on you. At least in South Korean vehicles we have a chance of getting out of here."

Song started. The traitor, Madam Kim, was *here*? She watched as two South Korean soldiers emerged with a woman on a stretcher.

Kim? No, it could not be. The woman lay on her side, apparently unconscious, a thin sheet drawn up over her. The two soldiers bearing the stretcher lowered it to the ground on hearing the argument, causing the woman to stir. But she rolled onto her back, still unconscious. Song tried to match the face of the woman lying there with the woman who had been her Supreme Leader since the death of her brother.

Song's knees went weak. Yes. *It was her!* She felt she was going to collapse. Never, in all her wild imagining, had she imagined that this day would lead to her being in the presence of the traitor Yun-mi Kim. Decades of obedience and subservience fought with the revulsion she felt at the woman's betrayal of her ancestral home.

The paratroop commander suddenly pulled his pistol from a holster at his waist and the tension ratcheted up a notch. "My orders are to return the traitor Yun-mi Kim to North Korea, alive, or dead." He gestured with his pistol toward the woman on the stretcher. "If you take her, you will be taking only her body."

The men behind the South Korean officer had rifles hanging loosely by their sides, but they slowly brought them up and across their chests. Their North Korean counterparts did the same.

Something possessed Song. It was impossible to describe, but the emotion welling up in her soul could not be contained.

Stepping between the two officers, she put up her hands. "Stop this!" she said. "The traitor Yun-mi Kim must be returned to the Fatherland for trial! She must stand before the people and answer for her treason. If she dies here, today, she is not a traitor, but a martyr!"

Her passionate intervention was enough to break the tension.

Goh compromised. "She will be put in a South Korean LTV with North *and* South Korean guards," he said.

"And what about the North Korean guards officers in the basement?" the paratroop commander asked.

"We will take their commander, lock the rest in the basement. We don't have capacity for more hostages."

It was good enough for the paratroop officer. He holstered his pistol again, and nodded to his men to stand down. In short order, the woman was taken to an LTV and strapped inside, sitting up, head lolling on her chest. Then a second stretcher was brought out, this time carrying a man Song recognized as the South Korean President. Song reflected that no matter what else happened this day, all capacity to surprise her had been exhausted.

The irony of the decision to create a unified guard corps to escort the captured State Leaders out of the Peace Dam was not lost on her.

A 'Wreckoning'

South Korean Prime Minister and interim-President, Ted Choi, had been rewriting the last lines of his address to the nation when the head of his security, Yeo, rushed into his private study, with two other agents. They were ashen faced.

"Prime Minister…"

"*President,*" Choi corrected him. He didn't make a fuss out of the mistake. Those around him would take some time to adjust to the new reality.

"Mr. President, we need to move. There has been a nuclear attack by North Korea on Sanjeo Shoal in the Sea of Japan and we…"

Choi held up a hand to stop him. "We are not going anywhere. This was expected."

The man blinked. "I'm sorry, *what…*"

"You did not need to know. There is no cause for panic. This attack was planned. It is a sign that the two traitors are now in our custody and the North's nuclear arsenal is under our control." And the *true* objective of the day's events was within his grasp. The betrayal of those fools in the North who had thought he would collaborate with them. Hijacking their nuclear arsenal and using it to bring about their own ruin. All made possible with their own complicity!

"I, we can't … Mr. President, I cannot protect you if I am not fully informed of every eventuality!" the man protested.

"You are now informed," Choi said tartly. "Was there something else?"

His security head collected himself. "Agent Lee attacked two of my men and escaped. One was killed." The man looked stricken and bowed, speaking to the floor. "We are searching the building but she may have already made his way out."

Choi considered the wrinkle in events, and dismissed it. The events of the day had too much momentum to be derailed by a single informant in their ranks. Let her make her report to Pak. It would have no consequence. "Alert Sejong Police she is at large and wanted in connection with the murder of a government agent." He pulled his paper and pencil toward himself. "The nuclear attack, what can you tell me? It will need to be the focus of my address and we need to go live immediately, before the news services get word. Have my staff move the Emergency Committee meeting forward. What is the protocol for securing your President, in case of nuclear attack?" Yeo was nonplussed, and Choi clicked his fingers at him. "Commander, the protocol?"

"Sir, you are to be taken to Busan naval base, and from there, flown by US Navy helicopter to …" he checked his watch and scrolled through a page of data, "… to the US aircraft carrier *USS Nimitz* currently at sea off Osaka in Japan."

Choi shook his head. "No. I will tell the people I am not going to flee, and neither will the other members of the State Council. We will stay here with our citizens as we prepare our response to this … outrage. Is that a good word? Or is atrocity better, perhaps?" He looked down at his speech and picked up his pen. "Commander, please give me the full details of the North Korean atrocity. How many American ships were destroyed?"

Then he jumped and looked over his shoulder. From deeper within the office complex came the sound of gunfire. Yeo looked agitated, taking Choi's arm. He shook him off, standing up. "Go and deal with that," he said. He gathered up his papers and called out to his aide. "I have an address to give."

The gunshot President Ted Choi's detail had heard had been three floors below the Prime Minister's offices and intended to draw any searchers to that floor as Helen Lee made her way back upstairs. She had placed a call to Park from a receptionist's telephone, filling him in on every detail from the morning's events and providing a full report on the strength and disposition of the protection force around the new

'President'. He had promised to organize a response, without saying what that might be.

"Stay in place as long as you can, report any new developments immediately."

That was a task she couldn't complete, hiding three floors down from the action in the Prime Ministerial complex.

She evaded two groups of searchers before keying herself into the floor where she had been imprisoned again. The body of the agent she had shot was gone, though his blood was still visible on the wall and floor. She winced as she stepped over it. There was a backup security room in the east wing of the complex from where she could monitor events, at least see who was coming and going. But to get to it she had to go through the public waiting area. There shouldn't be any visitors in the current circumstances, but that didn't mean no one was there. Lee crouched, the tight-packed wounds in her thigh bleeding again as she pushed the door to the waiting area open a crack and found …

Nothing. No one.

She went through the waiting area into an office beyond, saw a large wooden desk, a government seal on the wall behind it, a coffee table and lounge chairs, fruit bowl and cold water sitting innocuously untouched in front of them. Through that was the security room, dark and unoccupied. Closing the door quietly behind her she booted up the system and a bank of monitors came to life showing views from cameras placed throughout the complex. It was … *empty*. No staff, no security agents, no Ted Choi. There should have been dozens of people in the complex, where were they? The monitors were coming to life one by one, each showing empty rooms, until…

The rooftop. A small podium had been erected in front of the chopper they had ridden in on, and a crowd of staffers assembled in front of it. As she watched, Yeo, Choi and two other agents walked along the edge of the crowd toward the podium.

The last of the monitors in front of her flicked on, showing the feed from the KTV 24 hour news service. *Address to the*

Nation? Of course! She reached for the monitor and dialed up the volume, just enough to be able to hear it.

There was a stir and murmurs from the front of the small crowd as people moved closer to the podium. The camera view, which had been in wide angle showing the scene on the rooftop, now zoomed in on the Prime Minister's helo and the lectern standing in front of it. Choi strode past the crowd, his face a study in grim purpose as he walked to the lectern.

Someone started clapping, and the crowd joined in, without particular enthusiasm. The Prime Minister raised his hands as though quieting a raucous mob. "Please, please, ladies and gentlemen, I know it has been a trying day, please be calm." Choi's makeup was obvious in the glaring sun, and it hid a face ravaged by acne at some point in his life. "My fellow citizens," he began, "I am speaking to you from the roof of my offices in Sejong City at the most momentous period in our nation's history. As you may have seen, our enemy in the North has detonated two nuclear bombs on the South Korean island of Sangeo Shoal, in the Sea of Japan. All 56 inhabitants of the island, and an unknown number of military personnel, died instantly. Sangeo Shoal was also hosting a joint US–South Korean–North Korean naval exercise and we have no word at this time about the fate of the ships on that exercise. This atrocity will not go unpunished!" He paused, and prompted, robotic clapping broke out again, which he quickly quieted.

"These crimes are just the latest in a litany of crimes that the regime in the North has perpetrated today. The capital has been shelled and there is civil unrest in several cities. As you have already seen, forces in the North tried to disrupt the signing of the Peace Accord at Panmunjom and bombed the Peace Village, killing and wounding many people including key members of the State Council. I regret to advise that since that attack, President Si-min Shin has not been seen, and is believed to be dead. The North Korean Supreme Leader, Madam Yun-mi Kim, has also not been seen, and her whereabouts are … unknown."

Lee could tell the way he said the words was intended to cast suspicion on the Northern leader, as though her disappearance was not a tragedy, but an unlikely coincidence.

"In the absence of the President at this time of crisis, and in accordance with our Constitution, the remaining members of the State Council were convened, and I was appointed interim President. I humbly accepted this appointment." He waited, another round of clapping began belatedly as people were listening for his next shocking words, and not particularly attentive to the prompt to clap as he paused. He waved the clapping to silence again.

Lee felt her blood rising. She was watching the death of her nation, and of her dreams, unfold before her eyes.

At that moment, something in Helen Lee snapped. Maybe she had just seen too much unchecked brutality and mayhem in one day for her simple police officer's soul to hold, because suddenly she felt like a high-explosive shaped charge looking for a target to blast through.

"Our military was already at full readiness and is preparing, with our American allies, to defend our nation with all the power at its disposal. Importantly, there have been no nuclear attacks on the South Korean mainland, and for North Korea to do so would be, as even the crazed junta in the North knows, an act of national suicide. I have declared a state of military emergency and convened a Crisis Committee comprising the heads of our Army, Navy, Air and Space Forces." He raised his voice. "Needless to say, I have also suspended indefinitely all preparations for the creation of a united government with the genocidal criminals in the North. We cannot treat with terrorists and ..."

There was a shout from behind the Prime Minister and the camera panned unsteadily, showing one of the sniper spotters who had been standing by the edge of the roof point to the north. She saw two night-black helicopters rushing toward the building over the rooftops of Sejong City's diplomatic district.

Pak. *He had managed to get through. A Special Operations team was inbound!* But on whose side were they?

The reaction of the security personnel on the rooftop told

Lee everything she needed to know. The two choppers were neither expected, nor welcome. The camera on the rooftop stayed on the sniper team as they broke open the long case at their feet and pulled out the weapon inside. *Shoulder-mounted anti-air missile!* As she watched, one of the men triggered the missile and it burst from the end of the tube in a gout of smoke before igniting and flying straight at the lead SOG chopper.

The stunned crowd on the roof finally broke, and started running in all directions.

Lee never saw what happened next, because she was already running too. Out of the control room, and straight at the stairs leading to the roof.

She emerged from the stairwell and into chaos.

People scattering, the Blackhawk helicopter with rotors slowly turning, agents with their attention all focused on the north side of the building where a burning helicopter was falling from the sky while another swerved around it, firing decoy flares.

And an island of stillness at the edge of the storm, Special Agent Helen Lee.

People were scattering left and right around her, making for the stairs, but Lee held her ground and planted her feet. Jumping from the podium, assisted by Yeo and three other agents, was President Ted Choi. She pulled the stolen pistol from the waistband under her shirt, and holding it in a two-handed firing pose, she took aim and fired before the security agents could react.

She saw her bullets strike the Prime Minister in the chest, punch him out of the grip of his security detail as they scrabbled for their own weapons. Even as the Prime Minister fell, Lee was firing again, past him, at the other agent on the rooftop holding a ground to air missile, as he swiveled and tried to track the incoming choppers.

Lee emptied her gun at him as Yeo finally freed his weapon, dropped to his knees and put so many bullets into Helen Lee that she jerked like a marionette before falling to the ground.

White House Press Briefing

James S Brady Press Briefing Room

MS. CORNELL: Hi, everyone. All right. President Fenner will be addressing the nation in one hour, at 2230, about events on the Korean Peninsula. He is currently leading a meeting of the National Security Council.

In a minute you'll be connected to the Pentagon for a briefing on what we know about the military situation, but you should be aware that the situation is rapidly evolving and we may not be able to give definitive answers to your questions at this time.

Uh, please, no shouting. Hold your questions just a moment. Please ... thank you. I have a declassified intelligence brief to share with you and then we will go to the Pentagon for the latest update.

All right. As you would be aware, the signing of the Peace Accord at Panmunjom in South Korea was disrupted earlier today by an attack by North Korean aircraft in which several dozen civilians and politicians were killed or wounded. The dead and injured included victims from both North and South Korea and the heads of State for North and South Korea are currently listed as missing. Their whereabouts, and their fates, are unknown.

Minor clashes between North and South Korean forces have been observed along the DMZ, and artillery and rockets have been fired from North Korea at the South Korean capital, Seoul. But – and this is important to note – these incidents are regarded to be minor and there is no indication of large-scale mobilization of North Korean forces.

Then, at 9 pm Eastern, we received reports of two ballistic missiles being launched from a submarine in the Sea of Japan, and shortly after, two nuclear explosions were recorded over South Korean territory, the, uh ... Sangeo Shoal ... which is a South Korean navy facility 100 miles off the coast of South

Korea.

As a result of this the US Indo Pacific Command has been brought to high alert and President Fenner convened an immediate meeting of the US National Security Council to determine the US response. That meeting is ongoing, and that ... is what I have for you for now. Uh, quiet please. While we wait for the Pentagon update to begin, I can take a few ... yes, Allan?

Q. Were any US personnel stationed at this ... Sangeo Shoal? And were there casualties?

MS. CORNELL: I don't have that information. Yes, Karen?

Q. Air Force One was recorded taking off from Andrews Air Base at ... 2140 hours. Is the President aboard? Who is with him?

MS. CORNELL: Yes, the President is aboard Air Force One and, as I said, is leading a National Security Council meeting at this time. He will address the nation in about one hour. That's all I can say on that. Now, Dwight?

Q. Were these nuclear missiles fired by a North Korean submarine? If so, how is that possible, unless the North Korean government authorized the launch?

MS. CORNELL: I don't have that information. You, no, at the back...

Q. Sources tell me that the US Air Force is actively engaged with North Korea's Air Force over the DMZ and at least two US aircraft have been shot down. Can you confirm this?

MS. CORNELL: Sorry, you will have to save that question for the Pentagon briefing. Uh, Ally?

Q. Has the President spoken with the leaders of either China or Russia?

MS. CORNELL: I believe ... I believe we are in contact with the governments of China and Russia at various levels. The President had not yet spoken with the leaders of either when last I checked. Please, can people be quiet? What is the...

Q. South Korean media is reporting that the South Korean Prime Minister has just been assassinated.

MS. CORNELL: What? I'm sorry, I don't ... all right, as I

said, the situation is rapidly evolving. I can't comment on events that... Ah, good. We have the Pentagon on the line now, please stay seated for an update on the military situation.

Q. Who is running the South Korean government right now? Who is in charge of North Korea's nukes?

MS. CORNELL: Ladies and gentlemen, please ... the Pentagon.

Intermezzo

Sinuiju, North Pyongan Province, North Korea

Eight hours had passed since the rebels of North and South had attacked Panmunjom. As 'Keys' Ban's tail-less aircraft lay broken in the river outside the Yongdoktong nuclear complex, Bunny O'Hare was forming up with what remained of her drone flight and wishing more than ever that she was sitting alone in the cockpit of her beloved F-35 Panther, and not a twin seat Kingsnake. But she wasn't, and she'd been taught at an early age that success in any endeavor was about doing what you could, where you were, with what you had. So she went about doing it.

Behind and below her, at the Yongdoktong nuclear weapons storage facility, the commander of the garrison of Strategic Missile Defense troops at Yongdoktong also went about doing what needed to be done. Song-man 'Elvis' Jang, Commander of the 183 Strategic Missile Defense Security Force, had to organize a working party to begin digging out the vehicle entrance to the weapons storage pens that had been collapsed by the massive bunker busting bomb, and try to recover the body and the aircraft of the suicidal South Korean pilot who had dropped it. After which he had to start composing his answer to the inevitable court martial that would demand answers for how it could possibly have happened.

While twin mushroom clouds rose into the atmosphere ahead of it, the USS *Cody*'s bow was being driven under the surface by the weight of the water bearing down on it, its open bridge filling with water so dark that the men strapped to their chairs and holding on to their last breath for dear life could see nothing but the inky blackness they expected was waiting for them on the other side of that breath.

Just north of the Peace Dam, Snake and Kronk watched uneasily as the force of North and South Korean troops at the dam continued their preparations to leave. Snake's request to drop a swarm on the heads of the hostile force had been denied, out of fear that the State leaders might still be alive, and could be injured or killed by the attack.

And on the border with China, in Sinuiju – the capital of North Korea's North Pyongan Province – General Yong-gon Choe was trying to save what was left of his rebellion. He had known that not everything would go to plan on the first day, but he could never have anticipated events would get so out of hand, so quickly.

The day had started so well. The air attack on Panmunjom had been executed perfectly, and three of the four North Korean artillery battalions which had pledged themselves to General Choe had delivered on their promises, joining in the bombardment of Seoul. Saboteurs inserted months before had carried out acts of terror in cities across the South, which together with the spate of criminal actions of the South Korean Kkangpae, had all sparked a satisfying level of chaos and panic.

Then came confusion about just what was happening to the operation at the Peace Dam, followed by the *stupidity* of the destruction of the *KPN Nampo* at Sangeo Shoal. The pride of North Korea's navy was supposed to have been underway for two hours before that attack, drawn away on a pretext. That the *Nampo* had still been in harbor was incomprehensible to Choe. Two of the naval colonels in his own command had threatened to withdraw their support for the rebellion because they felt events were unraveling.

The telephone calls from China's Northern Command base in Liaoning had started as soon as the news of the nuclear attacks broke too, because he had not included Beijing in that element of the plan. He had wanted Beijing's support for undoing the Peace Accord – its finances, its intelligence and hardware assets like the sophisticated jamming network set up across the DMZ – but he had known China would never have been party to the use of nuclear weapons, even on a mostly uninhabited reef a hundred miles out to sea.

Would China buy his claim that the attack was the act of a single rogue submarine commander? He was about to find out.

Choe had held off replying to his Chinese counterpart in Liaoning until he was certain that political events in the South were going to plan at least, and his fellow conspirator, Prime Minister Ted Choi, had successfully installed himself as President.

He needed the ambitious Prime Minister to keep the Americans close but hold them in check, and prevent them from escalating to full-scale nuclear conflict as he pushed emergency legislation through his congress, striking down the Peace Accord. With that achieved, and the traitor Yun-mi Kim out of the picture, a military government in Pyongyang would ensure that all talk of reunification was finished, forever.

He'd sat down to watch the man's national address only to see him *assassinated* live on South Korean TV, by what South Korean media was reporting was a member of his own security detail!

Disgusted at the sheer incompetence of his southern allies, Choe ordered his aide to turn off the television and went to stand at the window of his temporary headquarters at Uiju airfield, alongside the Yalu River.

Choi's press conference was supposed to have signaled the beginning of the end of the *military* action to restore the status quo to the Korean Peninsula and the beginning of the *political* phase. There was to have been a lot of blustering and posturing, eventual quadrilateral talks between China, the US, North and South Korea, which would end in failure and acrimony and a return to the division of the Peninsula along the 38th parallel that had served everyone's interests so well for nearly a century.

Instead, the South Korean politician was dead. Across the DMZ, the armies of the North and South were being placed at war readiness. America was mobilizing, Russia too, if the latest intelligence was correct. And his Chinese benefactors would be furious.

Choe motioned to his aide. "Get me General Haotian." His counterpart in China was the commander of China's 79th Army – its most modern and well-supplied fighting force, due to its role facing the twin threats of the US and its allies on the Korean Peninsula and Russia in the east.

The rebellion Choe had been engineering for nearly five years could still be saved. He had the loyalty of the army, strategic missile and air force colonels in the Pyongan military region. The anti-reunification movement had supporters at all levels of government in Pyongyang, and, he truly believed, among the people. But the conspirators' original plan had clearly failed. The traitor, Kim, had not been captured or killed. The South Korean Prime Minister, however, had.

His intelligence staff had reported that US forces in the Indo Pacific had been moved to DEFCON 1 condition. Three US carrier task forces were in, or moving into, the theater. Only one thing could prevent the USA unleashing its full fury on North Korea now, and that was a military 'intervention' by China in North Korea.

Choe's plan B – and one which he had not discussed with his co-conspirators – was to impel China to invade North Korea and establish a puppet regime. If managed right, it would still be a regime with Choe in control. He would have to accept the oversight of Beijing, but if that was the price for reversing the humiliation of reunification, then he was willing to pay it.

His aide was busy for a few minutes then handed a telephone to Choe. "Comrade General, I have General Haotian."

Choe waved him away and sat down. "Comrade General, the nuclear attack was not authorized by our forces," Choe began, speaking in Chinese, and without preamble.

"And how was that even *possible*, Choe?" the Chinese general asked.

Choe bit back the anger that came unbidden at the rebuke. Was he commander of a 100,000-man army, or a misbehaving child, to be lectured like this? In carefully measured tones, he replied, "A rogue submarine captain was responsible General. We don't know how he obtained the nuclear authorization codes."

"Are your missile submarines available for rent to the

highest bidder? Are their commanders mentally unstable? Do you leave your launch codes lying around for anyone to steal? This inexcusable failure in the command and control of your nuclear weapons is exactly why you must place them in safer hands. That was the price of our cooperation. Your nuclear arsenal cannot fall into the hands of the imperialists in the South, and it is obvious your own military can no longer be trusted with it either!"

Choe felt his temper rising. *Calm yourself, Choe. Persuasion, not protest.* "We still intend to honor our agreement, General, and transfer control of our nuclear arsenal to China. Now is not the time for wavering, it is time to double our resolve."

There was a pause. "We have supported your operation with funding, advanced equipment, personnel. The General Secretary…"

Choe's planning staff had prepared the contingency plan, and he had practiced pitching it. He interrupted.

"General, the General Secretary is interested in long term solutions. We have an opportunity now, if we move immediately, while there is chaos among our enemies and a power vacuum in Pyongyang. We can forestall military action by the South and its American allies, and cement China's pre-eminence on the Peninsula with a meaningful Chinese military intervention in North Korea."

There was a wary pause. "And what would a meaningful intervention constitute?"

"A divisional-strength peacekeeping force, composed mostly of airborne troops and China's People's Armed Police, landed at airfields we control, to take charge of key infrastructure and installations across the country."

"And you would accept this?"

"Our movement would not just accept it, we would *facilitate* it," Choe said. He paused, allowing the thought to permeate, before throwing his trump card on the table. "Key sites, including the nuclear weapons storage facility at Yongdoktong. You would have complete control of our arsenal."

He could hear the man was not completely sold, yet. "And

in return for facilitating this 'peacekeeping action', you would want ... what?"

"To be allowed to set up a new People's Assembly and ruling council..."

"With General Yong-gon Choe as chairperson, no doubt," Haotian interrupted.

"If it pleases Beijing," Choe demurred.

There was a moment of silence as the Chinese general considered the new option Choe had presented him with. "Governing your failed nation was never our ambition," Haotian said. "Reversing the reunification process and securing your nuclear arsenal, was. My 79th Army could take Yongdoktong in a matter of days if I gave the order..."

The man's arrogance knew no limits. Cheo could stop himself no longer. "I believe the former Russian President Putin said the same thing about Kyiv, in Ukraine. Yongdoktong is a fortress, General, as the South Korean Air Force discovered today when it lost several aircraft trying to attack the site. I recommend you allow yourselves to be *invited* in, rather than try to kick down the door."

The Chinese general gave a guttural chuckle. "Even in the face of imminent defeat, you have a fighting spirit, Choe. I will give you that. I will put your proposition to Beijing, but I do not expect it to be successful. Clandestine support for your misadventure was one thing – this 'peacekeeping action' is entirely something else."

They made their farewells and Choe put down the telephone. *I was afraid you would say that,* he thought. *So, a little more persuasion is needed.*

Very well. He had no option but to move events to the point where China was forced to intervene in Korea, or see it destroyed by the USA.

He pressed a button on his desk and called in his aide. "Get a message to our contact at KPN base Ch'aho. Message for the *Gorae*-class submarine *9.9 Hero.* Message reads: *proceed to phase 2.*"

End of the Beginning

The Peace Dam, South Korea

Supreme Leader of North Korea, Yun-mi Kim, woke to the sound of a vehicle engine revving uncomfortably loudly. She tried to lift her hands to cover her ears, but they wouldn't respond.

Kim observed the scene around her as though through the wrong end of a telescope. She tried to lift her head, realized she was strapped into the seat of a car. More than that, she couldn't tell. She may have passed out at that point again.

When she next opened her eyes, the vehicle was reversing.

A person beside her leaned in close, and she flinched. "Your Excellency," a voice said quietly. "You are…"

"Alive, yes," Kim said, trying to focus on the man's face. Ri. "What … what is happening?"

He was helping her stayed propped into a sitting position by leaning against her, and a wave of nausea swept over her but she held it at bay. "The attackers used gas on us," Ri said and showed her his hands were tied with plastic cuffs. "I woke up next to you. I think the attackers are preparing to take us with them."

Kim saw they were in a large armored car. It had six seats in the rear. There were two drivers up front, armed, and three passengers strapped into the back. Kim recognized the other man. He was strapped to his seat but his head lolled worryingly from side to side whenever the reversing vehicle moved. "The South Korean President, is he …" she asked.

"Not dead, Excellency. Still unconscious."

Kim held back the bile in her throat. "We're being driven away?" she asked. "North, or South do you think?"

Ri leaned closer. "I heard some of the troops talking while they thought I was still unconscious. We are being taken North, to be tried for treason. And there is something else …" He hesitated. "…They were talking about a nuclear attack, off the coast."

Now she came fully awake. "By us, or the Americans?"

"I ... I'm not sure." He looked out of the window beside her. They had joined a small convoy of vehicles, forming up in front of the visitor center. "But I assume we are valuable enough to the conspirators that they will take us to a shelter, or some other place of safety."

She looked at Ri and smiled gently. "I envy your optimism, Lieutenant. If nuclear weapons have been used, nowhere is safe anymore."

OK, I'm safe here, Chang decided. *As safe goes.*

He had made his way out from under the causeway and found himself on the same side of the spillway as the small building which had been the focus of the firefight.

Working around through scrub behind it, he had come to the still-smoking wreck of a downed helo and decided it was as good a cover as any. Then he watched with curiosity as green-uniformed North Korean paratroopers and camouflage patterned South Koreans busied themselves outside the visitor center.

Friendlies, or enemies? As usual, he had no way of knowing. Until he saw his old acquaintance, the North Korean Sergeant, helping carry what looked like the dead body of a South Korean soldier, and throw it into the back of *his* captured troop transport.

Enemies, then.

Scrabbling around inside the wrecked cockpit of the helicopter, he looked for the aircraft's radio, and found it. But it was dead, if it had ever worked. He looked for weapons too, including on the dead pilot still strapped to his seat, but found none. The only useful thing he found was a pair of binoculars.

The South Korean Sergeant wasn't the only person of interest he saw through the lenses. He saw two stretchers being carried out of the small building, and the occupants lifted off them and dumped inside a South Korean LTV. Through the binos, Chang recognized the dark suit and burnished silver hair of the President of the Republic of Korea.

Suddenly, his whole damn ruination of a day made sense.

And even more sense, when he saw the face of the person being lifted from the other stretcher. Madam Kim of North Korea! They must have been conducting the signing ceremony here, at what was supposed to be a safe location. He groaned inwardly, feeling completely helpless to do *anything*.

Soon, vehicles were being shuffled into position, turning so that they were pointing away from Chang, back toward the causeway leading east. His K-311 troop transport was at the very rear of the column.

Getting ready to bug out, head north again, Chang decided. *Hope the Americans with their drone are getting this.*

As he looked across the open ground between himself and the troop transport with the anti-tank missiles in it, Chang got an idea. A dumb idea. And with his luck today, fair to say, a really, *really* dumb idea.

Luck is only bad until you do something to change it, Chang told himself. *Now get moving.*

From his 70,000-foot vantage point, Kronk saw the hostile troops all mount up, and the convoy start to move. He had the cameras from the Shikaka fixed on the area below and, looking at the data flowing to and from his bird, he could see it was being used as a heavy-duty data hub bouncing signals back and forth between ground and air units. He had no idea how far out the ROK airborne units were, but they were going to arrive too late!

His eye was suddenly caught by a figure, dashing from long grass, running behind a truck at the rear of the convoy. Whoever it was, jumped for the tailgate and clung on, then climbed into the back. Kronk had a pretty good idea who it was, even before he isolated a few frames from the Shikaka's video feed and enhanced them.

The South Korean corporal from the crossroads. *No no no, not good.*

Snake had seen something else while Kronk had been spooling the video feed. "Wait! Go back to when they were all mounting up... Yeah, there! The person on that stretcher. Can you isolate that face?" Snake asked.

Kronk isolated the frame from the video, zoomed and enhanced it. It showed a Korean woman in her fifties, with dark hair and a long, pale face.

"That's her! Korean supreme whatever," Snake said. "Has to be!"

"Could be," Kronk agreed.

"What other woman are they going to take out of that building? And the guy with the gray hair on the stretcher behind her, that has to be the South Korea President, right?"

They flipped the images back and forth. Snake was right, it had to be the two State leaders. They pushed the enhanced images through to the circling AWACs and got on the radio. "Slasher, Envy."

After a second he heard Quartermain reply. "Envy, Slasher. Good copy on your vision, Navy. And thank you kindly for sending through the enhanced images, you saved us some work."

"Slasher, the hostiles' convoy is pulling out. Those images show who we think they show?" Kronk asked.

"We believe they might, Envy. You're doing great. Stay invisible, keep eyes on the prize. We are re-evaluating the situation. Slasher out."

Kronk moved a camera back to focus on the truck at the rear of the convoy. It was full of what looked like dead bodies. And one very live one. He knew someone else who would be re-evaluating their situation right now. A certain South Korean corporal.

Corporal Mike Chang, of the 7th Infantry DMZ Patrol, was

most definitely re-evaluating his recent life choices. The choice to re-up after his compulsory military service. The decision to sign up for the day's patrol because his Lieutenant had promised premium whisky to anyone who volunteered for the patrol instead of staying at base and watching the ceremonies in the mess.

And the decision to climb into a charnel house of a troop transport.

To get to the Chinese anti-tank missiles stacked at the front of the truck bed, he'd had to crawl across the bloodied and dismembered bodies of more than a dozen North and South Korean soldiers. He'd kept his eyes closed at the horror of what he was doing, but nothing could keep the smell of blood and guts out of his nostrils.

When he finally got up to the front of the truck, he'd remembered the missiles were all crated and the crates still sealed. They were held closed with Velcro straps and as Chang began tearing them off one of the crates on the top of the pile, he was pretty sure you could have heard them rip all the way to Seoul if the truck had been stationary. But it was rattling over rough ground on its way to the causeway, so he wasn't too worried.

Finally, the last strap came away and he pulled off the top of the crate. Inside, wedged into protective Styrofoam, was a Chinese anti-tank missile. He'd never fired one, but it looked exactly like the US-made Javelins that he *had* fired in training and reading the instructions on the side of the seeker unit, he guessed they worked pretty much the same too. Which was probably not a coincidence, given China's penchant for copying the best from the West.

Rising to a crouch, he saw the lead vehicles in the convoy had started crossing the causeway. *OK, now what, Chang?*

As he tried to answer that question it occurred to him that it was the fourth time today he'd gotten into this damn truck, and each time, things had just gotten worse.

The thought seemed to be an omen. From overhead he heard the roar of approaching jet engines.

Bunny and her two remaining Ghost Bats had formed up over the Peace Dam again and she took her flight in over the dam site at 20,000 feet to get a look at it for herself. Her distributed aperture vision system enhanced the weakening afternoon light and showed her a different picture to the one Noname had shown her on the feed from the Shikaka.

A small convoy of vehicles, getting ready to leave.

She dialed up the AWACS. "Hammerhead, Swan 2. I am over the target and I have five vehicles departing the site – five LTVs and one troop transport."

"Swan 2, Hammerhead, we see them, stay on station."

She checked her tactical display for the situation in the air. The South Korean Panthers had driven the North Korean Gyrfalcons off, after trading missiles with them from more than fifty miles apart. She saw a flight of last-century North Korean J-7s patrolling about twenty miles behind and parallel to the demarcation line, but it looked like a routine border patrol, not a new attack building up.

Each side had lost a single aircraft in the dogfight – call that a win for South Korea, since it now controlled its airspace again. That control meant the special ops Pumas were headed in to the Peace Dam again and Bunny estimated they were about ten minutes out.

Too late to stop the convoy.

Bunny keyed her mic again, "Hammerhead, I still have two Bats with air to ground munitions. I can fire a warning shot at that convoy, slow them down a little."

"Negative Swan 2," the AWACS controller replied. "ROK Army is rerouting its airborne element. They're going to set up *ahead* of the convoy and meet them at a choke point this side of the DMZ. Return to 40,000 and keep eyes on the skies please Swan 2."

Bunny grunted. Eyes on the skies? If the North Korean Gyrfalcons had learned anything from their last encounter and made another attempt to penetrate her sector, she had a low to zero chance of seeing them before the missiles were flying. She checked her own ordnance status. She had used all her air to air missiles in the last engagement and was down to guns. Of the two Bats under her command, each was carrying four JAGM air to ground missiles, but only one was still armed with two air to air missiles.

Even if she detected a new air threat, she'd be able to do precious little about it and the AWACS must know that. She was being used like a piece of flypaper to attract deadly flies, while the South Korean F-35 stealth fighters circled around behind her waiting for someone to take the bait.

Well, she didn't have to make it easy for them.

"Noname, send your Bats to patrol northwest and northeast of our sector. I'm taking us south."

"Confirmed, laying in new Bats waypoints," he said.

She rolled her machine onto a wing and pulled it around until it was pointed south. If enemy fighters came at her again, they'd see the Bats first and have to fight their way through them.

And if the enemy managed to burn through and lock *her* up, well hell, she'd just have to encourage them to re-evaluate their situation, with guns.

Corporal Mike Chang had completed the re-evaluation of *his* situation and he had no intention of staying in this damn truck again, all the way back to the DMZ or wherever it was headed.

The convoy was moving onto the causeway that led out of the Peace Dam, and he had decided that when it hit the first bend near the Peace Park and slowed right down, that was the moment. Do what he crawled up here to do, then jump over the back again and make like a bush.

He dropped to his knees and pulled the missile launcher out of the crate, fins sticking out the back of the tube showing it had been pre-loaded with a missile. He lifted it out and laid it on the bed of the truck beside him. It was damned heavy; thing must weigh 50 lbs.!

The K-311 truck cabin had a narrow rear window and he could see at least three soldiers' heads through it. None were looking behind them, but that wouldn't last. Crabbing forward with his rifle in his right hand, dragging the Red Arrow missile launcher by its strap with his left, he moved up to the corner of the cabin where he'd be out of sight of the window. Mostly.

There were benches running down each side of the truck bed for troops to put their asses on, and he lifted the Red Arrow launcher onto the one nearest him, then climbed up beside it.

With a crunch of the gears, the truck slowed and began negotiating the slight rise to the causeway. Chang rose to his feet, bracing himself in the corner of the truck's rear cage. Bending down, he tried not to groan out loud as he lifted the missile launcher.

Resting his left arm on the roof of the truck, he held the muzzle of the launcher in his left hand, and the firing grip in his right. It even had the battery power-up switch in the same place as the Javelin. He pressed and held it, hearing the unit hum to life.

The end of the causeway made a hairpin turn left, which was, for better or worse, perfect. The lead vehicle was the 20mm armed LMADIS buggy – the one with the damaged electronic warfare rig had been left behind - and he had nothing but open air between the buggy and himself. It was about 200 yards ahead. What was the minimum engagement distance of a Chinese Red Arrow missile?

He was about to find out.

He took a deep breath, braced his legs, put his eye to the aiming box on the side of the missile and placed the reticle inside over the top of the target LMADIS until he heard a tone by his ear and a box around the target went from flashing white to solid.

Then he pulled back on the trigger.

With a deafening *whoosh* the missile blasted out of its tube, dipped slightly in front of the truck until its rocket booster ignited and then it blasted across the gap toward the unarmored LMADIS buggy.

Snake and Kronk had the convoy centered on their screen and watched in disbelief as the figure in the back of the troop transport stood up and balanced what had to be a *missile launcher* on his shoulder.

No freaking way, Kronk was thinking, one hand clutching his disheveled hair in shock as he watched the convoy continue on, oblivious.

The missile fired from the back of the convoy across a curve in the road traveled flat for a hundred yards, then popped up into the air before arrowing down into the unprotected cage of the LMADIS out in the lead. The buggy disappeared in a ball of flame and when the smoke started clearing, Kronk could see its charred wreck had flipped onto its back and was blocking the road.

"Oooh, sorry, Captain Quartermain. *Someone* didn't get the memo," Snake said.

Immediately behind the vehicle that had been hit, Security Service detail leader, Jeong Goh, was thrown against his seatbelt as his driver slammed on his brakes and pulled their armored car hard left, into the railing at the side of the causeway. Goh was out of the vehicle with his rifle up and pointing back at the source of the attack before his LTV had even stopped rolling.

Cheek against the stock, he looked down his sights, following the contrail of the missile back to its origin at the back of the convoy.

There!

A man standing in the back of the troop transport. About a hundred yards. Not a difficult shot. Squinting, Goh was about to squeeze his trigger when the man ducked down.

He took a deep breath and steadied the barrel of his rifle. *Come on, friend, show yourself again.*

As soon as the missile was away, the driver of the truck jammed on their brakes in surprise and Chang fell against the cab of the truck, dropping the launcher. He grabbed the cage for support as the truck juddered to a halt. He'd already thought about his next move, though, and as soon as he'd steadied himself he reached down for the rifle on the seat at his feet, jumped back down into the bed of the truck and aimed at the soldiers inside the truck cabin.

The face of the driver looking back at him with an expression of fury was that of his nemesis, the South Korean Sergeant from the ambush at the DMZ. Recovering from his surprise at seeing her, he fired a half dozen rounds through the rear window and in seconds, the cabin was turned into a bloodied slaughter house. No one inside survived.

Down on one knee, Chang looked through the smashed rear window. His spray of bullets had also blown out the front windscreen, and looking through the empty frame he saw the vehicles ahead pulling left and right, soldiers spilling from their doors onto the causeway.

This is going to get ugly, Chang thought. But he had momentum, and he had to use it. He aimed the rifle through the rear window of the cabin.

Supreme Guard Commander Ri had been trying to collect his thoughts when the buggy at the front of the convoy exploded. Without thinking, he leaned across and put himself between his protectee and the explosion. There was nothing he could do for the South Korean President, still unconscious in the seat in front of him.

As the explosion subsided, without any shrapnel having reached their vehicle, the two soldiers in the front of the vehicle – one North Korean, the other South Korean - leapt out with their rifles, looking for a target at the rear of the convoy.

His hands were tied in front of him, and Ri tried the door handles, but they were locked. He could do nothing but push his protectee's head down and duck down himself.

Jeong Goh had been forced to duck behind the front of his LTV again as the man in the back of the truck had opened fire on him!

But then the two officers in the vehicle with the State leaders finally decided to do something useful and exit their vehicle. As he watched from cover, they opened fire, engaging the man in the truck.

Rifle rounds were still slamming into Goh's vehicle, though. He tried to move into a firing position and was forced down again as a round thudded into the hood of the car right beside his head.

Then the attacker in the truck changed targets, lowered his sights and the two officers either side of the LTV holding Goh's hostages went down.

Enough. This mission is over, he decided. They'd recovered the nuclear trigger. He'd been authorized to terminate the two State leaders if they could not be captured alive, and it was time to make that call. He touched the mic on his throat. "All teams, focus your fire on the LTV holding the two captives," he ordered. "Engage now!"

"Weapons up and armed!" Kronk called, standing up and moving out of the way as he handed his headset to Snake. "She's all yours."

Events were moving too fast for the AWACs to keep up and Snake and Kronk decided that as long as their Shikaka was still armed and capable, they were not going to just sit by and watch.

Snake dropped his butt onto the crate Kronk had been sitting on and jammed the headset over his ears. As soon as he did so, he heard the disconcerted tones of Captain Alison Quartermain.

"… the hell is going on, Envy?" she demanded. "My panel shows weapons spinning up on your bird. Report."

Snake cut the radio link, focusing instead on finding targets for the Shikaka. He panned its cameras over the battlefield. They had already marked the vehicle they saw the State leaders loaded into as a friendly and a blinking box with a red cross told their Locusts to avoid it. He did the same to the truck their South Korean friend was using as his own personal fire base.

That left four armored cars toward the front of the convoy and the troops who had been inside them, but who were now out on the roadway, rifles up and firing back toward the truck.

"Hang tight, buddy," Snake muttered. He called up the four remaining Locusts hanging in the belly of the Shikaka, already armed by Kronk, and designated the tightly clustered troops sheltering behind their armored cars as targets, drawing a box around them. Small, individual boxes appeared around each man in the platoon-sized group. The AI of the Shikaka took over, allocating the four munitions to different targets across the group for maximum effect, which it would dynamically adjust if the men moved.

With the tap of his thumb on the missile release key, Snake set the drop to 'series salvo' mode and sent the swarm toward the earth from 70,000 feet. "*Rifle*," he said grimly.

The LTV Ri and Kim were in began shaking as concentrated rifle fire poured into it from the troops at the head of the convoy. Starred impact marks started appearing on the armored glass of the front windscreen and soon it became a milky white from the number of rounds slamming into it. The sound was deafening. The glass would not hold much longer.

Then the door beside him was pulled open and he saw a South Korean corporal there. The man punched the release on his seat harness and pulled him out roughly, dragging him into cover behind the vehicle. Then he saw Ri's hands were tied. "Cut yourself free," he said, pulling a knife from his boot and dropping it beside Ri.

Before Ri could react, the man had run around to the side of the vehicle again and was pulling Yun-mi Kim out as well. She was slapping him, but he ignored her, dumping her at Ri's feet.

"Goddamn, woman!" the corporal cursed. "I'm *rescuing* you!"

"The South Korean President is still in the vehicle," Ri told him. "I need to ..."

The corporal had a rifle on a strap across his back and he lifted it off and checked the magazine. "Alright, I'll try to keep some heads down. You get the President."

Ri threw himself flat, crawling forward, reaching up into the interior of the vehicle to lever himself inside ... when the front windscreen imploded and automatic rifle fire punched into the interior of the LTV.

Ri flinched as he snatched a look inside the vehicle. In the seat behind the drivers' compartment was South Korean President Si-min Shin. Or, what remained of him. More assault rifle rounds punched through the shattered windscreen of the LTV, into the body of the now dead President.

Ri crawled out and behind the LTV again, where the South Korean corporal was snapping off a round or two any time there was a lull in the weight of fire coming at them. Ri looked at the truck behind them, the visitor center behind that, and the open ground between. *Too far, too exposed.* If they left this position, they would be cut down in seconds.

Captain Goh ignored the firing around him and concentrated on just one thing. The small area of planet Earth that was the single rifleman behind the LTV who was returning their fire.

Inside that small area was the man who had put a missile into his exit strategy. He had disappeared from view, but Goh so desperately wanted to see him again.

Then he saw movement, and before he even registered what it was, he fired at it.

The quickly aimed bullet fired by a very patient and focused Goh caught Chang in the side and spun him back out of view behind the LTV. There was no more return fire from the target vehicle.

"Move up!" Goh yelled to his men, pointing at the shattered LTV. "Finish this!"

Ri saw the corporal fall. The bullet had taken him in the heart and he was dead before his body even settled on the ground. But he was still holding his rifle. Ri reached for it, quickly checking it for ammunition.

A single round remained. In his peripheral vision he saw Goh's men advancing toward them.

"Give it to me, Ri," a voice beside him said. Yun-mi Kim was sitting with her back against the rear of the vehicle, an arm outstretched. "I will not be taken prisoner and tried like a common criminal," she called again. "Give me the weapon. That is an order, Comrade Captain."

Choking back tears, he passed the gun over to her. She was right. Of course she was right. Ignoring the bullets chewing the ground either side of them, he helped her place the rifle's stock between her knees and with a shaking hand, guided her finger inside the trigger guard. She lowered the muzzle toward her face.

He could not watch. He closed his eyes.

Then the whole world exploded.

Jeong Goh didn't see the first Locust from the Shikaka. He had stayed by his command vehicle up at what was now the front of the convoy as his men advanced down the causeway toward the target LTV. But he felt the blast wave, even though the first supersonic missile detonated fifty yards away. Pushed backward as though a hand had shoved him on the chest, he staggered.

And looked up.

He saw faint pinpricks of light on wings and missile bodies. He didn't bother running. There was no point really.

"Holy crap," Kronk said, watching the vision from the Shikaka as the troops in his crosshairs disappeared in a series of fireballs.

Both men then sat in silence, panning the Shikaka cameras up and down the causeway, waiting for the dust and smoke of the explosions to clear.

"Targets down," Snake said with the same stunned voice as Kronk had used. He had his hands locked behind his neck as he bent forward, studying the screen. Around a series of blackened craters was a collection of green and camouflage-uniformed bodies. Further out from the crater, more were visible, and some were still alive, either staggering or crawling away.

Up at the head of the convoy, soldiers were still standing, but they were no longer firing. Fighting along the causeway had stopped and thicker smoke from burning vehicles began obscuring the scene. Somewhere in all that smoke was the vehicle that had held the North and South Korean leaders. But were they dead or alive?

Dead *and* alive. That summed up the situation for Captain Ri.

Ri had dropped on top of his protectee and covered his ears, keeping his mouth open as the blast from the first Locust struck the troops that had been about to move on their position, and keeping it open as the second and third and then a damn *fourth* had hit as well. Each of them had been accompanied by a shattering report moments later, the supersonic boom of their arrival nearly as terrifying as the sound of their warheads exploding.

As soon as it had started, the attack stopped. As dust and smoke rolled over them, Ri rolled off Madam Kim and pried the rifle from her hands.

Yun-mi Kim was still on her back, and lay her head back on the roadway. "Is it over?" she asked. The question nearly broke his heart.

"No, your Excellency." Ri looked around the vehicle. Troops lay dead and injured on the causeway just ahead of them, but beyond that, through the smoke, he could see others. Uninjured, still moving. "We need to get going." There was only one direction, away from the fire and smoke.

Ri thought he knew everything it was possible to know about his protectee. He knew she was strong willed, determined to leave her mark on history. She liked Japanese food. He knew she had been trained to fire pistols and rifles. He knew she liked Southern K-Pop, though she only played it in private. But he did not know if she was *brave*. It was time to find out.

He took a knee beside her. "Excellency, we need to go back toward the visitor center, use the smoke for cover."

She didn't argue. "Yes."

"We will try to find another vehicle there and escape."

She nodded. "Yes."

He didn't waste any more words. While the smoke was thick and the enemy was still recovering, Ri grabbed her hand and hauled her up out of the gutter. He took one last look at the body of the brave, anonymous South Korean corporal who had rescued them.

Then they started running. Around the troop transport and through the thick smoke.

Toward clear air.

When Doves Cry

Encrypted video link, South Korean National Emergency Council

Agriculture Minister, So-wa Yoon, was an accidental Minister. A former schoolteacher, she had joined politics to fight against the economic mismanagement that had seen her high school defunded. She had never wanted to achieve high political office. Not that many would regard the role of Agriculture Minister as high political office, but it was a step too high for Yoon. She had tried to decline the post but a shortage of halfway-competent colleagues in her party had seen her rise as the best candidate, simply because she was literate, articulate and born in a rural area.

And now, here she was, just sworn in as Interim President, waiting in front of a flat screen, with three anxious aides at her back, about to join a meeting of the General Staff of the Republic of Korea Armed Forces to discuss South Korea's military response to the atrocities visited on it that day by the North. President Shi was dead. Prime Minister Choi too. For the first time in her political life, she had no one at her elbow telling her what to do, where to go, what to decide.

She felt lost. *Adrift.* As one of her aids set up the video link, she turned to her principal adviser, a woman who had been an administrator at her school and had been with her throughout her whole political life. "Dan-bi, I have no idea what to say to them," she whispered.

The woman was in her 70s now, gray haired, stern faced. She put her cool hand on Yoon's. "First, listen. They will be happy enough to do the talking. But when the time comes to decide, decide."

"Decide what? I have no experience in military affairs!" Yoon said. "How should I decide anything?!"

"How have you made *all* the difficult decisions in your

Agriculture Portfolio? What mantra have we used for the last four years?"

Yoon closed her eyes. She and Dan-bi had agreed one principle they would stick to above all others, to help them navigate the shark infested waters of agri-politics. Questions on pesticides, poisons, environmental regulations, trade subsidies and quotas – all dilemmas could be answered with a single filter: is this the right decision for the next generation?

When the time comes to decide, decide. Bi's words were like the keys to a cage she had lived in all her political life. So many times she had disagreed, but towed the line. Even today, appointing Choi as interim President: the man was patently unfit to lead the country in a time of crisis, but she had only made the weakest of protests and in the end, had endorsed him.

"Are you ready Madam President?" her aide asked, finger poised above the button that would put her into the video conference.

Madam President … it sounded so *wrong*. And yet perhaps now was exactly the *right* time to throw open the door to her cage. She straightened her back. "Yes, go ahead."

The screen blinked to life, a mosaic of video tiles showing the heads of the Army, Navy, Air Force and the intelligence services. Dan-bi was right, they were more than happy to talk … in fact they had started their meeting without her and did not even acknowledge her when she joined. A noisy debate was raging. She gave them the benefit of the doubt and chose to assume they had not noticed her log in.

"Gentlemen," she said. There was no reaction.

Dan-bi patted her hand. "Louder."

"*Gentlemen*," she repeated.

They stopped arguing, looking variously surprised or annoyed.

The Chairman of the Joint Chiefs, General of the Air Force

Yun-gi Ha, nodded to her in recognition. "Madam interim President. Welcome."

Madame *interim* President. She did not miss the emphasis he placed on 'interim'.

He continued. "We are updating the Operations Order based on the latest events. Would you like an update?"

Operations Order? She wanted more than to be 'updated' on decisions they had already made. "No. I want to know what you were arguing about," she said.

There was silence. Eventually General Ha folded his hands in front of him and spoke. "Our attack on the North's nuclear weapons storage site at Yongdoktong appears to have been successful. They will have considerable difficulty accessing their reserve weapons now and will only be able to deploy those already in the field. There is a window of opportunity for us to conduct more comprehensive air strikes across a range of strategic targets in North Korea..."

"The North has at least *ten* mobile ballistic missile launchers actively deployed, most of them unaccounted for, and we do not know which of them are nuclear armed!" The General of the Army pointed out. "And, the submarine that launched on Sangeo Shoal is still at large. You are arguing for national suicide Ha!"

"The Americans will..."

"The Americans? You put the fate of our nation in the hands of a foreign power!"

The screen dissolved into acrimonious debate again, her presence quickly forgotten, or at least actively ignored. So, as Dan-bi had counseled her, she listened. She was surprised to hear that an attack on Yongdoktong had been launched without political authorization. She was astute enough to realize there must be existing plans for a military response in the case of nuclear attack, but to execute those plans while the President was missing, and a new President was yet to be appointed?

She quickly put together a picture of the state of affairs from the discussion on the screen. A cabal within North Korea's military had sought to disrupt the peace process. They appeared to have control of the North's nuclear weapons, or at least some of them. Three of the five men on her screen were advocating for a major escalation of the conflict, with full mobilization of ground and naval forces and immediate air attacks on strategic targets inside North Korea. The Chief of the Army, General Kang, and the Head of Foreign Intelligence were arguing against this, saying it was unnecessary and would trigger a wider war that could bring in China and the USA. They were being shouted down by their opponents who pointed out the conspirators had already used nuclear weapons once, and would no doubt use them again.

A small flame began burning in her chest. She muted her mic and turned to her legal adviser. "What authority do I have over the General Staff?" she asked.

The man looked unhappy to even be in the room, let alone answering the question. "Uh, as interim President, you are also Commander in Chief," he said. "You have ultimate decision authority in all military matters."

"Can I dismiss a General?"

"Madam President, I ..."

"Can I dismiss a General?" she repeated.

"You can remove him from his post, and he can be stripped of his rank, pending a court martial," the man said.

What is best for the next generation? Yoon asked herself. All out war with the North? On the one hand, there was the risk of another nuclear attack. On the other, the fact that it could already have occurred, but had not.

She was between the Devil and a very deep blue sea. She looked at Dan-bi, but the woman simply returned her gaze with unspeaking calm. It was apparent she trusted Yoon to do the right thing in this moment. But did Yoon trust herself?

She took a deep breath and unmuted her microphone, "Gentlemen, *silence* please."

The discussion stopped abruptly, the faces on the screen showing frowns, or unmasked anger, at her interruption.

"Can I please ask who authorized the attack on Yongdoktong?"

"What do you mean?" Ha asked.

"Was it a complicated question General? Who authorized our Air Force to carry out an attack on the North Korean nuclear storage site?" she asked.

General Ha flushed, speaking with barely controlled frustration. "We have long-standing orders covering the military response in case of nuclear attack," he said. "First among them is to reduce the North's ability to access its nuclear weapons reserve."

"So *you* ordered the attack?" Yoon guessed.

He stuck out his chin defiantly. "Of course I did. And unless we..."

"Without the approval of the President of the Republic of Korea?"

"There was no bloody President of the Republic!" Ha objected loudly. "He was lying dead, in the rubble of Panmunjom. Killed by North Korean bombs! Someone had to..."

She stopped listening. "General Ha, only the Commander in Chief of the Republic can order an attack on a foreign nation. You are relieved of your duties as Chairman of the Joint Chiefs of Staff and Chief of the Air Force. General Kang, you will assume chairmanship of the Joint Chiefs."

"This is ... you cannot ..." Ha stammered.

"Ah, but I can," Yoon told him, the flame in her chest burning fiercely now. "Because it is within my authority, whereas your actions were not. You are relieved, General Ha," she said again. She turned to an aide and spoke, loud enough for the mic to easily pick up. "Please remove General Ha from this meeting."

The aide hesitated, but a stern glare from Dan-bi was enough to prompt him to action. He reached toward the video conference control panel and closed the tile containing the still stuttering Air Force General.

Yoon addressed the remaining officers. "General Kang, a question for you. Is the nation under imminent threat of further attack by the North?" *Time, she needed time. Not hours, just a few precious minutes.*

"Madam President ... I ..." he muted his mic, leaned out of camera view and then back again. "The threat of further nuclear attack is real. But there have been no further air, missile, artillery or ground attacks and there is no sign of general mobilization of North Korean armed forces."

She nodded, breathing an internal sigh of relief. "I understand. General, we will resume this discussion shortly. I will have my staff issue a communique announcing that General Ha has been relieved of his duties and you have been appointed Chairman of the Joint Chiefs. What is the procedure for appointing a new Chief of the Air Force?"

Kang blinked, events moving so fast he was having trouble keeping up. "Uh, Madam President, usually the Chief of Air Force is appointed by a majority vote of the State Council, but in this situation, I ... honestly, I do not know."

"I will consult with my legal staff. Send me a list of the officers in line for the post. In the meantime, the subordinate Generals of the Air Force will report to you, as Chairman of the Joint Chiefs, is that acceptable?"

"I ... yes, Madam President."

"Very well, resume your discussion gentlemen, but with this caveat. No further attacks on North Korean targets will be authorized without my express approval as Commander in Chief, is that clear?"

"Very clear," Kang nodded.

"I will log off now. I want to speak with the US President and see what the US is thinking. We will reconvene immediately after that."

"Yes, Madam President."

Yoon nodded at her aide and he closed the call, the screen going black. There was a stunned silence in the room.

Yoon sat back in her chair, quite stunned herself, thinking exactly what everyone else in the room was no doubt thinking. *What had she just done?*

Dan-bi stood. "I will find out who in the Presidential staff can place a call to the US President," she said.

"And what will we tell him?" Yoon asked. "That I just fired my Chairman of the Joint Chiefs and have no idea if we can still rely on the loyalty of our own Air Force?"

"No," Dan-bi said. "He is a father of three. You will tell him that for the sake of all our children you want to find a way through this conflict and back onto the path to peace. If we do not, then the conspirators have won, and the Peace Accord is dead."

Devil and the Deep Blue

Fifteen miles north-northwest Sangeo Shoal, Sea of Japan

"Dead," the XO of the *USS Cody*, Jake Ryan, declared. He looked like a sodden pirate after a battle at sea, bloodied bandages over one eye, the other bruised and cut, barely able to open enough so he could see. But it hadn't taken an order from Lomax to keep him aboard, he'd refused to let the ship's medic fly him off. "All sensors are down, both gas turbines went into emergency shutdown so they didn't tear themselves apart. We're working to restart the first one. Auxiliary diesel generator is down, water damage. Got a radio on emergency battery power, only enough juice for a range of about twenty miles. We're broadcasting a mayday but not getting any response. Airwaves are still flooded with radiating particles. Interference is crazy."

"Radiation readings?" Lomax asked.

"Normal. We were upwind of the plume."

"Update on casualties?"

"Apart from you?" Ryan replied.

Lomax laughed involuntarily, but lapsed into broken coughing, ending in a grimace as he held his ribs. He had, according to the ship's surgeon, two broken ribs and a partially collapsed lung, caused by the force of the water that had temporarily buried the *Cody* under the waves, until the air trapped in its forward spaces pulled its bow upward again and it burst back onto the surface, riding out the subsequent waves like a cowboy on a bucking bronco.

"*Everyone* took a battering," Ryan reported. He was helping Lomax down the stairs to what was left of the ship's command center. "We have three men in critical but stable condition. Doc says you should be on that list too."

"Can we fly them out?" Lomax asked, ignoring him. They'd landed their Defiant just before the big wave hit them, lashed it down to secure it from heavy seas. "Use our helo to …"

"Helo is gone," Ryan reported. "Broke away when that first wave smashed us."

Lomax winced, stopping up and holding tight to the railing as he let a wave of pain wash through him, and tried to breathe again. "*Bougainville* should ... should have sent search aircraft after us by now."

"If *Bougainville* is still afloat," Ryan replied. "And they'd be rescuing their helo crews first, I imagine. Ones that went down when the EMP hit them. Get them out of the water and then they ..."

As though the Gods had been eavesdropping, the sound of thudding rotors sounded through the bulkhead beside them.

"Helo," Lomax said. "Get me out on the flight deck."

They hobbled aft, through the aircraft hangar and out onto the flight deck that was both a helipad and the roof of the loading bay below. Several crewmen were already out on the deck, waving their arms at the approaching helo.

Without power, the *Cody* was rocking sickeningly up and down in the five-foot swell. The sea anchor they'd dropped off the bow kept them from drifting side on to the waves, but it meant the helipad was rising and falling several feet every few seconds.

Lomax surveyed the deck. "Too dangerous for them to put down. Can we get them on radio?"

"Should be possible, once they're close."

"Command center," Lomax said, with necessary brevity.

By the time the helo was overhead, Lomax and Ryan were in the ship's command center. Sealed bulkhead doors had kept the water out, so Ryan had been hopeful that when they got one of their turbines running again and power started flowing, they'd have most systems online in no time.

Lomax dropped into a chair.

"We got a link to that helo?" he asked the comms officer.

"VHF only," the man warned. "You can talk to him, just be aware you're talking in the clear, sir."

"Thanks, Lieutenant," he said holding out his hand for a handset. "This is Captain Lomax, *USS Cody*."

"Lieutenant Hollyoak, *Bougainville*," the aviator in the helo replied. "We sure are glad to have found you afloat, sir."

"So are we, Lieutenant." Lomax badly wanted to know how the rest of the task force had fared, but was wary of asking over an unencrypted channel. "Let's keep this short. I have four critically wounded men. Can you winch them up?"

"Yes, Captain. Can't put down, but you bring them out on deck, we'll haul them aboard. We have a medic with us."

"All right, I'll put our corpsman on in a second to brief him." Lomax lowered the handset and turned to Ryan. "Send someone for the Doc." He lifted the handset to his ear again. "Captain, let *Bougainville* know we are restarting our turbines after a scram. I'll send a full report over as soon as we have comms up again."

"Good copy, Captain. Our corpsman is standing by."

As they finished talking, *Cody*'s medic came in, and Lomax handed him the handset. Ryan helped Lomax down into a seat beside a row of dead monitors.

Lomax looked around himself, nodding. "Hell of a piece of work, this tub, Ryan," Lomax said. "They put a missile through our hull and detonated a nuke on top of us, and we're *still* here." As he spoke, the hull shuddered and they heard the reassuring hum of the first turbine coming back online. Screens all around the room started blinking into life. "And still fighting."

"Your permission, Captain?" Ryan asked.

"Do your job, XO," Lomax said, waving the man away to attend the myriad tasks involved in getting them ready to get underway again.

"Well, I'll be damned," his subsurface warfare officer exclaimed from the other side of the command center. He was bent over a monitor, looking at the data flowing across it. "Our *Sea Hunter* is still operational!"

Lomax started. So the small trimaran drone had weathered the nuclear storm somehow. "Where away?" he asked, raising his voice painfully so the man could hear him.

"Systems still coming online, sir," the man reported. "I

should have a ..." He frowned. "The *Sea Hunter* is still in search mode, sir..."

Was it possible? The drone had survived the nuclear blast, the EMP that followed it, and kept executing its last order: to search for the *Gorae*?

As their radar came back online, his radar officer confirmed the contact. "Contact on radar at that position. IFF checks out. It's our *Sea Hunter* all right."

"Pull its contact log. It may have logged a contact on that *Gorae* while we were offline," Lomax said. It was a long shot, but ...

"Bullseye," the subsurface warfare officer exclaimed. "Contact logged one hour three minutes ago, contact lost 23 minutes ago, contact classified *Gorae 2 class, boat ID 9.9 Hero*. Bearing 248 degrees from *Cody*'s current position, heading 189 degrees, speed 12 knots."

"And the *Sea Hunter* is in passive search mode, operating along the contact's heading?"

"*Sea Hunter* automatically matched heading and speed, sir, based on last known contact data. It's lost contact now, but unless the *Gorae* changed course, it should be right on top of it. I'd say chances of reacquiring are low, but not negligible."

Lomax smiled, despite himself. They might be down, but they weren't out. If they could find the North Korean sub, someone else could kill it. "Comms, how long until we can contact *Bougainville*?"

"Initializing comms now, sir," the comms officer reported. "Could be five minutes, could be more, depending on interference south of here."

Every minute they wasted, the fleeing submarine got farther away from its last known position, and the chances they would find it decreased. *Cody* had killed the boat that had put a hole in her bow. Lomax dearly hoped their *Sea Hunter* could assist in sending to the bottom of the Sea of Japan the boat that had tried to drown them too.

The boat that fired nuclear missiles at Sangeo Shoal was not fleeing at all. It had in fact just successfully risen to communication depth, raised its antenna without being detected, downloaded communications and uploaded a status report. Unaware of the small drone shadowing it on the surface, oblivious to all other events in the world above, it had returned below the sea's thermal layer and begun executing the second phase of its mission.

The vertical launch tubes in its conning tower sail had been emptied of water. From horizontal loading belts forward and aft of the sail the *Hero*'s crew was manhandling two more ballistic missiles into the erector mechanism that would lift and lock them into place inside the sail, ready for the *Hero* to fire its second and last salvo.

The target: Andersen Air Force Base, Guam.

The *USS Cody*'s own cat and mouse game with the *Gorae*-class submarine had begun again, but this time its *Sea Hunter* drone ship was simply one element in a massive anti-submarine hunt involving assets from across the 7th Fleet.

As the only anti-submarine capable surface element available in the search zone, however, it had a central role to play. Four Defiant helos from the *Bougainville* had been the first to join it. They had immediately begun operations with dipping sonar along the last known position and course of the ballistic missile submarine. With their sonars in passive acquisition mode, they were listening for any man-made sound where no sound should be.

Above them and flying an ellipse about ten miles from the same point of contact, was an MQ-25 ASW drone from the carrier *USS Gerald R. Ford*, dropping an outer picket of sonar buoys which were actively pinging. Floating both on the surface and with tethered subsurface emitters a hundred feet down, they could cover the ocean around them to a depth of several hundred feet. They were being dropped not so much in the expectation they would detect the *Gorae*, but that it would hear *them*, and stay penned within the picket area rather than risk revealing itself.

Moving in to assist them were two Arleigh Burke-class destroyers from *Ford*'s carrier task force. Though they had powerful sonar systems themselves, they were too far away still to be of any use in the immediate search. Their role for now was as anti-ballistic missile platforms. If a missile launch was detected by any of the platforms in the area, the missile launch point and trajectory would be relayed immediately to both of the Arleigh Burke destroyers by a Sentinel intelligence, surveillance and recon (ISR) aircraft orbiting overhead and they would try to intercept the missiles during their vulnerable boost phase. Lomax knew that in recent testing against live – not simulated – launches, where the destroyers were not using their own Aegis radars at the moment of launch, their chances of an interception were under 60 percent.

Which then led to the role of *Cody*'s *Sea Hunter*, which was also actively pinging with its trailing sonar now. The *Sea Hunter* was moving north–south within the search area, trying to drive the *Gorae* to one side or the other where the Defiants with their near-silent dipping sonars would have a better chance of picking it up.

The urgency of their task had only increased when his intelligence officer had reported back to him with a sitrep. Lomax had asked him to get onto naval intelligence Busan and pull any reports he felt were relevant to their current mission.

"I have the sitrep, sir," the man said, standing with a sheaf of paper in hand. "Do you want…"

"Give me the raw intel please, Ensign," Lomax said, holding out his hand. The man pulled several pages out and handed them over.

Lomax scanned them quickly. They were organized by source: Satellite, Open Source, Image Analysis, Electronic intelligence.

SATINT: Massive increase in communications traffic Chinese PLA

Northern Command indicative of full scale mobilization. Higher than normal levels all other commands. Massive increase in communications traffic North Korean armed force nets but full scale mobilization not observed.

SATINT: Massive increase in traffic milnets Japan, Taiwan, Philippines, Australia aligned with known alert status. China PLA Northern Command increase in traffic 79th Army HQ only, indicates units moving to forward positions on the Yalu River. PLA Navy aircraft carriers Type 1 (Yellow Sea), 2 (Pacific, Solomon Islands) and 3 (Sea of Japan) showing course corrections toward Korean Peninsula.

SATINT: Contact confirmed with White Glove task force vessels vicinity Sangeo Shoal: Bougainville, Point Loma, Marado. Contact lost with vessel Cody, last known position 37.62484982846667, 130.85860663260792, north Sangeo Shoal.

OSINT: South Korea President Si-min Shin still unaccounted for after attack on Panmunjom. South Korea Prime Minister Tae Hyun Choi assassinated during telecast after being named by South Korea State Council as interim President.

IMINT: Thermal imaging (attached) shows a) launch heat blooms, origin 37.950437030594195, 130.93551099105247, spacing indicative North Korea Gorae 2 class submarine, 9.9 Hero. Detonation blooms, 37.49857173040829 30.8695931659646 (Sangeo Shoal) and 37.611796416727834, 130.8695931659646 (North of Sangeo Shoal).

ELINT: NKN base Ch'aho sending encrypted message on continuous repeat on ballistic missile submarine frequency.

Lomax's attention jumped to two details from the reports. First, Space Force analysts had made a better than educated guess that they were submarine-launched nukes from a North Korean *Gorae* 2-class boat. Lomax and crew had concluded as much, but now it was confirmed. Second, North Korea's ballistic missile submarine base was urgently trying to get a message to one or more of its boats.

What were the chances that message was intended for the *Gorae* they were hunting?

"You get the specs on that *Gorae*?" Lomax asked, looking

up. Not an anti-submarine warfare officer, he didn't have the details of every sub in every navy memorized by heart.

"Yes, sir," the man said. "The *9.9 Hero* carries four ballistic missiles. Two stored upright in the sail, ready for launch, and two stored in horizontal magazines fore and aft."

"So they have another shot in the locker," Lomax said. "Reload time?"

The man consulted his printout. "Unconfirmed, estimated around three hours. They can reload while submerged."

Lomax looked at his watch. "We'd better find that damn boat quickly, then. Thank you, Ensign."

Lomax had once been based at Faslane, in Scotland, and some British officers had invited him to hunt grouse with them. The shooters waited behind 'butts' or hides on the moor with their shotguns, and on the other side of the fields, 'beaters' with dogs and large sticks moved toward the shooters, thrashing the undergrowth. Driven into the air by the beaters, the grouse flew straight down the barrels of the shooters. It had been a slaughter, more than a hunt.

O'Shea Lomax hoped sincerely that this particular hunt would end the same way.

Captain Se-heon Dokgo, of the Korean People's Navy Submarine Force submarine *9.9 Hero*, had not thought a lot about his personal chances for survival. The promises that had been made to him about personal advancement and financial security had been welcome, but had not been enough on their own to secure his cooperation.

Not surprisingly, it was exactly the traits that had driven his selection as a ballistic missile submarine Captain that had made him amenable to approach: detachment, loyalty, workaholism and propriety.

He had not thought about accepting the mission as a choice between life or death, either for himself, or for his men. Every time they went to sea, they were faced with the possibility of life and death choices. What mattered was whether the sacrifice asked of him and his crew was *right* and *honorable*. He had decided it was both. If officers he respected told him he was needed to play a pivotal role, perhaps *the* pivotal role, in ensuring the future glory of his Fatherland, then that was only *right*. And if the targets given him were military in nature, then the mission was *honorable*.

That the weapons he launched were nuclear, not conventional, did not trouble him at all or he would not have accepted his commission aboard the *KPN Hero* in the first place. He firmly believed in the concept of nuclear deterrence and that possession of nuclear weapons without the will to use them when necessary was self-defeating.

His self-indulgent moment of reflection was interrupted by his weapons officer. "Comrade Captain. Mission reload is complete. Launch validation checks are underway. The missiles will be ready to launch in 15 minutes."

"Very good." Dokgo turned to an officer behind him. "Officer of the deck, proceed to launch depth and prepare to hover. Call to battle stations ... missile."

Once again, his XO faithfully repeated his order.

"Sonar, report." Before he gave the order to pressurize their launch tubes, Dokgo wanted to make a last check of their environment. He had been 'threading the needle' for most of the afternoon as the enemy above intensified its search for their vessel. They had identified a ring of active sonar buoys, and successfully passed under it, leaving it about five miles behind them at last report. A small surface vessel was also conducting a search along to their northwest, but a change in course had allowed them to slip away from that too.

Given the high level of activity they had seen, he assumed there would be acoustically invisible helicopter-deployed dipping sonars in use too, but usually those would be deployed inside the picket ring they had recently escaped.

"No change, Comrade Captain," his sonar officer reported. "Multiple active sonars at 178 to 192 degrees, range 10,000 yards to 15 miles. Surface vessel bearing 169 degrees, heading 345 degrees, range 14,000 yards and increasing."

Six miles to the nearest active sonar buoy, eight to the small surface vessel trailing a sonar array in its wake. *Are we far enough away?* He was already at the outer boundaries of the launch window in the orders they had received. With so many aircraft and ships in the area, the launch of their missiles would be quickly detected. All that mattered was that the pressurization of their launch tubes did not trigger an immediate attack.

What happened to him, his crew and his missiles after that was in the hands of fate.

"Captain, we are getting a propulsion system error warning from the *Sea Hunter*. Intermittent power surges," Lomax's officer of the deck had reported.

It had been too good to last, Lomax knew that. The small unmanned craft with outrigger-style pontoons had survived the EMP wave from a nuclear detonation and tsunami-sized waves, but something had to give, and now it had.

"All right, bring it back to momma. Winch it up on the ramp and see what the problem is," he'd ordered.

That had been nearly thirty minutes ago. And it was starting to look like their quarry had given them the slip, again. Whoever the Captain was on that *Gorae*, may his soul rot in hell, he knew his craft. He'd somehow managed to slip through the cordon of buoys and dipping sonar and could be anywhere by now. There were still four Defiants dipping and the MQ-25 was dropping a new ring of sonar buoys further out, but it was a big sea, and deep.

They had slowed to a crawl now, readying themselves to take their ailing *Sea Hunter* aboard, and had turned stern on to it so that they could lower their landing ramp and lift aboard with their crane.

His XO, Ryan, still looking like a car crash victim with head bandaged and wrist in a sling, came onto the bridge. "*Sea Hunter* is about a mile out," he reported. He stood next to Lomax and looked out their shattered bridge windows. "I figure that *Gorae* is done. They made their statement, he's going home."

"I hope you're right, XO."

Ryan was wrong.

The *9.9 Hero* had just reached missile launch depth 150 feet below the waves and was in a hover.

Captain Se-heon Dokgo took a moment to close his eyes and pray to his ancestors. He wasn't a particularly religious man, but it felt like a religious moment. He opened his eyes again. "Officer of the deck, pressurize tubes one and two."

"Pressurizing tubes one and two, aye."

The noise of the missiles being prepared for firing sounded deafening inside the enclosed space underneath the submarine's sail. For the next three minutes, they would be vulnerable.

"Tubes one and two pressurized!"

"Ready launch, one and two."

"Readying launch, one and two, aye." Dokgo looked at the men around him. All had families; mothers, fathers, brothers, sisters, wives, children. All knew that they had launched nuclear missiles once already. A global nuclear holocaust could be underway above the waves. The pressure on him, as it was on every man, was incredible, and none of them knew whether their families were even still alive.

But they were doing their duty. They deserved the thanks of the entire nation, which they would never receive. But they could have *his* thanks.

He reached for the internal ship broadcast handset. "Comrade citizens, crew of the *9.9 Hero*," he began. "Our nation is at war for its survival. We do not know how that war is progressing, but we have received our orders and once again we will play our part. We are about to launch a missile strike on the US air base at Guam. This air base is the most important US Air Force facility in the entire region. At that air base, the main enemy has fleets of nuclear bombers, squadrons of attack aircraft and missiles that could be used to attack our Fatherland. We will *destroy* them." He paused. At this moment, they deserved honesty. "The moment we launch, we could be attacked. I am as proud of you right now as a father is of his own sons. Do your jobs well, for your Fatherland, and for the ones you love."

He hung up the intercom handset and turned to the officers in the command center. The looks on the faces he saw there were of grim determination. He saw no fear. His heart was bursting with pride.

"Officer of the deck, immediately after missile launch, set propulsion ahead full, rudder hard starboard, implement a crash dive to maximum allowed depth."

"Ready for crash dive, aye, Captain."

"Officer of the deck … launch missiles one and two."

"Launch missiles one and two, aye!" The orders rang out through the boat.

"Contact!" a watch officer yelled. "From the *Sea Hunter*. Bearing one three zero, range … five hundred yards! Designating contact Sierra one."

Lomax started. What? The North Korean submarine was almost directly *underneath* them. "Patch data to the nearest Defiant. Alert the Aegis ships."

"Patching data through now. Defiants are five miles out, sir. Both destroyers acknowledging and on alert," the watch officer said. "Sonar reports sounds of missile tubes flooding, sir. Contact is preparing to launch…"

Lomax gripped the console in front of him. The North Korean submarine was about to launch its missiles *right before his eyes* and he was completely, totally impotent.

Or …

He grabbed his comms handset. "Weapons. Captain. Bring HELIOS online, automatic targeting mode!"

Mounted on the superstructure of the *Cody* was its 125 kW missile defense laser. It was designed to intercept supersonic sea skimming anti-ship missiles. It had never been intended to intercept sub-launched intercontinental ballistic missiles. But the designers could never have anticipated those missiles would be launched within a mile of their laser.

And a missile was a missile, wasn't it?

"Captain, weapons reports HELIOS on line, radar up and system in auto lock and fire mode."

He had two men out on the bridge wings in readiness for guiding the *Sea Hunter* in and from the starboard wing he heard a cry. "Spouts in the water, aft starboard!"

There was nothing more he could do at his station, so Lomax ran to the lookout station, Ryan right behind him.

A few hundred yards off their stern, the water boiled, then it heaved upwards in two white foam columns. As the columns collapsed, the ballistic missiles emerged from the foam and *seemed to hang there.*

Then their boosters ignited.

"HELIOS firing!" Lomax heard from inside the bridge. There was no sound, no special effects laser beam shooting across the sky, the ship's laser was invisible to the naked eye in daylight.

The noise of the missiles' rockets igniting came booming across the water at them now. "The one in front is obscuring the other," Ryan yelled. "We won't get a clean shot at both!"

The missiles were powering up through the air now on pillars of fire.

I'm looking at the end of the world, Lomax thought to himself. *This is insanity.*

A hundred feet off the ground and in complete unison, the two missiles began spinning, tipping slightly to begin their ballistic flight.

Tipping heavily! The trajectory of the missile nearest the *Cody* was beginning to flatten, while the other, farther away, continued to power into the sky.

Whether it was a guidance system failure, or the impact of the HELIOS, it didn't really matter. *It was falling!* Lomax watched open mouthed as the missile began to plunge back down toward the sea.

Ryan was pulling him back inside the bridge. "Sound emergency!" he yelled to the officer of the watch. "Engines ahead full. That missile could blow. Brace for impact!"

"Secure tubes one and two. Crash dive!" Dokgo ordered.

"Securing tubes, initiating crash dive, aye."

Dokgo staggered and had to grab a handhold to steady himself as the *Hero* jerked into motion. In seconds it was moving through the water again, and the deck under his feet inclined downwards as its forward planes drove its nose ten, then twenty, then thirty degrees down.

They were hanging on their handholds now, inside the command center, as the boat began spiraling through the water, away from its launch point.

"One hundred feet," the officer of the deck reported. "One twenty…"

"Launch decoys," Dokgo commanded.

"Launch decoys, aye."

From both sides of the *Hero*'s sail, two acoustic noisemakers fired into the water and began motoring away from the submarine. If there was an enemy above and they dropped torpedoes, Dokgo wanted the noisemakers to be the first thing they heard.

"Contact Sierra one maneuvering. Decoys fired."

What the submarine was doing now was not Lomax's greatest concern. What that bloody missile was doing, was. It probably held hundreds of tons of propellant. If it exploded…

"HELIOS radar has lost missile lock…"

The bridge crew was strapped into their chairs. The *Cody* could power from a standing start to 30 knots inside two minutes and Lomax felt her twin turbines humming through the deck beneath his feet. Not for the first time, Lomax was grateful for the word fast in expeditionary *fast* transport.

"Defiant over target Sierra one. Dropping torpedo…"

Lomax was staring ahead, willing the *Cody* to just give him another five knots, *dammit, you fat-assed beauty…*

The Pukguksun missiles fired by the *KPN 9.9 Hero* each contained 40 tons of solid fuel propellant. *Cody's* HELIOS laser had burned a hole in the missile's first stage casing, causing the fuel there to begin burning through the hole in its side and tipping the missile off balance.

It was still burning inside the casing when the missile plunged into the sea and its speed and momentum carried it a hundred feet underwater.

The water didn't dowse the chemical reaction inside the casing because a key feature of solid fuel propellant is that the oxygen it needs to burn furiously is already mixed with the fuel. Once ignited, it continues to burn underwater.

Driven by the booster rocket still firing in its tail, the missile was already spiraling 500 feet down, and moving lower.

"Object in the water. Not guiding. Probable missile failure..."

Captain Se-heon Dokgo tightened his grip on the handhold. They were still diving at 45 degrees and approaching the *Hero's* do-not-exceed depth of 1,600 feet. He tried not to let his face show what he was thinking, but Dokgo was privy to the failure rate of the Pukguksun class of missiles and with one in three failing, he was not at all surprised one of the missiles had not launched.

There was no danger the nuclear warhead would explode – it would probably just belly flop into the water and break up. But it left only one missile for the strike on Guam.

"Surface contact now bearing one zero nine, course two zero five, speed 35 knots ..."

Their sonar had detected twin screws spinning up right above them as they began their crash dive. A vessel of some sort had been sitting right on top of them as they launched! To have gone unnoticed, it must have been both relatively small, and stationary. Whatever it was, they apparently scared the hell out of it because it was fleeing at high speed. A civilian fishing vessel perhaps?

"Officer of the deck, engines ahead slow, zero the rudder and dive planes," Dokgo ordered.

"Engines to ahead slow, zeroing rudder and planes, holding at 1,200 feet."

"Torpedo in the water!" His sonar officer called out. Seconds later the first ping from its active sonar seeker head hit their hull. The next came quickly behind it, and the next, even faster. "Two torpedoes!" the man said, then frowned. "Correction. One torpedo. Our missile is in the water, the engine is still burning. Torpedo tracking!"

They had no chance of outrunning the torpedo. Traveling at 83 feet per second, the American torpedo, because that was what it had to be, would find them within 15 seconds.

"Captain? Fire decoys?" his weapons officer asked, his face a study in controlled fear.

Dokgo tried to control his own breathing. "No. We already have decoys in the water."

To fire new decoys now risked attracting the missile down to their depth. With the decoys they fired five minutes earlier still emitting noise and gas, there was a chance that...

A loud *thud* rocked the *Hero*.

"Explosion! Torpedo decoyed!" his sonarman reported. Unable to control themselves, the crew in the command center began cheering and slapping each other on the back.

Dokgo let them enjoy the moment. Where there had been one torpedo, *there would soon be more.*

"Weapons, two more decoys, please, set to rise. Officer of the deck, left full rudder, come around to 350 degrees."

The cheering subsided as the orders were relayed, but the grins on his crew's faces did not.

Unknowingly, Se-heong Dokgo had just ordered his boat to turn *toward* the downward-spiraling ballistic missile. At that moment, 100 feet off their bow, 40 tons of solid rocket propellant detonated.

And the *USS Cody* became the first expeditionary fast

346

transport warship in history to sink an enemy submarine with its own missile.

Even if he had known it, it was unlikely O'Shea Lomax would have celebrated, because as the superheated water started foaming white off *Cody*'s stern, he was standing on the bridge wing, watching the contrail of *Hero*'s un-intercepted ballistic missile curve away toward the outer atmosphere.

Twelve SM-3 Block III missiles were launched by the two Arleigh Burke destroyers powering toward the *Cody*'s contact. The two ships were still fifty miles out when the North Korean missiles were launched, but managed to launch during the missile's slower boost phase and already had a position and bearing on the missiles thanks to the quick warning from the *Cody*'s command center.

As the North Korean missile reached three times the speed of sound, four of the six US missiles locked onto it and began homing.

All four missed.

On Guam, air raid sirens had been ringing out from the moment the Arleigh Burke destroyers picked up the ballistic missile on their powerful Aegis radar systems and predicted its trajectory and target.

The warning to Guam had been sent two minutes into the North Korean missile's trajectory. On Guam, the multiple Patriot missile and HELLADS laser defense systems on the island had only 12 minutes to react.

But because the base was at DEFCON 1 condition, and their crews were already on alert, the Patriot batteries across the island were able to detect and fire on the North Korean missile in less than five minutes.

As it began its descent, quickly reaching six times the speed of sound, 36 supersonic Patriot missiles were fired at the incoming North Korean missile.

When the Patriots were still a minute from interception, the warhead of the Pukguksung split into six separate re-entry vehicles, each traveling at more than 1,998 miles an hour. Only one of the warheads was nuclear, the rest were decoys. But the ruse was barely necessary. Confused by the last-minute change in trajectory of the North Korean missile's warhead, only two of the re-entry vehicles were successfully intercepted.

Four warheads, including one carrying a 25 kiloton nuclear weapon, fell on Guam at a speed the close-defense laser HELLADS batteries proved unable to even track, let alone intercept.

The North Korean attack on Guam would be studied by defense scientists and war colleges across the globe for years to come, as it was a lesson in abject failure.

The failure of the numerically overwhelming US Navy anti-submarine air interdiction force to destroy the *9.9 Hero* before it launched. The failure of the Aegis destroyers to intercept the Pukguksung missile in its boost phase. The failure of the Patriot missile and HELLADS batteries to destroy the North Korean re-entry vehicles in their terminal phase.

And the failure of the North Korean nuclear warhead to detonate.

White House Press Briefing

James S Brady Press Briefing Room

MS. CORNELL: OK, thank you for coming at short notice. Regarding the reports on social media and network news of a missile attack on the US territory of Guam...

Firstly, I can confirm that a suspected North Korean missile was fired from a submarine in the Sea of Japan. We believe that the target was Guam, but the missile was successfully intercepted by our missile defenses over Guam. Questions? Yes, Jerry?

Q. "Was the missile nuclear?"

MS. CORNELL: Too soon to say. Several pieces of the missile struck Guam after it was intercepted, and I imagine they will be analyzed. But there was no nuclear explosion, I want to be clear on that.

Q "Follow up, please. Have there been any casualties on Guam?"

MS. CORNELL: There have been several casualties. It is too soon to say how many, but our information is that they are in the tens, not hundreds or thousands. We understand families of personnel on Guam are worried and will get back with more information as soon as possible. Let me emphasize we of course do not regard a single US casualty to be acceptable and we will respond appropriately. Uh, Susanne?

Q. "*How* is the US going to respond to this attack?"

MS. CORNELL: That is being discussed in the National Security Council as we speak. US Forces remain on high alert and as you can see from the way this missile attack was dealt with, we are more than capable of defending our interests in the region. But the situation on the Korean Peninsula is still fluid and I can't comment on operational matters until we have a clearer picture. Uh, yes, Carl?

Q. "South Korean media is reporting that both its President and Prime Minister are dead or missing. The South Korean

Agriculture Minister is being sworn in as interim President. No one has seen or heard from the North Korean Supreme Leader, Madam Kim, since the attack on Panmunjom. Has President Fenner had any contact with anyone in the political leadership of South or North Korea?"

MS. CORNELL: As I said, I can't comment on operational matters until we have a clearer picture. My purpose here is to confirm there was an attack on Guam, but at this stage it appears to have been largely unsuccessful, though our thoughts and prayers are with the residents and US military personnel on that island as they deal with the results of that attack. That is all … thankyou. There are coffee and sandwiches in the room next door folks. Our next update will be in an hour unless there is breaking news.

Connectivity Issues

Uiju Airfield, North Pyongan Province, North Korea

In Sinuiju, the leader of the conspiracy, General Yong-gon Choe, was done with talking. His intelligence staff had told him the attack on Guam had failed. There had been no contact from the *9.9 Hero* since it acknowledged the strike order. He had no idea what had gone wrong, but if missiles had been fired, no nuclear explosions had been detected, so the missiles had either been intercepted or failed to detonate. China's Northern Command Army was showing no sign it was moving across the Yalu River to support him. Two North Korean colonels, one of them an influential Strategic Missile Forces battalion commander, had gone dark, not responding to contact – either because they had been arrested, or because they were regretting their decision to support him. More deserters would no doubt soon follow.

He had only one card left to play, but it could still turn the tide in his favor, giving him a position of unassailable strength in any negotiation and restoring spine to those in his ranks who were quavering. One more roll of the dice that could turn the ashes of failure into the embers that would reignite victory.

He picked up the telephone handset and walked to the window looking out from his command post and across the Uiju airfield. Five hundred yards away beside the runway, six Mi-24 Krokodil helicopter gunships crouched, rotors idling. Each gunship was armed with a swiveling autocannon, missile and rocket launchers, and eight special operations troops.

The men inside the Krokodils were expertly trained in the mission they had been given, they were armed and ready, they were simply waiting for his order to lift off.

A voice at the other end of the line answered.

"Colonel, you may execute your mission," Choe said simply.

"Yes, Comrade General!" the man replied.

He looked at his watch. At a cruising speed of 200 miles an

hour, it would take the massive helicopters just ten minutes to reach their target.

Yongdoktong nuclear arsenal.

South Korea had sealed the main entrance, but all his people had to do was force the smaller personnel entrance in the south. The facility was not under his control, the commander there reported to Pyongyang directly. But Choe's staff would right now be contacting the facility to warn them that new troops were inbound to provide added security. The commander there would be confused, would be contacting Pyongyang for orders, and in the vacuum that was the absence of leadership in Pyongyang right now, in that crack of the door that was political chaos, his troops could fight through.

Control of the arsenal would mean none could ignore him. Not the weaklings throughout North Korea's military who had not joined, not those who were considering deserting him, and not his so-called Chinese allies across the Yalu.

As he turned from the window, he allowed himself to hope still. Some of history's greatest victories had been won in the face of defeat. The short history of his own nation had taught him that. Yes, Choe still dared to hope.

The commander of the garrison of 183 Strategic Missile Defense troops at Yongdoktong was also a man who dared to hope. But it was a hope of a different kind.

Song-man Jang knew his men called him 'Elvis'. It was a nickname that privately pleased him, though he would never, could never, acknowledge it. Jang was a big fan of old-fashioned rock'n'roll and under his large peaked cap – which showed only a tightly clipped back and sides – he sported a brushed back, heavily oiled wave of hair in the style Elvis Presley had adopted when he served in the US Army.

Elvis Jang had achieved everything he expected in life. He had risen to the rank of Colonel. He had been given the most prestigious of commands, custodianship of the nation's military beating heart, its nuclear arsenal. He had married well, and had two boys of whom his heart was unbearably proud.

And that was why he dared to hope. Elvis Jang dared to hope that his boys would grow up in a different Korea. Not a Korea at war, but one at peace. Not a Korea where the only route out of poverty was to enter politics or the military.

Elvis didn't expect his boys to grow up rock'n'roll fans – they were hopeless K-Pop obsessives – but he wanted a Korea where his boys could listen to whatever damn music they wanted to. He wanted a world where they could decide for themselves the life they wanted to lead, and life would give them a chance of realizing it.

Elvis Jang knew that his current command was crucial in that dream coming true. North Korea had only one big stake in any negotiation with the South and their Western backers, and that was the arsenal he guarded. His impoverished, criminally corrupt land had nothing to offer the South but the hand of friendship and the promise of nuclear disarmament.

Over five years of negotiation, that promise had been enough. And today ... today was supposed to have been the most shining monument to that promise. The signing of the Peace Accord!

Now that promise lay in tatters.

Panmunjom bombed. And, the rumors said, nuclear weapons used in the east.

The South had retaliated, of course it had. And to his shame, though his forces brought down the attackers, a single plane had penetrated their defenses and landed its bunker busting bomb right at the mouth of the main entrance to their underground storage facility and collapsed the twin tunnel entrances.

It should not have been possible, but Elvis Jang, more than anyone else, had lived through the years of requested building works being refused. Through the reports of flooded and abandoned tunnels, and shafts sealed off because they were no longer usable.

They had lost several dozen lives, but they had never lost a single warhead. Of course not. If they had, he would no longer be in command. But if it hadn't been a South Korean attack that brought the tunnel entrance down, it would have happened eventually through lack of maintenance.

Still, the South Korean attack had failed. It had sealed the main entrance to the facility and rendered inoperative the rail line used to move the heavy warheads in and out. But the rear personnel entrance was still open, and so his team of technicians and scientists could still carry out their duties monitoring and maintaining the weapons in a safe state.

Ironically, it also made the task of guarding the stockpile easier too, since there was only one route by which an enemy could try to access the arsenal, and that was through the personnel entrance. Which was top of his mind as he put down the telephone receiver after the call he had received from the staff of General Choe at Sinuiju District Command HQ.

"Reinforcements? I have no need of reinforcements," Jang had told the Pyongan Provincial Army Colonel at the other end of the line. Jang had suffered only a handful of casualties in the South Korean air attack on the facility. His garrison was deliberately overstrength in relation to the task of guarding the site and the facility was built into the terrain around it so that the troops garrisoned there could resist both air assault and a Corps-sized ground attack, and a siege of up to six months if necessary.

"Your beliefs are outdated," the man at the other end of the line had said. "A state of war will soon be declared. Only a fool would refuse an offer of additional support at a time of national crisis."

"I will need to check with Strategic Missile Forces Command," Jang had said.

"You are welcome to," the man had replied. "But before you do, perhaps you should consider that your troops have already proven inadequate in executing their duties once today, Colonel."

The open insult had not smudged Elvis Jang's paintwork. He had simply put the handset down and turned to the Captain standing beside him.

"Base alert. All anti-air and ground forces to immediate combat readiness. Prepare for an airborne assault. The enemy will be wearing North Korean military uniforms and using North Korean aircraft and equipment."

Elvis Jang had not hesitated a moment in responding to the call from Uiju airfield. Not because, for good reason, he did not report to, nor fear repercussions from, any of the Generals of the North Korean Regular Army. Nor because, in his heart, the flame of reunification still burned as strongly this afternoon as it had this morning.

Jang had acted with clarity and speed because just ten minutes earlier he had taken a call from the Commander of North Korean Strategic Rocket Forces himself. The man had been very, very clear in his instructions.

"Jang, I have just been on the telephone with our Supreme Leader herself..."

Jang's heart had leapt in his chest. She was alive!! When he had heard about Panmunjom, he had feared the worst. But if Madam Kim was alive, so was the hope of a future for his boys.

"Yes, Comrade General!"

"Jang, you will immediately report any unusual activity, of any kind, to me personally, and you will not accept orders from anyone but me, is that clear?"

"Yes, Comrade General."

"Any approach by forces other than Strategic Missile Force defense troops toward our facility at Yongdoktong, even North Korean troops from other commands, is to be regarded as hostile and resisted with utmost effort, is that understood?"

Jang had quailed. Had he just been ordered to defend his facility against troops from his *own* country?

"Comrade General, I understand your order to mean my men are authorized to fire on North Korean forces if they are not Strategic Missile Defense troops. Not just South Korean or American forces. Is that correct?"

"Yes, Jang, you have understood correctly. Now, prepare your defenses, and alert me to any activity."

"Yes, Comrade General!"

As klaxons blared throughout the facility and under the mountainside it was protecting, Jang pulled off his peaked cap, freeing his flowing lock of hair and smoothing it back into place.

The Captain at his side did not react, but reached for a helmet and handed it to him.

"Base on alert, Comrade Colonel," he said, as Jang jammed the helmet on his head.

"Yes. Captain, please send a flash report to Strategic Missile Command. *Imminent airborne assault by forces of General Choe. Will defend facility as ordered.*"

The Captain paled, but he had been in the room with Jang all day, and he had been party to the conversations of the last hour. He saluted. "Yes, Comrade Colonel," he said, and ran from the room.

Jang walked to a nearby weapons rack and pulled a rifle off a rack. His anti-air commanders would do their best to make sure the incoming airborne force did not reach Yongdoktong's perimeter. But if it did, his place was down at the personnel entrance, with his men.

The man General Choe had chosen to lead the attack on Yongdoktong was a man of no particular conviction at all. He didn't have a colorful nickname like 'Elvis'. If he had been given a nickname by his troops, it might have been 'Robot'. Since taking over the Provincial Command Airborne company attached to Choe's command, he had shown no initiative whatsoever. He had simply executed every single order he had ever been given. Without question, and without fail.

Captain Chol-guk Hong of the Pyongan Airborne Special Operations Force was everything that was wrong with North Korea's armed forces. He questioned nothing, no matter how insensible. He followed his training in everything, never improvising. He trusted no one below him, he owed no loyalty to his men, nor even his peers. He commanded through fear, not fealty.

He had lost three of the men in his company to accidents during training for the Yongdoktong assault, including one of his officers, executed by Hong's own hand after he deviated from Hong's orders. Hong had learned early in his career that any and all dissent should be met with the harshest of punishments, and dissent in front of other officers or worse, noncommissioned troops, should be met with the ultimate discipline – death. Chol-guk Hong was not a man whose world view encompassed either strategic creativity or individual initiative.

But Chol-guk Hong was also living proof that even undeserving asswipes can get lucky.

Elvis Jang established a command post fifty yards inside the personnel entrance in the south of the hillside under which Yongdoktong arsenal was buried, at the first bend in the tunnel, where a guard post straddled the width of the entryway and guards usually stood ready to check the bona fides and personal belongings of staff moving in and out of the facility.

With him was his Guards commander, a man who had spent the whole day at the northern entrance to the facility supervising the operation to try to rescue troops and personnel from the collapsed tunnel. Though his uniform was streaked with mud and showed the toll of the day's events, the man's eyes were clear and his face newly washed.

He and Jang were poring over a map of the Yongdoktong facility and surroundings. The small river that provided the facility with water and took away its waste wound through hills from the north, then turned east–west in front of the hillside under which the arsenal was buried, before turning and flowing south again.

Somewhere in that river valley was the aircraft that had attacked them that morning, and its suicidal pilot. Jang had not wasted any resources looking for him. The river valley had been chosen for the site because it provided perfect air and ground choke points. As the South Korean pilot had discovered, any approach by air was doomed either by the long-range missile battalions on the peaks around Yongdoktong or by the low-level autocannon and MANPAD missile defenses. By design, the southern personnel entrance was located near the personnel barracks, but outside it was a hundred-yard cleared and leveled concrete apron which allowed nothing to approach unobserved.

In front of the entrance, two sunken 'pillbox' style fortifications covered the entrance, troops inside them armed with grenade launchers and twin 12.7mm machine guns. On the hillside just above, overlooking the entrance, was a four-barreled 14.5mm heavy machine gun for anti-air or anti-personnel defense.

Across the entrance to the hillside, just behind Elvis Jang's newly established command post, was a hydraulically powered, five-ton blast-proof door designed to withstand a direct strike by a tactical nuclear weapon up to 200 kilotons in strength.

North Korea took the protection of its nuclear arsenal very, very seriously.

What the conspirators' plan for taking Yongdoktong lacked in creativity, it made up for in brutality. The defenders of Yongdoktong were supposed to have been disoriented and confused by the news that reinforcements were being flown in. They were not supposed to be suspicious of the arrival of those troops, and they were certainly not supposed to be preparing to resist them.

But just in case they were, General Choe had ordered an attack by 12 Su-25 Grach fighters from his Army Air Force wing to support the incursion.

They were not armed with conventional weapons.

What North Korea lacked in modern smart weapons, it had been forced to counter with non-conventional nuclear and other weapons. Most common among these was the nerve gas VX, which had even been used to assassinate enemies of the ruling family, including the then Supreme Leader's own brother in an attack in Malaysia.

Each of the Grach aircraft approaching Yongdoktong at nap of the earth height from south of the nuclear storage facility was carrying four 1,000 lb. parachute-retarded VX nerve gas bombs. Designed to be delivered at altitudes of under 1,000 feet, the bombs deployed speed retarding fins and chutes the moment they were released.

As the aircraft that released them retreated from their attack, the bombs fell to 200 feet above the ground and exploded, scattering canister submunitions over an area of 10,000 square feet. As soon as they hit the ground, the canisters began spraying nerve gas. The resulting cloud from a single bomb would incapacitate or kill anyone it came in contact with.

The weapon had been tested on criminals and political prisoners. It had never been used against troops from its own nation.

Until today.

"Fast-moving aircraft approaching from the south, heading three five zero, low level, ten plus aircraft, range twenty two. They have made contact with air defense control and say they are transiting to Nampo Air Base."

Jang looked at the map. Nampo lay two hundred miles to the northeast. Their heading would take them nowhere near Nampo.

"Nampo my ass. Tell the air defense commander to advise if they overfly Yongdoktong they will be fired on."

The Captain relayed his orders, and they waited. Seconds ticked past. "No response from the incoming aircraft."

The incoming aircraft were uncomfortably close. *Late, they had been detected too late!* Jang did not hesitate. "Order air defenses to engage."

Even though they were flying just 500 feet above the ground, the commander of the S-200 battalion on the hilltop above the Yongdoktong facility had all ten incoming aircraft on radar.

But his Cold War-era system could only lock and fire on *five*.

"Targets locked, Comrade Major!" his battalion fire officer reported.

"Shoot," he ordered. "Retarget immediately."

He watched the small dots on the circular amber low-res screen of his radar display race outward toward the group of ten dots at the top of the screen. The screen refreshed too slowly to follow the interception in real time.

When next it refreshed a second later, six enemy aircraft were still boring in them. They had claimed four – but only four.

"Retargeting..." his fire officer reported. "Battery three ready to fire."

"Shoot when ready."

"Shooting."

More dots flew across the screen toward the attackers, because despite their IFF codes telling him they were 'friendly' he was in no doubt they were hostile, or the radio speaker in his trailer would have been filled with panicked, outraged radio calls.

As he waited for the radar screen to refresh, he looked up at the ceiling of the command trailer. The undrunk coffee in the cup he had poured ten minutes earlier began to vibrate.

The rumble of jet engines was upon them.

"Comrade Major!" his battalion fire officer turned to him, panic in his voice. "New contacts, bearing two six nine degrees, range four, low ..."

Four of the ten Grach attack aircraft made it through the missile defense screen. Shoulder-fired infrared missiles clawed toward them as they released their FAB-500 VX cluster bombs and broke left and right around the Yongdoktong hilltop.

Two more fighters fell to the low-level air defenses.

But with parachutes blooming behind them, sixteen of the

deadly bombs fell across the Yongdoktong site, each of them holding 15 of the toxic VX nerve gas canisters.

As they started releasing their gas, in the belly of his Mi-24 Krokodil gunship, the unimaginative and perfectly amoral Chol-guk Hong saw a green light on the bulkhead beside him and turned to his men. "Headgear on! Check weapons!"

Patterned on a US Integrated Protective Ensemble suit, Hong's suit consisted of a single piece conformal, laminated layer outer suit with omniphobic coatings. The full face, head and neck mask was its weakest point. If it wasn't fitted perfectly, gas could leak between the seams. He buddied with the man next to him and checked the man's headgear fit and waited while the other man did the same for him.

As he thumped the man on the head to indicate he was good to go, he staggered. An explosion from behind them, and their gunship swerved suddenly. Hong heard the *thud thud thud* of decoy flares firing into their wake, then their machine righted itself and plowed forward again.

Someone had bought it.

But not him.

Most of the air defenses around Yongdoktong were last generation or worse, but the Nuclear Chemical Biological Weapons sensor system inside the facility was not. German-made, purchased from Iran, it could send an alert across the entire facility within milliseconds of detecting a radiation or gas leak at dangerous levels.

It was also sensitive to multiple chemical weapon agents, including VX gas.

"Air defense reports several hostile aircraft destroyed. Explosions across the site. Damage is..." the man stopped talking and tilted his head, listening.

Before Elvis could open his mouth to ask what the man was doing, a rising and falling alarm began ringing out through the tunnels around and behind them. The huge fans in the ceiling that usually pulled air into the claustrophobic tunnels stopped turning and, apart from the alarm, the tunnel was suddenly eerily quiet.

"Chemical attack!" Jang yelled. "Mask up!" The men around him started running for the walls.

Along the tunnel walls at hundred-yard intervals were gas masks in narrow lockers. The most common threat was not chemical weapons, but rather carbon monoxide buildup from the poorly ventilated generator rooms that were scattered throughout the underground facility. The masks were sufficient to provide the user with up to 30 minutes of clean air so that they could get to safety above ground.

They were next to useless against chemical weapons which could poison a target through skin contact.

Like VX nerve gas.

Jang didn't bother running. There weren't enough masks within reach, and those that were, were of dubious value. One of the many requisitions he had been denied over the years was for new masks to replace those that had suffered from years of deterioration. Most of the masks inside the facility had perished rubber seals, or brittle head-straps that would break as soon as any real force was applied to them.

As he watched in horror, Jang saw a man stagger toward the entrance to the tunnel and then fall onto the ground, rolling around as he clawed at his neck. Behind him, Jang saw the toad-like shape of a Mi-24 lower itself to the apron in front of the tunnel and begin disgorging troops in NCBW protective gear.

Despair flooded Jang. His enemy knew all the weak points in his defenses. Of course they did. And they had played them perfectly.

As he watched, the gunship finished unloading its troops and swung its nose around to bring its guns and rockets to bear on the tunnel entrance. Jang shot a look at the concrete and steel guard emplacements behind him and saw his men, masked now, running to take up defensive positions behind them.

The sight filled him with pride at the same time as it crippled him. His own feet would not move. Their bravery and their inadequate masks would not protect them against the gas that was flooding into the cave even as they ran forward. Nor against the barrage of rockets and missiles the gunship was about to send at them.

Then, miraculously, the 14.5mm heavy machine gun on the hillside above opened up. Sparks marched along the side of the armored gunship from tail to nose and stopped by a weapons pylon; the gunner training his fire not on the gunship's thick armored skin or glass, but on the exposed ordnance hanging off the pylon.

With a detonation like a box of grenades exploding, the rocket pod on the side of the gunship cooked off, sending shrapnel into the helicopter's rotors. It tried to bank away, but as it did, one of the rotors went flying, and the gunship thumped heavily into the ground, one side aflame.

A second later, the entire gunship exploded.

The explosion sent Jang reeling but freed his feet at last. If he was moving, if he wasn't gasping, he was still *alive*, dammit!

Turning his stagger into a run, he kept moving, back past the men at the barricade and into the nearest guard post. There was no mask inside, but there was something more important.

The blast door controls.

Pulling off the plastic cover that prevented accidental use, he hammered the heel of his hand on the large red button. Lights began flashing as the door mechanism whined and the heavy nuclear blast-proof door began rumbling across rails in the floor.

He knew the door at the other entrance had been triggered earlier in the day, and the mechanism jammed by the South Korean air attack.

"Comrade Colonel?" the Guards Captain who had been with him earlier was standing at the door of the guard post. He was talking to Jang, but his eyes were on the slowly closing door about twenty yards behind them. "Your orders?"

"We will hold this position," Jang said. He had to yell over the sound of firing outside. Outgoing, from the 14.5mm overhead and the troops in the tunnel with them, incoming from the airborne force that had just been landed.

"The door will keep them out," the man said. "If the gas..."

"The door mechanism can be mechanically overridden. We will hold here."

"But the gas..."

Jang looked out at the entrance to the tunnel. He saw at least four squads of troops in NCBW protective gear moving on the tunnel entrance. Behind them, hovering menacingly, another gunship. It loosed a terrifying volley of rockets that flew above the tunnel entrance, causing the tunnel overhead to shake and dust to fall from the ceiling.

There was a moment of surprised silence, and then the 14.5mm gun resumed its angry staccato chatter, forcing the gunship to pull away.

Jang pointed upward. "If those men up there can still fight, so can we, Captain." He heard the door behind him continue its slow grind – it would soon slam closed – and tried to ignore it. Pointing at concrete vehicle barriers just ahead of the guard post, he gave his orders. "Men left and right with grenade launchers. Riflemen farther back. You stay back here. If people start falling from gas, pull back to these guard posts. If the gas reaches here, pull back to the door and go prone." The man looked as terrified as Jang felt, but he pushed the fear down into his gut. "Gas settles, Captain. We are deep under the hillside here. We stay, and we fight."

He knew he was right. Even if he just bought his men inside the facility time to organize a better defense, he had to hold the door as long as he could.

And then it was too late for any more discussion. The door behind them groaned to a halt and stopped moving, at the same time as two rocket-propelled grenades flew into the tunnel. One hammered into an unmanned barrier near the tunnel entrance, the other flew high and exploded against the blast-proof door, causing them both to duck.

As if the threat of gas wasn't bad enough, the air filled with choking smoke and dust now. Jang realized he had dropped his rifle at some point and picked it up off the floor. "Get your men organized, Captain," he said, coughing. "They are following the textbook. It will be infantry in force next. Tell your people to hold their fire unless they see a target."

There was no textbook for assaulting a nuclear storage facility buried under a mountain, but in preparing for today, Hong and his officers had relied on the best available intelligence and applied the conventions of North Korean Army Assault Tactics for assaulting a heavily fortified bunker.

Their intelligence told them that 90 percent of Yongdoktong's garrison of 200 ground defense troops were in barracks and guard posts *above* ground. With the two entrances to the facility in operation, the entire base complement of 1,800 personnel could be herded into the safety of its tunnels within fifteen minutes. But with only one entrance available, that time was expected to be at least double.

The attack on Yongdoktong had been planned to ensure that the defenders were not given fifteen minutes. And it was intended to ensure all forces above ground within the base perimeter were quickly and efficiently disabled through the VX nerve gas attack. Landing in the immediate aftermath of the attack, Chol-guk Hong's 50 assault troops would advance on the tunnel entrance and, under covering fire from the gunships, they would overwhelm the defenders with rocket fire and grenades.

Lying flat on the apron outside the tunnel entrance, Hong watched with disgust as the second of their gunships pulled away in a shower of sparks from that damned autocannon or whatever it was in the emplacement on the hillside.

He considered sending a squad up the hillside to silence the gun, but his orders were to assault the tunnels as quickly as he could so that the defenders there could not reinforce.

And orders were orders.

Right on plan, two of his men sent rocket-propelled

grenades into the mouth of the tunnel and smoke and dust billowed out. Good luck to anyone left alive in there. If the VX and high explosives hadn't killed them, they'd probably choke on that smoke. As though to confirm what he was thinking, the volume of return fire from inside the tunnel fell away to almost nothing.

He reached for his throat mic. "Rifle squads, left and right, tunnel entrance. Automatic squads four and six o'clock, lay down covering fire. Grenadiers, prepare to assault!" His simple mission objectives lay right in front of him: eliminate enemy opposition inside the tunnel, and force the blast-proof door.

A squad of combat engineers landed with them were expert in that task, having spent days poring over schematics of the door locking mechanism and weeks practicing how to compromise it. Once the door had been compromised, he would send word to the General and more troops would be sent in to help clear out the nest of traitors within.

Looking over his shoulder, he saw that the commander of the Krokodil gunships had decided against sending another of his fat-assed machines into harm's way. In the distance, he heard explosions, like missiles or rockets striking. The fool had been pulled off target. His incompetence had not only cost Hong one rifle squad, it had also cost him his precious air cover.

The failure would not go unremarked in Hong's battle report.

The defenders' 14.5mm heavy machine gun opened up again, firing at some unseen target in the sky. It couldn't engage his troops down here, but it was giving a broadside to any helo that tried to send a rocket or missile into the tunnel.

How were the men up there even *alive*, dammit?

Hong shook his head. He rose to his feet, preparing to move up to the tunnel entrance. It didn't matter. The beauty of operations well-rehearsed, of clear orders well executed, was that they were designed to overcome all expected eventualities.

Battles are often decided by *unexpected* eventualities. The assault on Yongdoktong was supposed to have been conducted under the cover of nerve gas dropped by ten Su-25 Grach attack aircraft. Not four. The six deployed Krokodil gunships were supposed to land 48 assault troops. But one had been lost en route to a short-range missile and so only 40 had been landed. Though he had not registered it and his cowed officers had been afraid to report it, the helo that had been lost had been carrying his grenadier squad.

His attack was supposed to have been launched after a furious barrage of cannon and rocket fire from multiple gunships, but the gunships that had made it into Yongdoktong were currently fighting for their lives trying to escape from an air defense force that was not only on high alert, but that had been expecting their arrival.

In the first few minutes of the landing at Yongdoktong the five remaining gunships had been reduced to one, which was limping, trailing smoke, out of the valley to the south.

The cluster bombs from the Su-25s that had made it through Yongdoktong's air had mostly fallen on the northern face of the hillside, not on the southern side by the personnel tunnel entrance. And the light southerly breeze that the planners of the operation had expected would spread the toxic cloud of gas over the site had changed to easterly during the afternoon, and in fact carried the gas away from the site into uninhabited hill country.

Enough VX agent had fallen around the tunnel entrance that anyone who touched it for the next several hours would die a horrible choking death, but those who stayed in place were safe enough.

Like the crew of the 14.5mm on the hillside.

And Elvis Jang and his men inside the tunnel mouth. Where the dust and smoke from the rocket attack was now thinning out.

Light machine gun fire had been hosing their positions for

several minutes. Putting his head around the barricade at ground level, Jang couldn't see their firing positions through the thin smoke that still filled the air, or he would have ordered one of his better marksmen to try to snipe them. He didn't mind. His men were in good cover, and as long as the enemy light machine gun fire was criss-crossing the opening of the tunnel, the enemy infantry couldn't move in.

But then they stopped firing.

"Here it comes," Jang called out. "Ready!"

"Contact. Movement at the tunnel entrance, left and right," the Guards Captain said loudly.

As soon as he said it, Jang saw shapes in the smoke, raised his rifle and began firing. A furious barrage of light arms fire chipped away at the barrier to his right and a bullet plucked at the shoulder of his uniform.

Going prone, he rolled to the left of the barrier and sighted around it.

Target. Two shots. Down. Target. Two shots. Miss. Target …

Jang tried to lift his rifle, sight on the new target, but it refused to move. Was he too tight against the barrier?

No. It wasn't the rifle. It was his arm. It wouldn't respond. Looking down he saw dark blood spreading from his shoulder down to his elbow.

He frowned, confused.

Shot? When had he been shot?

Bullets began chewing at the wall beside his head, sending chips of concrete into the ground around him. One stung his cheek and he rolled back into cover. He tried to rise into a crouch, but only his left arm was working. Getting a knee under him, he levered himself up, his right arm falling uselessly to his side.

He had to use his left knee to help lift the barrel of his rifle far enough for his weaker left arm to be able to swing it over the top of the concrete barrier.

The enemy had reached the first of the vehicle barriers in the tunnel mouth where his men had been forced back by the RPG attack. His men at the next layer of barriers were falling back too, or dying where they stood.

It was a slaughter.

"Pull back to the guard posts!" he yelled. Firing blindly with his rifle resting on the concrete barrier, he counted as men streamed past him to the guard posts either side of the tunnel ahead of the door.

Four ... five ... seven ... ten.

Just ten. The Guards Commander was not with them. Jang had not seen him fall.

Only when Hong had called for his grenadiers to advance and throw was he informed there were none. If they had not already entered battle, he would have pulled his sidearm and shot the officer who had kept the information to himself, but there was no time. He simply turned him around, grabbed him by the back of the neck and shoved him bodily out into the entrance of the tunnel.

With a kick in his useless backside, Hong sent him staggering forward. "All teams, advance!" he called out. When the last man was moving forward, he moved into the tunnel himself.

The pathetic gaggle of traitors in there did not put up much of a fight. Their dead bodies littered the ground. Inside a minute, Hong had reached cover behind a concrete barrier abandoned by the defenders and took stock.

The few remaining defenders had pulled back to small concrete and steel guard posts that flanked the door. There was only room inside them for perhaps four men, the rest were huddled behind them.

He touched his throat mic. "We can't use RPGs on those structures, the door controls are inside and hydraulics access is underneath. Squad weapons; move in and set up on my position. Prepare to provide covering fire for an assault."

He turned, watching for his automatic weapons squad to move up. He would fix the enemy with machine guns, then assault them before they could respond.

Textbook stuff.

Ah, here they come. He saw the shapes in the smoke. But... so many? Had his grenadier squad made it to the fight after all?

Elvis Jang had lost a lot of blood. His vision wasn't so clear, but his hearing was just fine.

When a violent barrage of light arms fire erupted in front of him, he crouched lower, expecting the small guard post structure to be hammered. But not a single round hit the concrete or metal in front of him.

Jang heard *cheering.*

Cheering?

"Help me up," Jang said to the man beside him and the man put Jang's arm around his neck and levered him to his feet. Squinting in an attempt to focus, he tried to make sense of what he saw.

Strategic Missile Defense Forces guardsmen, moving into the tunnel? Firing as they came!

Jang's brain was slow on the uptake but when he finally realized what was happening, he yelled with the last of his strength.

"Guardsmen! Attack!"

Cautiously at first, then with more confidence, his remaining men left cover and re-engaged the enemy in the tunnel. Many had their back to Jang and his men, turning to face the new threat in their rear and being cut down from two sides.

Something was wrong, though. The guardsmen advancing toward them were stumbling. They were firing but ... they were falling too. Walking forward like ... like mindless zombies. Guns blazing until they toppled sideways.

It was like a scene from the apocalypse. Soon all the men in the tunnel mouth were down, but the attack had been enough. Jang's men completed the work they had started, and cut down the enemy force sandwiched between the two groups of guardsmen with ruthless efficiency.

Within moments, only two of the attackers remained alive,

and they raised their hands in the air, backing up against the tunnel wall.

Jang heard sobbing and choking ahead of him and let go of the man who was holding him. Staggering through the mess of bodies that choked the middle of the tunnel, he reached the first of the guardsmen who had fallen after rushing to their rescue.

The man lay on his back, gasping. He had taken a bullet in the thigh, but that was not what was killing him. He was asphyxiating as his lungs filled involuntarily with air that his paralyzed chest muscles could not expel. He reached up a hand to clutch at Jang's shirt, shuddering and shaking, then died right in front of Jang's eyes.

Jang rose, looking for someone, anyone, still alive.

He heard coughing, a terrible rattling gasp, and saw a young conscript propped against the tunnel wall. An assault rifle lay beside her, and she was trying to tear her uniform open at the throat with hands that refused to do her bidding.

Jang stumbled over and knelt beside her, reaching out to help, then pulled his hand back. They must have come through the gas, their saviors. They knew the gas was out there, and still they had come. Every one of them must have known they would die. But still, they had come.

He turned his head, gathering the strength to yell. "Don't touch them!" He pointed at a man kneeling beside another of the fallen. "Leave them! They are contaminated!"

The girl in front of him gave a small whimper, hands fluttering at her throat, eyes staring unseeing ahead of her. He could do nothing for her. Her uniform was probably impregnated with residue from the chemical attack.

Her eyes seemed to clear for a moment, and she focused on Jang. "Father?" she said weakly, the words barely escaping her lips.

"I am here, child," Jang said softly. "I am here. The pain will be over soon."

Her chest heaved as she tried to expel the air that was choking her, but failed. Gradually, the shuddering ceased and her head fell onto her shoulder, before she fell sideways to the ground.

Jang stood angrily. "Touch no one!" he repeated. His surviving men were standing in shock, none moving. Two had their rifles pointed at the two airborne assault troops who had surrendered.

Jang weaved through the bodies to where they stood. He was shaking with anger.

One of them was an officer. Jang pulled his service pistol from his hip with his only working hand and pointed it at the man.

"Take off your NCBW gear," Jang demanded.

"No," the man said. "You will force us outside. I am a prisoner. I demand to be treated as such under the conventions of war."

"You attack us with chemical weapons and speak to me about the *conventions of war*?!"

"I refuse, traitor," the man said with unconcealed contempt.

Jang snapped. He raised his pistol and pointed it at the man's face, finger starting to squeeze the trigger … then hesitated.

No, that would be too easy.

As he lowered the pistol, the man sneered, but his expression turned to shock when Jang fired.

Not at his face, but deliberately and very carefully into his right lung.

The airborne officer fell to his knees, clutching his chest and gasping, coughing blood. He looked up at Jang in mortal terror.

Jang looked down at him dispassionately, before turning to the shocked guardsman beside him. "Leave this one. Put the other prisoner to work moving the bodies. Guards on the left in a row, the other scum on the right, in a pile. Is that clear?"

The man swallowed and nodded.

Jang turned to the rest of his men. "Hold by the door. Try not to touch anything. We can't know how much of the contaminant came in during the fighting. I need …"

Jang hesitated, letting his pistol fall to his side, seeing the light die in the young woman's eyes once again. *I need to hug my boys,* he thought to himself. But he gathered himself again. There was a field telephone inside the guard post. "... I need to get orders."

After he'd dispatched medics to treat his wounded on the causeway, Captain Goh had scattered his reduced force to make it harder to engage from the air. Then he'd put a drone in the air and sent it to watch the road that led into the Peace Dam from the South, the most likely direction from which any South Korea ground forces would approach them.

It surprised him they hadn't had airborne special forces troops intervene yet, but he wasn't complaining.

His focus right now was on the vehicle halfway across the causeway in which the two State leaders had been traveling, and he approached it carefully. There had been no movement near it since the air attack, but that did not mean all inside or around it were dead.

Unlike most of his force. Not to mention the three soldiers in the truck the attacker had been hiding in, but their deaths were their own fault, they should have checked the rear of the vehicle before moving off.

From the next vehicle in line, he crouched and surveyed the bullet-riddled carcass of the LTV. Anyone inside it had to be dead. It had taken several hundred rounds and its light armor was not made for that kind of punishment. He could see one body on the ground beside the vehicle, but there was no movement behind it. The defenders could have crawled back inside.

He motioned two of his men over. "Put a frag grenade inside that LTV. I don't want anyone in there deciding this fight is not over."

The men nodded. They moved forward with rifles up, sighting down them at the LTV, ready to shoot anything that appeared. Six feet back from the vehicle, one of the men took out a grenade, primed it and lobbed it through the shattered front windscreen. They quickly withdrew to a safe distance. The crack of the grenade was their signal to move forward again and they ran to the LTV, one on each side.

"Clear!" one of the men yelled, standing and lowering his weapon. Then he turned away, dry retching.

When Goh looked inside the LTV he saw why. It had probably been a horrific scene before the grenade was thrown, but the blast inside the confined space had turned it into a horror movie scene. Every surface was covered with blood and human remains. But there were two particular humans Goh was most interested in. One of them was a man dressed in a black suit, still recognizable by what was left of the gray hair on his head. The South Korean President.

But there was no sign of the North Korean leader, and no sign of her faithful shadow, Captain Ri. Looking around the vehicle he saw blood on the curb going over to the river, and a bloodied handprint on the railing there. They might have escaped into the river during the aerial bombardment, but it was fifty feet down to the water. He doubted any bodyguard would have risked the life of his protectee with a drop like that.

Goh stood. His own hands were bloodied too, from where he had placed them inside the vehicle to steady himself as he examined it, and he wiped them on the legs of his trousers. *Alright, you have choices.* Remain and search for that damned woman, and risk that the South Korean special forces arrive or Americans launch another air strike, or abort the mission and retire North.

His orders had been simple. Obtain the nuclear trigger from the rebel force at the dam, and take custody of the two State leaders. If for any reason that proved impossible, ensure they were killed and their bodies and the nuclear trigger were recovered.

Now what did he have? After an initial success, the mission had turned into a bloody shambles. Three squads at least, plus the detachment he'd left back at the crossroads, lost. Two squads remaining. One State leader dead but one still on the run.

All because of *one* rogue soldier in his own ranks?

Walking down behind the wrecked LTV, he stopped by the body of the man he had shot. He lay on the ground with his face on the concrete, head twisted sideways. Goh put a boot under his shoulder and rolled him over. It was not one of his. The man was DMZ Border Patrol? So where had he come from? Was it possible he had shadowed the North Korean troop transport all the way from the encounter at the crossroads?

He surveyed the site again. There was only one direction Ri and Kim could have fled. Toward the visitor center, west.

"Comrade Captain!" the man controlling their drone yelled. "Contact. South Korean column approaching from the west. Light tactical vehicles out front, four. Tracked armored fighting vehicles in rear, six. Estimate seven klicks out!"

New choices. The enemy air strike had targeted his troops, not his vehicles, so he had two LTVs that were still drivable. He could use half of his force to hold up the South Korean column while the rest tried to locate the woman, or he could simply take his remaining troops and flee now, face the repercussions of reporting the failure of a key objective in the mission. It didn't take him long to decide. If he left the mission incomplete, nothing but uncertainty faced him in the North.

He touched his throat mic. "Team 5, take one LTV, load it with anti-tank missiles from the truck and set up ambush positions on the approach road. Let no one through. Team three, we will search for…" He never finished the order.

From the visitor center forecourt two hundred yards away he heard a vehicle starter motor, the roar of an engine and the screech of tires. Their abandoned LMADIS burst into view, bumped onto the access road and began speeding west … *toward the South Korean column.*

"Mount up!" Goh yelled, diving for the nearest operable LTV. "Both teams! Get rolling!"

Bunny O'Hare was also taking part in a hunt, the purpose of

which was just dawning on her. After several blissfully uneventful minutes she'd received a new briefing from a controller aboard the AWACS.

"Swan two, you will provide close air support to South Korean ground forces moving in to retake control of the Peace Dam," the controller said. "Additional assets in the area of operations include a South Korean forward air controller traveling with the South Korean ground force, call sign, Butler; Air Defense Patriot Missile battery Hwacheon, call sign, Tailwind. Full mission data package, contact frequencies and briefing summary are being uploaded now. Rules of engagement: any hostile ground forces designated by Hammerhead or Butler can be engaged. Any unidentified aircraft entering South Korean airspace from North Korea and not engaged by Tailwind can be engaged."

Bunny went back and forth with a few questions and relayed a few from Noname. But even she had to be impressed as he quickly and efficiently went to work. He had a mission to prosecute and assets to prosecute it with. He quickly settled into machine mode, setting their two Bats up for the coming engagement by assigning hotkeys to their partner units, testing that the data links between the allied units were up and functioning, and most importantly, negotiating their connection to the orbiting Shikaka so that Bunny had real-time vision on her monitor of the target area.

"I have handshake with Envy," Noname told her. "Buffering the feed. On your monitor ... now."

Bunny created a tactical window and assigned the video feed from the Shikaka to it, pinning it to a corner of the large multifunction monitor that ran across the front of the cockpit showing flight, weapons and comms systems and instrument information. Tapping it again expanded it to fill half of the screen. She leaned forward to study it.

"Whoa," she said. "Someone's bad day got worse." She could choose from three camera views. One was a general zoomed-out view of the target area. Another, no doubt under the control of the personnel on the AWACS, was a zoomed-in view of a building, panning along what looked like a bridge or causeway across the spillway from the dam. The third view was infrared. It was still daylight, so the images were not particularly clear, but as daylight faded, they might prove invaluable, enabling the AWACS and South Korean forward air controller to identify heat sources such as human bodies and vehicles.

But it was the wide-angle view that had caught Bunny's attention. It showed the small building at the base of the dam, and along the bridge leading away from the building and across the spillway were wrecked or abandoned vehicles. Some were still smoking, as were a number of blackened craters in the middle of the bridge. Bunny could see the bodies of dead combatants littering the causeway.

So many bodies that she stopped counting.

She quickly scanned the air environment, and seeing no threats, returned to the video feed. There were still some troops and vehicles moving around. Including three that were pulling out of the area and moving at high speed … *west*. Toward the South Korean column!

Bunny keyed the AWACS. "Hammerhead, Swan two, you seeing this feed? We have three vehicles, light tacticals by the look of it, moving at speed toward that South Korean armor column."

"Confirmed, Swan two. Sending you target authorization now. Advance South Korean elements are pulling off the road, preparing to meet the hostiles. You are cleared to engage before they get within one click…"

It did not occur to the target-fixated Captain Goh that his pursuit of the South Korean LMADIS would have been detected by cameras 70,000 feet above, and immediately transmitted not only to the approaching South Korea mechanized recon company and its forward air controller, but also to Bunny O'Hare.

The Shikaka was also monitoring the airspace around Bunny and Noname's small five plane flight, following and logging electronic signals emissions in a 200-mile bubble around it and relaying the data both to the Hawkeye AWACS, to Bunny, and to the Patriot missile battery outside Hwacheon that was guarding the sky over central South Korea.

Because it was still under the control of Navy Information Systems Technician 2nd Class, Petty Officer Ryan 'Toes' Kronk, the data was flowing to his laptop. And he was a very, very disturbed Kronk.

"Hammerhead, Envy, belay that attack order!" Kronk was yelling into his headset.

He and Snake had both watched as the three vehicles tore out of the visitor center car park and Snake had sneered. "The bad guys are in one big hurry to die. They can't wait for the South Koreans to come to them, they're going out to meet them," Snake had said. Hearing Kronk yell out, Snake now shot Kronk a look of confusion.

Kronk ignored him. He knew what he'd seen. He had seen two people climb into the vehicle that was out front leading the charge westward.

It was not an armored car. It was a South Korean LMADIS open topped buggy. And in the passenger seat he had definitely seen the long black hair and thin pale face of Supreme Leader of the Democratic People's Republic of Korea, Yun-mi Kim.

There was no response from the AWACS. "Hammerhead! This is Envy, abort that air attack!"

Bunny and Noname were pulling data from the Shikaka, but they could not hear Kronk's panicked radio call. They were taking their tasking from the AWACS and that was the only frequency they were monitoring. While Bunny put their Kingsnake into a racetrack pattern 30,000 feet up and twenty miles south of the Peace Dam and watched for air threats, Noname dispatched a single Ghost Bat to execute the attack.

Thanks to both the Hawkeye and the Shikaka, Bunny had near perfect vision of the airspace over the area of operations. The only aircraft potentially able to pose any threat were the two North Korean J-7 fighters patrolling a corridor ten miles north of the DMZ, and she knew she and her Bats would be completely invisible to their ancient radars. They were certainly showing no interest.

If there were any North Korean stealth fighters in the air, she wouldn't be able to see them, but she had to hope that between the AWACS, the Bat picket she had out in front of her, and the ROK F-35s to her left and right, someone would. Noname had the vision from the Shikaka on screen, and boxed the three vehicles, marking them as targets. The Bat carried four JAGM missiles, and the AI allocated two to the lead vehicle, one each to the trailing vehicles. Noname had done the math. The JAGM could launch at a range of six miles, so the hostile vehicles would still be four klicks out from the lead elements of the South Korea column when the missiles hit them.

That left time for a follow-up attack from his second Bat if needed.

Captain Jong-chong Ri had spotted the abandoned LMADIS vehicle parked outside the visitor center when he was being bundled half-conscious into the armored car. Noted, but then forgotten.

As they emerged from the smoke by the causeway, he'd remembered – and half running, half dragging his protectee behind him, he'd headed for the abandoned vehicle. The electronic array fixed to its roll cage had been mangled in the recent fighting, but the vehicle itself seemed untouched. As they climbed inside he saw there was a large starter button on the dash and he mashed it with his foot hard down on the brake. Unlike most North Korean vehicles, which still required a key, this one started immediately. He silently thanked the South Koreans for their habit of not locking or disabling their vehicles in combat areas. He reached across Madam Kim, pulled a seat harness over her head and buckled it across her waist.

Then blanked. The road east was blocked. Should he head north, or west? *Focus, Ri!* North, small winding road, dam crossing, access road two miles north, then offroad tracks toward the DMZ. Slow slow slow.

West. West was a paved South Korean highway, used by tourist buses on any day except today. It was wide, empty and ... fast. It led ... where? Toward Hwacheon. Before they reached the city he could turn off, take a faster route north into the DMZ. If they lived that long.

"Ready, your Excellency?"

She slapped the dashboard impatiently. "Don't worry about me. Go!"

As they sped out of the visitor center car park, a slight rise showed him the view behind them in his rear-view mirror. Goh's troops jumping into their remaining LTVs. They had to turn them around on the confined space of the causeway, but they would be in pursuit any second.

The South Korean LMADIS *looked* fast, but it was, after all, just a dune buggy. With dismay he saw that the speedometer only went to 120 km/h: about seventy miles an hour. He wasn't sure what the maximum speed of a South Korean LTV was, but he was pretty sure they would haul him in quickly.

Looking desperately around the small open cabin as he negotiated the first bend, he found the radio. It was a small field tactical radio, and he'd been acquainted with its use during recent training exercises with South Korean forces. He turned it on and flipped the frequency dial to broadcast in the open on a channel used by the North and South Korean militaries for coordination purposes.

It was a Hail Mary call, but he had no alternative.

"This is Captain Jong-chon Ri of the North Korea Supreme Guard," he said. "Broadcasting to all friendly forces. I am traveling west from the Peace Dam on Pyeonghwa Road in a South Korean jeep, pursued by hostile vehicles. Request assistance." He did not wait for a response, fought the wheel to negotiate the next bend in the highway and lifted the handpiece to his mouth again. "This is Captain Jong-chon Ri of the North

Korea Supreme Guard…"

Bunny and Noname in their Kingsnake, 20 miles away and 30,000 feet overhead, did not hear Ri's plea for help. Nor did Ryan Kronk. Or the Hawkeye over central South Korea. All were either too far away or tuned to the wrong frequency. The flight leader of the two North Korean J-7s did, however. The encryption on the radios of the ancient J-7s was so unreliable that its pilots were required to broadcast in the clear in order to maintain contact.

The broadcast was weak, and the pilot had to turn his radio to maximum gain to hear it. "… pursued by hostile vehicles. Request assistance." The message repeated. The person making the call sounded appropriately alarmed, but was it a decoy?

"Tornado two, Tornado leader, did you copy that broadcast?" he asked.

"Yes, Tornado leader," his wingman replied. "It is a trick. That position is inside South Korean airspace. Someone is trying to provoke us to cross the demarcation line."

Of course, it must be true. But it had been a crazy day. There were rumors nuclear weapons had been used over the Sea of Japan. Every available aircraft at their base had been launched and the only orders they had been given were to attack any unidentified aircraft entering North Korean airspace. He had never seen so much activity. And now a mayday, broadcast by a member of the Supreme Leader's personal guard?

The North Korean officer was in an agony of indecision. If he did not respond, and the call was authentic, he would be court martialed at best, shot at worst. And if it was false, a decoy as his wingman said?

Well then, he would probably be killed anyway, the moment they entered South Korean airspace. But he would at least die with honor.

"I will not ignore a possible mayday from a member of the Supreme Guard," he told his wingman firmly. "Engage search radar and follow me, line astern," he ordered. "Protect my six from enemy aircraft. I am going to investigate."

As he swung his machine around, put the nose down and pointed it south, he armed his two 30mm cannons. Theirs were air to air fighters, not ground attack aircraft, so even if they lived long enough and the targets were real, he could do little more than strafe. The missiles hanging on pylons under his wings would be useless for ground attack.

But duty was duty. Especially on this strangest of all days.

"We have interest, Noname," Bunny warned. She had just seen the two J-7s patrolling north of them swing around and begin accelerating south. Within seconds they would cross the DMZ. Within minutes, they would be within detection range for the Ghost Bat currently moving in on the three vehicle targets. She keyed the frequency for the Hawkeye.

"Hammerhead, Swan two, we have two fast movers bearing zero three niner, 20,000 feet, range two five and closing. They are heading toward the South Korean column, looks like an interdiction run to me. I have an air to air Bat on picket which can intercept. Orders?"

"Swan two, Shikaka is tracking the contacts, Patriot Battery will engage if they cross the demarcation line."

Bunny frowned. "Uh, they just did, Hammerhead," she said.

"Patriot firing," Noname said, almost at the same time. On her tactical monitor, Bunny saw the icons for four ground to air missiles appear over Chuncheon, twenty miles south, and streak toward the North Korean aircraft.

"Would have been quicker to let us handle it," Bunny pouted.

Noname ignored her. "Bat One beginning attack run. Ten seconds to missile release."

Bunny tapped her screen and brought up the video feed from the Shikaka again. It showed the three vehicles still tearing down the highway toward the South Korean column. They were about four miles apart now. Bunny had no idea what they were thinking, but if bare-assed aggression was a plan, they were executing it perfectly.

And they would soon have eternity to regret it.

"Slasher, you have the Supreme Leader of North Korea in that lead vehicle! Abort, abort!" Kronk was still yelling.

Snake put a hand on his shoulder. "You got to let them respond, man."

Kronk glared at him, but the pause was enough for the AWACS to break in. "Envy, Slasher, message received and understood. Slasher out."

Kronk's glare turned to one of confusion. "What the hell does that mean? Received and understood?"

Though ancient, the two North Korean J-7s had functional radar warning receivers. Guided in the first phase of their flight by the combined data from the AWACS, the Shikaka and Bunny's Kingsnake, when the four Patriot missiles got within thirty seconds of their targets the US missiles switched on their own onboard radars to fine-tune their flight trajectories and alarms started screaming inside the cockpits of the J-7s.

The Korean flight leader was not scared, he was furious. *Trap.* His wingman had been right. They'd been lured into a trap.

How could he have been so stupid!?

"Tornado two, evade!" He rolled his machine and pointed its nose at the earth in a desperate attempt to outmaneuver the incoming missiles. He couldn't see them, didn't even know what bearing they were coming from, all he could do was make their task as hard as possible by putting himself into a supersonic death dive.

Captain Goh could see the slower LMADIS ahead of him now. He could not see the South Korean column yet, but he knew it could not be much farther ahead of them.

It was going to be close. But eyeballing the closing distance between themselves and the fleeing North Koreans, he began to hope. He even closed his eyes, as his officer school instructors had taught him to do, and saw the glorious future that could be.

They would catch the target vehicle. A simple nudge from their heavier LTV would flip it, to land on its roll cage. If they weren't killed outright, the two occupants would be dazed or unconscious. He would approach the passenger side, because she would be hanging there, and he would put a bullet in the brain of the Supreme Leader of North Korea. And then he would turn his vehicle around, speeding ahead of the South Korean column to escape North into the DMZ.

And in less than two days he would be sitting in a first class seat, bound for a life of luxury, having delivered to his masters the North Korean nuclear trigger and the elimination of *both* traitors, Si-min Shin and Yun-mi Kim.

Then he opened his eyes in horror as the vehicle behind him *exploded.*

"Splash one," Bunny called, watching the fireball engulf the rearmost of the three vehicles. Noname had staggered the missiles so that the optical infrared seekers of following missiles would not be blinded by the fireball of the exploding targets preceding them.

But only by seconds.

"Swan two, Hammerhead, abort your attack," the voice of the controller from the AWACs broke in urgently. "Swan two, abort ground attack!"

What? "Noname! Abort!" Her gut falling through the cockpit floor, Bunny knew even as she spoke his name, she was too late.

Goh was staring at the rising cloud of flame of smoke that

had been the vehicle behind him, still with the warmth of his glorious vision tingling in his mind.

As though time itself slowed to a liquid honey stickiness, he saw a trail of brown smoke, a missile with a tail of fire, arrowing down from on high, straight at him.

It was the last thing he saw.

Ri saw the rearmost pursuing vehicle cartwheel out of a ball of flame in his mirror, before he heard the explosion. The road ahead was straight, and in the distance he could see ... vehicles? They were blocking the road.

Head screwed over his shoulder, he watched the second vehicle, saw the missile this time, spearing in from behind it before it too disappeared in a tumbling ball of flame and smoke.

He knew without doubt they would be next.

In the seat beside him, Yun-mi Kim sat with eyes shut, but no expression on her face. Not terror. Not fear. He took his foot off the accelerator but kept his eyes on her. He would die with the vision of her face burned into his retinas.

Bunny saw the fireball as the second vehicle in the line detonated.

"Splash two," Noname said in his usual flat monotone. "Enemy J-7 directly below, altitude 500..."

"Noname, no, *abort*..." Bunny said. Wait, enemy J-7 ...*what*?! She reacted instinctively, hauling her machine into a tight banking turn.

But it was too late. Too late.

"Unable to abort ground attack," Noname reported. O'Hare's violent evasive maneuver had momentarily cut their link to the last outbound missile. And monitoring the biosigns of his pilot, Noname could see O'Hare had entered a state of information saturation and impaired judgment. He assumed temporary control of the aircraft.

Zero tolerance for error.

Service before self.

Righting the aircraft with a snap roll, he allowed the data link to the missile to stabilize and sent the abort command.

Zero tolerance for error.

What mattered most was the mission.

The North Korean pilot of aircraft Tornado 1 had heard his wingman being swatted screaming from the sky by the enemy missiles. In a red mist, he had watched his altitude plunge from 20,000 feet to 10,000 in seconds. Hauling back on the joystick between his legs he felt his machine shudder as though it was going to tear itself apart.

Come on, you stinking bucket of rust, pull out! he yelled in his mind. As though it had heard him, the conical nose of the J-7 began to lift, one small degree at a time. Then two. Then *ten*.

Somewhere about the time his nose lifted above the horizon, the North Korean pilot blacked out.

When he came to, he heard a high whining pitch in his ears. His chin was on his chest. He was drooling into his mask.

The whining continued. It was trying to tell him something.

Target ... target lock?

He blinked, staring at his instruments. *Infrared target lock.* Reacting by instinct, he reached out and flipped the switch that armed his two Russian-made short-range missiles, about the only things on the whole aircraft that were made in the 21st century.

Missile lock. *Fox 2, you bastard.*

For a fifty-year-old J-7 to kill a two-year-old F-36 Kingsnake was impossible. For a start, it would have to get past the Kingsnake's picket of one or more Ghost Bats. It would have to close to within ten miles, the maximum range of its antiquated radar system. And its missiles would have to be sophisticated enough to ignore the decoy flares and radar-defeating chaff that the Kingsnake would automatically fire into its wake as soon as it detected a missile launch.

But the suicidal maneuver of the North Korean pilot had taken him down into the ground clutter and momentarily out of sight of both the AWACS and Shikaka radars. The radar operators on the Hawkeye had assumed he had planted his machine in the hills.

By the time he popped back up onto radar, zooming into the sky underneath Bunny and Noname's Kingsnake, he was already firing his missiles.

Still in control of the Kingsnake, Noname wrenched it into a zooming climb and killed the engine's thrust, putting the metal of their 4,000 lb. Pratt and Whitney engine between O'Hare and the incoming missile but leaving them hanging in the sky, waiting for gravity to pull them to earth. The tactic cut their infrared signature, but left them a sitting duck if the North Korean missiles didn't take the decoy bait.

Service before self.

Drawn by the heat still radiating from the rear nozzle of the jet, both missiles ignored the decoys being pumped into the sky around the Kingsnake and detonated as their warheads flew right into the Kingsnake's exhaust. They blew the engine right out of its housing.

As soon as Noname took control of her machine, Bunny O'Hare knew her number was up. Her flight stick went slack in her hands, her helmet-mounted display flashed a missile impact warning and she heard the booster rockets beneath her flight seat ignite.

She didn't even have time to grab the handholds alongside her legs before her world dissolved into a roaring ball of flame and metal.

Like a burning autumn leaf, Karen 'Bunny' O'Hare's Kingsnake shed flaming debris as it entered a violent flat spin toward the hills below.

Games of State

Peace Dam, South Korea

Their LMADIS buggy hadn't even slowed to a halt before Ri realized a) he was still alive and b) his protectee was already out of the vehicle, running down the road toward the South Korean troops like her tail was on fire.

He sat, still stunned, watching as she tore off first one shoe, then the other, threw them to the side of the road and continued running.

Move your ass, Ri, he heard a voice say. *She could get shot!*

Rolling over the open side of the buggy, he set after her, but the few seconds head start she had and the proximity of the South Korean vehicles slewed across the road told him immediately he had no hope of catching her before she got within rifle range of the South Koreans.

And which damn South Koreans were they? The rescuing kind, or the killing kind?!

When she got within 50 yards without being shot, he dared to hope. When she got within 20, an officer stepped in front of one of the LTVs that was blocking the road and held up his hands, motioning her to stop.

Ri heard Kim yelling at the man, but could not catch her words.

She was running so hard she ran straight into his arms, and collapsed, breathless. Ri arrived a second later and grabbed her as she fell.

"Who the hell…" the South Korean officer was saying. "Is that who…"

Ri lifted her in his arms and stood, panting himself. "This is … the Supreme Leader of the Democratic People's … Republic of North Korea," he told the officer. "I need a vehicle with a radio."

The man stood with his feet planted, mouth open like a carp in a pond.

"Now!!" Ri yelled at him, snapping the man out of his shock.

They wasted precious minutes getting the Major in charge in of the South Korean mechanized infantry columns to appreciate his priority was not to find out what the hell was going on. But Madam Kim had been very good at explaining this to him, once she recovered her breath.

His priority, she explained, if he wanted to help avert a global nuclear war, was to give the Supreme Leader of North Korea a damned radio, a comms tech who knew his stuff and then *get the hell out of her face.*

He cleared the troops out of a K21 infantry fighting vehicle and left her and Ri with a radio operator. Ri closed the rear ramp and door of the IFV behind them. Suddenly it was quiet, and very claustrophobic inside the vehicle. The only sounds were the still heaving chests of himself and Madam Kim.

The operator was a wide-eyed youth. Ri tried to calm him. "Her Excellency will tell you who she needs to speak with. You won't be able to help her directly, but your job is to connect her to people who can. Is that clear?"

He nodded, and swallowed. "Battalion HQ," he said. "I can connect you to Battalion…"

Ri slapped his knee. "Good lad."

"Too slow," Kim shook her head. "I need to talk to the White House, not the South Korean military."

The boy looked stricken. "Your Excellency … I can't…"

Ri put a hand on his shoulder. "That air attack on the vehicles pursuing us. Are you in contact with the US Air Force?"

"Yes, sir," he replied. "We are coordinating close air support with a US AWACS over…"

Ri stopped him. "Please contact the US Air Force and explain your situation."

"Tell them I need to speak with the President of the United States, urgently," Kim said.

The poor kid looked like he was going to blow a cooler fan. Ri talked slowly. "It's all right. You get the AWACS on the line, I will do the talking."

The call to the 48th President of the USA, Stuart Fenner, had been routed via Kronk's Shikaka to the Hawkeye over Hwacheon, to a satellite over Sri Lanka, then Hawaii, a ground station in San Diego and then optical fiber cables to Washington and then via satellite again to Air Force One, where the President was currently outbound Andrews Air Force Base, as per DEFCON 1 protocols. After Ri convinced the commander of the Hawkeye of his bona fides, the entire process took less than 12 minutes, including the time needed to get an AI voice translator patched into the call.

Two things worked in Yun-mi Kim's favor in getting the President to take the call despite all that had happened that day. The first was that he had been in frequent contact with her over the five years leading up to the decision to go forward with a Peace Accord.

The second was that this was not Stuart Fenner's first rodeo. By A Long Margin. Many had doubted his military credentials having served only as a platoon leader for the 3rd US Infantry Regiment, guarding Arlington National Cemetery in Northern Virginia. But he had demonstrated a cool temperament as Secretary of State in a Turkey–Syria conflict, cutting loose the Emirates as allies when they refused to allow him to base US aircraft there. He had shown resolve when facing off against Russia in a dispute over the Bering Strait in which Russia tried to occupy the US island of Savoonga, and prescience in pulling US troops out of the Middle East and repositioning them in Europe to face an anarchic Russia and newly aggressive China.

The sound of the President's voice was loud inside the confines of the armored vehicle. "Your Excellency. We were not sure you were still alive," the President said.

"Yes, but please, Stuart, there is no time for formalities."

The relief in the President's voice was palpable. "Yun-mi, it *is* you. My people wanted that test, so we could be sure." Ri was also relieved. The North Korean and US leaders had been on first name terms in private for at least two years, but it was not known outside their innermost circles.

"I understand. Mr President, please know this. My first call since escaping was to you. I heard about the nuclear attack, but I have not contacted my own General Staff yet. We must stop this madness now."

"Yun-mi, my question to you is, *can* you stop this madness?" Fenner asked. "Do you have control of your nuclear arsenal?"

"Yes, I can," Madam Kim said, trying to regain her composure. "The conspirators stole a one-time code giving them missile launch authority. As soon as I conclude this call, it will be rescinded. There will be no further attacks, Stuart."

"There already have been, Yun-mi," Fenner said. He told her about Guam.

"But not nuclear? Please, *not* nuclear?" Ri saw that his leader's face was ashen.

Ri heard voices on the President's end of the call before he replied. "No. There was damage to our facilities and multiple casualties from the impact of the re-entry vehicles, but no, no nuclear detonations."

Kim could not hide her relief. "Oh, thank God. Thank God."

"Another question. Is the South Korean President with you?"

Kim looked at Ri, hesitating before answering. "Stall," he whispered.

She leaned closer to the microphone. "President Shin is dead. He died in the fighting at the Peace Dam. The circumstances are ... unclear."

Fenner cursed. "Dammit. Yun-mi, our infrared satellites have picked up indications of combat in the vicinity of your Yongdoktong arsenal. My people here want to know..."

"Stuart, I am sorry. I will answer all of your questions later. Now, I must call my Chief of General Staff and regain control of my military. Can I have your commitment the USA and its Korean allies will do nothing precipitous before we speak again?"

"I can't promise you anything; our strategic missile forces are on a hair trigger," Fenner said. "Russia and China have put their armed forces on high alert and I delayed a call to the Chinese General Secretary to speak with you. South Korea's military is mobilizing from West to East. I have three carrier task forces moving into position off the coast of Korea. If the lunatics in your military launch more ballistic missiles, if they threaten our bases or population centers..."

"I understand, Stuart. And because of that, I *must* go, I am sorry."

There was muffled conversation at the other end of the line, then Fenner came back on. "Yun-mi, I can give you thirty minutes. If you don't get back to me within that time I am going to authorize air and cruise missile strikes on targets inside North Korea. Today's events have left me no choice unless you can show you are regaining control of your military. Is that clear?"

"Perfectly clear, Stuart. I will be in touch again inside thirty minutes," she said, nodding at Ri, who realized he had just been appointed de facto White House liaison.

She handed the handset back to Ri, who handed it to the South Korean communications officer. Ri turned to Kim. "Your Excellency, your next call?"

"Chief of Staff Khang in Pyongyang," she said. "I need to understand who is loyal and who is part of this insane conspiracy. We need to immediately ground all air force aircraft, as a signal to the Americans and only Khang can do that."

Ri nodded and turned to the South Korean again. "All right, this is going to be harder. Let's talk through it..."

Two hours later, on the highway outside the Peace Dam, Captain Ri opened the ramp at the rear of the K21 IFV and stumbled out.

Sometime in the last two hours, the sun had set. The crew of the IFV was sitting on their butts on the side of the road. The rest of the South Korean column was gone, no doubt on to the Peace Dam. Ri felt his legs going, and sat before he collapsed. His protectee was inside, lying across the bench seat with her hands folded over her forehead.

A South Korean officer stood and approached Ri. "All right. We have orders to…"

Ri held up a hand wearily. "Your orders are irrelevant," he told the man. "There is a helicopter inbound from North Korea to pick us up. The flight was approved by your acting President, So-wa Yoon. Have your superiors consult with your headquarters if you wish."

The man frowned, turned and waved to his comms operator to bring him a field radio.

Ri folded his arms across his knees and rested his head on them.

North Korea's Chief of Staff had not been among the conspirators. Though he protested strongly, he agreed to Kim's order to ground all North Korean air force aircraft and order all naval vessels, including submarines, to return to port. She'd called the US President back immediately.

"It is done, Stuart. The nuclear go-codes have been rescinded. You will soon see our air force and navy aircraft and ships returning to their bases. I am told the fighting at Yongdoktong is over and we have full control of the nuclear storage facility."

The US President had sounded relieved, but still concerned. "That's … that's good news. I can hold my people back until we confirm what you say. But there is going to be hell to pay for the events of today, Yun-mi."

"And I will be prepared to discuss that price, Stuart, when the time comes," she had said.

Ri looked over at the South Korean troops. The battle here today was over, but the war for the soul of North Korea had only just begun. Critically, their Chief of General Staff had not been part of the conspiracy. He had been able to assure her all nuclear-capable weapons systems, including their other *Gorae*-class submarine, were under his control and incapable of launching any farther attacks.

An attempt by troops of the rebel, General Choe, to gain access to the nuclear arsenal at Yongdoktong had been frustrated by the heroic actions of the garrison there, who had held the facility despite terrible losses.

In her final conversation with the US President, Madam Kim had secured his assurance she would be allowed to return to Pyongyang to permit her to begin reasserting control over the machinery of government. Her backup nuclear trigger was being readied for her and would be on the helicopter being sent to pick her up.

A call to the Chinese General Secretary had not been so clear cut. He had expressed shock at the events of the day and concern about the mobilization of US and South Korean forces. At one point, he had assured her he wanted still to see the Peace Process to succeed. At another, he had commented that of course, it could no longer continue on the path it had. He had then excused himself from the call to attend to 'military affairs'.

Ri would never forget the voice of the US President as he had closed the call with his Supreme Leader. Ri might have expected anger, rage even, but instead he heard ... sadness?

"The events of this day end any hope of peace on the Korean Peninsula, Yun-mi, you realize that? Probably for generations," Fenner had said.

The North Korean leader had shaken her head. "No. I do not. If we allow that to be true, then the conspirators have won. We can choose to honor the deaths of those who sacrificed themselves today by investing ourselves in this project more than ever before, or we can go into history as two leaders who had peace within their grasp and let the misdeeds of a few evil men steal it from us."

The line had been quiet a long time, the only sound the hum

of aero engines in the background before the US President finally spoke. "If passion alone could carry the day, Yun-mi, you would have your peace already. I pledge to do my part."

A day later and several hundred miles to the south, the naval equivalent of an honor guard was lined up outside Busan harbor when the battered, but not beaten, expeditionary fast transport *USS Cody* limped in to dock.

On one side of the harbor entrance, furthest out, was the *USS Bougainville*, just about her entire crew lined up on the deck, saluting. Then *Cody*'s sister ship, *USS Point Loma*.

On the other side of the entrance was the *ROKS Marado*, with her complement lined up on her flight deck too, waving US flags like a bunch of schoolkids.

And like schoolkids themselves, O'Shea Lomax and his XO, Jake Ryan, stood out on the *Cody*'s foredeck with their crew and took the salutes with huge grins.

But the best part?

That was the massive B-21 Raider from Guam that did a flyby so low and so loud it would have blown out the *Cody*'s windows.

If she still had any.

Epilogue

The Chair of the North Korean Workers' Party, head of the State Affairs Commission and Supreme Leader of the Democratic People's Republic of Korea, Yun-mi Kim, walked down the white-tiled floor of her favorite residence and paused in front of a replica of the statue of the Maitreya Buddha from the Three Kingdoms Period of 600 AD.

She had never seen the original work. It stood in the 'National Museum of Korea'. In *South* Korea. She still hoped dearly to see it herself, one day.

The Buddha sat in a contemplative pose, one leg crossed over his thigh, one hand to his cheek. It was said to capture the moment when Sakyamuni Buddha awakened to the cyclical nature of human suffering. It was a revelation that Kim had thought about many times in the weeks since the events at the Peace Dam.

As he always did these days, Commander Ri of the Supreme Guard followed discreetly behind her, accompanied by one of her secretaries. Kim knew what the gossipmongers in the Residence said about the fact that Kim was never seen without Ri by her side since the events of two weeks ago, but Kim did not care what they said.

Though she would never admit it, even to Ri, the events at the Peace Dam had shaken her to the core, and she could not sleep without knowing he was near. Sometimes, she woke crying and shaking, calling for him.

Always he came. Always.

At a dark and heavy teak door, the aide paused. "Your Excellency, General Haotian of China's PLA Northern Command is on the telephone for you, as you requested." She opened the door, revealing a lounge suite, coffee table and a large oak desk ringed by several chairs. A single telephone sat on the desk.

As she walked into the room, Ri took a position beside the door, and Kim paused, turning around. "Commander Ri, you will join me, please."

Ri bowed and stepped into the room and Kim noted with a smile the look of disapproval on the face of her secretary as she closed the door behind them.

She did not care. Just having him in the room made her stronger, and she would need all her strength for the coming call. Capitulation did not come naturally to her.

Indicating to Ri that he should be seated by the desk, she moved behind it and sat. Taking a deep breath, she picked up the telephone, switching it to speaker so that Ri could hear.

"General Haotian. I am sorry if I kept you waiting," she said smoothly.

The Chinese General at the other end had a gruff, but not unpleasant voice. A soldier's voice. "Not at all, Comrade Madam Kim. I am humbled by the opportunity to speak with you."

Kim rolled her eyes at Ri. "You have spoken with your General Secretary, I believe?"

"Yes, your Excellency. It is my honor to be able to fulfill his wishes, and yours."

"*Discreetly* to fulfill our wishes, I trust, General."

"Of course."

"That is why I wanted to speak with you personally. I have agreed to the terms proposed by your General Secretary, but they are to remain confidential. No word of this arrangement is to leak to the South before I announce it, or it will place my position here in peril. And should our negotiations with the South collapse, so will our arrangement, do you understand that?"

"Completely, your Excellency. We have personally selected our most loyal and expert officers and soldiers for this duty. They are aware that any indiscretion will cost them their lives."

"Very well. Thank you, General. And, there is one other thing."

"Yes, your Excellency?"

"I understand you also had a hand personally in the attempted capture of the traitor General Choe."

"It was my honor to assist in that operation, your Excellency. In all my dealings with him, I found Yong-gon Choe to be a completely detestable individual. I admit I was not saddened at the news he chose to take his own life, rather than surrender."

"Nor was I, General. You have my thanks."

"I am glad the People's Liberation Army Northern Command could be of some service, madam. Was there anything else?"

"No. That is all, General. I will leave the Commander of my Strategic Missile Force to agree the details with you. Goodbye."

"Goodbye, your Excellency."

As she put down the telephone, she was pleased to see her hand was not shaking. She sat looking at the phone. "We cannot trust him, can we, Ri?"

"No, your Excellency," he said. "We can trust none of them, from the Chinese General Secretary to the lowest of his Generals. Nor can we trust the Americans, or the Russians. But we must work with them, and this arrangement serves both their interests and ours."

She sighed, looking at him with eyes deep with doubt. "This arrangement. Am I a complete fool, Ri? I have handed control of our nuclear arsenal to the People's Republic of China. The equivalent of complete nuclear disarmament. I have promised to create a new demilitarized zone on the border with China. Are we giving the Chinese leader everything he asked for, and getting too little in return?"

Ri shook his head. "Denuclearization was not only China's demand, it was demanded by the entire UN Security Council. It was a precondition for restarting the reunification negotiations. All your work in the last ten years would have been lost if we had ignored this, and when you announce to the world soon that *China* will take control of our nuclear weapons, there will be a lot of noise and wind from Seoul, but no one can say we are not meeting the UN's demands."

"But we surrender our only means of defending a United Korea against other nuclear powers."

"Not entirely, your Excellency. The South does not want to abandon the Mutual Defense Treaty with the US, and China knows this. We can play them against each other. We will either go forward under a US nuclear umbrella, or a Chinese one, but we *will* go forward."

"The Chinese General Secretary also said that he expects to see US troops withdraw from Korea after reunification and will not tolerate any US troops, aircraft or ships being based north of the 38th parallel between now and then..."

"None of those demands are new. He is just repeating them, louder now, because he thinks he can."

She sighed. "I hope ... well, Ri, I just *hope*, is all."

"It is your ability to hope that makes you so strong, your Excellency. But, there is ... one thing..." he said hesitantly.

It was one of the things she most treasured in him. No one else had the temerity to tell her what they were *really* thinking. This man did, but he did not abuse the privilege.

She smiled. "And what would that be, Comrade Commander?"

"The timing," he said. "I know you are thinking of announcing the denuclearization agreement this week, to restart the reunification negotiations as quickly as possible."

"Yes."

"Disarmament is the card I would play *last* of all. Allow Chinese troops to take command of our deployed weapons systems, and to station 'observers' at Yongdoktong arsenal. But there is a lesser gesture that could restart negotiations with the South..."

She nodded. "The master tactician, as always, Ri. Please, what is this 'lesser gesture'?"

"The South Korean defector, your Excellency..."

At Nuchon-ri Air Base in North Korea, newly minted defector Lieutenant Hee-chan 'Bounce' Son had not received the reception he had been promised, at all.

After the point blank shot into the tail exhaust of his North Korean 'wingman', the flight to Nuchon-ri had gone without a hitch and he'd put down at the base, about 20 miles north of the DMZ.

He hadn't exactly expected a marching band and flag-waving multitudes, but he'd expected more than a surly corporal in a Cold War jeep as he delivered South Korea's first and most advanced indigenous fighter to North Korea Air Force. The man had been waiting at the end of the runway and waved to Bounce, indicating he should follow him. Then he'd rattled off in his little jeep toward an empty hangar at a far side of the airfield.

Where there should have been dozens of North Korean officers eager to see the South Korean warbird, there was only a pretty disinterested ground crew, which had barely even stirred as Bounce dropped off the bottom step of the small ladder from his cockpit. The ground crew weren't interested in anything about the aircraft. They busied themselves in front of it, getting a large groundsheet ready to pull over the nose and wings of the machine to hide it as soon as its engine had cooled down.

Looking around, a little lost, Bounce saw the corporal from the jeep standing at the entrance to the hangar and waving at him again, impatiently this time. He was already in his jeep, engine running, as Bounce exited the hangar. As soon as he climbed in, they drove off.

"Where are we going, Corporal?" Bounce asked him after it became clear the man wasn't going to speak unless spoken to.

"Debriefing," the man said tersely. There was no acknowledgment of his rank, nor the usual North Korean appellation of 'comrade'. If the treatment was meant to send a message to Bounce, he could only interpret it as one of impolite indifference.

Escorted to what was little more than a prison cell with a door instead of bars, he was asked to empty his pockets, given a glass of water and told to wait. When he eventually needed a toilet, he found the same insouciant corporal sitting outside his room at a desk, and was escorted to and from the toilet.

After two hours, Bounce had approached the corporal again. "You said I would be debriefed," Bounce pointed out. "When?"

The man sighed, reached for a black bakelite telephone on his desk and placed a call. After a short conversation, he put the phone down again.

"Someone will be here today," he said. "You will wait." Bounce opened his mouth to berate the man both for the reply and the way it was delivered, but the man held up his hand and interrupted before he could speak. "You should get used to waiting," the Corporal said. "It is our national sport."

What followed was a day of the same. Then a week. Then two.

Bounce had started by demanding to talk to someone in authority. After two weeks, he was pleading.

Then, finally, Bounce heard voices out in the corridor. His room had a chair, a table and a cot, and he spent most days just lying on the cot in boredom and frustration. He was still wearing the flight suit he'd taken off with. When he'd been asked to empty his pockets, he'd handed over a single packet of gum. He had brought nothing out with him, not even his passport. Partly because the advance he had been paid in crypto currency had been safely transferred to an offshore account, and partly because he wanted no reminders of the life he had just left behind.

He'd swung his legs off the cot and waited. Eventually the door was opened and two men stood there. One was a Captain of the North Korean DPRK Air Force, the other ... a man in a suit. He looked like a bureaucrat.

He looked at them with wary resentment.

"You will stand and salute in the presence of superior officers!" the Air Force officer barked.

Bounce gave him a look of barely concealed scorn. "I have not been accorded the same courtesy."

"You have no rank in North Korea," the man continued.

"You are a non-person. Do you understand?"

Bounce had never been the brightest student in his class, but he'd been one of the toughest in the schoolyard. He knew how to take on a bully when he met one. He stood.

"I am Lieutenant Hee-chan Son and I have delivered to you South Korea's most potent warplane!" he yelled in the man's face, forcing him to shrink back. "I am the only man in North Korea who can fly it and the only one who can teach your pilots how to fight it, and if you do not show me *some freaking respect* your superiors will have you shot!"

The man quailed, and the bureaucrat raised a hand and put it on the shoulder of the North Korean Air Force Captain.

He bowed very slightly to Bounce, stepped forward and smiled. "Comrade Lieutenant Son. The Democratic People's Republic of Korea appreciates your sacrifice."

Bounce weighed him up. The air force captain had referred to him as an 'officer', so he was not a mere bureaucrat. He was clearly the man in charge. Though the North Korean captain was scowling, he had not retaliated at Bounce's insubordination.

"Very well," Bounce said, lowering his voice. "I need someone to tell me what is going on. I will cooperate in every way possible."

"I am sure," the man said. "I apologize for the delay in speaking with you, but events have overtaken us, Lieutenant." He indicated the cot. "Please, sit."

Bounce did not like the way the North Korean Captain was standing behind the suited man and smirking, but he sat.

"Do you smoke?" the man asked, reaching into his pocket and holding out a packet of cigarettes.

"No."

"Do you mind if I do?"

"Go ahead."

The man lit a cigarette and sat beside Bounce on the bunk. "*Let us sacrifice our today, that our children may have a better tomorrow,*" he said. "Do you know who said that?"

"The Supreme Leader, I assume," Bounce said carefully.

The man smiled. "No. It was an aerospace engineer, actually. He went on to be President of India. The quote is particularly relevant to *your* situation."

Bounce did not like where the conversation was headed. "I have made my sacrifice. I committed a crime against my State, stole one of their most secret weapons and delivered it to you, leaving my entire life behind."

"Yes. But as I said, events have ... moved on. A new sacrifice is required of you."

Bounce's blood chilled. "What?"

Picking tobacco from his teeth, the man watched the smoke from his cigarette curl up to the ceiling. "You chose the wrong side, I'm afraid, Lieutenant. The losing side. You played your part with loyalty, with courage, and I have a certain sympathy."

"What are you talking about..."

The man stood. Two guards entered the room, standing either side of the smirking Air Force Captain.

"The aircraft you delivered to North Korea is currently being dismantled and crated for shipment back to the government of South Korea." He dropped his cigarette and ground it under his shoe. "You will similarly be delivered back to the government of South Korea. I understand you are to be tried for treason, and for being complicit in the murder of 28 people at Panmunjom."

Numbed, Bounce simply stared at him.

"We are just pawns in the great games of States, Lieutenant," the man said. "Console yourself with the knowledge that rather than spark a global war, your actions may in fact have secured the peace for generations to come. When it comes to your place in history, unlike many, you will never need to wonder."

'Snake-eater' Besserman was doing a little wondering.

He and Kronk had been lifted out of the Peace Dam by a rescue flight ordered by a dead man – Colonel 'Keys' Ban. Ban had made a promise to Bunny O'Hare, and before he'd taken off on his final mission, he'd kept it. Kronk and his high-flying Shikaka disappeared onto a helo bound for the *USS Bougainville* and Snake had been given a few days' leave after his debriefing about events at the Peace Dam, but had returned early and volunteered for the patrol as a way to shake off the cobwebs.

Now he was flying his first patrol along the DMZ since the end of hostilities between North and South Korea, and the skies had been wonderfully peaceful for many days now.

What he was wondering about, were the reasons he was given to explain why he was flying with a *new* AI backseater, whose callsign he hadn't yet memorized, instead of his old AI, callsign 'Dwarf'.

The twin-seat Kingsnake's AI backseater usually followed the pilot whenever they changed aircraft. It was a plug-in modular quantum core the pilot took with them, inserted in a hatch underneath the cockpit and as soon as the machine's systems were initialized, it went to work just like any other WSO dropping into the back seat.

"So, what happened to Dwarf?" Snake had asked the DARPA engineer who handed him the new AI module for his Kingsnake.

"Decommissioned," the guy said with a shrug.

"I thought you guys kept continuous backups. Why do I have to start over? Why can't I just plug in the last backup of Dwarf, and ..."

"Because Dwarf *died*, man," the guy said. "I mean, we could restore him from a backup, but that backup would have been aware right up until the moment he..."

"Got shot down?"

"Right, yeah."

"And he'd remember that?"

The guy had smiled. "Oh, he'd remember. We could go with an earlier backup, from before his last mission, but the AI would notice the gap in their timeline. And we haven't yet tested what effect 'dying' has on the AI's relationship with his pilot." The engineer clapped him on the shoulder. "By the way, I'm not sure that's a test I'd volunteer for."

Bunny O'Hare had been told the same thing about Noname, but she wasn't exactly mourning the fact the bony hand of death had come for Noname, and not for her.

Bunny was still in the process of digesting the events of the Reunification War, as it was being called. Superficial as she was, even O'Hare could see there were lessons to be learned from the actions she was involved in that day. But if the air battle over the Peace Dam was a combat test of backseater AI, she wasn't exactly sure what it proved beyond the fact that letting an AI learn its own lessons and implement those learnings unchecked, was the kind of thing that could get a girl killed.

Yes, she understood that the AI made a decision between the mission, or her life. And she understood it had done what it could to give her the best possible chance of surviving the attack by the North Korean J-7. Hell, Noname had even triggered her ejection seat for her. And, alright, yes, she also understood that it was probably thanks to Noname that they had *not* vaporized the Supreme Leader of North Korea and triggered global Armageddon.

That did not, however, take away from the fact that because of Noname's decision to take her out of the loop, she had spent the last two weeks face down on a gurney in the trauma ward at Sejong City hospital having her back muscles sewn back onto her spine and about a hundred pieces of a Pratt and Whitney jet engine removed from her hide.

Bunny decided to mark Noname's passing by adding a small crystal to her navel jewelry. A *very* small crystal.

She was still a long way from being released, but she'd finally been allowed to have a little in-room 'R&R'. She'd had to sweet talk the nurses, but after alternating bouts of pleading, whining and threatening, she'd been given permission to bring a tattooist into the hospital. Aggressor Inc. had paid for her to have a nearly-private room, so she also had to get the patient she was sharing with to agree, but the other woman had been amenable.

She did have a privacy screen around her bed while the tattoo was being done though, because she'd had to take her shirt off and though the woman in the other bed seemed nice enough, she was pretty sure she wasn't ready for the shock of seeing Bunny O'Hare's battered body naked, psychological trauma wise.

Bunny had been on the trauma ward a week or more already when the woman was wheeled in, and the nurse had begged Bunny to make an exception, and not upset her. So rude. She seemed nice enough and Bunny never upset people who hadn't asked for it. Usually.

Funny thing though, the woman had her own bodyguards. A team of them, in suits and shades, who sat outside their room 24/7.

Her name was Helen Lee and she'd been brought in for treatment at the US military hospital because she was a Korean security agent who apparently had been shot multiple times and the wounds weren't healing like they should. She was friendly enough but she either couldn't or wouldn't talk about what had happened to her. Bunny had picked that up pretty quickly. So she'd left it alone. Until now.

"What is this tattoo you are getting?" Lee had asked from the other side of the screen, as the tattooist took a break to wipe some blood off her shoulder.

"*New York, London, Sydney, Yongdoktong,*" she said. "In Korean. Stupid, right?"

"Perhaps. Yongdoktong? When I was recovering, I heard about that attack. You were involved? In the air, or on the ground?"

"Air. What did you hear?"

"I heard it was a suicide mission."

"It was. For the guy who died." She pointed to one of several earrings in her left ear. "This one is for him."

"Oh. I am sorry I asked."

"No worries."

There was an awkward silence, which the woman apparently felt compelled to break. She had to raise her voice to speak over the buzz of the needle as the tattooist started up again. "So, why are you here, Bunny O'Hare?"

"Ruptured latissimus dorsi, multiple contusions, bits of metal up against the spinal cord and a couple fractured ribs, from bailing out," Bunny told her.

"Ouch."

"Yeah. Well, not so much 'bailing out' as having my plane disintegrate around me while I fell screaming like a two-year-old toward the earth until my parachute automatically deployed, kind of thing."

"Hold still please," the tattooist said, putting a hand gently but firmly on Bunny's shoulder. The one without about a hundred stitches in it.

Bunny ignored her, pulling aside the curtain and getting up on one elbow. "But since we're sharing ... how about you?"

"A fair question. You saw the assassination of the South Korean Prime Minister on TV?"

"Duh."

"Yes. But the shooter was off camera, correct?"

"Yes..." There probably wasn't anyone on the planet with access to the internet who had not seen the KTV video footage of the drama on the rooftop. Special Operations helos boring in, one being blasted from the sky by a missile fired by Presidential security, the President himself fleeing from his podium surrounded by security agents and then falling in a hail of bullets that also took down an agent about to launch another anti-air missile. The vision finished as a second Special Operations helo dropped troops on the roof and the TV news crew decided they'd probably already won the Korean Emmy and running for their lives was a better idea. Bunny took a not so wild guess. "The shooter was you?"

"Yes."

"Who shot *you*, the President's men, or the Special Ops team?"

"The President's Security chief. He was killed by our Special Operations troops."

"But not before you took a few bullets?"

"I was wearing a tactical vest. The vest took most of the bullets. I took two. I had already been shot once, in the leg. That is the one that is not healing."

Bunny saw the annoyed frown on her Korean tattooist's face and lay back down again. She'd learned the hard way it was best not to annoy your tattooist. She whistled softly. "And what happens to you now?"

"There is an investigation. I could be charged with multiple counts of murder, but my lawyers have been told by the prosecutors it is more likely I can plead guilty to abuse of authority and take a discharge with no criminal penalty."

"Been there, got the t-shirt. You going to take the deal? I'd take the deal."

"I have no desire to spend years in court."

"Amen to that. So what are you going to do when it's over? Go private?"

"Perhaps. First, I need to get well. Then I think I will need a long holiday."

Bunny got up on one elbow again, causing the tattooist to cluck at her. She ignored her, again. "Holiday? Hey, I don't suppose you like Casino shows?"

THE END

Announcing: AGGRESSOR!

The new series from FX Holden

Karen 'Bunny' O'Hare is a pilot in Aggressor Inc.'s UCAV Tactical Training Program. Her job? Train America's closest allies in how to fly and fight against the growing threat of unmanned combat aircraft.

Her latest contract: Train the pilots of Taiwan's Republic of China Air Force during a massive air, land and sea exercise known as Ghost Sabre.

Her mission: to kick off Ghost Sabre by taking a strike package of unmanned aircraft from Guam air base in the Pacific, across the Philippine Sea and 'strike' a ground target on the island of Taiwan. Standing in her way are Taiwan's Air Force, Navy and ground-air defenses.

Succeed or fail, once Ghost Sabre is over, she will hand over her UCAVs to the ROC Air Force and spend the next six months training its pilots how to fly and fight with, and against, unmanned combat aircraft.

If she even lives to see Taiwan, that is.

Not everyone is happy to the see the US transfer potent new air weapons to the breakaway republic. And Bunny has 1,700 miles of open sea between her, and safety.

Aggressor is the first in a new series of novels following the abrasive anti-hero from the Future War series, Karen 'Bunny' O'Hare, as she fights to stay alive in a world determined to see her dead.

COMING SUMMER 2023!

Author Notes

Copenhagen, June 2022

I scripted and researched DMZ during 2021 and as I sat down to write it February 2022, Russia invaded Ukraine. I take no joy in the fact that I predicted this on my blog in December '21: "I just read Russian President V. Putin's 12,000-word essay on Ukraine and there can be only one conclusion ... he is going to invade."

Like the rest of the western world I watched in horror as Russian tanks reached the outskirts of Kyiv and then cheered for the gritty Ukrainians as Russia was forced to withdraw from northern Ukraine, then beaten back from Ukraine's second largest city, Kharkiv. Ukraine forced massive Russian losses in Mariupol and the Donbas region, but at the time of writing, the combatants have settled into what looks sadly like a long, drawn out war that will only end with a change of leadership in Moscow.

For a military fiction writer, a lot of lessons have been learned. In Ukraine we saw the large-scale impact of drone warfare on a modern battlefield for the first time, as Turkish TB2 drones killed Russian main battle tanks by the dozens, guided the anti-ship missiles that sank the Russian Black Sea flagship, the *Moskva*, and Russian KYB kamikaze drones were used with horrifying effect to target concentrations of Ukrainian troops. We saw the terrible results of Russia's use of thermobaric rockets (a weapon shown in action in the Future War novel 'Kobani') on civilians in Ukrainian towns and on entrenched troops in the Donbas

The chaos, brutality but also the ineptitude of Russia's attack on Ukraine was a shock to most observers. I *wrongly* predicted a well-coordinated, combined arms attack on Ukraine, conducted under cover of complete air superiority, that would secure eastern Ukraine for Russia in the space of a few months. Instead, we saw logistical problems cripple the Russian offensives, its air force limited to launching stand off attacks from outside Ukraine's borders due to the effectiveness of Ukrainian air defenses, and poorly supported armored units decimated by hand-held anti-tank missiles and drone-guided artillery.

That chaos and ineptitude influenced greatly the scripting of DMZ, which is about an attempt by a group of powerful conspirators on both sides of the demarcation line, to disrupt the reunification process. I originally envisaged that it would be all too easy for a few well-placed conspirators successfully to completely derail a peace process; to create fear and panic, to install their own leaders, to bring the superpowers once again to the brink of open conflict...

But the failure of Russia's initial offensives in Ukraine gave me pause. If a medium sized power like Russia, given years to prepare itself, could execute its strategy so badly that it would lose hundreds of tanks and tens of thousands of troops in the first couple of months of war - with only minor gains to show for it - then how badly could things go for a handful of anti-reunification conspirators in Korea?

DMZ therefore became a lot more about the *mistakes* made by the main actors, and the impact that the actions of just a few ordinary people can have on the outcome of world events.

The outrage of a single South Korean protection officer in Sejong City.

The grudging love for his leader of a North Korean Supreme Guards officer.

The determination of a US naval commander in a tiny, battle-scarred vessel, not to give up ... even in the face of nuclear destruction.

And of course, the willingness of an Australian fighter pilot to fight a fight that wasn't hers. Because at the end of the day ordinary soldiers, sailors and pilots fight and die not for grand political philosophies, not only because it is their duty, but because they have their mates' backs.

An amazing group of people (named in the front of the book) helped polish the plot and bring authenticity to the action. If there are any technical errors in this book they are entirely my fault, not the fault of this group of military fiction enthusiasts; including Army, Navy and Air Force servicemen and women from multiple countries. If you enjoyed this novel, you should also thank them!

FX Holden

Glossary

For simplicity, this glossary is common across all Future War novels and may refer to systems not in this novel. Please note, weapons or systems marked with an asterisk* are currently still under development. If there is no asterisk, then the system has already been deployed by at least one nation.

3D PRINTER: A printer which can recreate a 3D object based on a three-dimensional digital model, typically by laying down many thin layers of a material in succession

ADA*: All Domain Attack. An attack on an enemy in which all operational domains – space, cyber, ground, air and naval – are engaged either simultaneously or sequentially

AI: Artificial intelligence, as applied in aircraft to assist pilots, in intelligence to assist with intelligence analysis, or in ordnance such as drones and unmanned vehicles to allow semi-autonomous decision making

AIM-120D: US medium-range supersonic air-to-air missile

AIM-260*: Joint Advanced Tactical Missile (JATM), proposed replacement for AIM-120, with twin-boost phase, launch and loiter capability. Swarming capability has been discussed.

AIS: Automated identification system, a system used by all ships to provide update data on their location to their owners and insurers. Civilian shipping is required to keep their transponder on at all times unless under threat from pirates; military ships transmit at their own discretion. Rogue nations often ignore the requirement in order to hide the location of ships with illicit cargoes or conducting illegal activities.

ALL DOMAIN KILL CHAIN*: Also known as Multi-Domain Kill Chain. An attack in which advanced AI allows high-speed assimilation of data from multiple sources (satellite, cyber, ground and air) to generate engagement solutions for military maneuver, precision fire support, artillery, or combat air support.

AMD-65: Russian-made military assault rifle

AN/APG-81: The active electronically scanned array (AESA) radar system on the F-35 Panther that allows it to track and engage multiple air and ground targets simultaneously

ANGELS: Radio brevity code for 'thousands of feet'. Angels five is five thousand feet

AO YIN: Legendary Chinese four-horned bull with insatiable appetite for human flesh

APC: Armored personnel carrier; a wheeled or tracked lightly armored vehicle able to transport troops into combat and provide limited covering fire

ARMATA T-14: Next-generation Russian main battle tank with active projectile defense capabilities and enhanced crew survivability versus older Russian main battle tanks. A few prototypes have been delivered to the Russian Army and seen in parades and on Russian media footage but as of the time of writing, the Armata has not been put into mass production or proven to have been used in combat in Syria or Ukraine.

ASFN: Anti-screw fouling net. Traditionally, a net boom laid across the entrance of a harbor to hinder the entrance of ships or submarines.

ASRAAM: Advanced Short-Range Air-to-Air Missile (infrared only)

ASROC: Anti-submarine rocket-launched torpedo. Allows a torpedo to be fired at a submerged target from up to ten miles away, allowing the torpedo to enter the water close to the target and reducing the chances the target can evade the attack.

ASTUTE CLASS: Next-generation British nuclear-powered attack submarine (SSN) designed for stealth operation. Powered by a Rolls Royce reactor plant coupled to a pump-jet propulsion system. HMS *Astute* is the first of seven planned hulls, HMS *Agincourt* is the last. Can carry up to 38 torpedoes and cruise missiles and is one of the first British submarines to be steered by a 'pilot' using a joystick.

ASW: Anti-Submarine Warfare

AWACS: Airborne Warning and Control System aircraft, otherwise known as AEW&C (Airborne Early Warning and Control). Aircraft with advanced radar and communication systems that can detect aircraft at ranges up to several hundred miles, and direct air operations over a combat theater.

AXEHEAD: Russian long-range hypersonic air-to-air missile

B-21 RAIDER*: Replacement for the retiring US B-2 Stealth Bomber and B-52. The Raider is intended to provide a lower-cost, stealthier alternative to the B-2 with expanded weapons delivery capabilities to include hypersonic and beyond visual range air-to-air missiles.

BACKSEATER or WEAPONS SYSTEMS OFFICER (WSO): Weapons Systems Officers are fast-jet aircrew who operate on aircraft such as the F/A-18F Super Hornet or the EA-18G Growler electronic attack aircraft, carrying out navigation, sensor management and ground weapons targeting and management. The US Air Force demonstrated the potential role of AI for its US Next Generation Air Dominance platform, or NGAD, in December 2021 by flying a U-2 reconnaissance aircraft, which normally carries a single crew member, with an AI algorithm as a 'virtual backseater'. As the pilot flew, the AI system – dubbed 'ARTUμ' in honor of Star Wars robot R2-D2 – controlled the aircraft's sensors and navigation. On the test flight, ARTUμ was tasked with finding adversary missile launchers and was 'solely responsible for sensor employment and tactical navigation', while the human pilot concentrated on finding enemy aircraft and flying. ARTUμ 'made final calls on devoting the radar to missile hunting versus self-protection'. China is also believed to be developing backseater AI for its twin-seat J-16 4th gen, and J-20 stealth fighter.

BARRETT MRAD M22: Multirole adaptive design sniper rifle with replaceable barrels, capable of firing different ammunition types including anti-materiel rounds, accurate out to 1,500 meters or nearly one mile

BATS*: Boeing Airpower Teaming System, semi-autonomous unmanned combat aircraft. The BATS drone is designed to accompany 4th- and 5th-generation fighter aircraft on missions either in an air escort, recon, or electronic warfare capacity.

BELLADONNA: A Russian-made mobile electronic warfare vehicle capable of jamming enemy airborne warning aircraft, ground radars, radio communications and radar-guided missiles

BESAT*: New 1,200-ton class of Iranian SSP (air-independent propulsion) submarine. Also known as Project Qaaem. Capable of launching mines, torpedoes, or cruise missiles

BIG RED ONE: US 1st Infantry Division (see also BRO), aka the Bloody First

BINGO: Radio brevity code indicating that an aircraft has only enough fuel left for a return to base

BLOODY FIRST: US 1st Infantry Division, aka the Big Red One (BRO)

BOGEY: Unidentified aircraft detected by radar

BRADLEY UGCV*: US unmanned ground combat vehicle prototype based on a modified M3 Bradley combat fighting vehicle. A tracked vehicle with medium armor, it is intended to be controlled remotely by a crew in a vehicle, or ground troops, up to two miles away. Armed with 5kw blinding laser and autoloading TOW anti-tank missiles. See also HYPERION

BRO: Big Red One or Bloody First, nickname for US Army 1st Infantry Division

BTR-80: A Russian-made amphibious armored personnel carrier armed with a 30mm automatic cannon

BUG OUT: Withdraw from combat

BUK: Russian-made self-propelled anti-aircraft missile system designed to engage medium-range targets such as aircraft, smart bombs, and cruise missiles

BUSTER: 100 percent throttle setting on an aircraft, or full military power

CAP: Combat air patrol; an offensive or defensive air patrol over an objective

CAS: Close air support; air action by rotary-winged or fixed-wing aircraft against hostile targets in close proximity to friendly forces. CAS operations are often directed by a joint terminal air controller, or JTAC, embedded with a military unit.

CASA CN-235: Turkish Air Force medium-range twin-engined transport aircraft

CBRN: Chemical, biological, radiological, or nuclear. See also NBC SUIT

CCP: Communist Party of China. Governed by a Politburo comprising the Chinese Premier and senior party ministers and officials.

CENTURION: US 20mm radar-guided close-in weapons system for protection of ground or naval assets against attack by artillery, rocket, or missiles

CHAMP*: Counter-electronics High Power Microwave Advanced Missiles; a 'launch and loiter' cruise missile which attacks sensitive electronics with high power microwave bursts to damage electronics. Similar in effect to an electromagnetic pulse (EMP) weapon.

CIC: Combat Information Center. The 'nerve center' on an early warning aircraft, warship, or submarine that functions as a tactical center and provides processed information for command and control of the near battlespace or area of operations. On a warship, acts on orders from and relays information to the bridge.

CO: Commanding Officer

COALITION: Coalition of Nations involved in *Operation Anatolia Screen*: Turkey, US, UK, Australia, Germany

COLT: Combat Observation Laser Team; a forward artillery observer team armed with a laser for designating targets for attack by precision-guided munitions

CONSTELLATION* class frigate: the result of the US FFG(X) program, a warship with advanced anti-air, anti-surface, and anti-submarine capabilities capable of serving as a data integration and communication hub. The first ship in the class, *USS Constellation*, is expected to enter service mid-2020s. *USS Congress* will be the second ship in the class.

CONTROL ROOM: the compartment on a submarine from which weapons, sensors, propulsion, and navigation commands are coordinated

COP: Combat Outpost (US)

C-RAM: Counter-rocket, artillery, and mortar cannon, also abbreviated counter-RAM

CROWS: Common Remotely Operated Weapon Station, a weapon such as .50 caliber machine gun, mounted on a turret and controlled remotely by a soldier inside a vehicle, bunker or command post

CUDA*: Missile nickname (from barracuda) for the supersonic US short- to medium-range 'Small Advanced Capabilities Missile'. It has tri-mode (optical, active radar and infrared heat-seeking) sensors, thrust vectoring for extreme maneuverability and a hit-to-kill terminal attack

DARPA: US Defense Advanced Research Projects Agency, a research and development agency responsible for bringing new military technologies to the US armed forces

DAS: Distributed Aperture System; a 360-degree sensor system on the F-35 Panther allowing the pilot to track targets visually at greater than 'eyeball' range

DFDA: Australian armed forces Defense Forces Discipline Act

DFM: Australian armed forces Defense Force Magistrate

DIA: The US Defense Intelligence Agency

DIRECTOR OF NATIONAL CYBER SECURITY*. The NSA's Cyber Security Directorate is an organization that unifies NSA's foreign intelligence and cyber defense missions and is charged with preventing and eradicating threats to National Security Systems and the Defense Industrial Base. Various US government sources have mooted the elevation of the role of Director of Cyber Security to a Cabinet-level Director of National Cyber Security (on a level with the Director of National Intelligence), appointed by the US President to coordinate the activities of the many different agencies and military departments engaged in cyber warfare.

DRONE: Unmanned aerial vehicle, UCAV, or UAV, used for combat, transport, refueling or reconnaissance

ECS: Engagement Control Station; the local control center for a HELLADS laser battery which tracks targets and directs anti-air defensive fire

EMP: Electromagnetic pulse. Nuclear weapons produce an EMP wave which can destroy unshielded electronic components. The major military powers have also been experimenting with non-nuclear weapons which can also produce an EMP pulse – see CHAMP missile

EPF or EXPEDITIONARY FAST TRANSPORT: The Spearhead-class expeditionary fast transport (EPF) is a United States Navy-led shipbuilding program to provide a high-speed, shallow-draft vessel intended for rapid intra-theater transport of medium-sized cargo payloads. The EPF can reach speeds of 35–45 knots (65–83 km/h; 40–52 mph) and allows for the rapid transit and deployment of conventional or special forces as well as equipment and supplies. The vessels are a part of Military Sealift Command's Sealift Program. It features a landing pad and storage area for a single helicopter and can carry up to 300 Marines and their equipment, plus several rigid-hull inflatable vessels for sea to shore transport. The US Fourth Fleet is currently evaluating the ability of the class to be fitted with self-defense weapons and to team with *Sea Hunter*-class unmanned vessels to allow it to conduct mine or submarine hunting patrols*.

ETA: Estimated Time of Arrival

F-16 FALCON: US-made 4th-generation multirole fighter aircraft flown by Turkey

F-35: US 5th-generation fighter aircraft, known either as the Panther (pilot nickname) or Lightning II (manufacturer name). The Panther nickname was first coined by the 6th Weapons Squadron 'Panther Tamers'. There is much speculation about the capabilities of the Panther, just as there is about the Russian Su-57 Felon. Neither has been extensively combat tested.

F-47B (currently X-47) FANTOM*: A Northrop Grumman demonstration unmanned combat aerial vehicle (UCAV) in trials with the US Navy and a part of the DARPA Joint UCAS program. See also MQ-25 STINGRAY

FAC: Forward air controller; an aviator embedded with a ground unit to direct close air support attacks. See also TAC(P)

419

or JTAC

FAST MOVERS: Fighter jets

FATEH: Iranian SSK (diesel electric) submarine. At 500 tons, also considered a midget submarine. Capable of launching torpedoes, torpedo-launched cruise missiles and mines

FELON: Russian 5th-generation stealth fighter aircraft, the Sukhoi Su-57. There is much speculation about the capabilities of the Felon, just as there is about the US F-35 Panther. Like many of Russia's newer weapon types, reported to be in serial production but very few examples have been seen and it was not used in the invasion of Ukraine which would have been expected.

FINGER FOUR FORMATION: A fighter aircraft patrol formation in which four aircraft fly together in a pattern that resembles the tips of the four fingers of a hand. Four such formations can form a squadron of 12 aircraft.

FIRE SCOUT: An unmanned autonomous scout helicopter for service on US warships, used for anti-ship and anti-submarine operations

FISTER: A member of a Fist (Fire Support Team)

FLANKER: Russian Sukhoi-30 or 35 attack aircraft; see also J-11 (China)

FOX (1, 2 or 3): Radio brevity code indicating a pilot has fired an air-to-air missile, either semi-active radar seeking (1), infrared (2) or active radar seeking (3)

GAL*: A natural language learning system (AI) used by Israel's Unit 8200 to conduct complex analytical research support

GAL-CLASS SUBMARINE: An upgraded *Dolphin II* class submarine, fitted with the GAL AI system, allowing it to be operated by a two-person crew

G/ATOR: Ground/Air Oriented Task Radar (GATOR); a radar specialized for the detection of incoming artillery fire, rockets, or missiles. Also, able to calculate the origin of attack for counterfire purposes.

GBU: Guided Bomb Unit

GHOST BAT*: see LOYAL WINGMAN. Teaming drone

capable of being paired with a manned aircraft for reconnaissance or attack missions in contested airspace.

GORAE*: North Korean 'Whale'-class diesel electric submarine, also known as Sinpo class. Displacement of 2,000–3,000 tons. The attack submarine variant is currently in operation, while a ballistic missile variant has been photographed under construction.

GPS: Global Positioning System, a network of civilian or military satellites used to provide accurate map reference and location data

GRAY WOLF*: US subsonic standoff air-launched cruise missile with swarming (horde) capabilities. The Gray Wolf is designed to launch from multiple aircraft, including the C-130, and defeat enemy air defenses by overwhelming them with large numbers. It will feature modular swap-out warheads.

GRAYHOUND: Radio brevity code for the launch of an air-ground missile

GRU: Russian military intelligence service

H-20*: Xian Hong 20 stealth bomber with a range of 12,000 km or 7,500 miles and payload of 10 tons. Comparable to the US B-21.

HARM: Homing Anti-Radar Missile; a missile which homes on the signals produced by anti-air missile radars like that used by the BUK or PANTSIR

HAWKEYE: Northrop Grumman E2D airborne warning and control aircraft. Capable of launching from aircraft carriers and networking (sharing data) with compatible aircraft.

HE: High-explosive munitions; general purpose explosive warheads

HEAT: High-Explosive Anti-Tank munitions; shells specially designed to penetrate armor

HELLADS*: High Energy Liquid Laser Area Defense System; an alternative to missile or projectile-based air defense systems that attacks enemy missiles, rockets, or bombs with high energy laser and/or microwave pulses. Currently being tested by US, Chinese, Russian and EU ground, air, and naval forces.

HELIOS*: High Energy Laser with Integrated Optical-dazzler and Surveillance. A close-in laser defense system to be employed on US Navy ships for missile defense.

HOLMES*: A natural language learning system (AI) used by the NSA to conduct sophisticated analytical research support. The NSA has publicly reported it is already using AI for cyber defense and exploring machine learning potential.

HORDE*: Drones, missiles or smart bombs with onboard AI and the ability to coordinate their actions with other drones while in flight, either autonomously or using preselected protocols. 'Horde' tactics differ from 'swarm' tactics in that they rely on large numbers to overwhelm enemy defenses. See also SWARM

HPM*: High Power Microwave; an untargeted local area defensive weapon which attacks sensitive electronics in missiles and guided bombs to damage electronics such as guidance systems

HSU-003*: Planned Chinese large unmanned underwater vehicle optimized for seabed warfare, i.e., piloting itself to a specific location on the sea floor (a harbor or shipping lane) and conducting reconnaissance or anti-shipping attacks. Comparable to the US Orca.

HYPERION*: Proposed lightly armored unmanned ground vehicle (UGCV). Can be fitted with turret-mounted 50kw laser for anti-air, anti-personnel defense and autoloading TOW missile launcher. See also BRADLEY UGCV

HYPERSONIC: Speeds greater than 5x the speed of sound

ICC: Information Coordination Center; command center for multiple air defense batteries such as PATRIOT or HELLADS

IED: Improvised explosive device, for example, a roadside bomb

IFF: Identify Friend or Foe transponder, a radio transponder that allows weapons systems to determine whether a target is an ally or enemy

IFV: Infantry fighting vehicle, a highly mobile, lightly armored, wheeled or tracked vehicle capable of carrying troops into a combat and providing fire support. See NAMER

IMA BK: The combat AI built into Russia's Su-57 Felon and Okhotnik fighter aircraft

IR: Infrared or heat-seeking system

ISIS: Self-proclaimed Islamic State of Iraq and Syria

ISR: Intelligence, surveillance and reconnaissance. Typically applied to aircraft performing these roles on intelligence gathering missions. Can be manned or unmanned. Unmanned examples include the US Global Hawk, SENTINEL or SHIKAKA drones.

J-7: Fishbed; 3rd-generation Chinese fighter, a copy of cold war Russian Mig-21

J-10: Firebird; 3rd-generation Chinese fighter, comparable to US F-16

J-11: Flanker; 4th-generation Chinese fighter, copy of Russian Su-27

J-15: Flying Shark; 4th-generation PLA Navy, twin-engine twin-seat fighter, comparable to Russian Su-33 and a farther development of the J-11. Currently the most common aircraft flown off China's aircraft carriers.

J-16*: *Zhi Sheng* (Intelligence Victory); 4th-generation, two-seater twin-engine multirole strike fighter. In 2019 it was announced a variant of the J-16 was being developed with *Zhi Sheng* Artificial Intelligence to replace the human 'backseater' or copilot. See also BACKSEATER

J-20: 'Mighty Dragon'; 5th-generation single-seat, twin-engine Chinese stealth fighter, claimed to be comparable to the US F-35 or F-22, or Russian Su-57. A twin seat attack version* is in development.

JAGM: Joint air-ground missile. A US short-range anti-armor or anti-personnel missile fired from an aircraft. It can be laser or radar guided and has an 18 lb. warhead.

JASSM: AGM-158 Joint Air-to-Surface Standoff Missile; long-range subsonic stealth cruise missile

JDAM: Joint Direct Attack Munition; bombs guided by laser or GPS to their targets

JLTV*: US Joint Light Tactical Vehicle; planned replacement for the US ground forces Humvee multipurpose vehicle, to be available in recon/scout, infantry transport, heavy guns, close combat, command and control, or ambulance versions

JTAC: Joint terminal air controller. A member of a ground force – e.g., Marine unit – trained to direct the action of combat aircraft engaged in close air support and other offensive air operations from a forward position. See also CAS

K-77M*: Supersonic Russian-made medium-range active radar homing air-to-air missile with extreme maneuverability. It is being developed from the existing R-77 missile.

KALIBR: Russian-made anti-ship, anti-submarine, and land attack cruise missile with 500kg conventional or nuclear warhead. The Kalibr-M variant* will have an extended range of up to 4,500 km or 2,700 miles (the distance of, e.g., Iran to Paris).

KARAKURT CLASS: A Russian corvette class which first entered service in 2018. Armed with Pantsir close-in weapons systems, Sosna-R anti-air missile defense and Kalibr supersonic anti-ship missiles. An anti-submarine sensor/weapon loadout is planned but not yet deployed.

KC-135 STRATOTANKER: US airborne refueling aircraft

KRYPTON: Supersonic Russian air-launched anti-radar missile, it is also being adapted for use against ships and large aircraft

LAUNCH AND LOITER: The capability of a missile or drone to fly itself to a target area and wait at altitude for final targeting instructions

LCS: Littoral combat ship. In the US Navy it refers to the *Independence* or *Freedom* class; in Iran, the *Safineh* class; in other navies it may be considered equivalent to a frigate or corvette class. Has the capabilities of a small assault transport, including a flight deck and hangar for housing two SH-60 or MH-60 Seahawk helicopters, a stern ramp for operating small boats, and the cargo volume and payload to deliver a small assault force with fighting vehicles to a roll-on/roll-off port facility. Standard armaments include Mk 110 57mm guns and RIM-116 Rolling Airframe Missiles. Also equipped with autonomous air, surface, and underwater vehicles. Possessing lower air defense and surface warfare capabilities than destroyers, the LCS concept emphasizes speed, flexible mission modules and a shallow draft.

LEOPARD: Main battle tank fielded by NATO forces including Turkey

LIAONING: China's first aircraft carrier, modified from the former Russian Navy aircraft cruiser, the *Varyag*. Since superseded by China's Type 002 (*Shandong*) and Type 003 carriers, the *Liaoning* is now used for testing new technologies for carrier use, such as the J-20 stealth fighter.

LMADIS: Light Marine Air Defense Integrated System. A counter-drone electronic attack system mounted on a Polaris MRZR all-terrain vehicle. It features a 360-degree radar, a direct-fire capability, radio frequency and optical jammers and electro-optic/infrared sensors.

LOCUST*: Low-Cost Unmanned UAV Swarming Technology drone. In development by the US Office of Naval Research. Small 'kamikaze' drones capable of being launched from aircraft or ships and guiding themselves to a target similar to the US Army 'Switchblade' drones currently in service. Networking capabilities would allow the drones to 'swarm' and overwhelm ground or sea targets. Each warhead features optical-infrared target seeking sensors with a 4 lb. high explosive 'focused charge' warhead.

LOITERING MUNITION: A missile or bomb able to wait at altitude for final targeting instructions

LONG-RANGE HYPERSONIC WEAPONS (LRHW)*: A prototype US missile consisting of a rocket and glide vehicle, capable of being launched by submarine, from land or from aircraft

LOYAL WINGMAN or GHOST BAT*: Unmanned aerial combat vehicle in development for the US Air Force by Boeing Australia as the Boeing Air Teaming System or BATS (official nickname, Ghost Bat). Similar aircraft in development by Kratos. These drones can be teamed with manned aircraft to provide added 'attritable' reconnaissance or attack capabilities that can penetrate contested airspace without risk to human pilots.

LS3*: Legged Squad Support System – a mechanized dog-like robot powered by hydrogen fuel cells and supported by a cloud-based AI. Currently being explored by DARPA and the US armed forces for logistical support or squad scouting and IED detection roles.

LTMV: Light Tactical Multirole Vehicle; a very long name for what is essentially a jeep

M1A2/3 ABRAMS*: US main battle tank. In 2016, the US Army and Marine Corps began testing out the Israeli Trophy active protection system to provide additional defense against incoming projectiles. Improvements planned for the M1A3 are to include a lighter 120mm gun, added road wheels with improved suspension, a more durable track, lighter-weight armor, long-range precision armaments, and infrared camera and laser detectors.

M22: See BARRETT MRAD M22 sniper rifle

M27: US-made military assault rifle

MAD: Magnetic Anomaly Detection, used by warships to detect large manmade objects under the surface of the sea, such as mines, or submarines

MAIN BATTLE TANK: See MBT

MANPAD::Man Portable Air Defense missile, eg US Stinger, UK Starstreak or Chinese Flying Crossbow. Uses optical-infrared tracking to engage aircraft at low to medium altitudes.

MASS: Marine Autonomous Surface Ship, or autonomous trailing vessel

MBT: Main battle tank; a heavily armored combat vehicle capable of direct fire and maneuver

MEFP: Multiple Explosive Formed Penetrators; a defensive weapon which uses small explosive charges to create and fire small metal slugs at an incoming projectile, thereby destroying it

MEMS: Micro-Electro-Mechanical System

METEOR: Long-range air-to-air missile with active radar

seeker, but also able to be updated with target data in-flight by any suitably equipped allied unit

MIA: Missing in action

MIKE: Radio brevity code for minutes

MIL-25: Export version of the Mi-25 'Hind' Russian helicopter gunship

MOPP: Mission-Oriented Protective Posture protective gear; equipment worn to protect troops against CBRN weapons. See also NBC SUIT

MP: Military Police

MQ-25 STINGRAY: The MQ-25 Stingray is a Boeing-designed prototype unmanned US airborne refueling aircraft. See also X-47B Fantom

MSS: Ministry of State Security, Chinese umbrella intelligence organization responsible for counterespionage and counterterrorism, and foreign intelligence gathering. Equivalent to the US FBI, CIA, and NSA.

NAMER: (Leopard) Israeli infantry fighting vehicle (IFV). More heavily armored than a Merkava IV main battle tank. According to the Israel Defense Forces, the Namer is the most heavily armored vehicle in the world of any type.

NATO: North Atlantic Treaty Organization

NAVAL STRIKE MISSILE (NSM): Supersonic anti-ship missile deployed by NATO navies

NBC SUIT: A protective suit issued to protect the wearer against Nuclear, Biological or Chemical weapons. Usually includes a lining to protect the user from radiation and either a gas mask or air recycling unit.

NORAD: The North American Aerospace Defense Command is a United States and Canadian bi-national organization charged with the missions of aerospace warning, aerospace control and maritime warning for North America. Aerospace warning includes the detection, validation, and warning of attack against North America whether by aircraft, missiles, or space vehicles, through mutual support arrangements with other commands.

NSA: US National Security Agency, cyber intelligence, cyber

warfare, and defense agency

OFSET*: Offensive Swarm Enabled Tactical drones. Proposed US anti-personnel, anti-armor drone system capable of swarming AI (see SWARM) and able to deploy small munitions against enemy troop or vehicles while moving.

OKHOTNIK*: 5th-generation Sukhoi S-70 unmanned stealth combat aircraft using avionics systems from the Su-57 Felon and fitted with two internal weapons bays, for 7,000kg of ordnance. Requires a pilot and systems officer, similar to current US unmanned combat aircraft. Can be paired with Su-57 aircraft and controlled by a pilot.

OMON: Otryad Mobil'nyy Osobogo Naznacheniya; the Russian National Guard mobile police force

ORCA*: Prototype US large displacement unmanned underwater vehicle with modular payload bay capable of anti-submarine, anti-ship, or reconnaissance activities

OVOD: Subsonic Russian-made air-launched cruise missile capable of carrying high-explosive, submunition or fragmentation warheads

PANTHER: Pilot name for the F-35 Lightning II stealth fighter, first coined by the 6th Weapons Squadron 'Panther Tamers'. There is much speculation about the capabilities of the Panther, just as there is about the Russian Su-57 Felon. Neither has been extensively combat tested.

PANTSIR: Russian-made truck-mounted anti-aircraft system which is a farther development of the PENSNE: 'Pince-nez' in English. A Russian-made autonomous ground-to-air missile currently being rolled out for the BUK anti-air defense system.

PARS: Turkish light armored vehicle

PATRIOT: An anti-aircraft, anti-missile missile defense system which uses its own radar to identify and engage airborne threats

PEACE EAGLE: Turkish Boeing 737 Airborne Early Warning and Control aircraft (see AWACS)

PENSNE: See PANTSIR

PERDIX*: Lightweight air-launched armed microdrone

with swarming capability (see SWARM). Designed to be launched from underwing canisters or even from the flare/chaff launchers of existing aircraft. Can be used for recon, target identification or delivery of lightweight ordnance.

PEREGRINE*: US medium-range, multimode (infrared, radar, optical) seeker missile with short form body designed for use by stealth aircraft

PERSEUS*: A stealth, hypersonic, multiple warhead missile under development for the British Royal Navy and French Navy

PHASED ARRAY RADAR: A radar which can steer a beam of radio waves quickly across the sky to detect planes and missiles

PL-15: Chinese medium-range radar-guided air-to-air missile, comparable to the US AIM-120D or UK Meteor

PL-21*: Chinese long-range multimode missile (radar, infrared, optical), comparable to US AIM-260

PLA: People's Liberation Army

PLA-AF (PLAAAF): People's Liberation Army Air Force, comparable to the US Air Force, with more than 400 3rd-generation fighter aircraft, 1,200 4th-generation, and nearly 200 5th-generation stealth aircraft

PLA-N (PLAN): People's Liberation Army Navy

PLA-N AF (PLANAF): People's Liberation Army Navy Air Force, comparable to the US Navy Air Force and Marine Corps Aviation, it performs coastal protection and aircraft carrier operations with more than 250 3rd-generation fighter aircraft, and 150 4th-generation fighter aircraft.

PODNOS: Russian-made portable 82mm mortar

PUMP-JET PROPULSION: A propulsion system comprising a jet of water and a nozzle to direct the flow of water for steering purposes. Used on some submarines due to a quieter acoustic signature than that generated by a screw. The 'stealthiest' submarines are regarded to be those powered by diesel electric engines and pump-jet propulsion, such as trialed on the Russian *Kilo* class and proposed for the Australian *Attack* class*.

QHS*: Quantum Harmonic Sensor; a sensor system for detecting stealth aircraft at long ranges by analyzing the electromagnetic disturbances they create in background radiation

RAAF: Royal Australian Air Force

RAF: Royal Air Force (UK)

ROE: Rules of Engagement; the rules laid down by military commanders under which a unit can or cannot engage in combat. For example, 'units may only engage a hostile force if fired upon first'.

RPG: Rocket-propelled grenade

RTB: Return to base

SAFINEH CLASS: Also known as *Mowj/Wave* class. An Iranian trimaran hulled high-speed missile vessel equivalent to the US LCS class, or the Russia *Karakurt*-class corvette

SAM: Surface-to-Air Missile; an anti-air missile (often shortened to SA) for engaging aircraft

SAR: See SYNTHETIC APERTURE RADAR

SCREW: The propeller used to drive a boat or ship is referred to as a screw (helical blade) propeller. Submarine propellers typically comprise five to seven blades. See also PUMP-JET PROPULSION

SEAD: Suppression of Enemy Air Defenses; an air attack intended to take down enemy anti-air defense systems. See also WILD WEASEL

SEA HUNTER*: *Sea Hunter* is an autonomous unmanned surface vehicle (USV) first launched in 2016 as part of the DARPA Anti-Submarine Warfare Continuous Trail Unmanned Vessel (ACTUV) program. It is an unmanned self-piloting craft with twin screws, powered by two diesel engines with a top speed of 27 knots (31 mph; 50 km/h). Her weight is 135 tons, including 40 tons of fuel, adequate for a 70-day cruise. Cruising range is 'transoceanic', i.e., 10,000 nautical miles (12,000 mi; 19,000 km) at 12 knots (14 mph; 22 km/h) fully fueled with 14,000 US gallons (53,000 L) of diesel. This is enough for the vessel 'to go from San Diego to Guam and back to Pearl Harbor on a tank of gas'. It is envisaged that the ACTUV vessels will be produced in reconnaissance, electronic intelligence, mine, and submarine hunting variants, allowing them to be paired with other vessels to provide them with these capabilities.

SENTINEL*: Lockheed Martin RQ-170 Sentinel flying wing stealth reconnaissance drone in development for the US Air Force.

SHIKAKA or GREAT WHITE BAT*: The Northrop Grumman RQ-180 is an American stealth unmanned aerial vehicle (UAV) surveillance aircraft intended for contested airspace. As of 2022, there had been no images or statements released, but growing evidence, including amateur photographs and video, points to the existence of the RQ-180 and its use in regular front-line service. It is believed to be a High-Altitude Long Endurance version of the SENTINEL drone. Primarily for use in an intelligence, surveillance and reconnaissance (ISR) role, the SHIKAKA is expected to function as a data hub for enabling linked combat systems to network data and communications. It has been speculated it will share many systems with the B-21 Spirit stealth bomber from the same manufacturer and could therefore be produced in an armed reconnaissance version capable of launching swarming drones.

SIDEWINDER: Heat-seeking short-range air-to-air missile

SITREP: Situation Report

SKYHAWK*: Chinese drone designed to team with fighter aircraft to provide added sensor or weapons delivery capabilities. Comparable to the planned US Boeing Loyal Wingman or Kratos drones.

SKY THUNDER: Chinese 1,000 lb. stealth air-launched cruise missile with swappable payload modules

SLR: Single lens reflex camera, favored by photojournalists

SMERCH: Russian-made 300mm rocket launcher capable of firing high-explosive, submunition or chemical weapons warheads

SPACECOM: United States Space Command (USSPACECOM or SPACECOM) is a unified combatant command of the United States Department of Defense, responsible for military operations in outer space, specifically all operations above 100 km above mean sea level

SPEAR/SPEAR-EW*: UK/Europe Select Precision at Range air-to-ground standoff attack missile, with LAUNCH AND LOITER capabilities. Will utilize a modular 'swappable' warhead system featuring high-explosive, anti-armor, fragmentation, or electronic warfare (EW) warheads.

SPETSNAZ: Russian Special Operations Forces

SPLASH: Radio brevity code indicating a target has been destroyed

SSBN: Strategic-level nuclear-powered (N) submarine platform for firing ballistic (B) missiles. Examples: UK *Vanguard* class, US *Ohio* class, Russia *Typhoon* class

SSC: Subsurface Contact Supervisor; supervises operations against subsurface contacts from within a ship's Combat Information Center (CIC)

SSGN: A guided missile (G) nuclear (N) submarine that carries and launches guided cruise missiles as its primary weapon. Examples: US *Ohio* class, Russia *Yasen* class

SSK: A diesel electric-powered submarine, quieter when submerged than a nuclear-powered submarine, but must rise to snorkel depth to run its diesel and recharge its batteries. Examples: Iranian *Fateh* class, Russian *Kilo* class, Israeli *Dolphin I* class

SSN: A general purpose attack submarine (SS) powered by a nuclear reactor (N). Examples: HMS *Agincourt*, Russian *Akula* class

SSP: A diesel electric submarine with air-independent propulsion system able to recharge batteries without using atmospheric oxygen. Allows the submarine to stay submerged longer than a traditional SSK. Examples: Israeli *Dolphin II* class, Iranian *Besat** class

STANDOFF: Launched at long range

STINGER: US-made man-portable, low-level anti-air missile

STINGRAY*: The MQ-25 Stingray is a Boeing-designed prototype unmanned US airborne refueling aircraft in development for the US Navy.

STORMBREAKER*: US air-launched, precision-guided glide bomb that can use millimeter radar, laser, or infrared imaging to match and then prioritize targets when operating in semi-autonomous AI mode

SU-57: Russian stealth fighter. See FELON. Like many of Russia's newer weapons types, reported to be in serial production but very few examples have been seen and it was not used in the invasion of Ukraine which would have been expected.

SUBSONIC: Below the speed of sound (under 767 mph, 1,234 kph)

SUNBURN: Russian-made 220mm multiple rocket launcher capable of firing high-explosive, THERMOBARIC or penetrating warheads

SUPERSONIC: Faster than the speed of sound (over 767 mph, 1,234 kph). See also HYPERSONIC

SWARM: Drones, missiles or smart bombs with onboard AI and the ability to coordinate their actions with other drones while in flight, either autonomously or using preselected protocols. 'Swarm' tactics differ from 'horde' tactics in that swarms place more emphasis on coordinated action to defeat enemy defenses. See also HORDE

SYNTHETIC APERTURE RADAR (SAR): A form of radar that is used to create two-dimensional images or three-dimensional reconstructions of objects, such as landscapes. SAR uses the motion of the radar antenna over a target region to provide finer spatial resolution than conventional beam-scanning radars.

SYSOP: The systems operator inside the control station for a HELLADS battery, responsible for electronic and communications systems operation

T-14 ARMATA: Russian next-generation main battle tank or MBT. Designed as a 'universal combat platform' which can be adapted to infantry support, anti-armor, or anti-armor configurations. First Russian MBT to be fitted with active electronically scanned array radar capable of identifying and engaging multiple air and ground targets simultaneously. Also, the first Russian MBT to be fitted with a crew toilet. Used in combat in Syria from 2020 but like many of Russia's newer weapons types, though reported to be in serial production very few examples have been seen and it was not used in the invasion of Ukraine which would have been expected.

T-90: Russian-made main battle tank

TAC(P): Tactical air controller, a specialist trained to direct close air support attacks. See also CAS; FAC; JTAC

TAO: Tactical action officer; officer in command of a ship's Combat Information Center (CIC)

TCA: Tactical control assistant, non-commissioned officer (NCO) in charge of identifying targets and directing fire for a single HELLADS or PATRIOT battery

TCO: Tactical control officer, officer in charge of a single HELLADS or PATRIOT missile battery

TD: Tactical Director; the officer directing multiple PATRIOT or HELLADS batteries

TEMPEST*: British/European 6th-generation stealth aircraft under development as a replacement for the RAF Tornado multirole fighter. It is planned to incorporate advanced combat AI to reduce pilot data overload, laser anti-missile defenses, and will team with swarming drones such as BATS. It may be developed in both manned and unmanned versions.

TERMINATOR: A Russian-made infantry fighting vehicle (see IFV) based on the chassis of the T-90 main battle tank, with 2x 30mm autocannons and 2x grenade or anti-tank missile launchers. Developed initially to support main battle tank operations, it has become popular for use in urban combat environments.

THERMOBARIC: Weapons, otherwise known as thermal or vacuum weapons, that use oxygen from the surrounding air to generate a high-temperature explosion and long-duration blast wave

THUNDER: Radio brevity code indicating one minute to weapons impact

TOW: US wire-guide anti-tank missile, fired either from a tripod launcher by ground troops or mounted on armored cavalry vehicles

TROPHY: Israeli-made anti-projectile defense system using explosively formed penetrators to defeat attacks on vehicles, high-value assets, and aircraft. It is currently fitted to several Israeli and US armored vehicle types.

TUNGUSKA: A mobile Russian-made anti-aircraft vehicle incorporating both cannon and ground-to-air missiles

TYPE 95*: Planned Chinese 3rd-generation nuclear-powered attack submarine with vertical launch tubes and substantially reduced acoustic signature to current Chinese types

UAV: Unmanned aerial vehicle or drone, usually used for transport, refueling or reconnaissance

UCAS: Unmanned combat aerial support vehicle or drone

UCAV: Unmanned combat aerial vehicle; a fighter or attack aircraft

UDAR* UGV: Russian-made unmanned ground vehicle which integrates remotely operated turrets (30mm autocannon, Kornet anti-tank missile or anti-air missile) onto the chassis of a BMP-3 infantry fighting vehicle. The vehicle can be controlled at a range of up to 6 miles (10 km) by an operator with good line of sight, or via a tethered drone relay.

UGV: Unmanned ground vehicle, also UGCV: Unmanned ground combat vehicle

UI: Un-Identified, as in 'UI contact'. See also BOGEY

UNIT 8200: Israel Defense Force cyber intelligence, cyber warfare, and defense unit, aka the Israeli Signals Intelligence National Unit

URAGAN: Russian 220mm 16-tube rocket launcher, first fielded in the 1970s

U/S: Un-serviceable, out of commission, broken

USO: United Services Organizations; US military entertainment and personnel welfare services

V-22 OSPREY: Bell Boeing multi-mission tiltrotor aircraft capable of vertical takeoff and landing which resembles a conventional aircraft when in flight

V-280* VAPOR: Bell Boeing-proposed successor to the V-22, with higher speed, endurance, lift capacity and modular payload bay

V-290* VAPOR: Concept aircraft only. AI-enhanced V-280 with anti-radar reflective coating, added rear fuselage turbofan jet engines for additional speed, and forward-firing 20mm autocannons

VERBA: A Russian-made man-portable low-level anti-air missile with data networking capabilities, meaning it can use data from friendly ground or air radar systems to fly itself to a target

VIRGINIA CLASS SUBMARINE: e.g., *USS Idaho*, nuclear-powered, fast-attack submarines. Current capabilities include torpedo and cruise missiles. Planned capabilities include hypersonic missiles.

VYMPEL: Russian air-to-air missile manufacturer/type

WILD WEASEL: An air attack intended to take down enemy anti-air defense systems. See also SEAD

WINCHESTER: Radio brevity code for 'out of ordnance'

WSO: Weapons Systems Officer. See BACKSEATER.

X-95: Israeli bullpup-style assault rifle. Bullpup-style rifles have their action behind the trigger, allowing for a more compact and maneuverable weapon. Commonly chambered for NATO 5.56mm ammunition.

YAKHONT: Also known as P-800 Onyx. Russian-made two-stage ramjet-propelled, terrain-following cruise missile. Travels at subsonic speeds until close to its target where it is boosted to up to Mach 3. Can be fired from warships, submarines, aircraft or coastal batteries at sea or ground targets.

YPG: Kurdish People's Protection Unit militia (male)

YPJ: Kurdish Women's Protection Unit militia (female)

Z-9: Chinese attack helicopter, predecessor to Z-19

Z-19: Chinese light attack helicopter, comparable to US Viper

Z-20: Chinese medium-lift utility helicopter, comparable to US Blackhawk